DOCUMENT 512

By

Thomas Lopinski

All Rights Reserved
Copyright © 2012

© Copyright 2012 by Thomas Lopinski. All Rights Reserved
Printed and Published by Createspace
ISBN: 1469980282
ISBN-13: 9781469980287

Cover design by Thomas Lopinski
Web design by Michael Scherenberg

No part of this book may be reproduced, stored in a retrieval system or transmitted, in any form or by any means, electronic, mechanical, photocopying, recording, or otherwise, without written permission of the author. For more information, contact Document512@yahoo.com or go to www.Document512.com.

This novel is a work of fiction. Names, characters, organizations, places, events and incidents are either a product of the author's imagination or used fictiously. Any resemblance to actual persons, living or dead, events, or locales is entirely coincidental.

SPECIAL THANKS TO:

Don Terbush, Tom Rowland, Ralph Wells, and Bill Smith (a.k.a. The Writer's Group), Bob Thixton, Peter Jones, Mike Scherenberg, Staci Pearson, Bob and Glenda McMurray, Felix Chamberlain, Lani Ludwig, Tricia Halloran, Jennifer Mandel, Timothy Wager, Steve Bender, Carl Wertz, Brittany Lewis, and Tom Fullerton. A very special thank you to my wonderful wife, Lisa, and my family—Amber, Yassir, Zayd, Farida, Anna, Katie, and, especially Sarah—for taking the time to read my book repeatedly and offer some great advice. But most of all, a very, very special thank you to my dear friend John "Chris" Gleichman, whose never-ending encouragement and brilliant insight made it all possible.

AUTHOR'S NOTE:

Thomas Lopinski

Years ago, a group of friends in LA allowed me to join their writer's group. The assignment was simple: write a few chapters, meet once a month at the Fox and Hound, talk about each other's work over dinner and a few pints, then play darts and drink a few more pints well into the night. It was a golden period in my life, and I have them to thank for sparking my interest in writing.

This book is a work of fiction that was created by taking bits and pieces of stories and concepts from countless articles, shows and books and blending them with my own imagination. Some of those resources were so influential that they are worth mentioning: *Chariots of the Gods and Gold of the Gods* by Eric Von Däniken; *The Chronicle of Akakor* by Karl Brugger; *The Dark Tower series* by Stephen King; *Lost Cities & Ancient Mysteries of South America* by David Childress; *The Elegant Universe* by Brian Greene; *Secret Cities of Old South America and Mysteries of Ancient South America* by Harold Wilkins; and the *Ancient Astronauts series* on the *History Channel*. A more complete list can be found at www.Document512.com.

CONTENTS

PART 1 - THE CAVES OF TIAHUANACO................1

PART 2 - WELCOME TO CUZCO........................65

PART 3 - DIVINE INTERVENTION....................119

PART 4 - THE CHASE................................169

PART 5 - MYSTERIES OF THE TUNNELS...............207

PART 6 - THE LOST CITY............................257

PART ONE

THE CAVES OF TIAHUANACO

CHAPTER ONE
THE DREAM

"Hurry! They're gaining on us," yelled Renee as she raced down the mountainside jumping from one terrace step to the next. She struggled to maintain her balance between the patches of grass and moss that stumbled out from underneath her feet. The farther down the hill she ran, the farther away from the bottom she seemed to be.

"There they are!" shouted a voice in the distance.

She glanced back just long enough to see three men on top of the ancient ruins pointing down at her. Two of them shuffled from side to side as they descended the mountaintop, dodging bushes and trees along the trail. The third one was sprinting as fast as he could, barreling over anything in his pathway.

"Be careful," said the man running next to her. She turned to see his backpack bouncing wildly on his shoulders. The man's stride was so long that he skipped from step to step with only one foot hitting the grass.

Renee's steps were uneven and unsure. Her shoes were too tight, which caused her swollen feet to ache every time they touched down. The commotion coming from both directions made it hard to concentrate. On some terraces, she took two steps, on others, three. It was only a matter of time before she lost her footing and hit the ground hard.

"Ouch!"

The man in front of her stopped just long enough to see her roll out of control. When their bodies collided, the force knocked him to his knees and carried them both sliding down the hill until his hip crashed into a boulder.

"That's gonna leave a bruise," he moaned as he slowly rose to his feet. "Are you OK?"

She reached for her leg and rubbed the back of it. "I don't know. It hurts—a lot."

The yelling coming from above grew louder as the three men closed in. One of them was now out in front of the others by a good twenty yards. Even with the distance between them, Renee could still make out the tattoos on his biceps flashing black and blue as he moved along. The sunlight danced off his partially shaved head as he leaped like a jaguar from one terrace to another.

"I'll carry you." The man bent down and tossed Renee's body over his shoulder as if she were a sack of potatoes and continued on.

At the bottom of the hill was a six-foot-high wall made of stone and mud encasing the last terrace. He eased her onto the edge of the wall and jumped down to the bottom. Renee looked up the hill again at the man leading the chase. She was now able to make out a long scar that stretched from one ear to the middle of his jaw. It looked fresh. He was yelling something in Spanish back to the others. She carefully slid down to the ground and disappeared behind the wall.

In front of them was a thick clump of trees and bushes. Beneath their feet was a gravel path that followed alongside the wall. The man glanced both ways. His first inclination was to go left, but instead he paused and asked, "Which way?"

She looked from side to side and then at the clump of shrubs in front and said, "Go straight."

"Go what?" he exclaimed.

"Go straight into the bushes."

"But there's no trail."

"I know but you'll find one—trust me."

"I've been hearing that a lot lately, and trust is the one thing I'm all out of."

Renee wiggled free from his grasp, careful not to put any pressure on her sore leg. She hobbled into the trees and said, "Come on, it's gotta be here. The writings on the rock back there said something about 'hopping and diving.' This must be the diving part."

"Like 'diving' into the bushes?" he said. "That's a new one on me. The 'hopping' part was bad enough coming down that mountain, but who's ever heard of diving into bushes?"

"I don't know. Do you have a better plan?"

She tugged on his hand and guided him into a narrow opening between two shrubs. They zigzagged between trees and branches dodging flying limbs as the undergrowth thickened. The rooted lianas vines looping around the taller palm trees and philodendrons made maneuvering almost impossible. Blotches of red dotted their forearms as thickets of thorny stems and bristled leaves assaulted anything that came near.

They could barely hear the three men in the background arguing. The men had stopped at the edge of the wall and were unsure of which way to go. Finally, the one with the shaved head pointed to the broken limbs and said, "*Allí.*"

The vegetation eventually started thinning out as Renee and her companion continued ahead. There were no signs of the terraces behind them and nothing in front that looked encouraging. Then, without warning, she stopped and said, "Hear that?"

"Hear what?"

DOCUMENT 512

"Quiet." In the distance, they heard a soft, white noise. "It sounds like a waterfall. Let's go."

They ventured farther into the woods as rays of sunshine drizzled through the thinning tree branches. Up ahead was a clearing of tall grass and scrubland. A light mist hung in the air and gently announced the approaching falls.

"We're here," she said.

Before them was a cliff overlooking a small but deep basin. The opening was a circle no wider than twenty yards in circumference but at least a hundred feet deep. Along the perimeter were several tree limbs and roots drooping saplessly into the hole. Although they did little to provide shade from the humidity and sun, they camouflaged the area completely from the view above. The water from two separate streams plunged down into the abyss at a rapid pace.

They both peered over the edge and spotted a pool of deep blue water. He turned to Renee and said, "You're not thinking about going down there, are you?"

She nodded. "I was wrong about the diving into the bushes part, but this time I know I'm right."

He gazed into the hole again in disbelief. Then something caught his eye. He squinted for a better view as the sun continued to rise in the morning sky. On the other side, the wall began to glisten ever so slightly. Within seconds, it grew brighter and brighter until the rocks reflected the sun's rays in every direction.

"Look, over there. See the rocks? They're shining."

Renee didn't have to squint to see it. The reflection on the wall was so bright now that it blinded her. A thin coat of mist sprayed over the crystal-laced spectacle, enhancing its luster even more. Then, before they could say another word, it was gone. The light vanished completely as the angle of the sun gradually changed.

"That was totally amazing," said Renee.

"Unbelievably amazing," said the man. The Levi's tag on his blue jeans seemed to be absorbing the golden sunlight and glowing. It formed an almost catlike face where the "5" and "2" were mirror images of each other. As she stood there mesmerized by what she was witnessing, the sides of the middle number began to push together gradually until it looked more like a "1" than a "0". Then the man moved and the vision was gone.

Renee regained her composure and removed her backpack. She tightened all of the straps and zippers, making sure that nothing was open or loose. Then she put it on backward, with the bag snuggled against her chest.

"That's enough to convince me. Here, do this." She motioned him to follow suit.

"I don't like the looks of this one bit," he said as he removed his pack. "That's a long jump."

"Oh, we can't jump—we have to dive."

"You've gotta be kidding."

"No, I'm not. The writings on the wall specifically said 'dive,' not 'jump.'"

"Well, what difference could it make?"

She checked the straps one last time and replied, "All the difference in the world. How many people do you think have dove into this hole? Like, none—and that's why they've never found the entrance."

"You think this is an entrance?"

"It has to be," she said. "It all makes sense."

At that moment, the bark off the tree next to him shattered into pieces. The gunshot sound followed a half a second later. They both ducked down instinctively as another bullet buzzed by and nicked a branch above their heads. Someone was yelling frantically in the distance.

"OK, you win by default," the man said. "The other options aren't looking very good right now."

She smiled and said, "On the count of three, we dive in—and be prepared for anything."

He rolled his eyes and said, "God help me."

Renee grabbed his hand. "Are you ready?"

He rose to his feet and looked over the edge one last time. Then he smiled and replied, "No, but I'm willing."

"Here we go, then. One, two, three…"

CHAPTER TWO

LA PAZ, BOLIVIA

As Renee dreamed of falling deeper into the canyon, glimmers of sunlight crept along her hotel room's plastered walls. The baker had just pulled up on his Moped to open the shop next door. He parked his bike around back in the alley, turned off the key, and cringed as the muffler backfired. The young girl instinctively shifted onto her side and began to stir from a deep slumber.

Her mind wandered aimlessly as it shifted from the chase scene to her hotel room. Images from her past soon weaved in and out of her present as she slowly gained consciousness. She dreamed that her schoolmates were arguing outside her hotel room door over who'd be taking the next shower in the floor's only bathroom. Then her dream moved to a playground where a couple of young girls were jumping rope in rhythm with a haunting chant:

"Cinderella,
Dressed in yella
Peed in her pants in front of the fellas."

The singing twirled around in her head as she twisted in bed trying to avoid an imaginary rope under her feet. Then the stage shifted to a local market in La Paz where teachers greeted her on the street in the same way they'd pass her in the hallway at school. Snapshots of the ancient ruins she was to visit later that morning played like a slide show in her head. Her dreams seemed so brilliant and colorful—and so different from anything she'd ever dreamed before.

Everything about this strange continent was different to her. After all, this was South America: a continent where the snow-peaked mountains stood watch over peddlers roaming the cobblestone streets below; a continent where tiled-roof houses hid generations of secrets deep in the canyon walls; a continent where corruption fed off chaos and chaos fed off corruption; a continent lost in the moment with a history that was begging to be discovered.

The dueling aromas of rotting garbage and brewing coffee were now drifting into the air. A few birds began chirping off in the distance. Soon car horns and flute players would serenade the streets below. As the peaceful stillness of the dawn lingered a little while longer, a click came from the bureau next to the bed. The silence was broken. A cheap digital alarm clock blasted a repetition of irritating shrieks throughout the hotel room.

The screeching went on for almost a half a minute before she reached up and hit the snooze button. She wasn't quite ready to greet the new day. Being four thousand miles away from home and sleeping on a lumpy mattress had taken its toll on her after a long and weary plane trip the day before.

Renee lowered her arm and tucked the pillow back under her head as she opened one eye to look at the clock. What she saw startled her. She wasn't sure if it was just an illusion conjured up by the high altitude, so she blinked a couple of times for good measure. Right before her on the nightstand was the same number that had appeared in her dream just moments ago. It was also the flight number on her plane ticket from the day before. Glowing on the face of the clock and casting a reddish aura over the bedside was the time, "5:12."

It wasn't in the Courier or Times Roman fonts commonly used in books and on billboards. No, this was the typeface only found in the digital world of alarm clocks, coffeemakers, and microwaves. The world where zeros and ones had replaced capacitors and rectifier tubes.

Each individual section of the numbers was made up of the same rectangular block-shaped line. The straight line that created the top and sides of the "5" also created the bottom. The same lines also created the "2." Even the "1" in middle had two identical thin rectangular blocks stacked up on top of each other. The "5" was a mirror image of the "2." No matter what angle you looked at it, whether it was upside down or backward, the numbers were reversible.

While she lay on her side counting the seconds before the numbers changed, another eerie shape came into focus. In the darkened space between the glowing numbers, a crudely shaped cross appeared. It was vague and missing most of the top portion, looking more like a *T,* but still it was there. She rubbed away the sleep from her eye and the image disappeared.

The dawdling beam of light radiating from the clock left her with a feeling that someone or something was watching her. She thought about opening her other eye to get a better look around but decided to close them both instead.

CHAPTER THREE
TIAHUANACO

The sign at the crossroad read, "Titicaca del Lago—25 kilometers." The sign underneath said, "Tiwanacu—5 kilometers," with an arrow pointing to the right. As the jeep approached, the driver turned right while downshifting into second gear without losing a beat. The bumpy dirt road heading into the small village of Tiahuanaco was even worse than the pothole-ridden road they'd been on all morning from La Paz. Up ahead, a shepherd hastily tried to move his herd of llamas off the path so the jeep could pass.

The snow-topped Andes Mountains appeared around every bend as they drove higher and higher. A set of nimbus clouds dotting the horizon moved like a pristine white glacier rolling along the heavens. At 12,500 feet above sea level, the monotonous cobalt blue sky would usually lull a person to sleep with its serenity and beauty. That wasn't the case today; between the dust storms coughing up centuries of old ashes and a road with more twists than a wound-up Slinky, the mountain was doing a pretty good job of keeping everyone on edge.

"I thought it would only take an hour from La Paz," said Renee's father. Roger Gorman's brown ponytail jumped from one shoulder to the other as he braced himself for the next curve. His khaki shorts and flannel shirt were no match for the bitter winds that battered him in the open jeep, so he grabbed a jacket out of his backpack and put it on. He searched for a clean part of his shirt to wipe off his glasses but quickly realized that his efforts were futile.

The driver didn't dare take his eyes off the road as he swerved to miss a series of seemingly never-ending rocks and boulders. He'd been doing this same thing since picking them up at the hotel back in the city that morning. When a straighter stretch of road appeared, Don Carlos glanced over at Roger and said, "We are at the mercy of The Gods, *señor*. These mountains will let you know when it is time."

Roger looked down at his compass, which was attached to a chain around his neck. It was moving erratically back and forth from north to west to east.

"Look at this. This compass is going crazy up here."

He showed it to Don, who shrugged his shoulders. "What can I say?"

"It can't be the altitude." He stared at the compass for another minute before putting it back under his shirt. Then he looked to the backseat, where his daughter sat clutching the roll bar. With her arm interlocked around the metal pipe, she seemed to be in a trance.

"How you holding up?"

Renee eased her grip and subtly waved back. She'd been trying to remember the details from her dream earlier that morning. What was she doing running away from those men? And who was the man running with her? It certainly wasn't her father. Then there were the visions of her friends from school. She knew why they were laughing.

The images were so vivid in her mind. *It must be the mountain air*, she thought.

Having dressed a little warmer than her father, she pulled her scarf up tighter around her neck. She'd researched the area they were heading into and knew that it got cold very quickly. She placed her other arm on her backpack and said, "All good here, Pop," and gave him the thumbs-up sign.

"I bet you've never been on a roller coaster ride quite like this."

"Well, not one quite this long."

Renee cracked a smile as her dad returned his attention to the road ahead. Roger sensed the nervousness in his daughter's voice and wondered whether bringing her along was really a good idea after all. His wife had protested dearly in the beginning. How could he even think of taking their only daughter deep into the backwoods of South America? In fact, most of her friends thought she was downright crazy for letting the young girl go.

Renee's friends were skeptical, too. Even though she was pretty athletic and smarter than most kids her age, she was still a typical teenager. That meant unprovoked streaks of stubbornness, an inability to know her own limits, and, of course, an attraction to boys. But there was one other particular characteristic—or weakness, depending on whom you talked to—that concerned everyone: her learning disability. Her parents tried not to talk about it, but there were reminders every day. Yet when everything was said and done and after seeing the glow in her daughter's eyes grow week after week, her mother finally relented and gave her blessing.

The mountainside terrain was barren and desolate. A few scattered bushes were splattered among the huge boulders that dominated the landscape. Occasionally, a set of eyes popped up from the ground as a startled chinchilla scurried for cover. The wind blew and died down like the breath of a snoring giant. It had been a good half hour since they'd seen another vehicle.

A few minutes later, the jeep pulled into a parking lot beside the site of the ancient ruins. A small billboard written in Spanish guarded the entrance.

"*Tiahua-co-na—Elevación: 3,870 m,*" said Renee. No sooner had she said it than she started to blush. She looked at her father, who'd turned around immediately. While attempting a smile, she said with a surrendering tone, "Soooo, go ahead."

He smiled back and said, "'*Tiahua-na-co*'—or '*Tiwanacu,*' as the natives call it."

The meaning of their esoteric exchange was lost on Don Carlos. He wasn't aware of Renee's dyslexic tendencies, nor did he even understand them. Growing up, she'd learned to deal with it pretty well by using little tricks and tools to avoid embarrassment. But the taunting was something else. That, she never got over. The kids at school could be so cruel without even realizing what they were doing. Whenever she wrote something backward on the chalkboard or transposed syllables during reading time, they'd have a field day. She could still hear them laughing four thousand miles away.

The first time it happened was the worst. It caught her completely off guard as she stood in front of her kindergarten class—so off guard that she peed her pants right then and there. Of course, she'd never lived that one down. That's when the chanting started:

"Cinderella,
Dressed in yella
Peed in her pants in front of the fellas."

By the time she'd reached junior high, the kids had moved on and stopped mocking her, at least to her face. They may have matured enough to show her a little more kindness and respect, but in no way did that mean she was fully accepted as normal. She knew very well that they'd never elect her class president or captain of the cheerleading squad. Those titles were reserved for the "perfect" kids. But with the help of a beautiful smile and a cunning ability to adapt quickly, she was able to manage her disability pretty well. Her father knew this and could only grin with appreciation when she recognized her mistake.

There were only two other cars in the parking lot and no one in sight. Renee's dad scanned the grounds and said to Don, "Why so few cars today?" Roger stood up in the jeep and cupped his hand over his eyes to get a better look. "There are no buses either."

Don Carlos put the jeep into first gear, shut it off, and pulled on the emergency break. "It's a holiday, *señor*. You are very lucky. A lot of the businesses in La Paz are closed."

"What holiday is that?" Renee asked as she jumped out of the backseat with her bag in hand.

"*Día de los Muertos*—'Day of the Dead,' as you might say in English." Don stared into the young girl's eyes with a foreboding sneer and continued, "On this day, all of our dead relatives come back to visit—whether we want them to or not. That is why no one comes today."

This last comment raised Renee's eyebrows. Roger grabbed his backpack off the floor and exited the jeep. "It wouldn't also have anything to do with the fact that half of La Paz was out celebrating last night and now is hungover, would it?"

Don laughed loudly as his double chin wiggled. "You are very right, *señor*. My apologies for not choosing my words better." He turned to Renee and placed his hand on her shoulder. "Don't worry, my lovely *chiquita*. None of my dead relatives would want to follow me up here to this forgotten place."

For the first time, Renee got a good whiff of the foul body odor exuding from Don's skin. It was overwhelming. Somehow, she managed to refrain from gagging as she returned the smile while holding her breath and nonchalantly moving to the other side of the jeep.

CHAPTER FOUR
THE RUINS

Don Carlos set his backpack on the seat and said, "I must check and make sure we have everything we will need for the *socavones*."

DOCUMENT 512

"The caves," translated Roger. "Yes, well, maybe we'll have enough time to take a quick look at the sites, too?" Roger's voice rose ever so slightly. The six-foot-tall American, whose twig of a body shrank like a wilting sunflower next to the short, fat Bolivian, politely smiled and waited for an answer.

"Indeed we do. We have a good six hours before we must think about returning," said Don as he walked away from the jeep. Renee and her father's eyes connected. This is what they wanted to hear. It would be a complete shame to travel all this way from the Illinois and not see the ruins of Tiahuanaco up close.

An enigma of speculation, this site's origins and purpose had puzzled researchers for centuries. Some believed that it was the home of an ancient society that died off after some catastrophic event. Other, more eccentric scholars argued that the natives were lured there for some special purpose and then abandoned by their gods, who left them to rot. A few colorful ancient astronaut theorists had even declared that the inhabitants were not from this world at all and just visitors who returned to their own planet after finding what they'd come for. Either way, many believed that this was the oldest city in the world.

The three set down the path leading to the ruins, passing a few mounds along the way. A half-full tour bus pulled in behind them as they walked on. Don, looking a little annoyed as he spun his head back around, said, "I guess we are not so alone after all."

After entering the temple site, they headed over to the Sun Gate. This ten-ton gateway was carved from a single block of granite. A large crack splintered through the center above the entrance door. Its upper portion was deeply carved with beautiful and intricate designs of human figures with wings and astronomical symbols.

Renee's dad stopped in front of it and proceeded to lecture the two on the history of the artifact. "The legend passed down from the Aymara Indians says that this god rose from Lake Titicaca during the time of darkness to bring forth light. His name was

Viracocha. He was the storm god but also their sun god. That's what the crown and thunderbolt in his hands mean. It's said that Viracocha made the earth, the stars, the sky, and mankind. He then wandered the earth disguised as a beggar and observed the people he'd created. Unfortunately, he wasn't very impressed with what he saw, so he destroyed everything with a flood and decided to start over from scratch."

"Yes, *señor*, maybe the same flood in the Bible, no?"

"Maybe," reflected Roger.

"I thought the Inca Indians came from around here," said Renee.

"Not up here. In reality, the Incas only made up a small portion of the total population in their kingdom. How they managed to rule over millions of other Indians is quite amazing. The Aymara Indians have survived up here for thousands of years and watched over this area. I'm not exactly sure where they are now."

"Oh *señor*, they have not disappeared. There are still Indians up here who protect the sacred sites from unruly tourists and bad governments," interjected Don. "Ever since that book come out back in the seventies, they have been busy."

Roger blushed as he pulled a paperback out of his backpack. He'd read it so many times over that the corners were missing and its cover was so faded that the title was barely visible. "You mean this one."

Don looked at the cover and nodded, "Yes, *señor*. This *Chariots of the Gods* book has changed everything for the Indians. People come up here looking for souvenirs. Grave robbers trample over the sites and take many things they shouldn't. Now the government does not even care what happens."

"That's too bad. I didn't know that was going on." Roger skimmed over the horizon and said, "They must keep to themselves."

"Ah yes, my friend, they are only seen when they want to be. They have eyes everywhere, so we must respect their customs and history. Otherwise—well, put it this way: there have been many grave robbers chased off by the point of an arrow."

Renee looked up at her father with concern. She knew some of what he'd been through at work with his colleagues and how they'd thought his wild speculations about ancient civilizations were more cuckoo than concrete. Although he'd managed not to show his bottled-up frustration around her, she was still worried that one day it would get the best of him.

Her father ran his fingers through Renee's hair and said, "Don't worry, my darling. We're just visiting and doing a little cave exploring. We'll try to stay as far away from the natives as possible. Right, Don?"

Don looked to Renee and offered a conciliatory, "We can." The wrinkles on his forehead told another story.

She could see in Don a distinct resemblance to her own mother. The same man had fathered them both many years ago. They didn't know they were half siblings until adulthood and not until Renee's grandmother, while on her deathbed, finally confessed to her family the true identity of her mother's father.

A story was told about a handsome South American who came to Illinois to work in the coal mines with his brother in the 1960's. The two men knew very little English and had no relatives close by, but managed to mingle in with the Midwesterners easily. They were hard workers and eagerly welcomed by management. Renee's grandmother was a waitress at a local restaurant. It didn't take long before pouring coffee and taking orders turned into secret rendezvous and a little bun in the oven. The story is a little vague after that, as no one knew whether the Bolivian sneaked away back to South America or was run out of town by her family. Either way, Renee's grandmother found herself at the altar with a more "suitable" beau just days before the baby was born.

After finding out she had a half brother in Bolivia, her mother immediately went looking for him, much to the chagrin of her younger siblings. They contacted each other a few times over the years but never quite developed a strong emotional bond. This trip to South America was Renee's first face-to-face meeting with her distant uncle. He greeted them both with open arms and couldn't have been a more willing and inviting host. Still, there were moments of uneasiness and uncertainty surrounding the relationship. It was hard to figure out a man who constantly talked in circles and rarely gave complete answers. Yet, when Don offered to take the two to Tiahuanaco and show them something no other foreigner had ever seen, they were both elated.

Renee's dad continued his lecture: "Anyway, it's thought that the shores of Lake Titicaca once came up to this height. That would explain a lot, since it's difficult to imagine these people carting off all of these boulders to the top of this mountain any other way."

"Isn't the lake like fifteen miles away?" asked Renee.

"Yes, it is. But there's only a few hundred feet difference in height, so it is plausible that the waters could have receded that much over a period of ten thousand years or more." Renee and her dad both nodded in agreement.

They moved through the entrance and headed deeper into the temple until they arrived at the Sunken Courtyard, which was covered with sculptured heads protruding from the walls. A strange feeling of being judged by a jury of half-human-half-celestial spirits came over Renee as she examined the figures.

"This place is really creepy."

Her father reached out to touch one of the more human-looking heads and replied, "You got that right. Lord knows what kind of sadistic rituals took place on this spot. Boy, if these heads could talk."

After a few more minutes, Don, who'd been sitting down on the sunken wall wiping his brow with a handkerchief, said, "My friends, I think it's time to go to the caves. We don't want to wait too long or else we will lose precious daylight."

Roger whipped around and answered, "I agree. Let's do it."

CHAPTER FIVE

CUZCO

"*Quieto!*" Three hundred miles away from Tiahuanaco, a young Indian darted under the cover of a marketplace canopy and knocked over a corner pole. The blue tarp collapsed onto the collage of red, yellow, green, violet, and turquoise below. Street vendors tried to protect their carts of rugs and leather goods as the crowd of shoppers scattered away. "Filthy *muchacho!*" cried one of the vendors as he shook his fist. The poor merchants sitting on the ground had it even worse off—their goods were quickly reduced to a puree of trampled fruit and vegetables.

Two *policia*, who'd been chasing the boy all morning, collided with several market goers while the tents drifted downward. "*Mierda!*" the skinny policeman shouted as he helped an older lady to her feet. His partner looked around for an alternate route around the crowd. The tightly stacked boulders rising high and lining each side of the street created an impenetrable wall. Their origins were the subject of many discussions between the local Quechua Indians: Were they the creation of the ancient Incas or an older lost civilization that had long ago disappeared? Either way, they'd fought back invading armies for thousands of years. The officer threw his hands up in the air and walked away as his partner hurriedly ran to catch up.

A man in his early thirties wearing sunglasses and a baseball cap walked out of the quiet alley and unknowingly right into the melee. He hadn't heard the commotion coming from the street when he turned the corner because his mind had been elsewhere. It'd been preoccupied with more important matters like where he was going to sleep that night and how he was going to find his next meal.

THE CAVES OF TIAHUANACO

Jason Finch had spent the last year carelessly roaming the streets and jungles of South America while his bank account ran out of money. His only real option now was calling back to the States and asking his family for more funds. Getting the cash would be no problem: his father owned more timber on the East Coast than the devil owned souls. Getting over having to admit defeat and tell them that they were right was another matter completely.

Ever since landing in South America with the rest of his fellow researchers, Jason had felt a deep connection to this country. When they all returned home after a conference in Buenos Aires, he decided to take a leave of absence from his job and travel around the countryside. His obsession with local legends and stories of lost cities had completely transformed him into a different person over the past few months—a person that even his own family didn't recognize.

The young man slammed into him as he rounded the corner. He looked down and pulled the Indian's hands away from his jacket. The boy looked to be about sixteen or seventeen, not quite an adult, but still with a sense of maturity in his mannerisms all the same. A set of mesmerizingly large deep-blue eyes seemed so out of place on his reddish-brown skin. The high forehead, slightly hooked nose, and firm chin closely resembled that of the hundreds of penniless street rats he was accustomed to seeing, but then Jason noticed the golden hoop earrings and silver choker around his neck. Street rats didn't wear gold in Cuzco.

As he struggled to free himself, Jason realized there was something else quite unusual about his hands. Their movement was different than anything he'd ever seen before. The boy had six fingers instead of five! Between the thumb and pointer finger was an extra digit, long and fully functioning. The sixth finger bent and stretched in unison with the others so fluently that it startled Jason and caused him to unconsciously release his grip.

DOCUMENT 512

"Excuse me, *gringo*," said the young Indian. His words were soft-spoken and almost a whisper. There was also a hint of a European accent in his voice. It sounded almost Slavic or maybe German. As Jason stared at the boy's huge eyes, they appeared to shrink ever so slightly right before him. He blinked a few times in disbelief and looked again. The young man slipped his hands away and darted down the alley before Jason could react.

He immediately checked all of his pockets in his jacket and pants to see if anything was missing. You never knew in a city like Cuzco. Pickpockets were more common than pigeons. He felt for his wallet, which was still snug against his chest inside his jacket. The Swiss Army knife was still snapped in its case on his hip. But most important and more valuable than any other tangible possession was the hand-drawn map that was still, thankfully, in his pants pocket. Without the map, his quest would be over and the phone call home would no longer be an option. It would be a necessity.

After reassuring himself that everything was intact, he surveyed the pandemonium unfolding before him. His instincts immediately kicked in as he walked up to one of the abandoned vendor stands and grabbed a handful of bananas and some beef jerky hanging on a side rail. In one swooping motion and without making eye contact, the items quickly disappeared into his pockets, as he ducked into another alley across the street and vanished.

CHAPTER SIX
IGLESIA DE SANTO DOMINGO

Across town and far away from the chaos of the plaza square, an old priest strolled inside the church grounds from one flowerpot to the next. Under each archway, he paused just long enough to trim around the flower stems and pull off a few dying buds. A fellow priest would walk by every few minutes and nod without saying a word.

The Cathedral of Santo Domingo had been built atop the ancient Incan temple of Coricancha. The Spaniards ruthlessly conquered the natives in the 1500s and systematically dismantled every monument and shrine they could find. They stripped away gold plating from royal temple walls, melted down the gold guttering that encircled these buildings, and even disassembled a series of gold pipes that fed pure water into the city from the melting snow in the mountain ranges above. Then they used these same stones and precious metals to build places of worship for the monks and priests who'd so blissfully christened their conquest as righteous and divine. It was the ultimate insult. When they'd finished, the Spaniards had made it crystal clear to everyone that the Inca empire was never coming back and anyone caught worshiping their pagan gods would be brutally rewarded with certain death.

It was said that the mummified bodies of thirteen Incan rulers were once entombed somewhere under the cathedral. They originally sat on huge golden thrones in elaborately decorated tombs trimmed in gold and silver. The mummies were covered from head to toe in golden jewelry and precious stones. On special occasions, the Indians paraded these deceased rulers around the city on ceremonial litters and would seek their guidance on planning future

DOCUMENT 512

battles or settling domestic affairs. To this day, witnesses swear that during *Día de los Muertos*, the same thirteen rulers can still be seen haunting the streets of Cuzco.

Pizarro and his conquistadors toppled and pillaged the city with only 168 men in 1532. Atahualpa, the Incan emperor, believed that the Spaniards were sent to fulfill a prophecy involving the return of Viracocha; therefore, he ordered his eighty thousand warriors not to fight even if they were attacked. This resulted in a massacre of the Inca people and Atahualpa's eventual capture. In an attempt to save his own life, the emperor promised that he could deliver enough gold to fill a large room from the floor to ceiling. Over the next few months, his servants transported tons of plates, discs, utensils, and trinkets to the temple.

In an odd twist of fate, the emperor's translator, who was secretly in love with Atahualpa's wife, spread rumors that the king was building an army to fight the conquistadors. This was all the reason Pizarro's soldiers needed to take his life. Reluctantly, Pizarro agreed. The next morning, Atahualpa was stripped down to his bare skin in a purification ceremony while a Spanish monk converted him to Christianity. Then the soldiers strangled him to death and gave him a proper Christian burial. A few days later, the Spaniards discovered that there was in fact no army approaching the city and that it had all been a hoax. Needless to say, Pizarro felt remorse. Even though the natives were considered heathens in their eyes, a king was still a king in any culture and should have been respected accordingly.

It was said that the emperor's wife predicted her husband's demise by consulting the mystical powers of a "Black Mirror". In a highly secretive ceremony that included a blackened lamp and a young virgin, the high priest asked her to tell him what she saw in her husband's future. The images reflecting back from the mirror caused her to shudder uncontrollably so she ordered her servants to scatter the rest of the gold and treasures over the countryside in tunnels and secret passageways that had been built under the city. They placed all of the artifacts and statues deemed sacred to the Incas in these tunnels. The high priest conducted a ceremony while the half-caste servants sealed and camouflaged the entrances. Then the purebred Quechua Indians who supervised the burial executed the servants, thus preventing them from ever revealing their whereabouts. Every generation thereafter, the Indians guarded the caves and their secrets with their lives.

"Father Delanda," a muffled voice resonated from the bottom floor of the church. "Father Delanda."

The priest hesitated and rose as footsteps echoed down the corridor. He placed the shears inside his pocket, careful not to dirty his white tunic, and brushed off the soil from his hands. Running up the stairs from the level below were the two *policia* from the plaza. They reached the top of the steps out of breath but continued to scamper across the brick floor toward the priest.

Within seconds, they were kneeling down before him, making the gesture of the cross on their chests. The padre seemed annoyed with the show of respect and signaled the men to stop.

"Father, Father," bemoaned the tall, skinny one.

"What is it, my son?"

"He's gone. I mean the Indian boy disappeared."

A look of annoyance now became subtle anger as the priest rubbed his hands and turned his back on the two men. "What do you mean, he's disappeared?"

The skinny officer looked to his partner for help but saw only dismay. His partner just shrugged his shoulders and lowered his head. "Well, we chased him to the market and…the canopy fell… and…"

The priest raised his hand in the air and silenced the officer. "Never mind how." He turned back around and gazed down upon the two like a hawk studying his offspring after an unsuccessful kill. His eyes no longer showed any signs of hostility; they slowly and gently warmed up as he relaxed his shoulders. Then he recited a scripture: "The Lord is gracious and merciful, slow to anger and abounding in steadfast love."

A sigh of relief came over the two men as the priest gestured for them to rise. As they struggled to regain their posture, the priest added, "He will not go far. Go back to the station and alert your chief. Tell him that I'm in need of his services once again. We must find this boy before somebody else does."

CHAPTER SEVEN
THE STATION

The two policemen walked away while Father Delanda grabbed his black cloak and draped it over his shoulders. Then he spun around and quickly shuffled down the corridor. His robe fell so low to the ground that it brushed against the stone pavement, deadening the sound of his sandals. He came to a stairway that led to the center courtyard. After entering the courtyard, he followed the path of bushes that crisscrossed at the center and ended up at the far corner of the building. There he ducked down into another darkened stairway that wound along the side of the interior stone walls and deposited him underneath the ground level. In the dimly lit hallway, he grabbed a burning torch off the wall and continued farther away from the church, deep into the tunnel. Within minutes, he arrived at a large wooden door with no markings or handles.

Painted on the exterior wall near the wooden door was a sign that read, *"Estacion."* It was barely visible through the clumps of ivy that stretched from one end of the walkway to the other. Above the wall was a railing and platform full of dockworkers moving in and out of the warehouses with wheel barrels and handcarts. They were unloading crates from the railcars running along the track at a frantic pace. On another set of tracks sat a passenger train boarding people for the three hour ride to Machu Picchu.

As the deafening noise of engines and steam filled the air, the ivy obscuring the door began to move. No one above noticed the vines splitting in half below the dock as an opening appeared in the wall. Father Delanda pushed the door open, exited quickly, and looked around to see if anyone had spotted him. There was no one in sight. He placed his back on the door and closed it with as much force as he could muster until he heard a clicking sound. The seam of the door once again disappeared into the foliage.

He continued walking along the wall and around the corner, away from the train station. Soon a crowd of vendors and tourists surrounded him. They were jammed into the streets, shouting and haggling over the prices of goods laid out on the carts and tables. The native Indians were easy to spot amid the tourists with their black hats and long ponytails. The ubiquitous sound of flutes and mandolins accompanied him down the cobblestone roads. No one took notice of the padre in his drab-colored cloak as he weaved his way through the scenery.

A few blocks away, he detoured down an unpaved side street lined with heavily weathered shacks. Swaying in the wind were loads of laundry clipped to wires and strings from one fence post to another. Little girls and boys chased each other down the block as their dogs barked behind them. Halfway down the street, he spotted a marker above a door written in white chalk. It was a bold white cross. He knocked on the door and it opened immediately. Before entering, he glanced one last time each way down the street just to make sure he wasn't being followed.

Inside was a sparsely furnished one-room abode cradling a set of rickety chairs that seemed to be propping up an old wooden table. In the corner were two small beds smoothly tucked and trimmed against the wall. The old woman who'd opened the door returned to the kitchen area without saying a word and resumed her work on the counter. She reduced the fire on a pot that was steaming over the stove.

"Something smells wonderful, Nina."

The old lady shrugged but didn't say a word as she continued cooking. The priest looked to the table, where a Quechua Indian sat carving a piece of wood with a knife. "She still doesn't approve, Father."

Father Delanda moved closer to the table, carefully pulled back a chair, and sat down. He pried a pair of flimsy glasses off his hairy ears, cleaned them on his robe, and said, "I know, my son." He looked over at Nina. "It's hard to change the minds of those that have been practicing heresy for countless generations. May God grant mercy on their lost souls."

The old lady muttered something unrecognizable under her breath as the priest and Indian chuckled. "You surely know how to get under her skin."

"I think by just wearing this robe I get under her skin."

The Indian smiled and nodded. "That you do." He laid down the knife and wood and reached under the table for a burlap sack. It clanked as he set it on top and untied the string.

The priest's eyes opened wide. He placed his gold spectacles back on his crooked nose, tilted his head back, and grinned. "So, what do you have for me today, my son?"

The Indian looked up as he reached into the bag and fumbled through his treasure trove. "I think you'll be pleased."

"I hope so, Huascar. Your last finding was—how should I say?—not as exquisite as I expected."

Huascar looked at the padre and said quietly, "But if you only knew the trouble I went through just to bring these things to you, Father. These are gifts from The Gods and there are not many left. That's why I give them to you."

The priest tried not to stare at the Indian too long. Something about Huascar's lazy eye always caused him to unconsciously follow it around. Huascar felt uneasy and looked away. He knew the padre didn't mean anything by it. The Indian had spent his whole life putting up with people studying his face. Most weren't as inconspicuous as the priest.

The padre nodded and said, "Of course."

Huascar pulled out two concave discs made of solid gold and laid them out on the table. They rolled around for a few seconds until coming to a halt. Father Delanda rubbed his hands and reached out. "May I?"

The Indian nodded and pushed them closer. The priest lifted one of the dishes off the table and carefully looked at it in the candlelight. It was covered with markings and glyphs. There were drawings of animals never seen on the soil of South America: camels, elephants, and chimpanzees.

"Amazing, utterly amazing. And this came from the same area as the others?"

"Oh *sí*, Father. The tunnel I found them in has been abandoned for centuries. I think an earthquake or something."

A grin came over Father Delanda's face. "That is good, my son. You have done well." He continued studying the drawings. "I can't imagine how old this is. There's no known record of camels and elephants in this area. How would they have known they existed?"

Huascar reached for his knife and stick and resumed his carving. "It is said, Father, in the chronicles of my people that they did exist. Legends have been passed down from one generation to another describing distant lands where our ancestors traveled back and forth. Only the high priests were allowed to go. They traveled with The Gods on wagons that glowed and spewed fire as they zoomed off into the darkness."

Father Delanda looked away from the disc and over at Huascar. "All conjecture, my son—quite impossible to believe. I must study this one closer back at the cathedral." He quickly added, "Under the most strictest secrecy, of course."

Huascar nodded. "Yes, no one must know."

The priest slowly spun the dish around 360 degrees and then looked inside. When he positioned it in the candlelight, the reflection off the bottom was so bright and intense that it made him squint. He recoiled and almost dropped it.

"Be careful, Father. There is very powerful magic hidden in these pieces."

The light emanating from the disc was now beaming toward the kitchen and reflecting off Nina's cooking utensils. She was visibly annoyed and waved her hand around while muttering underneath her breath. The priest took notice but let the light linger awhile before moving it away.

He again examined the exterior and ran his finger over two indentations. "What are these for?"

Huascar stopped carving and leaned in for a better look. He pointed the knife at the disc and said, "That's what held them in place. My ancestors used these discs to reflect the sunlight from above down into the tunnels."

"Ah," said Father Delanda. He laid down the saucer and picked up the other disc. It had similar markings on the outside and a hole through the center. He twisted it upside down for a better look in the light.

"See, this one hung on a pole." Huascar put down his knife and stick and used his hands to demonstrate. "Each one of the discs was perfectly placed at the right angle to reflect the sunlight. When you combined them together, it was just as bright below the earth as it was on top."

"Brilliant. Absolutely brilliant."

The priest cautiously peered inside the disc and then angled it toward the candlelight. Once again, a powerful stream of light shot out and illuminated the wall above one of the beds. He then picked up the second dish and placed it in the path of the first beam. The room exploded into a bursting supernova of glowing radiance and blinding light as the combined saucers fed off each other.

"My word, it's bright, and so quickly," he exclaimed as he lowered the dish. Nina was now watching from the kitchen. Her annoying growl had vanished and been replaced with a look of bewilderment. Once she realized that the priest had noticed her staring at the artifact, she turned away and resumed her work.

"Huascar, my boy. This is by far one of the most astonishing relics you've ever brought me. Definitely better than the last few."

Huascar placed one of his elbows on the table and indiscreetly rubbed his fingers together. "I was hoping you'd say that, Father. It's getting much harder to find these, you know—I mean the exotic ones, that is. I still have tons of ordinary pieces if…"

The priest cut him off. "No, no. I'm still not interested. Only the unusual ones like this. The ones with camels and elephants—and especially astronauts." He reached into his pocket, retrieved a small leather pouch, and tossed it across the table. Huascar caught it in midair.

The Indian placed the pouch in his pocket and said, "*Muchos gracias,* Father, but promise me you'll keep this secret just between us."

As with anything in life that brought prosperity, there was usually a risk. Huascar's risks were severe. The penalty for selling ancient artifacts was death. He was a descendent of the proud and chosen few Quechua Indians who were assigned to protect his people's secrets and riches buried underground throughout South America. That title meant he was a trusted and respected leader in his culture, as were his father and his father's father and his ancestors going back hundreds of years. This title instilled pride and moral character in most Indians, but for Huascar, it was more of a curse—at least until he'd figured out how prosperous it could be.

"Of course, my son. *Gracias, de nuevo.*"

Father Delanda placed the discs back into the bag and tied off the opening. He began to rise up from the table but then hesitated and said, "Oh, I almost forgot. I think we're going to need the services of your...friend."

Huascar's wandering eye started to twitch. "You mean the crazy one?"

"Yes, unfortunately, the crazy one. I need him to find someone for me—unharmed."

"This boy you've been looking for?"

"This young scoundrel who's been living under my church and stealing from the monastery." The priest leaned in toward Huascar and whispered, "I know how this man operates and he must not touch the boy. Is that clear?"

"*Sí*, Padre."

Father Delanda stood up and tucked the golden trinkets inside his frock. "Take care, my son." He walked over to the door and let himself out. Without looking back, he said, "I wish I could stay for dinner, Nina, but thank you for asking."

CHAPTER EIGHT
THE CAVE

Renee, her father, and Don Carlos left the sunken courtyard and headed further down the path toward Puma Punku. Built of massive blocks with some weighing over one hundred tons, the structure was one of mankind's most mystical feats. How these huge stones were transported from miles away over mountainous terrain without the use of wheels is still a hotly debated subject. Add on the fact that assembling these precisely cut monoliths, made out of a rock almost as hard as diamonds, would take advanced engineering skills from a people who didn't even have a written language makes it even more puzzling. Some of the stones still standing fit together so perfectly straight and without any mortar that it was impossible to slip a knife into the cracks between each stone. On the outskirts of the site, huge boulders lay sprawled out on the ground like sets of fallen dominoes.

Don led them past the site and down a hill, where the path became narrower. They walked for a long time away from the village until the barren land began to come alive. The denser foliage lowered the temperature a good five degrees from that at the temple site. The few trees they did find were dressed in layers of smooth bark with branches that drooped to the ground like a servant bowing down before his master.

They continued up a dirt path for fifteen more minutes before Don Carlos stopped to catch his breath. He wiped his brow with a handkerchief and said, "No need to hurry. You must catch your breath every once in a while at this altitude."

Renee's dad examined his compass and exclaimed, "This is amazing. Now the compass needle is pointing toward the middle of that mountain. Look at this."

He showed it to his daughter and watched her face light up. "Very cool."

"Here, you carry it for a while." Roger took the compass off and placed it around Renee's neck. Renee couldn't take her eyes off the needle as she rotated the compass back and forth.

Don Carlos glanced over her shoulder for a peek and added, "It is pointing to the caves."

They resumed their walk until the ruins were far off in the distance, resembling speckled bread crumbs scattered over the landscape. The path was climbing through the mountain valley and winding around boulders and cliffs while constantly moving inward toward a large crevice.

"How much longer?" asked Roger.

"We're almost there." Don Carlos paused and pointed to a cluster of small trees and bushes butted against the hillside off to the left.

Renee checked the compass and commented, "Funny how this thing now points only to that clump of trees."

When they finally reached the ravine, Don Carlos pulled out his machete and started wildly hacking away at the branches that had grown over the diminished path. Renee and her father kept their distance until he'd carved his way to the cave entrance, then they came up for a better look.

"This is it?"

"*Sí, señor.*"

The opening was just a slit between two rocks barely wide enough for a man to fit through. Roger studied the hole and said, "How do you get in there?"

"You must be careful and slide through on your stomach. You can kick your backpack in with your feet."

"Well, here goes nothing." Roger dropped his pack to the ground, kicked it in, and shimmied through the opening on his hands and knees. On the other side, he pulled his camera out and started taking pictures. "Amazing! You gotta see this!" Flashes of light flickered out of the cave one after the other.

Renee looked to Don Carlos, who motioned her to go next. She was small enough to hold onto her backpack and slide through easily. Before entering, she glanced back and noticed that the path her uncle just cut away had somehow closed shut. *No wonder this place is so hard to find*, she thought.

When she appeared on the other side, she found her dad staring at a drawing on the cave wall. "Come here. You have to see this," he said. Renee stood up and walked over as Don Carlos struggled to push his plump belly through the opening. "Take a look at this drawing. Notice how the two men have some kind of helmet on their heads. What's it remind you of?"

Renee looked up. "Astronauts?"

"Precisely. There's a drawing very similar to this in Italy that dates back ten thousand years. Coincidence? I think not."

A crinkle of doubt lined Don Carlos's face as he looked up at the drawing and said, "Astronauts?"

"Yes, I know it's a little hard to believe, but you must admit the similarities are there."

"No doubt," chimed in Renee.

Roger smiled as he snapped a few more pictures before returning his camera to his backpack. It was such a nice change to have his daughter agreeing with him after they'd grown so far apart over the past few years. That's what happens when a young preteen outgrows her dolls. Between stories about the Sandman, the Tooth Fairy, and Santa Claus, who could blame a girl for doubting her parents and questioning everything around her? Roger missed having that little starry-eyed girl who used to think he was the greatest man on earth, and Renee still yearned for that hero on a white horse.

That last summer had changed everything. When he took her to the King Tut exhibit in Chicago, they reconnected. She was fascinated with ancient history and amazed by how much her father knew. He'd always been infatuated with extraterrestrial folklore but knew better than to share it with just anyone. A little too much enthusiasm around the wrong friends and colleagues would clear a room faster than you could say "little green men." With his daughter, it was different. She got it.

Soon they'd combined the two subjects together and were sharing everything from novels and scientific journals to big bang theories and personal diaries. She would surf the Internet and he would bring home the books. They visited the pyramids in Mexico and the Mayan ruins. They flew over the Arizona desert in a charter plane to see the strange lines and drawings left by ancient

Document 512

Indians. It wasn't long before they both realized where they needed to go next: South America. The last unexplored frontier on earth.

Getting the time off from work for Roger was easy enough. His job required that he either use his vacation time or lose it by the end of the year as it was. Taking Renee out of school posed its own problems, but not enough to deter them. It was actually easier than they'd thought. Her parents had enrolled her in an Options For Youth Charter School in hopes that the smaller classes and individual one on one time would help with her dyslexia. Even though the verdict was still out on that, it definitely helped with scheduling the trip around her classes. When the pre-holiday rates dropped so low that they couldn't be ignored, Roger jumped on them and booked the flight.

"This way," Don Carlos said as he gestured with his flashlight for everyone to proceed into another room.

They followed him through an archway that led into a bigger cave covered in stalagmites and stalactites with two hallways leading off in different directions. A few tree roots had squeezed through cracks crawling across the walls like thinly stretched spiderwebs.

Roger's flashlight fixated on another petroglyph. "Unbelievable." He moved in closer and touched it lightly with his fingertips. "See these lines? See how they follow along this mountain range? Do you know what this is?"

"It looks like a road," replied Renee.

"Yeah, but a road to where? It's on top of a mountain and ends right on the edge. No, I don't think it's a road. I think it's a landing strip. About two hundred miles south of Lima is a place called the Nazca Plains. You know, the place we're going to in a couple of days."

Roger's arms swayed like a philharmonic conductor guiding his orchestra as he continued. "It's huge—probably thirty-five miles long and a mile wide. There're tons of these perfectly straight lines, some of them parallel, some intersecting each other just like this. Look at these figures flying through the air. Doesn't it look like some of them are landing and others are taking off?"

He took a deep breath and released it. "Many people think this area was the original landing site of aliens thousands of years ago. From here, they could have traveled all over the world—even to Italy and Greece."

"Italy and Greece," echoed Renee.

"Think about it. Greek and Roman mythology were based on all of these immortal gods with human characteristics. Who's to say that Zeus really wasn't just an alien with a big ego?"

Roger continued to wander in and out of speculation about aliens and other worlds. After years of rejection over his wild notions and theories, he was now being vindicated with every wave of his flashlight. The light beams danced over the walls and floor like a parade of ballerinas. As they passed over the two hallways, Don Carlos noticed shadows reflecting off a pool of water that covered most of the other room's floor.

Renee looked over just as the shadows disappeared. "What was that?"

Don Carlos smiled and ignored her comment. "I think we need to move on. You will be pleased with what we see."

Roger regained his composure and caught his breath. "Excuse me for rambling on like this. It's just…it's just that you don't run into cave drawings like this every day. In fact, you don't see stuff like this in an entire lifetime." He took one more look at the drawings and turned to his daughter, "I'm sorry for getting carried away."

Renee was still staring at the reflecting pools in the darkened room. She looked up and tried to smile innocently. "Don't sweat it, Pop. You had me carried away for sure."

"Follow me," Don Carlos said as he exited the room and headed down the other narrow hallway. These walls took on a much different appearance than the ones at the entrance. They were smooth and glazed, almost as if they'd been cauterized. There weren't any chisel marks or rough edges like they'd seen in the first room either. The walls met the ceiling at a perfect ninety-degree angle. As they moved the flashlights back and forth, speckles of gold dust reflected off the shiny surface.

Roger ran his fingers along the rock and said, "How could Indians have dug these out and finished them so finely? I mean, have you seen the crude tools they used?" A swarm of birds suddenly flew by within inches of his head, and he ducked out of the way. They disappeared so quickly that they were barely able to catch a glimpse of their red and white markings.

"For Pete's sake! Where'd that come from?"

Don Carlos showed little emotion, as if he'd totally expected the incident to happen. "There are many air holes in these caves. They shoot straight up to the ground above and sometimes provide enough light for you to see. Turn off your flashlights and let's try it."

They both clicked off the lights and let their eyes adjust. A subtle glow surrounded them as each person's silhouette gradually came into focus. "There is almost enough light to see. Maybe as we go further."

Don Carlos turned his flashlight back on and continued walking. Around the next corner were a series of lifelike humans etched into the stone walls. Their bodies, skinny and frail, stood with spears in their hands. They looked as if they were guarding something. An eerie feeling again came over Renee and her father when they noticed that the eyes were twice the normal size. What was their purpose?

At the end of the hallway, a huge, solid marble wall stained with either blood or rust stood before them. In the dim light, it looked like a dead end. Don Carlos stopped a few feet away and surveyed the stone. The flashlight shining on the black surface reflected his image back over a set of strange markings that covered it from one end to the other. The drawings moved up and down the wall in rows, with segments of four shapes in each block. Most of the characters consisted of squiggly lines cutting through squares and half circles, while some resembled stick people walking or bending down. Each symbol appeared unrelated to the next.

"Looks like something you'd see on an Egyptian tomb," said Roger. "But nothing I've ever studied. The symbols are similar but yet...something's different about them." He moved in for a closer look and raised his light. "I just can't figure out what it is."

"I know what you mean, Dad." Renee reached around to her backpack and pulled out a thin book with symbols and drawings on the cover. "I can, like, almost make out certain symbols that match the hieroglyphic stuff we studied this summer, but there's something...out of whack."

"Yes, there is, my friends." Don reached up and ran his fingers along the grooves that made up the middle row. "To the untrained eye."

He placed both hands on the wall and glided them over a set of shapes carved at shoulder height. His hands went back and forth until he found the exact spot he was looking for. With both his middle fingers firmly placed in two indented circles, he smiled and said, "I think I've found it. I need your help, *chiquita*."

Renee returned the book to her bag and moved in closer to the wall behind Don Carlos as he placed the rest of his fingers into the other holes near his hand.

"Please put your finger in between my thumb and index finger." Renee reached up and placed her finger against the wall. "Now feel for the groove. Do you feel it?"

"Yes," she said excitedly, "I feel it."

"Good. Now place your other finger in the same exact spot by my other hand."

Renee lifted up her free hand and placed it between Don Carlos's thumb and forefinger just as before. "There, I found it."

"Good."

With all five of his fingers in place along with Renee's, Don Carlos pushed the huge wall with both arms in one sweeping motion. It slid back effortlessly. With every inch the rock moved, the light streaming through the gap doubled in intensity. By the time he'd shoved the stone a couple of feet back, the whole room was so bright that they had to cover their eyes.

"Whoa, how'd you do that?" asked Renee as she backed away a few feet.

"With the help of The Gods," said Don Carlos with a grin. "Let's continue, no?"

"Let's do," said Roger.

They went through the door and around the corner. A large open area covered with vines and roots stood before them. The light shining around the room didn't seem to be coming from any one source. It lit up the entire place from every angle, leaving the room void of shadows or any hues of darkness.

Renee studied one of the vines and said, "You know, there aren't any bugs down here."

Her father walked up behind her adding, "How interesting. No bugs—and just the right amount of humidity. Plus, the air seems to be thicker. I'm not having any trouble breathing at all."

"Welcome to the hidden caves of Tiwanacu—a place of many mysteries that very few have ever seen," Don Carlos chimed in. "Come, we continue, no?"

"Yes," Renee and her father said in unison.

They followed Don away from the vines to a corner of the room that was not as well lit as the rest. There stood a crude-looking thatch-roofed hut. The room's temperature dropped another degree with every step closer they took. By the time they reached the entrance, Renee could almost see her own breath.

"It's like an icebox in here. How'd that happen?"

"This is how the gifts of the cave have come to us, my friend," said Don Carlos. "No one knows why." He threw back the leather flap at the doorway and peeked inside the hut. "After you."

He motioned for Roger and Renee to enter and followed behind them. Inside, tall candles were placed in each corner to light the inner walls. The only other item in the room was a stone tomb in the center that was propped open with the lid ajar to one side. There were intricate carvings on its stone sides depicting snakes, jaguars, and other animals. The top of the chest contained diagrams of symbols and letters similar to the glyphs they'd seen on the marble door. Renee's father moved in for a closer look.

"Look, there's that same drawing of a lake that we saw back in the other cave."

"Yeah, but, I dunno, this lake looks more like a river. See how it runs on," said Renee. "And there's that other symbol that looks like a snail."

"Hmm, I wonder what that means." Roger turned to Don Carlos and asked, "Can you read this?"

"Sometimes, *señor*."

"Sometimes?"

"*Sí*. It depends on where you start reading. That is the key. Sometimes I start in the right place and sometimes I don't." Don Carlos shrugged his shoulders and added, "I forget."

Roger didn't seem to be buying the explanation but decided not to continue the line of questioning. Renee moved in closer and studied the illustrations in the dim light. She slowly moved her hand over the tomb's surface, then she traced the lines of each symbol repeatedly with her finger. She murmured a few words under her breath before saying, "It says '*crustum*' and, uh, '*aqua*.'"

Don Carlos and Roger looked at each other with disbelief. They all exchanged glances and were silent. Finally, her father spoke. "That sounds Latin. I think it means "bread and water." Then he looked to Don Carlos for confirmation, "Well?"

Don Carlos was speechless. He studied the writings for a while, looked at his niece, and then looked back at the writings. After a few more moments of silence he straightened up and said, "Maybe, maybe not. It is said of my people that the ancient symbols of bread and water depict life and death."

"Life and death?"

"Yes," replied Don Carlos. "These are the most important symbols in my people's language. Every entry written down begins with praising the gift of life and ends with recognizing the certainty of death."

Renee's father looked at her and said, "How'd you read that?"

"I don't know. It just kinda came to me," said Renee.

"Anyway, help me with the lid," said Don Carlos.

The two of them grabbed a corner of the large stone and pushed. At first, it didn't budge, but on the second attempt, they managed to slide it off enough to see inside.

Roger's eyes widened as he exclaimed, "Holy…"

Don shined his flashlight into the case as Renee peeked around his shoulder and gasped, "Oh my God!"

Inside the tomb were the remains of a semi-mummified cadaver. The corpse was wrapped in a shroud of old cloth that gently protected parts of the body while others were completely exposed to the elements. Strands of red hair dripped down off the scalp onto a pillow that cushioned a well-preserved face. The man had long, skinny hands and exceptionally wide feet. At first, they didn't notice his unusual features until they moved the light around. When they did, Roger and Renee just looked at each other and said nothing. Every limb on the corpse's body had six fingers and six toes. Around the neck and seated on his chest was a large golden necklace.

CHAPTER NINE

THE TOMB

Roger moved his flashlight up and down the mummified body. He could not believe his eyes. A silver sword rested on the left side of the shoulder while a golden chalice sat on the right. Around the mummy's neck was a circular piece of jewelry about the same circumference as a baseball. The edges were uneven and rough, but the markings inside were finely carved. They spread out arbitrarily like branches on a tree, twisting and turning, while other lines flashed images of half-drawn shapes or letters. It looked as if the piece had never been completely finished.

A band made up of animal hair and fiber held the pendant in place around the corpse's neck. The texture of each strand varied, meaning that they must have come from more than one source. Several different-colored strings dangled off the main band with knots tied randomly throughout.

Renee studied the markings intensely. "I can't seem to make any sense of it."

Roger leaned in with the light and said, "It's a *khipu*. I mean the cord connected to the pendant. That's a *khipu*."

"What's that?"

"It's thought that the natives used them to communicate with each other. A crude language of some kind." He tried to pick up the medallion off the mummy, but it wouldn't move. He pulled at it again, but nothing happened. It was still firmly attached to the torso. "It won't budge."

Don Carlos smiled. He knew that Roger wouldn't be able to raise it off the ancient ruler's chest. He also knew who could. Ever since that conversation with his half sister from the United States years before, he knew. When Leslie Gorman mentioned that her daughter had a rare deformity with her toes, Don Carlos knew immediately what it meant. From that day forward, he set into motion a plan to lure the young girl to South America in hopes that she'd be able to accomplish what thousands of others had not been able to do: remove the mysterious amulet from the corpse. It was the moment he'd been waiting for.

"Maybe the little *chiquita* could try?" he questioned. His delivery sounded so innocent that it would have fooled his own mother.

Roger rose up and shrugged his shoulders. He looked to his daughter and said, "I don't know. What do we have to lose?"

Renee smiled and said, "Sure, why not."

Roger stepped to the side, allowing his daughter to move next to the tomb. She looked at both of them and then down at the mummy. For the first time, she realized just how old and decrepit the body was. Inside the crusty contours of the cheekbones and jawline were pockets of missing flesh that exposed the brittle bones underneath. She reached down, gently grasped the trinket with her fingertips, and lifted it with ease.

Don Carlos held his breath. When the necklace rose off the mummy's chest and swung freely in the air, he exhaled so loudly that it startled Renee. She hastily dropped the medallion and flinched.

"Oh, I am so sorry, my little one. I didn't mean to scare you. Please, please pick it up."

Renee looked to her father; he nodded reassuringly. She untied the *khipu* and removed the ornament from the corpse's neck. Then she positioned it closer to one of the candles for a better view. Flickers of gold and white reflected off its surface as it spun around.

"It's beautiful."

The compass on her neck was now within inches of the pendant. A low hum slowly rose in volume as the trinket began to vibrate. Tints of red and blue light radiated from its center. Then a sudden flash of tiny white sparks spurted out around the medallion's edges for a few seconds before quickly disappearing.

"Wow, what was that?" asked Roger.

"I don't know. May I see it?" asked Don Carlos.

Renee hesitated. Something in his tone of voice had changed. It was more assertive than before. The inquisitive gentleness was gone. She had no reason to be suspicious but still an urge to say "no" came over her. Instead, she slowly dropped the necklace into her uncle's palm and then placed her hands back into her pockets.

"*Gracias.*"

Don Carlos lifted the pendant into the air and studied it closely. Finally, after all of these years of trying, he was in possession of one of the most sacred artifacts of his culture. Legend had it that whoever possessed this talisman held the secrets of life itself. He rubbed the ornament for a few seconds, waiting to see if anything happened. Nothing did. This confirmed one of his theories, but he knew that there were many other ways to obtain the powers hidden within. It would just take a little bit of experimentation on his part to find them. Years of learning the customs of his people and listening to the stories passed down from his elders had prepared him well for this moment. Now all he had to do was determine which stories were true and which ones weren't.

Renee and her father exchanged looks but didn't say anything. They didn't need to. They knew that something was wrong. As Don Carlos fumbled around in his backpack, Renee slowly shuffled closer to her father.

Roger placed his arm around her shoulder and said to Don Carlos, "What's going on here?"

The leather flap covering the opening to the door began to sway back and forth. A slight breeze permeated the room. It was a warm breeze. Normally, that would have soothed them like a warm bath—but not today. Outside, a rattling sound echoed in the distance. The noise seemed to be coming from all different directions. It made them feel disoriented and uneasy. Then there was the faint patter of feet shuffling outside the hut. It lasted only a few seconds but still, it was alarming.

"Dad, what's going on?"

Roger looked to his daughter and then to Don and said, "I'm not sure. Maybe your uncle can explain."

The plump Bolivian pulled a pistol out of his bag and pointed it at his bewildered relatives. A devious grin stretched across his face as he began to back up toward the exit.

"I am so indebted to you, Miss Renee. You have made me a very happy man."

"Where're you going?"

"Oh, I must be off now. You have been so kind as to retrieve the necklace for me. Now it is time for me to say good-bye—forever."

"Forever?"

"Yes. Unfortunately, one of the drawbacks to removing a sacred ornament from one of the thirteen kings is that you have awakened the protectors of The Gods. As long as you are on this hallowed ground, they will be looking for you and will hunt you down. There is little time for me to stay and explain, so I must ask that you do not try to follow me." He swung the gun from side to side. "I'd hate to have to leave your poor mother a widow—and maybe even childless."

The warm breeze was now blowing hard against the outside of the hut. The burlap walls fluttered uncontrollably and made the wooden braces squeak. Underneath the flap of the door, a thick, dark-reddish fluid started seeping in. Steam rose from the floor. The rattling noise had returned outside and was growing louder.

Don Carlos wiped his brow as he backed up slowly toward the exit. He was too busy concentrating on Roger to notice the liquid oozing under his feet. Roger was aware of this and kept his eyes focused on Don Carlos. Renee sensed that something was about to happen and moved behind her father.

Another wave of fluid rushed in under Don's feet, causing him to slip and lose his balance. The gun swung wildly into the air as a shot rang out. The bullet ricocheted off a tall candlestand in the corner, sending it crashing down onto his chest. Don Carlos hit the ground hard as his head bounced off the floor like a basketball.

The stench of decomposing flesh mixed with hot air now consumed the room. Renee's father carefully walked over to Don Carlos and picked up the revolver. He opened one of his brother-in-law's eyelids and said, "He's out cold."

The rattling sound grew louder. Roger looked to his daughter and said, "We need to get out of here before whatever is making those noises finds us."

CHAPTER TEN

RATTLING THE GODS

Roger cautiously peeked through the flap, stuck his head out, and said, "Coast is clear." The floor outside of the hut was bone-dry. They skirted across the open room while looking for any signs of movement or sound. The air was chilly, a stark contrast from the heated sauna they'd just exited.

When they approached the area where the trees and vines overtook the landscape, Renee's father put his arm in front of her and said, "Hold on. I see something moving." He lifted up his flashlight. Covering the floor in front of them were hundreds of tiny mounds of dirt that resembled giant anthills. Dust bubbled up from the shells in these holes as long, thin claws slowly emerged on the surface. Behind each set of claws were a set of legs and a torso shaking off the dirt and wobbling along. Within seconds, spotted gray wings sprouted from their bodies and began to flutter.

"There's your rattling noise."

"What are they?"

"I think they're cicadas, although they're rather large and nothing like I've ever seen."

"Are they dangerous?"

"No, not at all. They'll eat anything, but I've never known them to attack humans. Try to step over them, though."

Roger carefully tiptoed between each insect as he held onto Renee's hand. He glanced up and noticed a few locusts hanging in the vines above and around them. Renee concentrated on following in her father's footsteps while trying to keep her balance. As they passed each pile of dirt, the insects started spinning in circles and vibrating their torsos. The crackling noise continued as the newly hatched cicadas systematically flew off the ground and joined the others on the walls and vines.

The mounds spewed more and more bugs as Renee and her father maneuvered between them, making it even more difficult to avoid contact. Renee instinctively picked up the pace, dancing from one spot to another until she heard a crunch. They both stopped and peered down at the stream of body fluid oozing around her feet. She lifted her shoe and saw a gooey strand of liquid that stretched from the puddle to her heel. The same fleshy odor from the hut sifted into their nostrils. The scent caused Roger to cough and gag.

As Roger covered his nose with a bandana, one of the locusts swooped down and grazed the back of his head. Another followed suit and dove for Renee. Within seconds, hundreds of them were jabbing their razor-sharp probes into Renee's and Roger's heads. They tried to fend them off by swatting aimlessly in the air, but the locusts just pounded their exposed arms and hands, quickly tenderizing them beyond recognition.

"Keep moving!" screamed Roger as he led her along. They continued swinging wildly and raced toward the marble wall, crushing bugs one after another under their feet. This only increased the flow coming up from the ground, which made it even harder to navigate through the stench. Thousands of cicadas were now singing and flicking their wings in celebration as they feasted on their new prey. Roger noticed that part of Renee's earlobe was missing and patches of blood saturated her blouse.

"I can't see!" she screamed. The venom oozing out of her wounds dripped down her forehead and blanketed her eyes. She stumbled over a rock, but her father caught her before she hit the ground. He took his handkerchief and wiped away the pus from her cuts while swatting the diving insects with his other hand.

"Do you have that can of mosquito repellent?"

"Yes, it's in my bag."

"Get it out and I'll try holding them off."

One of Renee's eyes had swollen completely shut. She could only make out blurred shapes of figures as she fumbled through her bag. "I got it," she exclaimed.

Roger grabbed the can out of her hand and sprayed it in the air. One by one, the cicadas retreated; the mist created an invisible shield over their heads. "It's working!" he yelled. Renee rubbed her eyes but could still only make out the silhouette of a man's arm in front of her.

"Let's get into the other room," barked Roger. A cloud of locusts hovered around them as they sprinted toward the marble door. "When we get through, we need to shut it somehow."

"I think I can do it," shouted Renee, "but I'll need your help."

The giant insects resumed their chase, flying over and around the mist and speeding toward their targets. Roger continued pressing the nozzle while pushing his daughter along. When they entered the next room, he discharged the last of the repellent and tossed the can. Renee blindly scoured the black marble with her fingers, searching for the indentations her uncle had used earlier.

"Here, I got 'em. Put your finger in between my thumb and pointer."

Document 512

A few locusts burst past the toxic force field guarding the doorway. Roger shielded his daughter from the onslaught and yelled, "Push!"

The door slid shut with ease, sealing off the room from the light and chaotic chatter. Roger pulled out his flashlight to assess the damage. The few cicadas that had made it through were spinning in circles on the ground in front of him. He squashed them under his feet causing liquid to seep out of the their cracked shells and sizzle in the dirt.

When finished, he turned to his daughter and asked, "Are you all right?"

"I don't know." Renee stood up and rubbed her eyes again. "It's still pretty blurry."

Roger pulled out his canteen and dabbed the water on his handkerchief. Then he gently patted his daughter's eyes. "How's that?"

"Not much better. They're still swollen."

"Let me try something else." He unzipped a smaller pouch on the front of his bag and pulled out a tube of toothpaste, then squeezed a bead onto his finger and rubbed it over her eyelids. Within minutes, the swelling subsided.

"Wow, that really worked. What made you think of it?"

Roger returned the tube to his pack and said, "It's a MacGyver thing."

Renee feebly tried to chuckle as she wiped away the last of the paste with the bandana. She cleaned it off and handed it back to him. "What's happening to us?" she asked solemnly.

He knelt down and tried not to stare at her missing earlobe. The last thing he needed was another crisis to deal with. While gently washing away the blood on her arms, he calmly said, "Honey, we have to be ready for anything that might come at us. Removing that necklace from the corpse has triggered some kind of reaction."

"But we left it back in the hut."

"I know, but it might be too late to stop the wheels in motion. The way your uncle talked leads me to believe that we've unleashed some pretty powerful stuff here. We need to get out of this place and fast."

"What's so important about the necklace?"

"I don't know for sure," said Roger, "but you saw the way it lit up when you held it. I think we've stumbled upon something here. Have you ever heard of a place called *Puerta de Hayu Marca*?"

"No."

"There's a circular indentation in a rock there that's about the same size of the medallion we saw—anyway, I'll tell you more later. But more importantly, I think this cave is some sort of missing link or missing piece to a puzzle."

"What puzzle?"

"Who knows, maybe life itself. Think about it. This lost civilization just disappears. Why? It doesn't make sense. I think it's still alive and well. Don Carlos knew this. That's why he brought us here…or, at least, you here."

Renee didn't know what to say. She opened her mouth a few times but nothing came out. All she could think about was being back home snuggled in her bed, safe and warm.

Roger grinned and said, "Let's move on."

As they turned the corner into the interior hallway, Renee noticed that the human figures on the wall were missing. She shook her father's sleeve. "Pop, weren't those Indian drawings here?"

Roger rubbed his hands over the wall. "I'm not sure—but I think so."

They continued down the narrow tunnel that led to the large cave with stalagmites and stalactites. Down one of the hallways, they saw a flickering light coming toward them. Roger whispered, "Look! That looks like torches. I think we've been discovered. Let's hurry."

As soon as they stepped into the cave, Roger stumbled over something. The floor was uneven and felt like loads of laundry were strewn out everywhere. Renee held on as they both staggered up and down while the aroma of rotten flesh returned. A faint, deep humming sound reverberated off the walls.

About fifty yards away, the subtle glow of sunshine was peeking out of the small hole where they'd entered earlier in the day. Roger shined his flashlight over the floor to see what was making it so difficult to maneuver. He gasped. On the ground, stretching from one wall to the other and piled three or four deep, were pancakes of human bodies.

The light coming from the other hallway was now chasing a set of shadows along the walls. "We're running out of time. They'll be here soon. Climb on my back and just hold on."

He plowed his way over the bodies, using them as railings and stepping stones, while his daughter held on for dear life. Then a hand reached up and grabbed his leg. Then an arm stretched out for his foot and ripped off the heel of his shoe. Another set of long fingernails tore away the bottom part of his trousers, leaving scratch marks on his leg. He could hear the sound of laughter rising ever so slowly and taunting him with every step. The faces were all looking up at him as he passed by while their arms reached up, grasping for anything. He pulled out his buck knife and slashed wildly, cutting off fingers and hands with ease.

The faces were familiar too: he'd seen them all before. There were colleagues from work, old classmates, friends, and neighbors. Sometimes he'd see the same people more than once but at different stages of their lives. There were his mother and father as teenagers, then as young adults, then as decrepit seniors. Everywhere he looked, there were more versions of each person—sometimes with long hair and beards, other times with no hair at all. What became very apparent as he watched them all laugh and snicker was that they weren't laughing *with* him. They were laughing *at* him.

He tripped again and almost dropped Renee. "Dad, you can put me down now."

Roger set her down but was still fixated on the faces glaring up at him from the floor. The more they laughed, the brighter they glowed. Now they were singing "cuckoo, cuckoo, cuckoo" like the bird on a clock.

Renee got her bearings and took a few steps forward. Then she grabbed her dad's hand and asked, "What was that?"

"I don't know, but do you see them too?"

She looked down at the floor and saw faces, but they weren't the same ones staring up at her father. Instead, they were faces from her past: children she'd only known in kindergarten, old boyfriends smiling and winking, cheerleaders with pom-poms raised high into the air. They weren't singing "cuckoo," however. No, they were chanting something else completely. And as with her father, it began ever so slightly, but grew louder and louder.

"*Cinderella, Cinderella, dressed in yella, dressed in yella...*"

The mocking continued: "*Cinderella, where's your fella?*"

She staggered over a few more bodies and slipped. As her knee hit the ground, several little hands reached up and pulled her down. The bodies quickly jumped on top of her and began pulling out her hair and tearing at her clothes. Renee screamed and tried to fight them off as she clawed her way back upright. Her father pulled out the pistol and fired a couple of rounds at the floor near her feet.

Renee jumped back as a bullet barely missed her toes. "Dad! You almost hit me."

"I'm sorry, the bullets went right through their bodies. I didn't think..." It was then that he realized what was happening. He reached down and pulled her away while slapping and kicking them away. "Let's get out of here—now!"

Both of them were being teased and tugged simultaneously. The chanting grew louder still: "*Cinderella...*" "*Cuckoo, cuckoo...*" "*Dressed in cuckoo, cuckoo yella...*"

The bodies reached up, pulling at anything they could latch onto. On and on the teasing went, back and forth from one rhyme to the other. Roger looked back and saw the faint outlines of warriors with spears running toward them from the other side of the cave.

"Grab your canteen," he shouted. They both reached into their backpacks and pulled them out. "Sprinkle it on the ground as you walk." They doused the floor as several hands continued to tug at their clothes.

"Be careful, don't use it all up too soon. We still have a good twenty yards."

The water was working. Steam sizzled off the clumps of flesh, and the putrid stench returned. "I feel lightheaded," Renee moaned as she tumbled over.

Roger snapped her up before the bodies could react. "I do too. Cover your nose."

With their elbows tightly pressed against their faces, they continued to sprinkle water along the path. Fewer and fewer hands were reaching up, but the singing didn't stop. Instead it got even louder: "*Cuckoo Cinda, peed in the winda…*"

Then, all of a sudden, the mounds subsided and the taunting ceased. Renee's canteen was almost empty. She swung the last few drops out as far as she could and sprinted for the opening. Her father was right behind her.

When they finally reached the exit, Roger looked back and said, "Go ahead. Holler when you're clear."

Renee slid through the opening and yelled, "I'm out."

Roger wasted no time shimmying through the hole. Within seconds, he appeared on the other side and was standing next to her. Roger hugged his daughter with all his might. "We made it."

"My ears are ringing."

"Mine too. Let's get out of here before whatever it was down that tunnel catches up to us."

They discovered that the path Don Carlos had cut earlier had completely vanished. There were no branches lying on the ground leading away from the cave and no signs of a trail. "Do you have anything to cut with in your pack?"

Renee reached in and pulled out a Swiss army knife. "This is it."

"That won't work."

They both pushed away the brush, breaking branches as they went along. The process was slow and tedious. Some of the limbs snapped back unexpectedly and tore through their shirts. Finally, the vegetation thinned out enough to where they were able to easily walk again.

The shadows cast by the bushes were long, indicating that they had maybe an hour or two before dusk. The temperature had cooled substantially and a chill now blew through their clothing.

Roger looked from left to right and said, "I'm pretty sure we came in this way."

They proceeded at a brisk pace as traces of a path appeared on the ground, reassuring them that they were indeed heading in the right direction. There were a few footprints scattered around in the dirt too. As they rounded a bend, they heard a haunting wail off in the distance.

Renee looked up at her dad and said, "Do you hear that?"

Her father nodded. "I think we need to pick up the pace a little bit."

CHAPTER ELEVEN
THE CHASE BEGINS

It didn't take very long for the altitude to overwhelm them. They stopped at the end of an open plateau and rested. Several trees and bushes were scattered along the trail leading down the mountainside. They could now see the valley and fields below for the first time.

Out of breath and frightened, Renee leaned against a boulder and said, "Do you think we lost them?"

"That's hard to say, since I'm not quite sure what was chasing us in the first place." Her father walked in a small circle to keep his legs loose while scanning the horizon for any movement in the brush. "I think that whatever it was back there in the cave that we thought we were seeing did a pretty good job of slowing us down."

"I know what I saw—and felt."

"Yeah, me too, but I'm not so sure that it was real. Do you have any scratches on your arms or hands?"

She looked down. "No. How weird."

Her father took a closer look at Renee's ear. It was all there and didn't show any signs of being bitten. Then he looked down at her shoes. There was a small blackened-out gouge on the side of her rubber heel where the bullet he'd shot earlier had landed. "Just as I thought. All I have are these cuts on my arms, which I think I did to myself." He looked up and added, "The only wounds we have are the ones *we* did to ourselves."

She looked at her pant legs, which should have been shredded from the onslaught of arms reaching up to grab her in the tunnel. They were intact. "How's that possible?"

"I don't know."

"All I know is that it felt pretty real to me."

"Yeah, me too, but it wasn't, was it?" Roger was walking in circles again. "For some reason, that cave knew how to tap into our innermost fears and then use them against us. I think it had something to do with the stench. You know, it must have had some kind of hallucinogenic quality to it."

"You mean that we got high off the smell of those dead bodies?"

"I wouldn't quite say 'high,' but something more along the lines of 'tricked.'"

Renee looked down at her compass. The tip of the needle followed her father's every movement. It shifted back and forth as he continued walking in circles. He reached down to tie his bootlace when an arrow dashed by his head. Almost immediately, another arrow swooshed by his shoulder and drifted through the nearby branches.

"Get down!" he yelled and yanked his daughter to the ground. Another slew of arrows landed in the dirt in front of them.

Roger retrieved the gun from his backpack and said, "Over there. Get to the trees."

He fired a round in the direction of the arrows as they crawled on their hands and knees. They'd just ducked behind a bush when another wave of arrows landed in front of them. He peeked through the limbs and saw a group of fifteen or so Indians coming their way.

"Hurry, we need to stay out of reach."

They darted from one place to another each time the Indians stopped to reload. Roger shielded his daughter as they sprinted to the next rock. The Indians spread out in the clearing and fired again. This time, one of the arrows hit Renee's backpack dead center. She tried to pull it out but it was caught on something. When she looked inside, her heart sunk. The arrow had shattered her cell phone. At fifty yards away, their aim was deadly.

"This isn't working. We need to make a break for that path leading down the hill. I need to draw their fire. Once I do that, we can take off for those rocks." He pointed to a cluster of boulders about fifteen yards away.

Renee nodded.

Roger pulled a shirt out of his backpack and quickly wrapped it around the outside of the bag. He tied the arms together and let the bottom dangle down, simulating a body. Then he extended it outward and shook it. A dozen arrows pelted the canvas within seconds.

"Run!" he yelled.

They both took off sprinting at full speed toward the rocks. The few seconds it took to run fifteen yards were more than enough for the skilled marksmen. The arrows flew by in rapid procession; one hit Roger in the shoulder as he stumbled for cover.

"Dad! You're hit." Renee grabbed her father and kept him from falling. The Indians moved in closer and were now yelping with joy.

"I'm all right. I can still move." A blood spot formed on his back where the arrow had disappeared deep into his shoulder blade. He twisted his head for a better look. Then he placed his back against a boulder and pushed on the feathered nock of the arrow. The point ripped through his chest and the front of his shirt triggering a soul-curdling scream: "Ahhhhhh!"

Roger grabbed the shaft tightly and said, "Break it off in the back." Renee reached up and snapped off the end of the arrow. Her father's legs buckled underneath his weight causing him to struggle with the air and ground around him for a sense of balance. "Holy shit, that hurt." He regained his footing and took a deep breath. Then he pulled the rest of it out through the front. Another scream.

Roger took another deep breath and looked out at the approaching Indians. It was only a matter of time before they overtook them. He could now make out their faces and caught a good look at the one who seemed to be in charge. His eyes were almost twice the size of a normal person's. Roger scanned the ground, grabbed a fallen shoot of bamboo, and tested its sturdiness and said. "This will work. Over there, grab that one and bring it here. And that one too."

Renee ran over and grabbed a few with long, jagged edges off the ground. Then she removed any branches and laid them in front of him.

"Good. Now listen to me. This is our only chance. I only have a couple of bullets left. I'm going to distract them and slow 'em down. You keep going and I'll catch up later."

"No, you'll never make it."

"I'll never make it if I have to wait on you. That's why you have to go first."

Renee realized that what her father was saying was true. She couldn't keep up with him and was definitely slowing him down. The blood was still dripping onto his shoulder and down his back. She grabbed the shirt from his backpack and ripped it into pieces. Then she wrapped them under his armpit and over his shoulder.

"OK. But you have to promise that you'll be right behind me."

"I will, but you have to promise me that if I don't make it, you'll keep going." She started to argue, but just then, another arrow zipped by her head. "We don't have any more time. "Go now."

He reached out and hugged her with his one good arm as tightly as he could. She squeezed him even tighter. There were no other options, and she knew it.

"I love you, Pop."

"I love you too."

Roger nodded and tossed one of the spears back at the approaching hunters, "Now!" The diversion was just enough to allow Renee to race for the opening. Roger took a few steps backward, fired another shot, and ran to another set of trees a few feet away. As he ducked for cover, a swarm of arrows landed nearby. He threw another bamboo spear and sprinted off to another pile of rocks. So far, the plan was working.

DOCUMENT 512

Renee pressed on. The opening in the brush was now only a few feet away. She glanced back to her father and saw that he was still standing. That was a good sign. She darted off again and ran until she finally made it to the edge of the mountain trail.

She hid behind a large boulder and caught her breath. The path leading down was finally in front of her. The Indians would have a hard time hitting a target constantly disappearing around the next bend.

A gunshot rang out and then a scream. She recognized it immediately. As she spun back around, the man she'd looked up to all her life collapsed to the ground with an arrow sticking out of his back. The Indians were now within a few yards. Her first reaction was to run back toward him, but he lifted up and mouthed the word, "Go."

Roger stumbled forward a few feet before falling back down. Renee could only stand there and watch as the Indians closed in. Her father was now flat on his stomach with his head twisted to one side. He painfully raised his hand into the air and made an "I love you" sign with his thumb, index finger, and pinkie.

"No! Please, get up!" screamed Renee. Her father's arm wobbled in the air and dropped.

Roger Gorman's captors examined their victim and then looked to see where the noise was coming from. Renee didn't hesitate; she sped off down the trail at full speed.

The path was only a few feet wide, with a rocky mountainside on one side and a steep drop-off on the other. She slid around the first corner and almost lost her footing. As she teetered on the edge, just inches of falling to her death, she thought about how ironic it would be to get so far and then accidentally disappear over a cliff. Of course, the Indians knew that all too well. In fact, they were counting on it.

As she continued down the mountainside, the noises behind her grew fainter. Each turn gave her new hope. She kept one eye on the path and another on the rocks and trees alongside her. The altitude depleted her energy quickly but the thought of stopping was too frightening. Her stomach ached with pain from exhaustion. Every once in a while, she thought she heard a howl or scream coming from above, but it never got any louder. Her pace slowed as the path leveled off and headed back into the fields on the valley floor. Once again, she was near the ruins.

CHAPTER TWELVE
HIDE AND SEEK

As the site of the ruins came into view, Renee felt a sense of relief. She'd made it. The winds were much warmer now as the sunlight was still enjoying its visit in this part of the valley. The evening shadows were slowly creeping over the mountaintops in the distance and would be there soon. There were a lot more tourists in the area but none of them took notice of her as she discretely walked down the path heading through the main area.

She knew that the Indians wouldn't follow her into the ruins, but there were still many unknowns. At this point, she wasn't sure about anything. Anyone could be waiting for her around the next turn. She spotted a group of tourists laughing in a corner of the courtyard and playfully acting out some recreation of an ancient battle, but she just kept walking.

Once she'd passed the site and entered the parking lot, a thought occurred to her: *Where was she going to go for help?* Don Carlos's jeep was still there, but what good was that? As far as she knew, he was either dead or with the Indians looking for her. Maybe she could go to the authorities. As she contemplated this option, she remembered something her father had grumbled when they got off the plane in La Paz, "Damn police. They're more corrupt than the criminals down here." Then she wondered what they'd do with a teenage American girl all by herself thousands of miles away from home. Nothing good came to mind. She pulled her cell phone out of her bag. It was hanging together by wires with a huge hole right in the middle.

Behind her and coming down the walkway were the tourists she'd seen back in the courtyard. They were ambling along so carefree, laughing and joking the whole time. She had to act fast. The parking lot had maybe a dozen cars and three buses. The buses were all lined up in a row at the far end.

An idea came to her. She calmly walked over to the line of buses and bent down to tie her shoe. Nonchalantly, she studied each bus. The first was fairly new with tinted windows. Its door was shut and looked impenetrable. She kept searching. The second one was a good twenty years old. It looked like her old school bus from elementary school except that the front cabin was square shaped. Half of the windows were down and there was no one inside. It felt so inviting. She strolled over and, after surveying the area to make sure that no one was watching, gave the door a solid push. It opened without resistance. Quickly, she darted in, staying low to the ground. Then she grabbed the handle and snapped the door shut.

The bus was jammed with backpacks, coolers, blankets, and pillows. She grabbed one off a seat and shuffled down the aisle. The last three rows were filled with more equipment and supplies stacked to the ceiling. There were tents leaning against the backdoor and a pile of canvases sprawled over a few seats. Carefully, she slid underneath the covers and tried to hide.

The laughing sounds grew louder, so she dug herself in deeper. Outside the front door, the group stopped and started cursing in German. Even though the words were foreign to her, Renee definitely understood what they were saying. She also understood why: she'd accidentally locked them out. Renee could hear the tension building with each grunt and moan as the bus rocked from side to side every time they tried to force the door open. All she could do was helplessly sit there as the camaraderie between them hastily churned into chaos.

Finally, a female's voice rose above the others and silenced them. Renee then heard shuffling noises and a metallic scraping sound coming from the front of the bus. After a minute or two, a squeaky hinge moved and the door opened. Cheers of joy rang out from the group as they boarded the bus. The rumbling sound of random conversations and laughter filled the air again.

She tucked herself farther back into the pile of supplies as the Germans sat down in their seats. The engine whined for a moment and fired up. Another cheer rang out. The driver threw the bus into gear, gave it some gas, and turned left while all the passengers leaned right. Then the brakes squealed and the vehicle abruptly came to a halt. The driver put it in neutral and started yelling. The front door had opened again. Within seconds, everyone was quiet.

Renee heard footsteps and then a man's voice saying, *"Gracias."* She couldn't make out the rest of the exchange but could tell they were speaking Spanish. The conversation soon ended and then there were footsteps. Someone was slowly walking down the aisle toward the rear.

Renee started to shake; she prayed for an invisibility cloak of some kind to miraculously appear. This couldn't be good. The shifting canvas crinkled every time she shivered while the footsteps continued to come slowly and steadily. The laughter and joy that had filled the bus moments ago had vanished, leaving a silence thick with anticipation.

Then she heard a woman say something in a hostile tone. The words were muffled, so she lifted up the tarp up to hear more clearly. Then it hit her—a smell so putrid that it seemed to sift right through the fabric and into her pores: the smell of her uncle. The suffocating body odor forced her to hold her breath in order to keep from moving and blowing her cover.

Document 512

A woman sitting in the back of the bus stood up in the aisle and blocked Don Carlos from continuing any further. "That's far enough, Mister. There's no reason for you to be snooping through our supplies."

The bus was completely silent. Nobody spoke for a long while. Occasionally, someone would cough and try to end the standoff, but it didn't work. Don Carlos studied the woman for a long time but couldn't get a read on her. Then he focused his attention on the pile of supplies stacked up behind her. It was precariously packed in a way that one wrong tug might bring the whole heap down. That wouldn't sit well with the Germans, and he knew it.

"Of course, *señorita*. There is no need to go any further. Thank you for your time."

He turned around and walked back toward the front of the bus, stopping at each aisle and looking under the seat or over a passenger's head. The lady stood her ground and didn't take her eyes off him until he was completely out of sight. The bus door squeaked shut and the driver threw it into first gear. It slowly rolled forward, gathering speed as the driver shifted into second and floored it.

Renee finally exhaled.

PART TWO

WELCOME TO CUZCO

CHAPTER THIRTEEN
THE GRINGO

The night clerk at Mesón del Cuzco snored peacefully behind a padlocked fence with his body snuggled around the cash drawer on the desk. To his right stood a wooden board lined with room keys hanging like ripened chili peppers ready to be plucked from a vine. The barricaded office was sturdy enough to withstand almost any attack of brute strength—but not smart enough to prevent someone with a broom handle from sliding a key ring through a small opening on the counter.

Jason Finch quietly plucked the set of keys off the handle and placed the broom back in the closet. He knew better than to take the front set of stairs up to the third floor. It was riddled with squeaky boards and rusted nails. Instead, he followed the carpeted floor down the hallway and past the exit sign to the door at the end. From there, he shuffled up the second set of stairs without being heard.

This wasn't his first attempt at sneaking into a room late at night. On the contrary, he'd perfected this ploy to an art form over the past few months. There were many nights when he'd actually entered this same hotel as a paying customer. The night clerk even knew him on a first-name basis. He liked Mesón del Cuzco, with its twenty or so odd-looking rooms, because it was clean and reasonably priced. Although that was the case with most places in Cuzco, this one had a certain vulnerable charm to it when it came to security.

This lack of security was one of the reasons why he was now sneaking passed the clerk instead of waking him up. He'd been traveling throughout South America for over a year and had managed to avoid most of the pitfalls tourists usually get themselves into. Thieves and con men were everywhere, so you had to keep your eyes open for any kind of a setup. What he hadn't anticipated was the possibility of a female tourist, from Canada of all places, being more interested in his wallet instead of his chiseled looks and strong physique. At least, she said she was from Canada. Who knew if even that part of her story was true or just part of the con?

She'd played him like a game of chess: moving in slowly and capturing his heart piece by piece. It lasted just long enough to gain his confidence. Her sultry green eyes and innocent smile seemed so sincere. She laughed at all of his jokes—and why not? He was a funny guy. He was the designated jokester in his family, the one who could liven up Thanksgiving dinner with just a spoon and a few mashed potatoes. But she had one other gift that drove him crazier than anything else: she made him grit his teeth. Every time he got near her, an uncontrollable urge to grind them back and forth got the best of him. All he wanted to do was eat her up.

She was there for similar reasons too: adventure. That sealed the deal for him. Sometimes, she showed more desire to push the envelope than he did. They visited all the sites together and rambled through the countryside with reckless abandon. They stayed out late and drank the locals under the table. He soon discovered that she was capable of just about anything. Unfortunately, that anything also included deception.

One night after a few beers, Jason finally divulged his true purpose for staying in South America so long. He showed her the map that he'd been given months before by a dying Indian. The one possession he guarded more than anything. Then he recounted the story that the Quechua Indian had told him on his deathbed.

When Jason left Buenos Aires and arrived in Lima, he befriended a tour guide who kept him out of trouble and in possession of his money. The Indian was cheap, so Jason overpaid him and fed him well. As the weeks went on, the guide came down with pneumonia and never got better. He was dead by the end of the second month.

Before passing away, the Indian told Jason a story about the ceremonial closing of the secret tunnels that ran under the city of Cuzco. In these tunnels were ancient golden artifacts that the natives had worshipped for thousands of years. No man could find the entrance to the tunnel without knowing where to look for the clues. Once inside, the tunnels would lead you to the ancient city of Akakor, where a civilization as old as the artifacts themselves once existed.

The Indian died before explaining more of the puzzle but not before giving Jason a map that showed a version of South America very foreign to today's observers. Up and down the coast were thick lines drawn with small half circles protruding out on each side in seemingly random spots. To the north was the word "Parima" written close to a crudely drawn bow tie. In the center, a maze-like symbol sat next to a set of jagged points; it had a line below it and some markings too small to decipher. A pyramid sketched into a clump of trees followed to the east along the Amazon River. In between were several tributaries that branched off and aligned with clusters of black dots and squares. Along these rivers were the names "Akahim," "Akanis," and "Akakor" written in several places. Jason assumed that this was the mapmaker's way of hiding the true whereabouts of these cities and, thus, the riches hidden within. Unfortunately, the secret to reading these clues was buried with his friend.

DOCUMENT 512

The Canadian girl was fascinated with this map, and they talked about it for hours. They tried to fill in the gaps with their own explanations and fantasies, which led to even more exhilaration. When Jason told her the story behind Akakor and the lost civilization, he realized that he'd said too much. After that, he avoided the subject, which only made her more curious and set her plan into motion. Warming up to the night clerk and convincing him to give her the other key to Jason's room was easy enough. A low-cut blouse and a push-up bra did the trick nicely.

They'd gone out to dinner that night to their favorite hangout. After a couple of cocktails and ordering food, she told him that she'd forgotten something back at her room. Then she raced to his hotel and pulled up the loose board in the closet that she'd discovered weeks before. The secret hiding place contained his bankroll and other valuable possessions, but not the map. She quickly assessed the situation and decided that the money was better than nothing. The clerk didn't even notice the bag she was carrying as she (and her bosoms) bounced down the stairs.

By the time Jason realized she wasn't coming back, he was half drunk and preoccupied with another *chiquita* who was dancing for tips. Who knows? As far as he knew she might have even been part of the setup. Either way, it worked brilliantly and the Canadian was never seen again.

The night clerk felt a little guilty about being duped and offered Jason a free room for a few nights until he could get back on his feet. When it was obvious that nothing was going to happen anytime soon, he finally had to kick Jason out on the streets. That's when the clerk began snoring and sleeping through the night. He had a job to do, but he also had a conscience.

Jason turned the key gently and opened the door. There was always the chance that the keys had been mixed up on the board downstairs and the room was already occupied. That scenario could be deadly. The light shining through from the street lamp meant that the curtains were open—a good sign. He glanced over at the well-made bed and then switched on the light. The coast was clear. He plopped the key on the second bed and took off his leather jacket and ball cap. Then he pulled out some of the beef jerky he'd acquired earlier in the day for a midnight snack and settled in for the night. Before he could finish the second bite, he was fast asleep.

The first glimmers of sunlight that morning doused him like a bucket of water. He'd made it a point to always take a room on the east side of the hotel. The chances of a maid barging in on him were pretty remote at five o'clock. Before leaving, he flipped open his cell phone and placed a call. His brother would just be waking up in Virginia and getting ready for work. Unlike his adventurous younger sibling, Kyle Finch was a respected professor who'd settled down to a good life with a wife and two kids. He didn't despise the family's good fortune like his brother did. Instead, he embraced his parents' money by letting them put him through one of the best colleges on the East Coast. Then, for a graduation present, he let them buy him a house far beyond his salary range.

Hopefully, Jason could catch him before he got out the door. Most days, the phone just rang and rang. How could he blame Kyle for not picking up though? Their conversations had slowly digressed over the last few months from spirited stories of adventures through the jungles to dreary tales of stolen bananas.

He hit the speed dial number and put the phone to his ear. It rang four times. "What's up?" Kyle answered.

"Not much. How are things back in the real world?"

"Same old, same old. I'm just about to head out the door. I have to be at the school early this morning."

"I understand. Hey, I wanted to tell you about this boy I ran into today—or should I say he ran into me. It was the strangest thing…"

"Make it quick, bro. I have to leave in a few minutes."

"Yeah, yeah. Anyway, this kid had the deepest blue eyes. I mean, I know that's not strange, but he was an Indian. Red as an orangutan's butt."

"Yeah."

"Well, the most intriguing thing about him was that he had six fingers on each hand."

"What?"

"No shit. There were six digits on each hand and they all worked."

There was silence on the other end. Jason could tell that his brother had stopped walking around the house and was listening wholeheartedly. "Very strange."

"What's it remind you of?"

"I know, I know, the Brugger book, but I've told you before that all turned out to be a hoax."

"So they say," Jason retorted as he pulled out his map. "But I have proof that states otherwise."

Kyle let out a long sigh and answered, "Well, I'm not gonna argue with you about this again, so I'd suggest you just read over your book and try to figure out what it means."

"I don't have it anymore. I lost it…"

"Yeah, I know, with the other stuff. They've got a library there, don't they?"

"Sure, but that book's been out of print for twenty years."

"Well, just hope that the library you go to is more than twenty years old. Gotta go."

"All right."

"Keep me posted."

With that, the phone went dead. Jason looked down at a screen that was blinking off and on. He would now have to sweet-talk the waitress at the local diner into letting him borrow her charger once again. That usually meant the rolling of her eyes, a lot of arm waving, and a little cursing in Spanish. She always gave in, though. Why wouldn't she for such a cute gringo?

CHAPTER FOURTEEN
BIBLIOTECA

The Plaza de Armas was nearly vacant at daybreak as Jason headed toward the center fountain. His first order of business was to wash up a little bit and maybe even do some laundry. No one even noticed as he removed his shirt, dipped it into the water, and gave himself a sponge bath. He then wrung it out and set it over the back of a nearby bench to dry. The morning air was too chilly to be ignored, so he put his jacket back on, sat down, and lit a cigarette.

Out of necessity, he'd managed to keep his cigarette consumption down to two a day: one in the morning for breakfast and one in the evening for dinner. The diet was working, but he would have definitely gone for a warm tortilla with beans instead. Since he had a few hours to kill before the *biblioteca* opened, he decided to go to the local diner and visit his favorite waitress. She was always good for a free cup of coffee and maybe a few coca leaves as long as the conversation was lively. That was never a problem for Jason. Occasionally, she'd even throw in a free meal when they came available. Tourists were always sending their orders back to the kitchen. That never happened with the locals. Any warm meal was a good meal for them.

The waitress was complaining this morning about a young Indian boy she'd found rummaging through the garbage in the back alley. It seemed he'd knocked over two trash cans and left a heck of a mess when he ran away. She tried to coax him back, but he only stopped long enough to make eye contact with her. All she could do after that was talk about his big blue eyes.

"Which way did he go?" asked Jason.

DOCUMENT 512

"Hell, I don't know," the waitress said in a sassy tone that punctured her heavy Spanish accent. "Out of the alley and into the streets is all I saw. Why do you care? You have a thing for little boys?" She flirtatiously swayed back and forth, giving Jason a look that shook with attitude.

"I'd be living in Thailand right now if that were the case."

"Thailand. Where's Thailand?"

"Near Bangkok," he teased.

The waitress nodded, grinned widely through a set of missing teeth, and asked, "You'd rather Bangkok than me?"

"Now, now, now, Dulcina. You know I'm spoken for."

"*Sí, sí, sí*, this lost girl of yours who left you high and dry and took all your money. You have to come up with a better story than that, gringo. Mix them up once in a while, at least. I can take no for an answer, but at least make the excuses worth listening to."

Jason shook his head and grinned. "I gotta go, honey."

He got up, reached into his pocket for a tip, pulled out an empty lighter, and laid it on the counter. Dulcina rolled her eyes and started picking up the dirty dishes.

"Sorry. You know how it is."

"Go on, my friend. Don't forget your cell phone."

The streets were now bustling with market goers and vendors. Jason took in a deep breath of clean mountain air and headed back across the plaza. The *biblioteca* was located at the northern end of the *municipalidad* building. Everything in this town seemed to be within walking distance of the plaza. He skirted up the steps and opened the huge glass doors leading into the library. The signs were both in Spanish and English. He located the one that said "Bibliotecario/Librarian" and walked up to the counter.

The librarian looked up, quantified him as an American immediately, and asked, "May I help you?"

Jason placed both hands on the counter and said, "Yes, you may. I'm looking for a book. It's been out of print for quite a while now."

"That would be located in the archive section to your right and up the stairs. What's its name?"

"I believe it was written by a man named Brugger. *The Chronicle of Akakor.*"

The lady straightened up in her chair. She looked left and then right without moving her head. Then in a low voice she said, "It should be there—a thin book."

Jason couldn't decide what to make of her behavior. Librarians were a strange bunch, he knew, but her nervousness made him feel a bit uneasy. He thanked her and headed down the corridor to the stairway. Before going up, he looked one last time and saw that she was busy on the phone.

The slender book was not where it should have been filed under the *B*s. In fact, many of the books in this section seemed misfiled. Jason scanned through each shelf quickly and found nothing. Several covers didn't even have writing on their bindings. It soon became obvious that the only way to find what he was looking for was to pull out each unmarked book for a closer inspection. Unfortunately, there were many. The first two rows garnered nothing, but one on the third shelf caught his eye. Its title was *Document 512*.

Something about this book looked inviting. Its cover was made of worn-out leather that had deteriorated with age. The chopped off, uneven pages appeared to have either been eaten away by small insects or damaged by being outdoors in the elements for many years. When he flipped through it, some of the handwritten pages nearly disintegrated in front of him.

He went to the nearby table and carefully sifted through it. The cover didn't have an author's name or any other identifying words besides the title, which had been burned into the leather. The book didn't have a table of contents or index either. He thumbed to the last page and there, written in large, cursive letters, was the name "Francisco Raposo." Underneath the name read, "Transcribed into English by Mrs. Richard Burton, 1865."

Jason opened the book to the first page. There was only one sentence: *"In good words and clear script, this is the historical account of a large, hidden, and very ancient city, without inhabitants, discovered in the year 1753."*

"For ten years, in the hopes of discovering the far-famed gold mines of the great explorer Moribeca, which through the fault of a certain governor were not made public, and to deprive him of this glory he was imprisoned in Bahai till death, and they remained again to be discovered."

Parts of the page were missing, so he flipped to the next and picked up the story from there. *"After a long and troublesome peregrination, incited by the insatiable greed of gold, and almost lost for many years, we discovered a chain of mountains so high that they seemed to reach the ethereal regions and that they served as a throne for the wind or for the stars themselves. The glittering thereof struck the beholder from afar, chiefly when the sun shone upon the crystal of which it was composed, forming a sight so grand and so agreeable that none could take eyes off these shimmering lights...*

"Upon closer observation, and spotting a cavernous entrance which dug its way deep into a cliff in our path, we ventured closer. There was a strange man guarding this entrance, garnished with clothing, which were foreign to our eyes, including a medallion that draped down on his chest..."

Jason heard a door open and shut downstairs. There was a low murmur of an inaudible conversation going on. He slid the book back into the bookcase and placed a small piece of white paper next to it so it would be easy to find later. Then he continued looking. Wedged between two much larger encyclopedias on the fourth row was *The Chronicle of Akakor*. It was also in bad shape and worn on all four corners.

Karl Brugger was a German journalist who met a local Amazonian Indian named Tatunca Nara back in the early seventies. Their meetings and Tatunca's stories became the basis of the book. The title was supposedly the same title of the chronicle that the Amazonian tribe kept and had guarded for centuries. It contained a complete history of their origins along with a philosophy that had been passed down through time from the ancient gods who roamed the planet some fifteen thousand years earlier.

The mere notion that an ancient Amazon tribe had written down anything was remarkable in itself, as most scholars agreed that there were no written languages in South America until relatively recent times. These scholars, of course, rarely took into account the fact that Pizarro and others had totally destroyed every artifact and structure the Indians had created within a matter of years.

Brugger claimed that the chronicle dated back 10,500 years and described in detail the beliefs handed down by The Gods who ruled over them. But the most intriguing part of the book dealt with the underground tunnel system that The Gods built, which ran for hundreds of miles, from Chile to Peru to Ecuador and over to Brazil. It was there in these tunnels that the secret mysteries of mankind were hidden: the origins of life, the formula for longevity, the Incan gold, and maybe an ancient city still inhabited by a few chosen Indians—Indians who were waiting for their gods to return to earth and carry them away.

Most scholars considered these notions fantasy, especially after it was discovered later on that Tatunca Nara wasn't the Indian chieftain he claimed to be. Yet even with this revelation, Jason knew there was more to the story. Why was the name "Akakor" written on this tattered map that the guide cherished more than anything? Why was Karl Brugger murdered outside his apartment shortly after the book was published? Why were only a few hundred copies circulated before it was pulled from the shelves? Now it only existed in a few libraries and private collections around the world. It was the one possession Jason regretted losing the most to his Canadian desperado.

DOCUMENT 512

He took the book back to the table and began flipping through the pages. After a few seconds, he found the section entitled "The New Prince." This chapter described Tantuca Nara's adventure deep into the sunken kingdom to a secret temple complex that only a few chosen leaders had ever visited. Inside the temple were a group of six-fingered and six-toed humans lying in a liquid that rose to their breast and had preserved them for thousands of years. He recalled his encounter with the teenage boy in the market. Something told him that this Indian's six fingers and the story about a new prince were linked together.

The book said that these embalmed dignitaries were past rulers of the kingdom known as Ugha Mongulala. Throughout the history of these people, only a few sets of leaders had actually been born with six fingers or six toes. According to scripture, this was a special gene passed down from their creators. When the trait did appear, it was a sign that a new beginning was about to unfold.

The Second Union of Ugha Mongulala ruled during the Second Catastrophe—a time when the mountains shifted and the streams ran backward. This was the period when Lake Titicaca separated from Tiahuanaco. The Third Union reigned during the Third Catastrophe, when the Great Flood came. The last set of six-fingered rulers had the terrible misfortune of meeting Pizarro and his conquistadors during his conquest of the Incas. They interpreted his arrival as a sign that the ancient gods were returning to earth. With a combination of superior weaponry and the introduction of smallpox, the Spanish nearly wiped out their culture completely. Only a few survived and were able to escape under the guidance of Tupac Amuru, whose warriors mysteriously disappeared into the jungle.

As Jason read on, he noticed the candle on the table flicker. A draft that hadn't been there minutes ago was coming from somewhere. He looked up and saw a reflection moving in the glass bookcase in front of him. Before he could react, a burlap bag was jammed over his head and he was jerked off his chair onto the floor. He heard the muted sounds of two men talking in Spanish as a hand grabbed his arm and clasped a set of handcuffs on his wrist. They then flipped him onto his stomach, but he managed to roll back over and kick with all of his might.

"Umph!" one of the assailants grunted as Jason's kick landed squarely into his stomach. The next thing Jason felt was a hard thump on the back of his head. A jolt of pain shot through his skull. His eyelids fluttered and then there was silence.

CHAPTER FIFTEEN
COPACABANA

In Renee's dream, she heard a white noise in the distance that grew louder with every step she took. Then it appeared: a tall, gushing waterfall so big that it created its own rainbow. Above it was the moon setting over the mountaintops and welcoming the day. The roar of the continuous downpour was soothing and inviting. She nonchalantly walked in and out of the shower streaming down on her shoulders while humming an old children's song.

"Tommy and Tammy sitting in a tree, K-I-S-S-I-N-G..."

She could see her reflection in the darkness of the water. It was the image of a little girl in a white dress. She was spinning in a circle with her arms outstretched to her sides—singing and spinning, and singing and spinning...

"...K-I-S-S-I-N-G..."

Soon the little girl disappeared and was replaced by the image of a white cross dangling from a necklace. Then she realized that the cross was hang-

ing off her own neck as she bent over and touched the water—still spinning around and around like a weather vane blowing in the air. The water was so warm that she dove in and swam down deep into the lake. The current soon overtook her and pushed her through the aquatic plants and reeds until she ended up on a sandy shore next to a huge cave.

In front of her on the beach were several children picnicking in the sand. They pointed at her as she passed and chanted:

> Cinderella,
> Dressed in yella
> Peed in her pants in front of the fellas.
> She made mistakes
> With the letters she makes
> And tripped on her big feet falling in the wella.

She tried to ignore them and started walking away, but another group of older boys soon surrounded her. This time, they pushed and shoved while twirling her around in the circle and pointing to her feet. "How'd you escape from the circus?" one jested. "Where's your cousin Bigfoot?" said another.

Then a young man about her own age sitting off to the side walked over and lifted Renee into the air, carrying her into the cave. She couldn't take her eyes off his as the boy's smile faded into the darkness. The minutes passed as the cave narrowed until she heard water again. Then she saw the light and realized that they were both back at the same waterfall.

The boy stopped and said, "Lead me where you want me."

A jolt from the bus bouncing off a pothole quickly erased that image. Renee opened her eyes and realized that she was still under a tarp. In the distance, she could still hear the sound of a rushing stream, but it was fading fast.

She wasn't quite sure how long she'd fallen asleep, but from the look of the flickering lights that dashed across the darkened bus, it had been at least a couple of hours. The rocking sensation combined with an exhausting race down the mountainside had drained her completely. Yet her dream seemed so vibrant and real. Her dreams had all been very strange since setting foot in this country.

The bangs of her silky dark hair were now pressed against her forehead, ratted and rigid. From the looks of the damp pillow beneath her head, she'd obviously been crying in her sleep. Who could blame her after what she'd been through? Losing your father and almost your life in a strange land far from home was a lot for a fifteen-year-old to absorb.

Instinctively, she grabbed the compass. It was the last thing he'd given to her. She couldn't believe that he was gone. Her eyes watered, but she wiped them clean. This was not the time to start crying. She looked down at the compass and noticed that the needle was pointing at her backpack. When the bus turned a corner, it continued to point at her backpack. She tapped on the cover but nothing. Her fingers fumbled through the bag until she felt a round, hard object. When she lifted it out and studied its smooth surface, she understood why the Indians were chasing them. In her hand was the one item that had changed her life forever: the ancient medallion from the corpse back in the cave.

Her father must have slipped it into her bag when they were running away, she surmised. He knew at that point his chances of escaping were slim. By giving it to Renee, there was a good possibility that something productive could still come out of his miscalculated gamble. She studied it intently and wondered why he'd carried it away in the first place. Sure, there was something mystical about it. The flashes of light that it emitted when she placed it next to the compass were unusual but could probably be easily explained with a little physics and chemistry. The fact that she was the only person who could lift it off the dead corpse was a different story, though, and much harder to write off as coincidence. Still, did it actually have magical powers—and were they worth dying for?

It was definitely nothing like any other necklace she'd ever seen. The rugged edge around its perimeter was a stark contrast to the smooth serpentine carvings in the middle. She could envision the goldsmith hammering out the circular border with another lighter metal and then taking a cup of liquid gold and dripping it into the middle like chocolate syrup on ice cream. But what did the design mean? Its interweaving pattern was unique; there were gaps between the curvy lines that appeared to be unnatural and incomplete. She put it back in her bag but this time hid it in one of the side pockets for easy access.

The bus engine winded down as it shifted gears. Its brakes squealed when it turned into a parking lot and came to a stop. Then the passengers yawned and moaned as they started to disembark. A few minutes later, the last tourist walked down the steps and shut the door behind her. For the first time that day, Renee felt a sense of relief and quiet solitude. The silence accompanying her yielded only to the softness of her own breath. She was still alive, and that was a good thing.

She slowly lifted the plastic tarp off her head and got to one knee. A good thirty yards away, on the other side of the parking lot, was a glowing neon sign that read "Hotel Rosario Del Lago." She had no idea where she was.

She put on her backpack and cautiously began ambling up to the front of the bus, when something caught her eye. There was a silhouette in the window a few rows up that wasn't there a few seconds ago.

"Good evening, *fräulein*," said a soft and tender female voice with a heavy accent.

Renee stopped in her tracks.

"Don't be afraid. I'm not going to hurt you."

Dashing for the door wasn't a very promising option so Renee exhaled and sat down in one of the seats.

"Das is your name, young lady?"

"Renee. What's yours?"

"They call me Lena."

"Um, where are we?"

The lady laughed. "Where are we? A tiny little village located on the banks of Lake Titicaca in the middle of nowhere called Copacabana."

"Titicaca," replied Renee.

"Ya, Titicaca. Were you expecting someplace else?"

"I guess I was kinda hoping I'd end up back in La Paz or something."

"Ah, now we're getting somewhere," said Lena. "So you're from La Paz? Might I ask how you ended up in the back of our bus—and more importantly, why that plump little pungent man with a drooping moustache was looking for you?"

Don Carlos. She had forgotten about him. How did he manage to catch up to her at the bottom of the mountain? Why did he need her to remove the pendant from the ancient body? There were so many unanswered questions and so many reasons to be cautious.

Lena realized that her line of questioning was frightening her new little friend. She would eventually get the answers she was looking for; she always did. "Hey, I gotta better idea. I bet you're hungry."

Renee nodded.

"Come on. Let's go in and have some dinner. It's on me."

They bypassed the main dining room to the quieter bar area, where Renee hopped into a booth in the corner. It was dimly lit, with dark brick walls and just the perfect atmosphere for a couple to unwind after a long day. Outside the window was a spectacular view of Lake Titicaca. The moonlight glimmered off the small waves that splashed against the docks and piers.

The bartender looked over to the table and shouted, *"Dos?"* Lena nodded, and he brought out two menus and glasses of water. The conversation was slow at first, mainly small talk about the hotel and food. Neither one of them was quite ready to start talking.

Renee finally broke the ice. "Thank you."

The comment surprised Lena, "*Danke*, for what?"

"You know, for stopping the man back on the bus from getting me."

"Ah, I see. Who was that man?"

Renee hesitated before replying. Something inside told her to be vague. "That was, uh, like, our tour guide."

Lena nodded and remained silent. She was hoping that the young girl would continue, but Renee wasn't sure what to say next. Finally, Lena asked another question. "So, did you get separated from this tour group and…"

"Sort of," said Renee. "It was only me and my father and the tour guide."

"Your father. That's a very small and exclusive tour." Lena was starting to get suspicious. She leaned in and said, "Listen. Whatever happened back there at the site is over. Nobody can hurt you now. It's just you and me here. You don't have to tell me anything if you don't want to, but please make sure what you do tell me is the truth." She rubbed Renee's hands and looked at her with her warm green eyes. "You know, the truth is a fruit that should not be picked until it's ripe. I can wait."

Her words melted away any inhibitions Renee may have had. She now felt like she was sitting across from her own mother and began to cry.

Lena went to the other side of the booth, put her arm around the young girl, and stroked her hair. "Now, now. Go ahead and let it out—if it makes you feel better."

Renee laid her head against Lena's chest and sobbed even harder. Luckily, the bar was fairly deserted, so no one took notice. After a few minutes, Renee regained her composure and straightened back up. Lena handed her a napkin so she could blow her nose and wipe her eyes clean.

"My father. He didn't make it."

Lena's forehead tightened as a confused and concerned look came over her. "Didn't make it? What are you saying? He didn't make it back?"

"He's dead. He was killed, murdered by the Indians on the mountain."

Renee told Lena all about the day's excursion to the ruins. She told her about the drawings, the hieroglyphics, and the mummy with red hair. She decided not to reveal the identity of her uncle for the time being. That one she still had to sort out. When it was all over, an hour had passed and they were both growing tired. Lena offered Renee a warm bath and the other bed in her room. It was too inviting not to accept.

"When we get to the room, we'll call the American Embassy and find out what to do." The Embassy was closed and the call center told Renee that the quickest thing to do would be to go to the police department in Cuzco the next morning and file a report. They'd contact the office in Lima and promptly look into the matter.

"Do you wanna call your mother?" asked Lena.

"Not yet. In the morning."

Her answer took Lena by surprise. Why wouldn't a young girl all alone in a foreign land not want to call her mother? There was something more to this story and she knew it. There was more to the story that even Renee didn't know. She needed to think things through. She wasn't so sure what her mother would say or do if she called. What if she insisted that Renee go back to her uncle's house? That might be deadly. What if her mother told her uncle where she was? A few hours rest couldn't hurt at this point.

Renee took a shower and immediately fell asleep on top of the bed with a hotel robe wrapped around her. Lena grabbed an extra blanket out of the closet and draped it on top of her. She spent the next few hours going over in her head what the young girl had just told her. It was quite a tale and a lot to experience in one day. In a morbid sense, she wished that she could have been there in the girl's place. She had a feeling though that there'd be more adventures to come.

CHAPTER SIXTEEN
LAKE TITICACA

Renee was still groggy the next morning as she boarded the hydrofoil that would take her across Lake Titicaca to Puno. Lena didn't have much time to explain her own travel plans, but told Renee that her next stop was in Cuzco. She offered to escort Renee to the police station and make sure she was safe before heading off. Over breakfast, they met with the other Germans in the group who were scheduled to visit Amaru Muru for the day and parted ways.

There was some unfinished business that needed to be dealt with before leaving, though. Renee's mother would be worried sick if someone didn't check in. The only problem was how to explain her father's death when she didn't quite understand it herself. The phone just rang and rang before it went to voice mail. Just after the beep, Renee had second thoughts on what to say. Leaving a message just wouldn't be right. This conversation had to be in person. Instead, she rambled on for a few seconds about nothing and finally said she'd call from Cuzco.

When she hung up the pay phone and turned around, an old Indian woman wearing a derby hat and poncho was standing in front of her. She reached into a bag and pulled out a loaf of bread, which she then handed to Renee and said, "Bread, water."

Renee shook her head and said, "No, *gracias*."

As Renee started to walk down the hallway, the lady grabbed her arm tightly. She stared straight ahead as if in a hypnotic trance. "You've been here before."

"Excuse me?"

"You've been here before—many years ago."

Renee was speechless. The old woman continued, "You must worship and bow down to your ancestors: you must kneel before our maker…"

Lena came out of the restroom fiddling with her belt and tucking in her shirt. "That'll probably be the last clean bathroom we see…" She hesitated as soon as she noticed the Indian woman. The old lady let go of Renee's arm and walked away before anyone else could say a word.

"What was that all about?" Lena asked as they both watched her head down the hallway and disappear through a side door.

"Beggars," replied Renee.

The hydrofoil was swift and breezy, zipping in and out of the bay with ease. As the shores of Copacabana faded behind them, the loudspeaker came on in the cabin. The boat captain pointed out the Pilcocaina Sun Temple and then detoured over to the shores of Sun Island. He told a story about a sunken ancient city buried at the bottom of the lake. When the water levels were low enough, the Indians could touch the submersed rock formations with their poles. Renee wondered if they were remnants of the other half of Tiahuanaco that had drifted away thousands of years ago after a massive earthquake. If only her father were there to explain.

As they leaned against the railing and peered over to the shores, Lena reached out and put her arm around Renee. She knew how to read people very well, and this little girl was screaming for a hug. The boat zipped across the water and the morning air rejuvenated their spirits. For a few moments, they were mesmerized by the lake's beauty. The only images going through their minds were those of the mountainous snowcaps off in the distance and the rocky bluffs lining the shores along the way. The locals were pushing their handmade canoes with long wooden poles off the reed islands out into deeper waters. With the exception of an occasional cackle from a speckled teal gliding across the water, the only noise in the bay was the drone of the hydrofoil's engine.

"When we get to Cuzco, I'll take you to the police station. They'll know what to do."

Renee looked up and said, "How am I going to tell my mother?"

Lena tried to see past the watery pupils and deep into this young girl's mind. She could only imagine how hard this must be for her. "The authorities can call and let your mom know." She paused for a moment and added, "You might want to leave out the part about the cave and hut. I'm not sure they'd understand."

"You're probably right."

Renee leaned into Lena and rested her head against her shoulder. She welcomed the peace and tranquility. Her body had been in survival mode for way too long, leaving her little time to reflect or even analyze the situation. As she gazed over the horizon and watched the sun rise higher into the sky, she realized that there weren't any really good options.

She reached into her backpack and pulled out the necklace. This little trinket was solely responsible for the predicament she was now in. Did it really have magical powers like Don Carlos led her to believe? It was uniquely beautiful, with its both crude and intricate design, but was it extraordinary?

Lena noticed the pendant and its strange reaction to the compass. It was moving up and down like a Geiger counter.

"That's an interesting necklace you have there."

Up to that point, Renee had been absorbed in her own little world, trying to remember every word her father had said to her. She hadn't planned on telling Lena about the necklace, but now it was too late. The cat was out of the bag. "Yeah, it's a present from my father."

"I see."

Renee looked down and noticed the compass needle dancing in time with the pendant. "Weird, huh?"

"Ya, indeed. Can I see it?"

Renee handed the compass over and watched as Lena pulled it away from the medallion, causing it to shiver uncontrollably. Then she slowly brought it back in until the tip stood rigidly at attention and handed it to Renee. "Very interesting. Quite a magnetic field."

The speaker cracked again as the boat captain continued his halfhearted audio tour in broken English. "We now are approaching the Island of the Sun. Legend says that the sun is born there and those who bury on its soil are one with The Gods."

Renee felt heat rise from the vibrating medallion, so she lifted it out of her hand. A subtle red glow appeared around its perimeter as she pointed it toward the splendid formations of igneous rock layered on the shoreline. The red soon morphed into a darker shade of blue and then a very light purple before flickering white and disappearing altogether.

A figure began to take shape inside the intricate designs as Renee and Lena looked on in silence. At first, it resembled a stick person with a long, slender body and a short line intersecting in the middle. But then the two legs jetting out on the bottom transformed into the tip of an arrow that pointed toward Cuzco. Renee felt Lena's eyes upon her and looked away. The image was gone.

"What was that?" asked Lena.

"I don't know," replied Renee. She quickly returned the pendant to her bag.

Lena sensed the uneasiness in her new friend's voice and decided to drop the subject. As she gently placed her hand on Renee's shoulder, she cautioned, "I wouldn't tell the authorities about that either."

CHAPTER SEVENTEEN
THE INTERROGATION

Jason awoke crying out in pain. His head had rolled off the small pillow and bumped into the metal bed frame. The huge new lump on the back of his skull quickly reminded him of his recent encounter in the library. When he opened his eyes, a single lightbulb hanging from a wire stared back at him as a hint of urine sifted into his nostrils. He knew that smell—and also exactly where he was: in jail.

He rose to his elbows and noticed that he was alone. *How unusual,* he thought. It was more common to be sharing a cell with ten other hungover drunks rounded up from the night before. This evening was different. There were no barking inmates pleading for more food or water. There were no sneers or grunting threats coming from a darkened corner.

A guard came by and gave him a piercing glance that had "*machismo*" written all over it. He didn't say a word but just kept walking. A few minutes later, he returned with a meal tray and slid it along the floor through a gap in the bars. "Here, gringo. Eat while you can," he snorted as he strutted down the hallway and out the door.

Jason wasted no time shoving the food down his throat, cleaning up every last drop of gravy with his bread. This was no easy task with a pair of handcuffs tightly gripped around his wrists. The water tasted like rust, but it didn't matter. He slid the tray back over to the bars and reached for his pack of cigarettes. They were gone. He quickly checked his other pockets but they were empty too. Everything was missing, including the map. This couldn't be good, he surmised. Usually, the jailers let you keep a few things in your pockets. After all, what was a person to do but smoke and read while waiting to be hauled in front of the local magistrate? Something was different this time.

An hour went by before another guard came by his cell. He pulled out a set of keys and opened the door. Two *policia* in gray uniforms with red trim entered the cell followed by Father Delanda. The guard looked to the skinny policeman, who waved him away.

Father Delanda slowly walked around with his hands behind his back and studied the new prisoner. The unshaven face, worn-out clothes, and disheveled hair couldn't hide the well-built American's handsome features.

The priest paced the room for a few minutes before speaking. "So, please tell me, Mr. Finch, what's a scientist like yourself doing spending your days in our lovely country researching rare books that have been out of print for over twenty years?"

"What is this, the Spanish Inquisition?"

The two *policia* glanced over to the priest with the eyes of a vulture just waiting for a signal to strike, but none came. "I guess you could say that," answered Father Delanda.

The comment threw Jason for a loop. His question was more of a joke, as he'd never dreamed that anyone would actually respond in such a manner. This was not a good sign at all. He studied the three men cautiously. "Who's asking?"

"I'm sorry, my son. My name is Father Delanda."

"Glad to meet you, I think."

The priest pulled Jason's tattered map out of his pocket and opened it carefully. He lifted it up to the light, pretending to search for something buried in the yellowed paper. He adjusted his glasses before pulling out a lighter. As he held the flame close, he replied, "No, I don't see any of these names on my map." The corner curled up like a dead leaf begging for water as he added, "No, I don't see any of these roads on my map either."

Document 512

Jason leaped forward but the two officers were between him and the priest within seconds. Father Delanda lowered the flame and said, "So, my son, would you like to tell me about this map and its connection to the book, or will we have to do this by some other means?"

Jason hesitated just a little too long and was rewarded with a hard blow to the shoulder from the policeman's baton. The hit sent him diving to the floor, where his head bounced off the bedpost again. The pain bumper pooled from his shoulder to his head and back again so rapidly that it made him dizzy.

The officer grabbed his shirt and pulled him back up. He then slammed Jason against the wall and propped him up on the bed.

"I'm sorry, young man. My colleague doesn't know his own strength sometimes." The priest then pulled an old and rusted device out from under his cloak. There were two bolts holding two jagged plates together with a third bolt in the middle. The middle bolt had threads and a double-sided handle.

"It's funny that you mentioned the Spanish Inquisition. How good is your history?"

"I know enough to be dangerous, I guess. I mean, I know that the church put thousands of people to death just because they thought they were heretics."

"The Catholic church does not put anyone to death, my son. The local magistrates were responsible for that."

"How convenient."

One of the guards reached up to strike him again, but the priest shook his head and said, "That won't be necessary." Then he slowly began twisting the handle, causing the threaded bolt to scream for oil as the two plates opened wider.

"Let me tell you a little bit about the Inquisition—or should I say, inquisitions, as there were several. First, there was the Medieval Inquisition, followed by the Spanish, which was probably the most famous, followed by the Portuguese, and then the Roman. There was even the Peruvian Inquisition conducted in Lima as recently as the eighteen hundreds. But the one common denominator between them throughout the centuries was that they were presided over by the same group of Dominican friars. This group called themselves 'Ordo Praedicatorum,' but were better known as the Black Friars."

Father Delanda opened his cloak to reveal a scapular hanging over his chest with the letters *O* and *P* engraved on it. "This organization was made up of the greatest theologians and philosophers of their time. They preached the gospel and combated heresy by any means possible. Are you familiar with the methods they used to obtain confessions from these heretics?"

Jason shook his head.

The priest rotated the squeaky handle again and said, "This one's my favorite. It was a gift from the late Master General Alonso and dates back to the days of the great Tomás de Torquemada." Jason was silent as the padre continued to walk around him. "I guess you're not familiar with his legacy. Let's just say, he was often referred to as the Hammer of Heretics. This lovely device he called a thumbscrew."

He handed it to the skinny policeman while the other officer whacked Jason across the chest, knocking his breath out, and dragged him over to a chair. Then he placed Jason's handcuffed arms flat on the table and inserted his thumb in the device.

"If you move, it will hurt even more," whispered the skinny one. He turned the thumbscrew until the two plates were firmly against the top and bottom of Jason's thumbs.

The priest bent down and looked him into his eyes. "I believe you know what will happen if you do not tell me what I need to know."

Jason nodded.

The priest stood back up and continued, "Now, where were we? Ah yes—well, let's try another subject. My colleagues tell me that the section of this book you were looking at had to do with a prince, one with six fingers and six toes. Please tell me what you know about this prince."

"Not much. I mean, it's kind of hard to read when you have a burlap bag over your head."

Father Delanda nodded and the officer spun the handle on the thumbscrew a full turn. The pointed teeth dug into his fingernail, splitting it open and sending a few drops of blood trickling onto the table. Jason winced and tightened his shoulders but refused to scream. The pain wasn't as bad as he thought it'd be. It wasn't until he moved his hand slightly that the metal teeth scraped his nerve endings, shooting a stinging jolt up his arms. Then he lowered his head and exhaled, "Ahhhhh."

Think of something, you idiot, he told himself. The last thing he wanted to do was let the priest believe he was some kind of *Braveheart* masochist who enjoyed having his thumbs crushed. His brain was churning in overdrive trying to come up with a story, but nothing came to mind.

The good father lifted up Jason's head, then placed his other hand on the table and gazed into his eyes. "You know, the Black Friars wrote extensively on the effects of this device during the Inquisition. Most confessions were obtained after only one turn of the handle. By the second turn, the victim's fingernail was shattered into so many pieces that blood was everywhere. The teeth on both sides of the plates would press against the bone so tightly that a man would lose all feeling in his hand. Anyone insane enough to hold out for a third turn would be entertained by the sound of his own bone crushing under the pressure. If that didn't do the trick, then they moved up to the knuckle and started all over again."

A set of doors opened and footsteps approached down the hallway. A female voice was speaking, but Jason couldn't make out what she was saying. It was a child's voice. The priest signaled the two officers to remove the device and back away from Jason.

"Are you sure you can't stay?" asked the young girl.

"Ya, I'm sure. I have to catch a train to Lima in less than an hour. Otherwise, I vill miss my flight back to Hamburg," said the other female voice. She spoke in English, but with a heavy German accent.

"But it could be days before my mother gets here."

"I know. Das is why it's best for you if you stay here until she arrives. What could be safer?"

The two young ladies came into view. They stopped and peered into the cell, looking from the officers to the priest and finally to Jason. Jason stared at the woman and couldn't believe his eyes: it was his lovely Canadian con artist dressed in a white blouse and blue jeans. She was absolutely stunning.

Lena stared back as if meeting for the first time. Without the smallest twitch or raise of the eyebrow, she nodded to the two policemen, bowed to the priest, and said, "Father."

The priest replied, "Good evening, my dear. I hope we find that you're well tonight."

"Ya, we are, Father. In fact, maybe you could help us out here." She again surveyed the room before adding, "But maybe you are too preoccupied with other matters?"

The priest, realizing that he was in a predicament where his duty to a higher power was calling, answered, "Not at all, my dear. How can I be of help?"

The lady put her arm around the young girl and said, "My name is Lena and this is Renee. I found her a few hundred miles back near Lake Titicaca. She's lost her father in a tragic accident up in the mountains. Her mother is being contacted by the local authorities and will arrive from the United States shortly."

Lena glanced over to Jason but didn't make eye contact. Jason was still stunned. He'd written her off months ago and figured that she'd be thousands of miles away by now. He couldn't help but think about the irony associated with the whole situation. Here he was on the inside of prison bars looking at a woman who'd probably committed more crimes than all of the other inmates combined. To add insult to injury, she was about to walk away unscathed.

Lena then noticed the map in the priest's hands. She knew exactly what it was by its yellowed and soiled exterior. The tumblers in her brain were revolving fast, tapping that inner quality she had of thinking on her feet and coming up with a new plan instantaneously. "I was wondering, Father, if it's not too much trouble, could you maybe spend a few minutes with her? This whole ordeal has been very traumatic and a few words from the church might be the best medicine right now."

Father Delanda glanced at the two officers and then over to his prisoner. Jason wasn't going anywhere. A few minutes couldn't do any harm. "I'd be glad to, my dear."

The priest signaled the guards to open the cell door and placed the map back in his pocket. He turned back to Jason and said, "We will continue our conversation later, my son."

Jason didn't move or look up. He was holding the cracked fingernail with his other hand, trying to stop the bleeding. Then he took a deep breath and let it out.

The priest signaled the guards to leave the room and walked over to the two women. Lena introduced herself and Renee again and told the father that she couldn't stay. She summarized the previous day's events quickly and then hugged Renee very tightly. "You'll be fine now."

"Thank you for everything," said Renee.

Lena looked at Father Delanda and gave him a long hug. "Please take care of her for me. I really feel bad for having to leave like this but I can't miss my flight."

"No problem, my dear."

She stepped away and hurried down the hall. When she reached Jason's cell, she glanced over and winked but didn't slow down. He was still stunned by the sight of his partially shattered fingernail but her shrewd gesture brought him out of his trance. Quietly, he strained to hear the conversation outside his cell.

Father Delanda escorted Renee over to a bench and sat her down next to him. "Now, please tell me what's troubling you."

Renee recounted her battle with the Indians and their visit to Tiahuanaco. When the priest asked why they ventured away from the ancient ruins, she hesitated. The policeman behind the front desk had just taken notes and asked for basic details: her father's name, her mother's phone number, where was the body now, and so on. She hadn't really thought out a good story and wasn't a very good liar. Father Delanda had already picked up on this.

He placed his hand on hers and said, "Listen, Renee. I am here for you and with that, I bring the glory of God and all of his resources. I cannot help you, though, if you do not help me understand everything that has transpired."

"Is this, like, a confessional, Father? I mean, in confidence?"

He leaned in and did his best not to show any emotion. Just the mention of a confessional was enough to make him giddy. After all, they'd produced so many wonderful results in the past. Then he cracked a self-indulging smile and whispered, "Of course."

Renee peered down the hallway to make sure they were alone. "Well, the real reason the Indians chased us is because my dad...I mean, he..." She cleared her throat. "We went into this cave and found all of these drawings on the wall: hieroglyphics, and spaceships, and this mummy with red hair..."

Jason's ears perked up. The plastered walls and concrete floor acted as a great sound conductor as long as he didn't move or breathe too loudly. He knew of the mummies with red hair from one of the books in his library. The author had explained in detail the ancient myths about the thirteen Inca emperors who were buried in the tunnels deep into the Andes Mountains. If they were found, one would undoubtedly also find the gold and treasures hidden nearby.

The book told how a conquistador named Polo de Ondegardo stumbled across three of the mummies a few years after Pizarro's men murdered Atahualpa, the Inca ruler. The mummies were stripped of their jewelry and their bodies smashed into pieces. The shear brutality that the Spaniards employed was disheartening. Their mission was simple: destroy any signs of a pagan god or culture not subservient to Christianity and the king. When the men went back to the site the next day, they discovered that each shattered body had been completely restored. Each mummy was dressed in new articles of clothing and jewelry. This, of course, frightened Polo and his soldiers to the point of hysteria. They assumed that evil spirits were involved, so they tried to hide the entrance with rocks and foliage on their way out.

Father Delanda knew this story too. He didn't even twitch when Renee mentioned the mummy. He just remained calm and collected. Years of service to the Lord had conditioned him to absorb such shocking revelations from patrons without showing any emotion. While avoiding eye contact with Renee, he said, "Please, my dear, go on."

Renee continued her story and told him about the necklace and compass. She broke down crying as she recalled her father's final moments and her escape. Father Delanda comforted her. "There, there. That is enough for now. Would you like a glass of water?"

Renee shook her head. "I'm all right."

"Now, Renee, this medallion that your father took from the mummy. It obviously means a great deal to these Indians. Otherwise, they wouldn't have taken such drastic measures to get it back." He tapped his fingers lightly across his lips and added, "In fact, I doubt they'll ever stop looking for it. I believe that you are in grave danger, my dear, while you still possess it."

Renee dropped her head down and said, "I know."

"May I see it?"

She hesitated. What would the priest think if it started glowing again? Maybe she could just reach in slowly and grab the chain instead of the metal. As she rummaged around from side to side and then down into the bottom, she felt nothing. Then she frantically tossed everything out of the bag and onto the floor.

"It's not here!" she cried as combs and makeup clanged off the concrete. "It's gone!"

"What do you mean it's gone?"

"I mean it was in here this morning, you know, when we took off from Lake Titicaca but now it's gone. I don't know what could have…" She stopped in midsentence after remembering the last time she'd seen it. "Lena."

"The German?" asked the priest.

"Yeah, I showed it to her this morning."

The priest instinctively reached into his own pocket. Jason's map was gone as well.

CHAPTER EIGHTEEN
CELL MATES

Jason calmly moved back over to the bed and sat quietly. He was concentrating on making himself invisible. The bleeding had stopped but the throbbing pain in his thumb hadn't. He leaned against the wall on the bottom bunk and slowly submerged himself into the only shadow left in the room. Soon his body blended into the wall like a coat of paint.

Father Delanda was shouting orders to the officers while listening to the chief of police explain their options. He stroked the young girl's hair and assured her repeatedly that everything would be fine. Different guards, policemen, and plain-clothes cops shuffled in and out of the room every few minutes. It was both controlled and chaotic at the same time.

Eventually, most of the guards left and things quieted down. Father Delanda addressed Renee once again. "My dear, I'm going to accompany the chief of police and pursue this...Lena lady. If you would be so kind as to wait here until I return."

"But why can't I go with you?"

The padre knelt down to eye level and said, "I fear for your safety. We don't know who this lady is, and we don't know if the Indians are still looking for you. You'll be safe here."

Renee began to protest but he cut her off before she had the chance. "I promise that I won't be long." He brushed her hair back out of her eyes and continued, "I'll have one of the guards bring you something to eat, and you can lie down in a cell here and get some rest."

His words were gentle and sincere. The commotion had subsided and Renee looked emotionally exhausted. The father waved one of the guards over and escorted her to a cell two doors down from Jason's. "Get some rest, my dear. I'll be back before you know it." The guard opened the cell door, took the blanket and pillow off the top bunk, and placed them over the ones on the bottom.

Renee gave the priest a long hug and said, "Please don't be too long."

"I won't."

The guard left her door unlocked and switched off a couple of the hallway lights off as he left the room with the priest. Neither of them noticed Jason on their way out. In a matter of minutes, his situation had gone from one of total destitution to one of complete anonymity. He knew that it wouldn't be long before the priest realized his mistake. There wasn't much time to act. He didn't want to sound too eager by starting the conversation prematurely, but he also didn't want Renee falling asleep on him. At least she knew that he was there and wouldn't be totally surprised to hear from him. But what was he going to say?

WELCOME TO CUZCO

After a minute had gone by, he broke the silence. He rolled off the bed, walked over to the table, and dragged the chair across the floor making just enough noise to get Renee's attention. Then he sat down and tapped his fingers on the table.

"Sounds like you had a pretty tough day."

There was no response. Renee was lying on a pillow motionless in the bed. Part of her was too tired to speak; the other part was too scared.

Jason thought for a moment. It was obvious that his first comment wasn't going anywhere. He took another stab at it. "My name's Jason." Still there was no response.

This approach was going nowhere. He needed to try another angle, and he needed to do it quickly. Then an idea came to him.

"When I knew her, Lena went by the name Joanna." He waited a few seconds before continuing, "She didn't have a German accent back then; it was Canadian."

This last comment made Renee take notice. She put her hands behind her head and stared up at the top bunk. She wasn't quite yet sure what to make of this stranger.

Jason decided to keep trying. "You know, the last time I saw Joanna or Lena or whatever she calls herself, you know what she said to me? She said, 'Love is a fruit that shouldn't be picked until it's ripe.' Can you imagine that? She was talking about love." He half-heartedly laughed. "That was the last thing she said to me—before she snuck away and took everything I owned."

His words hit home as Renee recalled the conversation with Lena last night in the restaurant. This could not be a coincidence. She was beginning to wonder if her whole encounter with this mysterious lady was an accident at all.

"She told me that *the truth* was a fruit which shouldn't be picked until it's ripe."

Jason smiled a sigh of relief. He'd broken the ice. "Love, the truth, a sucker. I guess you can substitute about any word you want into that phrase."

As soon as he'd said it, he realized his mistake. He'd just called her a sucker. The only thing he could do now was to remain silent and hope she wouldn't take his comment the wrong way. The next few minutes melted by slowly, but he did what he knew he had to do and kept quiet.

Finally, she spoke. "How long did you know each other?"

"Oh, a month or two," said Jason. "Just long enough for her to gain my trust and ripen me up. How about you?"

Renee hesitated to answer. Should she be embarrassed for being duped so easily or proud of finding out so quickly? It didn't matter at this point, she decided. "One day."

Jason knew exactly what to say next. "It only took her five minutes with the priest."

Renee giggled and was now leaning on her elbow. "Where do you think she took off to?"

"I know where she's heading," said Jason immediately. "She has your necklace and my map. The question is, does Father Delanda know where she's heading?"

"Father Delanda? What does he have to do with everything?"

"I'm not sure yet, but I do know that if he finds her before we do, there won't be a need for either one of us any longer—if you know what I mean."

This thought hadn't occurred to her before. It didn't make sense, but yet it did. The priest had been nothing but kind to her, but so had Lena. "How do you know that?"

"What do you think the priest was doing in my cell when you two showed up? I can guarantee you that we weren't playing euchre. In fact, I'd be missing a couple of thumbs right now if you'd showed up five minutes later."

Renee replayed the events from the last forty-eight hours in her head. When she was done, she realized that there was a lot of truth in what this mystery man was telling her. There were just too many coincidences between his story and hers. Still, something made her reluctant to believe anyone at this point—after all, she'd just been duped by Lena and her uncle. This time, she'd have to rely on her gut feeling.

"This map you had—or that the priest had. What, I mean, where does it take you?"

"To a secret tunnel hidden deep in the Andes Mountains, right here in Cuzco."

Renee was sitting up in bed at this point with the blanket thrown back. This was much more than coincidence. This was fate intervening. She walked over to the cell door and said, "Tell me more."

"I will—but on the way. We don't have much time. We need to get out of here and fast before the priest realizes what's going on."

"How do we do that?"

"Well, for you it's easy," replied Jason. "For me, I'll need the keys to these handcuffs and to my cell."

The door at the end of the hallway opened. A guard with a plate of food headed for Renee's cell. She hurriedly lay back down as he entered and placed the tray on the table.

"*Coma algo por favor, señorita.*"

She smiled and nodded. "Could you please help me up?"

He didn't seem to understand English but knew what an outstretched arm meant and went over to help. As she got to her feet, Renee reached down and tried to grab the set of keys off his chain. They didn't come loose and the guard felt a tug on his belt loop. He turned to see what was pulling on him when Renee collapsed to the floor. She grabbed his pant leg on the way down to distract him. As he reached down to help her back to her feet, she studied the key chain and figured out the latch. This time she was successful.

When he sat her down on the chair, he started asking more questions in Spanish but Renee just shook her head. "I'm fine, thank you." She brushed off a few more questions until he finally gave up. "No, please. I'll be fine, *gracias, gracias.*" The guard stood up and nodded, then left the room.

As soon as he was gone, she grabbed her bag, opened the door, and ran straight over to Jason's cell. She fumbled with a few of the keys before finding the right one that let him out. Then she found the key to remove his handcuffs.

"Thank you," said Jason as he rubbed his wrist. "That feels so good."

She noticed the dried blood on his thumb and asked, "Are you all right?"

"Yeah, I'll be fine."

"How do we get out of here?" she asked.

"I'm not sure, but I have a feeling that most of the guards left with the chief and priest. We might be able to just walk right out of here if we time this right."

They both stood by the door at the end of the hallway. Jason peeked out of the small window and saw his backpack on a table with a few jackets and hats. On the other side of the room, a sergeant was talking on the phone at the front desk. In the middle was the door to freedom.

"There's someone at the front desk. We have to lure him away somehow."

Renee pulled out a business card from her pocket, "How about a frantic 911 call?"

Jason nodded. "A phone call might work, but we need him to walk away, not run out."

"How do we do that?"

He looked down at his cell phone and then out the window; then at Renee's backpack. "I think I've got it." He dialed the number to the station and could hear it ring in the other room.

"*Comisaria.*"

"*Buenas noches, éste es Padre Delanda.*"

"*Si, padre.*"

The sergeant was buying Jason's halfcocked impersonation. He went on to ask the sergeant to retrieve a folder from the chief of police's office.

"*No problema.*"

The sergeant laid down the phone and left the front desk. Jason and Renee immediately opened the hallway door and exited into the front lobby. As they walked past the front desk, Jason grabbed his jacket and bag off the table. An officer approached the door from the outside and turned the knob. "Don't stop walking," whispered Jason.

The front door swung open and a large, overweight man lumbered through it nonchalantly. He looked exhausted from a long day on the job. He gave Jason a concerned glare as their eyes met briefly. Then he looked down at Renee and smiled while holding the door open. "*Buenas noches, señorita.*"

"*Gracias.*"

The two exited the building and skipped down the steps. "Keep walking," whispered Jason. They turned right and briskly shuffled to the corner of the block. Without stopping, they turned right again and were soon out of sight.

CHAPTER NINETEEN
THE PRINCE

A boy sat quietly on the other side of the street as the door of the police station swung open. He kept his head down between his legs and didn't even look up. Most importantly, he kept his hands hidden. He'd learned quickly that people with six fingers and six toes were considered freaks. Over the past few days, he'd encountered and experienced about every reaction imaginable from the locals and tourists. Some people looked shocked when they noticed his fingers but politely went about their way without creating a scene. Others reacted as if they'd seen *el diablo* himself. On one occasion, a mob of indigent women chased him for miles, wanting to burn him at the stake.

Adjusting to life in the city was no easy task for the young prince. Little things that most people took for granted—knowing when to cross a stoplight or how to use a toilet—were foreign to him. He couldn't understand why so many birds and animals he'd grown up around were locked in cages behind windows. He did quickly learn his place in the Peruvian culture, though. After all, on a scale of one to ten, with tourists being a ten, the indigenous Indians ranked somewhere around one or two, which was just slightly above "better off dead."

So he sat quietly on the other side of the street. This had been his position for most of the night. From a pedestrian's point of view, it would appear that he was trying to stay warm in the mountain's chilly evening air. In reality, he was on a stakeout.

He knew that the best way to avoid capture was to pursue the very same people who were following him. The trick was to remain undercover and not be detected. His elders had taught him this important lesson and many others. As far back as he could remember, his elders had lectured him on the ways of his people and basic survival skills. Before he'd lost his first tooth, he knew how to build a fire and skin a small animal. His short childhood was filled with daily history lessons about his ancestors and the proud royal bloodline he was a part of. There were lessons on cooking, botany, medicine, warfare, and the different cultures that coexisted inside and outside of his Amazonian homeland. His head was so filled with facts and stories that sometimes he couldn't think straight.

WELCOME TO CUZCO

The one thing his elders didn't teach him was how to live on the city streets. They never anticipated the heir to the throne ever leaving the serenity and safety of his Amazon kingdom for the streets of Cuzco. The boy himself couldn't have anticipated any of the events that had occurred over the last few years. Fortunately, he was well trained on how to expect the unexpected—and that had kept him alive.

So the boy sat quietly while a few youngsters gathered around a shallow pit on the sidewalk. They warmed their bodies with a small fire where a tree once stood. He didn't dare venture into their little circle. Instead, he curled up in the dark corner of the doorway leading into a neighborhood apartment building and avoided eye contact with anyone.

He avoided eye contact but that didn't mean he missed what was going on. It didn't mean that he'd overlooked the constant stream of officers coming in and out of the station. It didn't mean that he'd missed Father Delanda and the chief of police frantically leaving the station and jumping in a black unmarked car. It didn't mean that he'd ignored Jason and Renee as they casually walked out the front door and strolled down to the corner. He saw it all.

Ever since he first eluded the two *policia* at the market, he'd been following them around the city. Staying on their tail was easier than tying your own shoelace. Once he learned their basic pattern, it was just a matter of repetition. They were so predictable. What he hadn't predicted was seeing them drag Jason from the library to the station earlier that morning. He recognized the man from the market immediately. It just seemed to be too much of a coincidence that this same man was crossing his path again.

So the boy sat quietly and waited. The ubiquitous sound of a flute playing off in the distance drifted in the night air. He risked being noticed and possibly captured on a hunch that this American somehow figured into his fate and future. He understood that chance encounters usually had a deeper meaning. His teachers taught him to be conscientious of these incidents because they were usually much more than they seemed. As Jason and Renee headed around the corner and disappeared, the young man slowly rose to his feet and followed.

CHAPTER TWENTY
THE TUNNELS

After the Spaniards conquered Peru and destroyed all of the Indian temples in Cuzco, they erected monuments to their Lord Jesus and erased all evidence of any pagan god before them. Years later, one treasure hunter set out to discover the remaining riches on his own. In his search, the man became lost and wandered through the maze of tunnels under the city for several days. He was abandoned by the few that knew of his quest and written off as dead.

A few days later, the congregation gathered in the Church of Santo Domingo heard a rapping sound under the floor. The flock of worshippers began murmuring about demons and devils. The priest quieted them and directed a few to remove a slab of stone from the floor. To their amazement, a man came up out of a tunnel carrying a gold bar in each hand.

When they tried to talk to the explorer, they soon realized that he was never going to tell them where to find the gold. The treasure hunter was delirious and babbled on incoherently about the caves. Some said that he went crazy from wandering aimlessly in the underground tunnels in complete darkness. Others said that he'd been inflicted by the "Curse of the Caves," a spell cast on any outsider who dared to enter the sacred tunnels uninvited. The church decided to destroy the entrance so this would never happen again.

Father Delanda knew this story well. He'd spent an exhaustive amount of time in the Museo's library researching these ancient tunnels. He'd also gained the trust of Huascar, his Quechua Indian confidant, who'd told him many similar stories about his people. These ancient passageways were believed to be older than any civilization known to man—tunnels carved so perfectly and sturdily that they'd lasted thousands of years underground.

The priest had an idea where the German girl was heading. A weathered map like this might have looked foreign and useless to most people, but portions of it made complete sense to him. He recognized the ancient names of Akakor and Akahim from his library readings. He also knew that the primitive animals roughly sketched along some of the rivers and lakes represented specific tribes of Indians, some well known and others thought to be extinct. Other parts of the map only made him ask more questions.

The most perplexing question wasn't about what was on the map, but rather how the American got his hands on it in the first place. It looked so authentic and original. Why was this map not in a museum somewhere, and why hadn't he discovered it first? Many maps had surfaced over the years that were drawn by early explorers and outlined the continent so well that they were still viable today. But this one didn't resemble any of them. This map was so out of proportion that the person who drew it had either never visited the shorelines of South America or was drawing from memory. Either way, it made him think of more questions than it answered.

"Where to?" asked the chief of police.

The priest didn't respond. He reached into his pockets one more time for the missing map. How could he have been deceived so easily? When one gets to be as old as he was, you'd think he'd seen everything. Yet this girl had outfoxed the hunter.

"Father, are you all right?" The driver was now looking in the rearview mirror awaiting an answer.

Father Delanda whispered under his breath, "The truth shall spring out of the earth, and righteousness shall look down from heaven." He looked up and replied, "To Sacsayhuaman."

CHAPTER TWENTY-ONE

SACSAYHUAMAN

The stars were on full display tonight as there wasn't a cloud in the sky. It was easy to see the rabbit on the moon as it hung on the horizon. Renee and her father always started every night of stargazing by zeroing in on the moon. "Look, the rabbit has come out to play," she'd say. Renee first noticed the silhouette and pointed it out to her father at the age of five. Funny how the child's mind works when it comes to those things. Most adults just see clusters of stars and maybe the Big Dipper if they're lucky. Children, on the other hand, find diamonds, fairies, and kites. Tonight, the rabbit pointed north.

Jason held Renee's hand as they crept along the shadows created by the terraced walls along this ancient fortress. Single stones four stories tall and weighing one hundred tons dominated the landscape. They snapped into place like giant Legos inside other finely cut rocks. It was hard to imagine how any amount of manpower could have actually lifted these boulders into place much less arranged them so precisely. The grassy field before them was abandoned at this time of night. There was only an hour of darkness left before the dawn gave their cover away.

"What are we doing here?" asked Renee.

"I have a hunch," replied Jason. He paused and looked around for any movement. "The map had a group of rocks drawn on it next to what looked like a tunnel. It was near the area where Cuzco would've been had it been notated. I've been here several times looking up and down these stones, but I think you might be able to help me find it once and for all."

"Why's that?"

"This necklace that your father took. The one that this Lena woman took from you. Do you remember the image you saw back at the lake?"

"Uh-huh, the stick person-arrow thingy."

"Yeah. I have a feeling that might be the missing part of the puzzle here."

"I don't get it," said Renee. "How would that figure into something like a secret passageway here at Sacsayhuaman?"

"I'm not sure. I just have a hunch. I'll show you at daylight. At this point, what do we have to lose? Lena either came here or took off straight to Machu Picchu when she left the police station. There's no way we're going to be able to get on a train with the authorities looking for us. She probably went directly to the train station and caught the one leaving last night. Let's just hope the padre hasn't figured this all out yet." Jason let out a deep sigh. "If he studied that map at all before losing it, it will come to him soon enough."

They sat down against one of the huge walls of stone and rested. Renee shivered and tried to shield herself from the cool breeze occasionally sweeping into their corner. Jason took off his jacket and put it around them both. She smiled and whispered, "Thanks." After she'd wiggled around enough to get comfortable, she added, "Tell me something."

"Sure, anything."

"Is your name really Jason?"

He chuckled as he pulled a bandage out of his bag and started wrapping his thumb. "Yeah. That is definitely my real name."

"What's Lena's real name?"

"I'm not sure. She called herself Joanna when I knew her."

"How long ago was that?"

"A few months ago."

"Were you, you know, in love?"

Jason didn't answer. He just looked away and cleared his sinuses. Then he gradually turned back and studied the features on her face. The night was fading away and he could make out her high cheekbones and budding nose. "You have some Indian in you, don't you?"

Renee blushed and put her head down. "A little, I guess. My mom didn't talk about it much growing up. Just lately she started telling me about my ancestry. That's part of the reason we're down here and all—my father and me. To see my uncle."

This time Renee looked away and sniffled.

Jason didn't like where this conversation was going, so he decided to answer the question she'd asked back at the police station. "The map was given to me by this dying Indian. He didn't call it a treasure map, although those who've seen it would think that's exactly what it is. He referred to it as his 'compass' to help him find his way back home."

"Where's home?" asked Renee.

"Paradise, or as the Spanish would say, *El Gran Paytite*—a place far away from civilization, hidden in the rainforest. A place where there's no violence or greed and no need for worldly goods. A place where there are no locks or doors because they don't understand the concept of stealing. It's where the ancient gods took their chosen people and hid them away to protect them from all of the needless destruction in this world—Nirvana."

"He told you that?"

Jason chuckled. "Not quite." He realized that this girl was no fool. "You're a pretty sharp kid."

Renee said nothing. A minute or two went by as they listened to the morning songbirds greet the day. The peaceful solitude tucked away in the darkness was now unraveling in the morning light. Jason finally rose up, brushed the dust off his pants, and added, "And yes, we were in love—at least I was."

They moved away from the wall into the center grassy area. He peered across the field and said, "Do you see that one rock that stands taller than the others?"

"Over there?"

"Yeah. I think that's part of the puzzle. Watch what happens when the sun comes up more."

The morning sun soon rose beyond the mountaintop. It glistened over the rock and cast a series of small shadows on its surface. The angle was such that certain lines and figures engraved into the stone slowly came into focus. There were several shapes, but three images stood out in the middle. Two of the shadows formed crude circles on the bottom that were connected by crevices between the rocks. The cracks were tall and jetted straight up past several other layers of rocks. Each layer crossed the crevice perpendicularly and created a distinct image in the wall.

The first symbol had three lines crossing the main stem that fanned out wider as they moved toward the center. It resembled an old TV antenna. The second figure had one line intersecting the center with a circle on the bottom. It was the spitting image of the female gender symbol. The last shape looked like a crudely drawn stick person with an elongated body. It was identical to the image Renee had seen back at Lake Titicaca.

"That's it," exclaimed Renee.

"Take a good look because it'll disappear any moment," Jason said. Within seconds, the sun rose higher in the sky and the symbols were gone.

"What's it mean?"

"I'm not sure. I was hoping you could answer that one."

Renee took out a notepad and pen from her backpack and began writing down what she'd seen. Frantically, her pen sketched the side of the mountain and its symbols. Jason pointed out a spot that she'd drawn differently than what was on the rock. When Renee ignored his comment and kept drawing, he decided to back away a step. She continued to draw and scribble glyphs from deep in her memory.

After a few minutes, she finished. Jason peered over her shoulder and looked at her paper. The symbols and lines didn't make any sense to him. He knew enough about Inca and Mayan cultures to identify most letters and petroglyphs, but these drawings were different. All he recognized were the three images they'd seen on the wall and the shape of a house. Renee looked up at the wall once again and said nothing.

"So, what'd you see?"

Renee looked frustrated. She raised her head and said, "I'm not sure. There's something about a white house and diving, but I can't fill in the rest." She pulled out her symbols book and thumbed through the pages.

In the distance, they heard a car door slam. Then another vehicle pulled up, popping gravel and sliding to a sudden halt. Time was running out.

"I think we have company." He put his arm around her and started leading her over to the wall. "We need to start diving then."

"No, we don't," said Renee. "Those are future clues."

"What do you mean, future clues?"

"Those symbols are for the next part. Don't you see? It's like a journey where you get a clue once you've made it to one place that will help you find your way to the next."

"I don't get it. How'd you devise that from a few drawings on a rock?"

"In Lake Titicaca. The last clue was there. That's where the journey began, I think—or that's where the last stop was before this one."

WELCOME TO CUZCO

Jason shook his head and stopped. "You lost me."

"You see, thousands of years ago, there was this tunnel that stretched from Tiahuanaco to Cuzco. My dad and I were actually in it. The earthquakes probably closed it up or something, but I think this was supposed to be the next stop in the journey."

Off in the distance, a man was shouting. Jason glanced over and saw a few men approaching on foot. "OK. You can explain this to me later, but we need to get outta here now. What's the clue from Lake Titicaca?"

"The stick person." She pointed to a place in her book and then to the group of rocks they'd been watching. "We need to get over there."

Jason leaned over to look at her drawings. In the corner of the page was the number 512. "Interesting."

"*Alto!*"

Four officers were coming toward them. The skinny one and his partner led as two other larger men trailed closely behind. In the rear, Father Delanda and the chief of police shuffled along.

Jason and Renee raced over to the wall that formed the legs on the stick person. It was actually a recessed cove about two feet deep and four feet wide. They both ducked into the shadows to catch their breath. The huge slabs of rock before them seemed daunting and uninviting.

"What do we do now?" he asked.

"I'm not sure, but I have an idea." Renee started skimming her fingertips over the surface. "This worked back in Tiahuanaco. Let's see if we have any luck with it here."

At first, she felt nothing, but after slowing down the pace and gently gliding her fingers over the stone, the grooves came alive. Whenever she came to an indentation, she placed her middle finger in it and pivoted her hand around to feel for other pockets. If she didn't feel anything, then she'd move on to another spot. It was slow and tedious work.

"Stop, stop!" This order was much louder and more distinct. The police were only a hundred yards away.

"We don't have much time. You keep looking and I'll try to slow 'em down."

Jason took a few steps forward when a voice called out, "Stop or I'll shoot."

His eyebrows perked up. He wasn't expecting guns. The skinny policemen fumbled for his revolver as Jason searched his backpack for any kind of weapon.

Renee glanced back. "How you doing?"

"Define *doing*." He tried to smile but could only conjure up a worried grin. "Just keep working on that wall. I'll come up with something."

At that moment, he heard a faint swooshing sound as one of the officers groaned and covered his neck. Then there was another *swoosh*. The gun in the skinny man's hand went flying into the air. The policemen circled the wagons, trying to figure out where the attack was coming from. *Smack!* Another officer reached for his forehead and fell to his knees.

"Stop or I'll sh…"

Before the biggest cop could finish his last word, a rock hit him in the leg and knocked him off his feet. The skinny officer picked up his gun and started shooting aimlessly into the rocks. The other police joined in.

"Cease firing!" yelled Father Delanda as he reached the group of officers. "Don't worry about that. Get the two Americans."

Jason retreated backward toward the darkened cove. The *policia* darted off after him with their guns drawn. Every few steps, another rock would go hurling through the air and land another victim. The biggest officer fell hard to the ground with a blow to the temple. The other three tried shielding their faces and pushed on.

"I found it!" screamed Renee. "The indentations are on the bottom of the wall. The lady at the lake said that I must worship and bow down to my ancestors." She bent down and placed both middle fingers and thumbs into the shallow grooves on each side of a set of stones.

"I need you to help me," she said. "Place your finger in between my thumb and index finger—on both hands." She now had all of her fingers in place along with Jason's. With a grunt, she pushed and the wall started moving. The whole section of rocks shifted downward and inward like a Rubik's cube on ball bearings. One section replaced another until an opening appeared. Jason looked one last time at the approaching officers before thrusting forward with all of his might.

The walls were now open enough for their bodies to slip through. He grabbed Renee and lunged into the hole. They were halfway through when Jason felt a tug on the back of his jacket. The skinny policeman had managed to make it past the gap before it completely closed on the outside. He yanked on Jason's collar, forcing him to the ground. Renee fell with him. Seconds later, they heard the sound of metal blades scraping against each other. There was a thump as the tension on Jason's coat relaxed. Then there was another thump.

"Do you have a flashlight?"

"Yes."

She fumbled in the dark through her pack and switched it on. Lying next to her was the officer's severed head. It rolled a few feet before coming to rest against a nearby wall. The man's nose and ears were caked with dirt, and his eyes stared straight up at her with a look of absolute horror.

The sound of her scream echoed down the tunnel for a good ten to fifteen seconds causing dust to fall from the ceiling before finally dissipating. Renee spun away from the bloody head and buried her face into Jason's chest. He put his other arm around her and braced himself with one knee. He didn't dare stand back up.

PART THREE

DIVINE INTERVENTION

CHAPTER TWENTY-TWO
LAST TRAIN TO MACHU PICCHU

The train station was filled with Indian women holding woven blankets above their heads as tourists did their best not to make eye contact. The men with briefcases full of silver jewelry were a little luckier. Every few minutes a visitor would stop and make a quick purchase before boarding the train. A burnt-orange-colored engine with yellow stripes warmed up on the track as the Andes Mountains loomed overhead and passengers lined up on the platform. Its noise was deafening.

In the far corner of the station, a woman moved in and out of the crowd and cautiously approached the ticket booth. She handed ten dollars to an Indian woman and took her smallest blanket, which she wrapped around herself like a poncho. She paid the woman another ten dollars for her black derby. Next, she pulled her blonde hair up around her head and stuffed it under the hat. Her disguise was complete. No one even noticed as she bought her ticket and mingled in the crowd. A lone guard dressed in a dark green jacket and ball cap stood next to a restroom chatting with a young lady. He pointed to her map and smiled as the woman thanked him and then walked back to her husband.

Document 512

Lena could tell that the authorities hadn't been put on alert yet. The atmosphere at the train station was too festive. A slender, blonde-haired female about five feet six and weighing around 125 pounds would have garnered their attention otherwise. She meandered through the crowd and boarded the train without a hitch. Then she found a seat next to an old woman who was half-asleep and riding alone. Lena closed her eyes and laid her head on the window.

She tried to clear her mind long enough to relax. Too much information was sometimes as bad as not enough. The quickest way for her to reboot was to think of a time when life was simpler. That would be her childhood: a time when her biggest problem centered around which color to paint her Barbie doll's fingernails.

She never knew her real parents. The man who eventually adopted her was a career officer in the U.S. Army. Even though he said he found her wandering the streets of Berlin, she never did quite buy into that story. Early on, she started to suspect that he knew more about her past than he cared to mention. Every once in a while, he'd catch himself midsentence and change the subject without any explanation. The slip-ups seemed harmless enough at first, but as she grew older they began to bother her.

Her mother was a different story. Since she was not able to have kids of her own, her husband assumed that she'd relish the chance to raise a child and mold her into whatever type of woman she desired. Instead, her mother resented it. She was jealous of the young girl from the moment she entered their lives and made it perfectly clear that Lena was not wanted.

When her father was home, life was pleasant and exciting. He told her countless tales about his time in the military, igniting a deep desire in her for adventure. They went on trips together to museums and historical sites in every city he was stationed in. When he was gone, her mother constantly put her to work cleaning the house and doing menial chores. Lena chose to remember the times with her father, and it calmed her nerves.

The whistle blew and a doorman yelled for last call in Spanish and then English. Tourists waved out the windows and slowly found their seats. As the doorman began taking tickets, another man in a dark coat and hat jumped onto the train. He started ordering the attendant around while waving his hands back and forth. The chubby doorman seemed annoyed. He reluctantly nodded and continued his job as the man in black walked into the next car.

This was not good, and Lena knew it. The chances of getting caught were rising by the minute. The only advantage she had was the fact that dusk had settled in, making visibility difficult. The train's overhead lights were few and far between. Still, she had to figure out how to get her ticket stamped without drawing anyone's attention.

Between her hat, blanket, and dark suntan, she could almost pass for a native. She still needed something else. Her eyes searched from left to right. Behind her, a little girl started whining and moaning to her mother. Then the lady's baby began crying. Lena had found a way out.

She turned around and looked over the situation. The poor woman was trying to feed her baby while the little girl pulled on her coat sleeve and begged to go to the restroom. In Spanish, Lena asked the lady if she wanted her to hold the baby. The woman was bewildered at first and caught off guard. Her daughter continued to whine and hold onto her crotch and complain. Lena conjured up the most caring smile, with droopy eyes and all, and started baby-talk to the infant. It was working. The lady thanked her and handed over the little bambino and his bottle. Then she said something to the old woman next to them and scurried off to the front of the car with her moaning child.

The stagnant smell of bodies cramped into a small compartment intensified. Then the lights flickered and the train began to move. When the doorman asked Lena for her ticket, she handed it to him while playfully rocking the infant in her arms. He punched a hole into it and handed it back without any hesitation. By the time he'd reached the back of the car, the man in the black jacket had returned. He shouted to the attendant, who shook his head and went back to taking tickets. The man took one last glance over the train car and then jumped off as it left the station.

The train soon began its steep climb out of the city into the surrounding hillside. A series of gut-wrenching turns and twists known throughout Peru as the "Zigzag" followed. The trip seemed much longer than the three hours stated on the marquee. The lights continued to sputter every time the train tottered back and forth across the tracks, making it impossible to rest. The smell of dirty clothing and wet boots swirled in and out of the few windows that actually opened. The sound of the Urubamba River, which meandered alongside the track, was muted by the engine noise. Lena squeezed the map in her pocket. There was no way she'd be able to study it at her seat, so she ventured into the *baño*.

The light in the restroom was dim but at least it stayed on constantly. The far-reaching Andes Mountains and Amazon River were easily recognizable on the map. Some symbols like waterfalls and animals were obvious, but most of the names were foreign to her. She studied the strange hieroglyphic markings up and down the coast. What was the square box with *L*-shaped lines jetting out of it on three sides that was drawn in next to Lake Titicaca supposed to signify? Broken lines traced the trails stretching all the way from Ecuador down to Chile—or were they possibly roads? Along the Amazon were several symbols resembling mountains, mazes, and staircases. In the area where Cuzco should be was the handwritten Spanish word *Chincana*.

"The place where one gets lost," she whispered.

The words *Machu Picchu* appeared nowhere on the map, yet she knew this ancient city was somehow tied into everything. The purpose of this green and grand ancient site had always been a mystery to humanity. Some people speculated that it was a sanctuary for the Nusta women or "virgins of the sun" that were sent there to hide from the invading Spaniards. Others believed that it was the playground or vacation homes of the Indian elite and their families. The fact that the Spaniards never did find it spoke volumes about its importance to their culture. The Indians wanted to keep this city hidden from the pillaging Spanish at all costs.

There were supposedly many caves under the site as well. It was believed that a group of Inca warriors split off from Tupac Amaru's army and disappeared into one of these caves in order to evade Pizarro's attacking forces. Legend had it that they disappeared into the Mountain of the Moon and traveled deep underground to a hidden kingdom. Others said they used magic to make themselves invisible to the soldiers and walked right by them. Either way, they were never heard from again. Lena knew that the secret to finding the lost city and its gold began at Machu Picchu.

CHAPTER TWENTY-THREE
THE PATH

Renee's breathing was loud and heavy. She still couldn't believe what had happened to her over the last forty-eight hours. What had started as a well-planned educational vacation had now become an unpredictable roller coaster ride through hell. Back in the States, her life had been about as peaceful and picture-perfect as a girl could ask. Never could she have imagined being attacked by Indians, watching her father die, running from the police, and almost being decapitated in such a short time. As she reflected on all of this, she noticed that there weren't any tears. She was all out of tears.

Jason heard the sniffles and just held on tightly until she calmed down. Even though they'd only been together a few hours, he felt that he knew her pretty well. Between overhearing the story she told Father Delanda and watching her calmly decipher the hidden passageway, he'd realized that this young teenager was special. Most girls, in fact, most people would have buckled under the pressure long ago.

"You OK?"

Renee didn't respond. Instead, she cleared her nose and took a deep breath.

"That was a pretty amazing thing you did back there. Saved our butts," Jason continued.

The recent events were still racing through Renee's mind. She tried hard to focus and regain her composure but all that kept coming up was the image of her father falling to the ground back on the mountaintop.

"I can't believe this is happening," she said. "It's just too much. And why me?"

Jason loosened his grip. "It's not by chance. There're just too many coincidences."

"What do you mean?"

"There's a reason that it's you. Think about it. What are the chances of me running into you and my ex-girlfriend at the same time? What would be the odds on both of us having an in-depth knowledge of this lost Indian culture? And the number in that book of yours—I know that number."

Renee raised her head. "How?"

"Back at the library in Cuzco. I came across this book called *Document 512*."

"512," Renee repeated. "What was it about?"

"From what I could gather, it's about a man who led an expedition into the Amazon back in the seventeen hundreds. He was looking for lost gold mines but instead found a hidden ancient city." Jason sighed and added, "I didn't have much time to look it over before those goons from the police station found me."

Renee considered this new bit of information and didn't say a word for the longest time. Finally, she broke her silence. "We need to find that book."

"I think you're right."

Jason moved the flashlight around, careful not to steer it toward the decapitated head and its former body. Instead, he pinpointed the beam on the area where the blades had sprung out of the walls. The slits were barely visible. They'd been lucky this time, but how long would it be before the next booby trap got the best of them?

"Let's remember to lower our heads each time we go into another room."

Renee wiped her face with her sleeve and said, "There was this old woman back in Copacabana who just walked up to me and started talking like she was in a trance or something. She told me to kneel down before our maker."

"That's odd."

"Yeah, that's only part of it," she added. "There were markings on the wall and floor out there. I mean, like, they were drawings or maybe hieroglyphics. I couldn't read most of them but the ones I did translate were *ambulo, sub,* and *directus.*"

"They sound Latin," said Jason. "*Ambulo* sounds like 'ambulance' or maybe 'amble.' Yeah, that makes more sense—'amble.' *Sub* is a prefix like in 'submarine'; which means 'under.' And *directus* sounds like, well, 'direct.'"

"*To walk under and direct.* What the heck does that mean?"

"I'd assume the other words you couldn't read would fill in those blanks. Maybe *walk under* had something to do with us entering this cave. If we hadn't fallen down when we came in, both of our heads would be playing pool with our *compadre* over there."

"I guess so."

"You know, I saw a few symbols and drawings on the wall out there, but they sure didn't look like any of the petroglyphs I'm familiar with."

"Me either, at first," said Renee. "When I stared at them long enough, the words just came to me. It was like all of the letters were drawn over the top of each other."

"Interesting. You mean like a 3D image, or did you see each letter forming separately?"

"Sort of a combination of both; more multidimensional, though. I could make out the letter *B* and then see the letter *U* connected to it on the right. Then the letter *S* somehow appeared over the top of both and so on. But it only worked with certain symbols."

Jason stiffened his back. "*B* and *U*: those letters are in our alphabet. Europeans have only been on this continent for about five hundred years. Those markings and that secret door must be way older than that."

"Hmm. Either way, they're not all Latin because some letters looked completely different. More like Greek or maybe symbols." She thought about what her dad had said back in the cave. His theory that these gods traveled all around the world establishing early Greek and Roman cultures seemed more believable than ever. She imagined how excited he would be right now if he were there with her.

"Wait a minute," said Jason. "How could the line for *B* end up on the left side of *U*?"

Renee lowered her head and grinned sheepishly. It was usually at this point of the conversation, between the awkward pause and the other party's realization that she had trouble reading words, that things started spiraling downward. Unfortunately, there was no way of backing out of this confrontation, so she decided to just answer.

"I guess I forgot to tell you. I'm dyslexic. Certain symbols, well, they appear backwards to me—and that's when I can make out the clues."

Jason was silent for a minute as he tried to put it all together. Why would there be Latin and Greek symbols imbedded into the ancient rocks of South American Indians? Maybe these clues could help him understand his map more clearly.

Renee misread his silence and was scrambling to find a way to diffuse the situation when Jason unexpectedly replied, "That is so cool. No wonder I couldn't figure it out. Do you think that these ancient Indians were dyslexic too?"

His comment wasn't at all what she expected. He thought it was cool! This had never happened to her before. For the first time in her life, someone saw her disability not as a burden but as an asset. At that moment, she had a newfound appreciation for her new best friend.

"I don't know. I just know that I am."

Jason shined the light on the tunnel walls. They were very similar to the ones Renee had described to the priest. They were also identical to the ones he'd read about in Von Däniken's book. All of them were smooth and flat, with ninety-degree corners at the ceiling and floor. They stood at least eight feet tall and six feet wide. He pointed the light to the ground, where a set of endless steps descended into the earth. A few feet away on the left wall was an unlit torch perched in a holder. A couple of pieces of flint rock sat beneath it alongside a golden jar of oil.

"Look over there. A torch." He slowly rose to his feet, keeping his flashlight above his head until he was standing upright. "No signs of swinging metal blades here."

He took the torch off the wall and dipped its end into the oil. Shiny bits of golden glitter dripped onto the floor as he positioned it between his knees. Within seconds of striking the two rocks against each other, the torch was lit.

"Interesting," he said.

"What?"

"I think that the oil is filled with gold dust."

"Why's that so interesting?"

"I studied gold and its properties in school. Something about gold being capable of reabsorbing itself in fluid."

"So?"

He looked over to Renee and said, "I have a feeling this torch will burn forever—or, at least, a very, very long time."

"How do you know so much about gold?"

"I'm a physicist."

She rolled her eyes as she got to her feet, dusted off her shorts, and said dryly, "How boring."

Jason grinned. "You so funny. Here, put the flashlight back in your bag in case we need it later." He threw the bag over his shoulder and added, "What do you say we venture on in—considering what's on the other side of that wall."

Even though they couldn't hear anything, they were sure that the priest and police were close by, yelling and screaming at the others for losing the two suspects.

"Yeah, I'd hate for them to figure out the trick to getting in here."

"Speaking of tricks, how did you figure that out so quickly?"

"I don't know. I watched my uncle open a door like that in Tiahuanaco. I just did what he did."

"Does your uncle have Indian in him too?"

"Definitely."

They cautiously sauntered down the steps into a darkened corridor until the ground leveled off. The torch provided just enough light to see the walls and floor, but that was as far as it went. Beyond ten feet, it was pitch black. They proceeded along the path as it wound through the tunnel, twisting and turning every few hundred yards.

After about a half hour of walking, Jason paused and said, "Are you sure about this? We seemed to be going deeper and deeper into this mountain and nothing's changed."

"Let's go a little farther. It hasn't been that long."

As the sound of their footsteps kept in time with their heartbeats, they soon began to lose focus on what they were doing. The walls seem to float by like dark rain clouds—never quite looking the same but never that different either. It was easy walking too. The ground was completely level, and the temperature was cool enough to keep them from breaking a sweat. After a while, they lost track of time and became fixated with the floor in front of them. Something was pushing them unconsciously to take step after step. The repetitive motion of feet and lungs along with the lullabying tranquility of the tunnel was mesmerizing.

They marched like zombies for a good hour before the torch flickered just enough to break them out of their trance. They both stopped and slowly became aware of their surroundings once again. Renee pulled out her flashlight, clicked it on, and pointed it down into the darkness. All she saw was more of the same. "Maybe we should turn around and go back. This tunnel just seems to like go on forever. Those men are probably gone by now."

"Do you think we could even get out the way we came in?"

"I don't know." She moved the flashlight beam around and something caught her eye on the floor. She swung the light back and screamed. On the ground about ten feet away was the decapitated head of the man who'd followed them into the tunnel.

Jason reached out and grabbed her before she could rush into his arms again. He had this ritual down by now. They stared at the lifeless eyes and dirt-covered face. Then he grabbed her flashlight and scanned the area around the head.

"How peculiar."

"What?"

"There's no body." He looked up and down and then behind them. "How did it get here?"

"Where are the steps?" she said.

"I don't know. They've disappeared too." He moved the light over the room again and said, "We must be walking in circles."

"How can that be? We're just following the path."

"I know, but maybe it's an illusion."

"What, the head?" Renee walked over and lightly tapped it with her foot. It rolled over and came to rest on its nose near her feet, which caused her to quickly step away.

"No, I mean the path. We're just following it where it goes and it keeps coming back to where we started."

"How do you explain the fact that the steps have disappeared?"

"I don't know."

Renee paced around in circles and rubbed her chin. "Remember the words that I transcribed outside."

"Yeah: *ambulo, sub, directus*. Walk, under, straight."

"Maybe those words are a clue. It kind of fits."

"It sure does. Do you still have your compass?"

"Yeah." She reached down into her blouse and retrieved it.

He shined the light on the compass as she held it out. "Move it around to see if it's working."

Renee moved the compass from left to right and the needle remained firmly positioned in one direction. "It seems to be pointing this way, but I don't know if that's north."

"What do you mean by that?"

"Well, back in Lake Titicaca, the compass kept pointing at the necklace. It was weird, you know. The necklace was a magnet or something. It didn't matter which way you turned it either." She pointed down the darkened path and added, "It could be pointing to it right now."

"Interesting concept," said Jason. "If that's the case, then it'd also be pointing right at Lena—and my map. Can I take a look at it, please?"

She looked down at the compass for a few moments and then squeezed it tightly. This was the last thing her father gave to her before they separated. She slowly lifted it off her neck and placed it in his palm.

"Thanks."

"Don't lose it. I mean it."

The reluctance with which she gave it up hit home with Jason. He could tell that it had special meaning. "Don't worry, I have no intention of losing it." He placed it over his head and added, "I have an idea." Then he moved to the center of the tunnel and pointed his body perpendicular to the walls. "The needle is pointing *this* way. If that's where Lena is"—he spun around 180 degrees—"then we need to go *that* way in order to get back to Cuzco and the library, and we need to keep walking in that direction no matter which way the tunnel goes."

"How can we do that?" said Renee. "What if the tunnel starts turning?"

"We keep following the opposite end of the arrow no matter which way the tunnel turns." He looked down the corridor and added, "Remember the stories about the explorers getting lost down here and wandering for days?"

"Yeah."

"Well, maybe they were lost because they kept following the tunnel where it wanted them to go. I think you have to lead the tunnel where *you* want *it* to go."

"Lead me where you want me," said Renee.

"What?"

"In my dream. I remember a boy saying, 'Lead me where you want me.' It makes sense now. Don't you see?"

Jason stared at his young companion and realized she was basing their next move off a dream she'd had. He admired her trust in instincts and fate, but his decisions were usually based on analyzing facts and hypotheses and then coming to a logical conclusion. That person had vanished since landing on the soils of South America. Now he was more interested in riding with the wind and taking whatever path it led him on. That's what he'd loved the most about Lena.

"Well, that's enough to convince me. Let's focus on the compass and see what happens. If it works, then we can always find Lena later by following the compass's point."

Renee nodded. "OK. Let's try it."

They resumed walking the dark tunnel slowly and cautiously using only the torch. Renee stayed right next to him and constantly monitored the compass. They walked for a couple minutes without any trouble. Then the path began to veer slightly to the left.

"Stay on course," ordered Jason.

She put her arm around his elbow and concentrated on the compass. As they ventured closer to the wall, something strange happened. Even though the path was clearly moving to the right, it seemed to widen as they followed the needle. As the minutes passed, it grew wider and wider. They could both still see the walls in their peripheral vision hovering off to the sides and fading in and out of focus, maybe even moving in between dimensions. Yet, in front of them was nothing; just blank dead space. It was almost as if they had two sets of eyes: one that could see objects nearby and one that could only see far away. They kept their course steady and followed the needle exactly. The path seemed to be descending too. Their steps were shorter and much quicker.

"We're going downhill."

"I can feel it."

Jason didn't dare swing the torch over for a better look. Instead, he kept his eyes on the compass.

CHAPTER TWENTY-FOUR

DIMENSIONS

For the next few minutes, it felt like they were still going in circles. The walls on both sides had now disappeared completely. Their visibility range was limited to a few feet and the path's slope kept taking them deeper underground. They found themselves gasping for more air the farther they went. As each breath became shorter, every stride seemed to stretch out longer. All the while, it became harder and harder to just stay standing. Something was weighing them down, forcing them to yield to some kind of gravitational ruler.

Neither said a word as they stared at the compass and followed the path. The feelings of breathlessness and added weight eventually subsided as they traveled deeper still. Glimmers of light began to reflect off the compass's metal casing, bending around corners and scattering like water from a rotating sprinkler.

Soon they saw both walls again and the light returned to normal. It was now bright enough to see well beyond the torch's range. They came to a T, where the path branched off in different directions. A slight breeze gently floated above their heads.

"Wow, that was weird," said Jason.

"No kidding. I could hardly breathe there for a while, not to mention the fact that my backpack felt like it was carrying a ton of bricks."

Jason extinguished the torch and placed it into an empty holder near the intersection. He noticed large golden discs mounted above them about every twenty-five feet and walked up to one. "My hand is blocking the light," he said as he put it in and around the saucer. "The sunlight from above must be reflecting off these discs."

Renee peered down the path they'd come from and asked, "Where do you think we are? I mean, did we just, like, leave one tunnel and enter another?"

"I'm not sure, but I'd say we're definitely in another tunnel."

"How's that possible?"

"I don't know, but I have a theory."

"I'm almost afraid to ask," Renee said apprehensively as her forehead puckered.

Jason smirked. He glanced at the floor and ceiling and then asked, "Have you ever heard of Entanglement or String Theory?"

"No."

"Well, I've done a bit of research on the subjects in my studies. I'm beginning to believe that this tunnel is acting like some kind of a massive superconductor.

"A what?"

"A superconductor has the capability to transport electron energy and single-frequency light without any resistance over long distances and for long periods of time. And since quantum entanglement allows two particles to behave as one no matter how far apart they are, we could…"

"Hold on there a minute." Renee raised her hand in the air. "Please speak English."

He nodded. "Understood. Simply put, entanglement says that everything is connected in some way and what happens to one member of a system also happens to every other member of that system even if they're separated by space and time."

"You mean, I'm connected to everyone else and what happens to them happens to me?"

"No, not like that. This occurrence is very rare in the universe. You see, there has to be a special set of circumstances in order for entanglement to take place—or in your case, maybe just a special type of person."

Renee blushed and lowered her head. "That's all nice and everything, but why haven't I heard of this entangled theory thing before?"

"I guess because it's only come to the forefront of science over the last few decades. In fact, it's one of the few theories that Einstein flat-out rejected because he just couldn't believe that God would roll the dice like that. He called them 'spooky actions at a distance.' Instead, he kept trying to come up with some kind of unified theory that would link his three-dimensional theory of relativity with quantum mechanics. Unfortunately, he never did— and what was even more unfortunate was the fact that quantum scientists eventually proved that they were right. Thus, the science of quantum teleportation was born. That's where one is able to make an object disintegrate in one place while creating a perfect replica somewhere else."

He could tell that she was still skeptical. "Imagine it this way: Let's say you tried to put your hand through this wall. Of course, it's not going to go through the first time. But if you did it a million times in a row, according to quantum mechanics there is the probability that eventually the protons would react differently and allow your hand to pass right through this wall and appear on the other side."

Renee's face was now crunched up like a wilted prune. "You think we've somehow transported ourselves into another tunnel—kind of like Captain Kirk?"

"Your knowledge of *Star Trek* reruns is impressive. I don't mean it quite like that, but it does explain how we got here—scientifically, at least." He continued looking around and added, "With quantum teleportation, there has to be a common denominator between places though in order for it to work—certain tangible materials, something that both sites have in common. In theory, you can transport from point A, meaning that other tunnel, to point B, say, where we are now, even if there's a wall between the two points just by having a common denominator or a hidden variable."

Renee wasn't really buying his hypothesis but didn't want to upset him. After all, her theory, based on a few drawings and a dream she'd had, wasn't much better. She shrugged and asked, "So what's the common denominator?"

"Well, it's hard to say, but there could be a number of different things. Graphene, for one, can transmit huge amounts of energy over slivers of tape. Nanoparticles or monatomic elements also can act like exotic matter, which can defy gravity and disappear right before your eyes." He then pointed to the disc above his head. "Then there's gold. Maybe even monatomic gold. That could be the key."

She stood silently and thought about what he'd just said. It didn't really sound like the type of teleportation she understood, in which a person moved from one place to another very quickly. Yet, on the other hand, she knew these tunnels were full of many inexplicable qualities and behaviors. The Gods had definitely rolled the dice a few times down here.

"Why gold?" she asked.

"Because it's everywhere in the universe, but at the same time, it's really unique. It comes from meteors and stars; you can find it in the core of our earth and even in the ocean. You can stretch it, mix it with other compounds, hell, you can even eat some forms of it. There are a few out there that'll swear, when in a monatomic form, it can disappear right before your eyes under certain conditions. Have you ever thought about why these tunnels were dug out in the first place and what it was they carted away? Do you think it was just rock? Why would they do that?"

His argument was starting to make sense. "So don't you need energy in order to teleport somewhere—and shouldn't it be really quick?"

"Not in theory." Jason looked down to the ground and said, "But for practical purposes, yes."

"So how do we transport ourselves out of this place to where we need to go?"

Jason bit his lip. "I don't know. It's just a theory—you know, trying to make sense of it all."

She chuckled. "It's a good theory and probably true, but maybe we shouldn't try so hard to figure it out, Mr. Scientist. Your head might explode."

Jason liked hearing her laugh. It was such a nice change from the frightened little girl he'd witnessed earlier. He smiled back and said, "Yeah," then he rubbed the top of her head. "Let's move on."

CHAPTER TWENTY-FIVE

TEMPTATION

The two had only been walking for a few minutes when Renee pointed and said, "Look, over there." Off to the side was a small cave. They both stopped at the entrance, checking it over for signs of metal blades. "What do you think? Do we dare?"

Jason took his bag and tossed it into the room. He automatically flinched when it hit the ground but nothing happened. "I'd say it's safe."

They both crept into the room and kept their heads low. There was no natural light, so Jason guided his flashlight over the walls and ceiling. Then he tripped over something lying on the floor.

"What the..." He reached down and picked it up. It was a golden bowl. He studied it closely in the dim light and exclaimed, "It looks like it's made out of solid gold."

Renee reached down and grabbed another item. "So is this."

The room was littered with golden cups, spoons, and forks. Jason picked up several utensils and placed them inside his bowl. "This must be the kitchen."

"Must *have* been the kitchen," Renee said. "I don't think it's been used in quite a long time. Look at this old makeshift stove. It's falling apart."

In the corner of the room was a pile of rocks stacked in a circle with an iron grill on top. To the side, scattered on the floor, were branches and small logs. A mat made out of straw lay flat in the opposite corner.

"I'd say this was more of a rest area than a kitchen," she added.

"I agree, but I'm not tired. What do ya say we keep going?"

"Sounds good."

They walked back to the opening and were about to exit when the pan shot out of Jason's hands. It slammed into the wall and stuck to it like a magnet. All of the knives, cups, forks, and spoons were also plastered against the wall. Jason tried to pull them off but couldn't.

"I think these walls are magnetized. That's weird, because gold doesn't have any magnetic properties. I mean, it's so malleable that you could stretch it across the universe and back, but it shouldn't be sticking to anything." He tried to pry one of the spoons off with his pocketknife.

"Then they must not be made of gold—not completely," said Renee. "There must be some other metal in them." Renee looked down at her compass. "Look. It's spinning wildly again—just like it did with the necklace."

"Of course," exclaimed Jason. "A superconductor needs energy but it doesn't have to be electrical. Do you know how high-speed trains work?"

"Yeah, sort of. Something to do with magnets."

"Precisely. Magnetism is so powerful that it can levitate trains and propel them down the tracks. Imagine if you could harness the magnetic field of the earth—or the universe. That must have something to do with this."

He placed his knife against the wall, but it just fell to the ground. "That's peculiar. This blade should've stuck to the wall too." He picked it up and tried again. A second time it fell. "It's not magnetic."

"What else could it be?"

"I don't know, something foreign to me. Maybe foreign to the whole planet."

"What do you mean?"

"Like I was saying earlier. I mean, look around you. Do you think Indians made these tunnels? How could they have possibly carved out all of these smooth walls? Not to mention, dug this far into the mountain."

"So who could've built them?" she asked.

"I don't know. But I don't think they were human."

"You sound like my father."

"There are more than just one or two believers, you know. It would explain a lot. Do you think we just ended up in this other tunnel by magic? No, there's something involved here that's way beyond this world and maybe the whole galaxy."

She could see that his pupils were dilated, and it bothered her. She wasn't sure if it was the talk of aliens or finding the gold that was setting him off. Either way, she didn't like it.

"Yeah, well that kind of talk got my father killed, so let's change the subject. I'm ready to go."

Renee started to leave the room, but Jason reached out and grabbed her arm. "We can't leave—the gold."

She brushed off his hand and said, "I don't think we have a choice."

"Well, let me try a couple of other things." He began scavenging through his bag. "Maybe something will counteract…"

"Jason, please, just leave it."

"Leave the gold. Are you kidding?"

His body was pumped on adrenalin, drunk on its own delusion, and boiling over with gold fever. More tools flung out of his bag as he rambled on. She was losing him and realized that something had to be done quickly.

"Jason, pleeeeease!"

This was not the voice of a polite little girl any longer. On the contrary, it was the voice of anger, with a hint of fear. When he ignored her pleas once more, she stomped up to one of the utensils glued to the wall and tugged on it. Surprisingly, it pulled away with ease. Then she snapped up another and another. Jason had stopped fumbling through his bag and could only stare in disbelief. When the last piece of gold had been removed, she marched out of the room back into the main area.

Jason instinctively followed and asked, "How'd you do that?"

"I don't know, but at least it got your attention. We can't take this stuff with us. Do you understand? There's something…not right about it." Then she tossed all of the utensils back into the room.

As the golden trinkets were bouncing off the floor and walls, Jason screamed, "No!" He ran in and grabbed a few pieces off the floor. With his precious treasure firmly secured against his chest, he raced back out through the opening. The items flew out of his hands, splintering off in every direction but out. Then he went back for more tableware and tried to toss them out of the room. Renee watched in horror as knives and forks spun wildly in her direction.

"What are you doing?" she screamed while ducking out of the way.

The utensils spiraled through the air, spinning methodically toward her forehead before curving into the walls in front of her. They both stood there in silence as the realization of what he'd just done sunk in. Her voice was hoarse from yelling as she tried to speak. "Ah?"

Jason took a deep breath and exhaled, "For a moment there, I really lost it, didn't I? Sorry."

Renee slowly stood back up with her eyes fixated on this erratic and crazy scientist. Something had snapped and brought out his dark side. She'd only known the man for a few hours and was now wondering if she knew him at all.

Jason saw the change in her demeanor. Her eyes were flashing yellow and the gate was coming down. He couldn't blame her, though. He wasn't sure if he knew himself anymore. Now he understood why all the explorers who'd come before him had gotten so carried away. Something in these caves triggered a reaction so unnatural that it overwhelmed the senses, polluting minds with thoughts of greed and evil and eventually drowning them in their own toxic nightmares. In fact, since figuring out the secret of moving from one pathway to another, he'd felt like a different person completely—almost possessed. If it hadn't been for his companion, who knows what would've happened.

"I'm really sorry. Something just came over me."

"Is it gone?"

He nodded. "Definitely." He exited the room empty-handed with his head down, still trying to understand what had just happened.

With a tint of trepidation, she sighed, "I hope so."

They regrouped in the main corridor and rested in silence. Jason was still a little tipsy and needed the time to clear his head. Then he stood up, looked around and said, "Which way?"

"This way. Let's follow the breeze."

They walked for an hour before coming to another intersection. This time there wasn't any need to discuss which direction they were going. One of the passageways was completely blocked with rubble piled to the ceiling. Dregs of gravel and silt squeezed around boulders while tree roots surreptitiously held everything in place. Spiderwebs were strewn from one vine to another as centipedes and small rodents scurried away from the light. From the looks of it, the tunnel had caved in a long time ago.

"Probably an earthquake caused this," he said. Then he ran his hand across the wall from top to bottom and added, "Or an explosion."

"Explosion? Why would someone do that?"

"Well, like I was telling you earlier about the explorers who used to come down here into these tunnels, they all went in, but nobody ever came out. Finally, the government decided to close some of the entrances with explosives in order to keep anybody else from getting lost."

Renee nodded. "After walking in circles back there, I can understand why." She took out her flashlight, pointed it down the other tunnel, and said, "I guess we only have one choice."

When she started to walk away, Jason reached out and stopped her. "Not so quickly. Something's not right here."

He studied the pile of rocks a little closer. "Something doesn't fit, but I can't put my finger on it."

Renee followed his lead and shined her light over the barricade. "What are we looking for?"

"Anything that seems…out of place. A rock that's a different color or size"—he bent down and rubbed the surface of a boulder that came up to his knees—"or a different type of material. See this, this is sandstone. Why in the world would a piece of sandstone be down here with all of this granite and sedimentary rock?"

"You're right. What's it mean?"

He laid his light on the ground and grabbed the boulder with both arms. "Shine the light down here." He tried lifting it until his face turned red and the veins popped out on his neck, but nothing happened.

"Try sliding it," suggested Renee.

"Why not." He repositioned his feet and pushed with all of his might. The rock moved easily and the wall behind them slid open.

"That's it," exclaimed Renee as she moved over to the opening.

"Be careful. Remember the booby traps."

She instinctively ducked down and stopped. The room was no more than a closet with walls about a dozen feet apart from each other. A wooden ladder stood in the middle.

A very faint sound was coming from above. At first, they couldn't make out what it was, but soon it became apparent.

"Do you hear that?"

Jason moved in closer. "Yeah. It sounds like a man…chanting."

"Oh dear, not that again."

As she looked around for any signs of bodies, music suddenly began to play. Loud church music blasted through the ceiling above the ladder as wooden boards creaked in synchronization with the bass notes thumping to a slow but steady rhythm.

"It must be an old pipe organ—with foot pedals," he surmised. Fifteen feet above, shards of light seeped through the cracks between the boards as the organ music continued its sermon.

"Where do you think we are?" asked Renee.

The music continued for a few minutes before abruptly ending. Jason listened as the shuffling of feet and a low murmur of voices resonated throughout the room. It grew louder for a few minutes and then died down.

"I'd say we're right in the lion's den."

CHAPTER TWENTY-SIX

THE LION'S DEN

The ceiling squeaked and croaked for another five minutes while they waited next to the ladder. Finally, Jason rose up, brushed off his pants, and asked, "Whatcha think?"

"It's been quiet up there." Renee stood up, switched her flashlight back on, and pointed it at the ceiling. "How do we get out of here?"

"Let's try the obvious first." Jason firmly grabbed each side of the ladder and climbed very cautiously. He looked from left to right and hesitated before each step. "So far so good."

"Be careful."

When he reached the top, he placed his palm on the wooden hatch above his head and pushed. It moved slightly. He pushed again a little harder and heard a click.

"Get back!" he screamed while quickly ducking and sliding down the ladder so fast that his legs collapsed under the force sending him hard to the ground.

"Are you all right?"

"Yeah, yeah, just taking precautions." He looked at the wood burns on his hands and then back up at the ceiling. Everything was still in place. "I guess it was a false alarm."

"I don't know. I heard the click too."

He brushed off his hands and said, "For a minute there, I thought a couple of metal blades were going to come swinging out of that wall."

"Me too. It must've been something else."

"Yeah, it sounded like a lock or a handle clicking from up there. In fact, now that I think about it, that would make perfect sense. Latches would be holding the platform in place. Otherwise, it'd just move around when you walked on top of it."

Renee nodded. Jason slowly climbed the ladder again, keeping a sharp eye out for anything unusual. A couple of steps up he paused and asked, "Can I use your light?"

She handed him the flashlight and he continued upward. At the top, he shined it around and found a small hole on the bottom of the platform. He reached up and felt a metal latch inside. Then he reached over to the other side and found another one hidden there.

"There're two latches. Let me see if I can move them."

Jason climbed up another step and placed the light in his pocket. Then he reached for the latch and slid it open. It moved easily. He did the same thing to the other side.

"It's open."

He slowly slid the platform over a few inches and heard another click. "This can't be good," he whispered as the ladder started wobbling under his feet. It quickly dropped to the ground as he lunged for a nearby rafter. Within seconds, the dirt floor swallowed up the ladder, leaving him dangling in the air.

Renee tried to jump out of the way, but her feet went nowhere. The gravel underneath her legs sifted into the newly created hole, slowly sucking her in along with it. She frantically tried to scratch her way back out, reaching for anything solid. It was no use. Her fingers kept slipping through the rocks.

As the ground siphoned her body away, she spotted a wooden two-by-four lying near the wall. She thrust herself back up out of the hole, flapping like an Olympic swimmer with her torso and legs as hard as she could. It kept her above ground for just a few seconds, but that's all she needed to find the board and cling to it for dear life. With the plank stretched above her head, she let the floor crumble around her. Her only hope was that it was long enough to wedge itself into both sides of the opening.

When the last grains of sand and pebbles disappeared, a cloud of dust shot out of the pit. The cool breeze that followed made her body shiver. The two-by-four had worked. After firming up her grip, she checked herself for any cuts and bruises. Everything was still in place.

"Are you all right?" yelled Jason.

She looked up to see him still hanging from the rafter. "Yeah, I'm OK."

DOCUMENT 512

CHAPTER TWENTY-SEVEN
MEAN JOE DEL

The Englishman threw down a wad of cash on the table in disgust. "Bloody Indian," he cursed as he walked out of the bar.

Joe Del Diaz tossed another dart at the board. The tattoo on his right shoulder of a jaguar poised to strike leaped forward as he extended his arm. It landed in the bull's-eye right next to the one he'd just thrown.

Another young lad stood up from his chair and growled, "I don't like being swindled, mate." He reached for the pile of bills. A dart immediately landed between his hand and the money.

"I wouldn't touch. If you smart," Joe said in broken English.

The man peered up at this daunting edifice, with its Mohawk haircut and tattooed biceps. He reached for a knife from under his vest and swung it wildly at Joe's face. The blade cut a shallow path from his cheek up to his ear. Joe jerked back, spun around, and released his own knife all in one motion. The gold-handled blade landed squarely into the Englishman's chest.

As the man fell back, Joe caught him by the shirt. Then he pulled the knife out, wiped the blade off on the man's shoulder, and let him drop to the ground. When the body hit the floor it knocked over a chair, which would have normally turned a few heads in the bar, but the music blaring out of the jukebox was so loud that no one even noticed.

Joe grabbed his money and headed for the door. He tossed a few bills to the bartender and nodded. The bartender understood. He dried off his wet hands and walked out from behind the bar. As Joe was exiting the front door, the bartender was dragging the bleeding corpse out the back.

Joe Del was one of six sons born to a tall and lanky garbage collector named Victor Diaz. Victor was a proud full-blooded Indian who worked seven days a week to keep food on his family's table. His wife had died while giving birth to her youngest son and left Victor to raise the boys by himself. They were all brought up with a firm hand rooted deeply in the Catholic faith and taught to respect their father without question.

Two boys died in a street fight with a gang from the other side of town. They'd teased the boys one day after seeing them riding on the back of their father's garbage truck tossing trash into the back. Victor made it a point of using all his boys on his route at one time or another. He said it built character and taught them an important lesson about modesty. The boys definitely learned a lesson about humility.

The two sons knew better than to pick a fight when it was seven against two. But they didn't know how to walk away from an insult to their father. They managed to incapacitate all but one of the gang members before being shot in the back and left to die. Joe returned the favor a few weeks later when he hung the last remaining gangster's body up on a lamppost—with his throat cut and both eyeballs removed—for everyone to see. That's when the legend of Mean Joe Del began.

Joe's father vehemently disapproved of his actions and quickly kicked him out of the house. When Joe refused to ask for forgiveness from the church, he also found himself excommunicated. After wandering the streets for days, a drug dealer took him in, gave him shelter, and eventually hired him to collect debts. It was there that he learned everything there was to know about the underworld of drug trafficking.

Within a few months, he'd become the most feared and powerful enforcer in Cuzco. Just the mention of his name usually motivated deadbeat addicts to pay up. A trail of dismembered body parts and missing relatives seemed to follow everywhere he went. These days, though, Joe worked for himself—a hired gun, or as Joe liked to put it, a "one-man army."

Document 512

Huascar was waiting at a table in an outdoor café when Joe casually strolled up and plopped down into the seat next to him. "You're bleeding, my friend." Huascar dipped his napkin into a glass of water and handed it to Joe.

Joe didn't seem alarmed when the blood from his cheek dripped onto the table. He motioned Huascar to hand him another one. "You be looking for me?"

Huascar tried not to stare as Joe calmly pressed the napkin against his jawbone. Joe didn't even notice. He'd always had trouble with Huascar's wandering eye and just tried to look away whenever possible. "Yes, this should be an easy one for you—and it pays very well."

"They all pay well," replied Joe with a half-cocked grin.

"Of course." Huascar leaned in a little closer and lowered his voice. "The good Father needs you to find a boy. This is not your ordinary boy, though. He is very elusive and smart."

Joe continued looking away while holding the second napkin to his face. The wound was drying up.

"The boy should be easy to spot," Huascar continued. "He has deep blue eyes and dark red skin, but there's one thing that makes him stand out over the others." He scanned the crowd of diners and whispered, "He has six fingers on each hand."

Joe's eyes opened wide as Huascar traced the outline of six digits on the table. He'd heard rumors of such people before but had dismissed them as childish folklore.

"The boy must not be harmed in any way," said Huascar. "That must be understood. Do you understand?"

Joe's shoulders relaxed as he leaned back into his chair and nodded. "Me can leave my mark above the church door when he found. Tell the padre to look at it every evening. When see it there, he meet me here the day following at noon."

Then he stood up and tossed the napkin on the ground. As the blood oozed onto the bricks and trickled down into the cracks, he guzzled the rest of the water in the glass and then disappeared around the corner.

CHAPTER TWENTY-EIGHT
SYMBOLS OR SIGNS

"I'm going to jump," said Jason as he firmed his grip on the crossbeam. "Maybe if I aim for the corner, I'll miss the pit. Then I can try and bring you up."

"Look." Renee released her index finger from the two-by-four and pointed over to the next rafter. A few feet away was a pole hanging from the ceiling with a loop at the end. It had three bars that tapered off in length in the middle and ran perpendicular to the main one. "What's that look like to you?"

Jason turned his head and realized what she meant. The iron bars formed the same symbol they'd seen on the fortress wall back at Sacsayhuaman.

"How bizarre. Where'd that come from?" he asked.

"I don't know, but I'm sure it's there for a reason."

"No doubt. I'm gonna try and swing over."

"Be careful. If you miss, then we're both goners."

Jason looked down at Renee and then into the deep abyss below her. "I don't think we have much choice."

The expression on Renee's face said it all.

He spun around on the rafter and faced the other way. Then he swung back and forth a few times and thrust himself toward the three iron bars. As soon as he took off, he realized that he was going to fall short. His fingertips barely scraped the lowest bar, but it wasn't enough. As gravity wrestled him to the ground, his hands swung wildly in the air grasping for anything. Renee braced herself for a hard landing. Just as he was about to come crashing down on her head, his fingers caught the round hole on the end of the pipe. The weight of his body tugged hard on his overextended knuckles, painfully pulling him closer to his death. He quickly reached up with his other hand and wrapped it around the pole.

A metallic sound of rust and gears climbing over each other filled the room. Jason slowly drifted down to the floor as he held onto the iron bar. The ladder they'd lost moments ago reappeared from the hole. Renee kicked her foot over and straddled the side railing as it shot up out of the dirt. In a matter of seconds, the floor had closed below them and Renee was on the ladder at the top of the ceiling while Jason stood on the ground.

He let go of the bar and sighed. While shaking off the throbbing numbness in his fingers, he looked up and said, "How in the hell did that happen?"

Renee hugged the ladder and closed her eyes. Then she chuckled.

He scratched his head and asked, "What's so funny?"

A memory of her uncle from the caves in Tiahuanaco danced across her eyelids. She opened her eyes and replied, "This is how the gifts from The Gods come to us."

"I guess I'll take it then." He moved up the ladder and added, "Let's get out of here before they change their minds."

They both carefully slid the platform over until there was enough room to climb out of the hole.

"Keep your voice down," he whispered.

Above them was the underside of a large pipe organ. The platform was right under where the keyboardist would have been sitting. No light was coming in through the stained glass windows, indicating that it was nighttime.

Jason looked over to Renee and said, "It looks empty."

He pushed himself out of the hole and then helped her up the ladder. Then he repositioned the boards back over the opening and locked it. They both shuffled across the floor and stayed low to the ground. There was no one in sight.

"Coast is clear," he whispered.

"Where do you think we are?"

Jason peered over the pews and up at the stained glass windows. The Virgin Mary's image was in one and Jesus on a cross in the other. "I have a hunch this is the Church of Santo Domingo."

"Isn't that where Father Delanda lives?" said Renee.

Jason just looked at her and nodded. "Let's get out of here as soon as possible. Hopefully he hasn't returned yet."

"Where are we going?"

"Uptown to the *biblioteca*."

CHAPTER TWENTY-NINE

THE CATHEDRAL

From the balcony of the cathedral, Prince Tana Nara heard the platform shifting underneath the pipe organ. He knew the sound very well. His elders had told him that he'd be the only one who knew how to enter and exit from the secret passageway. After all, the last person to use it was his grandfather some sixty years earlier.

Document 512

The tribe had made sure of that a long time ago. It negotiated a secret pact with the Peruvian government to seal the passageways to the tunnels and prevent any further intrusions into their underworld. The agreement only cost the tribe a few trinkets of gold and silver—items that meant little to the Indians.

He cautiously followed the shadows against the wall until he was in a position to peer down onto the floor below. The man standing behind the organ looked familiar. The prince squinted and then realized where he'd seen that face before: it was the man from the market and police station.

Then he spotted the girl. Up until now, he hadn't been able to get a good look at her. It was too dark at Sacsayhuaman to see her features while he was distracting the police. She was beautiful. Even though he'd never seen her face, it looked familiar. Her eyes, the high cheekbones, the long hair—they all dazzled him and aroused his interest.

Somehow, he sensed that she was not a threat and could be trusted. She had the look of a savior. The man was a different story. Their chance meeting at the marketplace didn't seem so coincidental any more. He knew that the stranger had done something bad enough to land him in jail. That wasn't enough reason to be suspicious, though. After all, the prince was running from those same *policia* when they first met. Still, he knew he had to be cautious.

The two made their way across the aisle and down through a row of pews that led them to a corner of the cathedral, where a large wooden door stood. The prince was very familiar with it too. He also knew that if they opened the door it would mean certain capture.

The prince raced across the balcony and jumped over the railing. His hands grasped the thick velvet tapestry lining the wall and broke his fall as he slid down to the lower level. The curtain slowed the prince's momentum, but it wasn't enough to keep him from rolling over on the ground with a thump. He thrust himself back up on his feet in one swift motion. Jason's knife was within inches of the boy's stomach when Renee jerked it away at the last moment.

"Don't!" she said as Jason tried to wiggle his way loose from her grasp. She held on and then jumped between the two of them. Tana realized that his daring entrance had startled them and backed away a few steps.

"Please be quiet," the prince whispered.

CHAPTER THIRTY
THE DOOR

The prince slowly crept over to the wooden door and placed his ear against it. He signaled for the other two to do the same. They felt the vibration of another door resonating and footsteps on the floor. Then they heard voices coming from the other side.

"I think the father has returned," Tana whispered.

His European accent immediately caught Jason's attention. He looked down to the prince's hands and noticed the six fingers. Then he gestured with his eyes to Renee, who noticed them too.

"You're the boy from the market."

The Indian straightened up and answered, "*Sí*, I am Prince Tana Nara of Akakor."

"Prince."

"Akakor."

Renee looked to Jason and shook her head. He just smiled and said, "I'll explain later."

"Do you live here or something?"

Tana grinned slightly and said, "No, not exactly." He looked over at Renee, who was fixated on his blue eyes. "I'm from a land far away. I've been staying here up in the loft because it's the safest place."

"Does anyone else know that?" asked Renee.

"No. Well, uh, maybe. Some policemen have been chasing me around the city lately. It's hard to stay invisible with hands like these." He extended both arms showing them his twelve digits. The Medusa-like tentacles were mesmerizing. "I think the father knows something, but I'm not sure."

"The father seems to know everything about everybody," said Jason.

"Yes, he does. I think he's a bit crazy-loco, though. I mean, he has wild eyes."

"Is he here?"

"We can check." The prince pulled out his knife and shimmied it into the peephole. Carefully, he slid the cover to the side, not making a sound. "Take a look."

Jason leaned in toward the hole and moved his head back and forth until he found the right position. Suddenly, he veered away.

"He's here. There's another guy in there too. I've never seen him before but he looks dangerous."

Tana peered through the hole and whispered, "That's Mean Joe Del Diaz. We should stay far away from him."

Jason nodded and added, "I wish we could hear what they're saying."

"Follow me," replied the prince with a smile.

They climbed the staircase back up to the loft and headed for the corner where the prince had been living. There was nothing there but a small blanket rolled up and tucked away behind a pew. The boy knelt down and gently removed the vent cover on the floor. He waved at them to move in closer while placing his finger over his lips.

"I don't know if they can hear us," he whispered, "but we can hear them."

Renee and Jason smiled and moved in closer. They heard Father Delanda talking below. "I didn't see your mark above the door today. What's the status on the boy?"

"He will not be difficult to find. One with six fingers it leaves big impression," replied Joe.

"I didn't ask for commentary. I asked what the status was."

There was silence. They only heard feet shuffling across the floor. Then a faint voice could be heard saying, "I very close."

There was another pause and silence. Finally, the father replied, "I have another person I need you to find. She's a blonde girl in her late twenties, early thirties. She speaks German."

"That could be anyone on streets of Cuzco."

"Here's a photo of her taken down at the police station. It's a little grainy, but I think it'll do."

"What I do with her?"

"Bring her to me—unharmed," said Father Delanda. "Do you understand?"

"*Sí.*"

Just then, the big wooden door downstairs in the cathedral swung open. Joe stormed through and raced up the steps. His knife was in one hand as he held onto the railing with the other and jumped two steps at a time.

Jason pulled out his knife and signaled the other two to get behind him. Renee grabbed the prince and embraced him tightly. Tana was surprised by the sudden show of affection. He held onto her, and inhaled the sweet smell of her hair for the first time. He wasn't used to being this close to a person, especially a young girl near his own age. She squeezed him harder as Joe's Mohawk appeared at the top of the stairs.

Jason fumbled through his backpack. He pulled out a flare and snapped off the tip. Smoke began to pour out of the end.

"You two jump over the railing and slide down the curtains while I distract him."

"That's not necessary," said the prince as he wiggled loose from Renee's grip. "There's another way out."

Tana ran over to the corner pew and yanked hard on the back of it. The pew lifted up in front and an opening appeared in the wall behind him.

"Go," said the prince as he gestured to Renee with his head. She immediately ran to the opening and slid through.

Jason looked back and then forward toward the oncoming maniac. He quickly backed up while keeping an eye on Joe and shouted, "Go ahead, I'll follow behind you."

The prince was still pulling on the pew with all of his might. "You have to go first. There're only a few seconds after I release it before it closes."

"What if you don't make it?" cried Jason.

"I will."

Jason tossed the glowing flare at Joe, who caught it in midair. This only seemed to piss him off more. He ducked into the opening and shouted back to Tana, "Come on."

The prince released the pew and stumbled back through the opening as Joe's knife flew by his head.

Father Delanda, who'd just arrived at the top of the stairs, screamed, "No! They must be alive."

The opening closed just as Joe made it to the wall. He yanked on the pew but nothing happened. Again, he pulled and pulled, but still nothing. Then he let out an angry yell and kicked it with his foot, sending the pew skidding across the floor until it smashed into the wall.

The priest walked up and remained quiet. Joe's eyes were on fire. The father waited a few seconds until they caught their breath.

Then he walked around the broken pew and ran his hand over the wall where the opening had appeared.

"Amazing. How'd he know?" Then he turned toward Joe and said, "They must all come back alive and unharmed. They do me no good dead."

Joe yanked his knife out of the wall. "If I wanted him dead, he be dead."

CHAPTER THIRTY-ONE

EL ALTO AIRPORT

Renee's mother exited the front doors of El Alto Airport in La Paz and walked a few steps to the curb. She was carrying just a purse and a small shoulder bag. Her luggage didn't make the flight. At least, that's what she was told by the airline.

She covered her eyes from the sun and looked out over the scattered buildings in front of her. Immediately, she noticed the beautiful snowcapped mountains that endlessly rolled over the landscape in the distance and realized just how far out in the sticks she really was. A car horn honked and startled her. Her long-lost half brother had pulled up to the curb next to her in his jeep and was waving.

"Hop in," said Don Carlos. She threw her bag in the back and jumped into the jeep. He shifted into gear and sped off.

She reached over with her hand and put it on his shoulder. He reached up and placed his hand over hers. When Don Carlos returned to La Paz, the first thing he did was call Leslie to find out if she'd heard anything from Renee. When Leslie told him that she was fine and heading to Cuzco with her father, Don knew that his cover hadn't been blown. A couple of days had passed by with no word from anyone, so Leslie called the Cuzco Police Department. That's when she found out that her daughter and husband were missing. She boarded the next flight to La Paz and called her half brother. All Don Carlos had to do was act surprised and offer to help in order to gain her trust.

"Any word?"

"No, Leslie. Nothing yet." He quickly looked to the rear while shifting gears and added, "Is that all you brought with you?"

"No, the airline misplaced my bag. Who knows, the damn thing could be halfway to Brazil as far as I know. I gave them your info and they said they'd call when it gets here."

"I see. We have time. There is no use heading off anywhere this late in the day. We will get settled in at my house and leave first thing in the morning."

"For where?" said Leslie.

"Even though we have no news of Renee, we do know where she has been. The police station in Cuzco was the last place she went to. We go there and see this priest. He will help."

Leslie didn't say anything. She just stared out over the vast open countryside. The magnitude was overwhelming. Just to think that her little girl could be anywhere out there was more than she could comprehend.

It was just a week ago that they were all sitting at the dinner table excitedly talking about the upcoming trip. She'd wanted to go with them but couldn't get the time off from work. Asking for a vacation just months after starting a new job wouldn't have sat well with her employer.

"Have they found my husband?"

Don's lip curled up under his moustache as he shook his head and focused on the road.

CHAPTER THIRTY-TWO

IN THE DARK

The secret passage led down a set of rickety wooden stairs to the ground level. Jason and Rene scurried down the spiraling steps in complete darkness as Tana guided them with his voice.

"Stay to the left and keep your hands on the rail. The right side is missing a few boards."

A crackling sound and then a loud grunt followed. "I see what you mean," said Jason.

"Slow down. We're almost to the bottom. Look at the floor and you'll see light."

As they rounded the last turn, a subtle golden glow met them at the bottom step. It was just enough light to make out the contour of the irregularly shaped rocks and jagged concrete walls. The smell of urine reeked in the air.

"Where are we?" asked Jason.

"The back of the church."

The vague outline of a door was in front of them. Tana walked over and slid the hinge to the side as quietly as possible. Slowly he exited, looked both ways, and then waved at them to follow.

"We must leave quickly. They'll be here soon."

The stench was overwhelming as they hopped over puddles of urine and trash. The small lightbulb mounted on the wall leading into the alley left many shadows and dark corners around them. They each kept both eyes peeled for any movement.

As soon as they were far enough away from the smell, Jason reached for the prince's shoulder and stopped him. "We must go to the *biblioteca*."

"It's closed."

"I know, but we must go there now, before it opens."

"Yes," said Renee. "It's very important." She'd been silent since they'd held each other on the balcony. The awkward encounter felt right at the time, but now she was embarrassed to think about it. She had no idea why she ran into his arms so willingly.

"If we must," he said. "It won't be difficult."

CHAPTER THIRTY-THREE
DOUBLE YOUR DOUBLE

Father Delanda paced the floor in his office. On the wall opposite his desk a blazing array of logs crackled and popped in an enormous fireplace. He knew chasing the three would do no good at this time of night. The streets were still bustling with people drifting in and out of the cantinas, and he wasn't sure which way they'd gone. He cursed himself for believing that the inept local police department could help him find this boy. Then he wondered what the connection was between these fugitives: Was it as serendipitous as it appeared, or did they actually know each other?

The man had spent over forty years of his life performing Mass for the local Catholics in Peru. He had a solid following and was well known in the community, so the church left him alone when it came to matters regarding his parish. In fact, almost everyone left him alone in Cuzco and for good reason. In a country so deeply rooted in corruption, there were only two choices on how to survive: either you played the game or you got played. Over the years, the good father learned how to take the game to a whole different level.

Providing for the poor and satisfying the Vatican's financial needs were no easy tasks for an honest man. He tried soliciting the rich socialites and leaders in his city, but that rarely produced anything. Then one day, after presiding over the confession of the local chief of police, his prayers were answered. What he learned that day was the same age-old secret that had been passed down throughout the centuries: how to maintain complete control over a congregation, not to mention, whole nations. Some priests would call it a miracle. Others considered it God's way of conveying his message. Outsiders would just call it blackmail.

Just a hint that the chief's deepest, darkest secrets could somehow be leaked to the public caused the man to literally shake in his boots. He offered up his services in any way possible so enthusiastically that Father Delanda couldn't turn him down. From that moment on, he recognized the powerful tool he'd been blessed with and went on to nurture many other loyal servants over the next few years.

When Von Däniken's books of aliens and other gods came out in the seventies, the good father received a visit from a high-ranking cardinal in Lima. The official was in town attending a conference for the prestigious Congregation for the Doctrine of the Faith, or CDF. They discussed the recent hoopla over these books and the theories of ancient civilizations predating the Bible by thousands of years. The cardinal also conveyed what the ramifications would be for the church if these stories continued to proliferate throughout South America.

When the dignitary left the cathedral, Father Delanda was a changed man. The meeting was more than inspiring; it was enlightening. *The Lord works in mysterious ways*, he thought as he recalled their conversation. He immersed himself in every book that came out over the next few years professing to confirm these outlandish claims. He visited museums and libraries throughout the area in a quest to understand how the legends and myths originated in the first place. As he better understood the history of the early monks and priests who spread Christianity throughout South America, he realized that they never did quite finish the job they set out to do. They never completely rid his country of its pagan gods and rituals.

It was then that he experienced what he believed was a true epiphany. It wasn't an enlightening dream or illuminating angel speaking to him in the middle of the night. No, this was a subtler message, something as gentle and simple as opening the mail. Still, when he read that letter, the sensation that flowed throughout his delirous body was just as powerful to him as the parting of the Red Sea.

The letter was from Erik Von Däniken himself. This could not be a coincidence, he concluded, considering the recent visit from the cardinal. Apparently, the author had been told about several golden artifacts of unknown origin that were sitting in the cathedral's basement. He politely asked for a meeting with the good father so they could discuss the possibilities of including some of them in his next book. Father Delanda was more than obliging— he even allowed his picture to appear in this book holding two mysterious relics in his hands. He was convinced that God had personally sent him a telegram telling him to take notice. After all, there's no better way to defeat the devil than to look him straight in the eye.

This connection opened many doors for the priest. He was introduced to other scholars and locals who were eager to share their secrets and beliefs. It was rare to have a man of the cloth more interested with learning about an ancient culture than suppressing it. Most of these scholars weren't focused on disputing specific claims found in the Bible as much as they were just trying to fill in the missing puzzle pieces surrounding the origin of life itself.

DIVINE INTERVENTION

The priest's unique theological perspective added colorful insight to their discussions. All the while, Father Delanda was gathering any information he could—along with whatever unusual trinkets his friend Huascar was handing over. Together, and like the conquistadores hundreds of years before him, he would present his findings to the church someday. Surely he would be rewarded beyond his wildest dreams—maybe even sainthood.

Over the next few years, his young Indian servant delivered a bounty that only Pizarro and his men could have appreciated. Father Delanda pushed Huascar to find only those trinkets with strange and unusual markings and rewarded him dearly. Those were the only ones he was interested in. He knew that calculating the age of these items was difficult, so any claim could easily be dispelled. What he didn't know how to explain were the drawings of animals from other continents and otherworldly creatures. That's why it was imperative that he got to them before anyone else did. Over time, the gifts came less frequently and became less exotic. He could feel the eyes of his forefathers upon him, congratulating him for a job well done.

The priest looked up at the plaque hanging above the fireplace. It read:

> For they have forsaken me and made this a place of foreign gods; they have burned sacrifices in it to gods that neither they nor their fathers nor the kings of Judah ever knew, and they have filled this place with the blood of the innocent—Jeremiah 19:4.

He read it every night before lighting a fire.

He opened a drawer in his desk and pulled out an old photo of a large gold medallion with unusual designs and indecipherable markings on it. He turned the picture over and read the inscription: "Sister Frida—Rio De Janeiro." To this date, he still had no idea who Sister Frida was. It drove him crazy.

The picture belonged to a Sister Margarita, whom he'd met while on sabbatical in Rio de Janeiro. She knew of his appearance in Von Däniken's book and believed, as many did, that the good father must have had similar suspicions about the existence of this lost civilization. She showed him a copy of *The Chronicle of Akakor*, written by the German Karl Brugger, and explained that this novel had her congregation in an uproar.

According to the locals, the stories in this book were linked to a legend about a mysterious amulet that had disappeared centuries before. This necklace, she was told, was the key to unlocking the powers of the universe. They believed that it was not of this world and any person who possessed it could do great things. Supposedly, she even knew how to find it and had pictures, but refused to share them with anyone.

"The risks are too great," she answered every time he asked.

The two corresponded often after that meeting, and the priest made every effort to get her to show him this mysterious medallion. It became an obsession for him, and he was determined to get his hands on it. When all of his efforts failed, it was obvious what needed to be done. There was only one person in Peru who possessed enough persuasive skills to get her to change her mind: Joe Del Diaz. His plan was simple: send Joe into Rio to "convince" Sister Margarita to hand over the photo and any other information she had about the medallion. Unfortunately for the good sister, Joe's methods were a little too extreme—and it cost her her life. From that day forward, Father Delanda realized that he had to be very specific about any orders he gave to Joe in the future.

Joe Del had learned from his mentor how to track his prey with all of his senses. When he'd felt the cool breeze brush by his head earlier that night, he knew that someone else was nearby. The scent of Renee's shampoo directed him to a vent in the ceiling. Had he been just a few steps quicker, he'd be a lot richer right now—and most likely celebrating down at his favorite *cantina*.

He sat quietly in one of the leather chairs and studied the photo while the priest contemplated his next move. Though it was grainy, he could still make out a substantial breast line and curvy torso. Lena's features were hard to forget. Beautiful blondes were scarce in Cuzco—at least in the places he hung out. His mind had just begun to wander and dream of his ultimate encounter with this young lady when Father Delanda interrupted him.

"It doesn't make sense. Why would they all be together—and here?" The father looked up at the stack of books covering his wall. "What is the connection between Sacsayhuaman and this church?"

The priest walked over to the bookshelf and scanned a row slightly above his head. He reached up to grab a book but hesitated. It was entitled *Malleus Maleficarum*, his most precious book on methods of torture. *No need for that right now*, he thought. He rubbed his chin and wondered aloud, "Why wasn't she with them? They would have gone looking for her—and probably did—but she wasn't where they thought she'd be."

Joe took one last look at the photo and placed it back in his pocket. He wasn't sure if the padre was just thinking out loud or actually talking to him. He decided that either way he needed to set things straight.

"We start with one. Now there four."

Father Delanda came out of his trance and swung around. "Yes, you are correct. I will double your fee."

Joe lifted himself out of the chair and stood up in front of the priest. His ominous frame cast a shadow over the whole corner of the room as the fire sizzled in the background. His scar was still fresh and oozed an occasional trickle of blood when he smiled. The priest tried not to be intimidated by this towering figure and postured himself in an unyielding yet pious manner.

"You double your double or no have a deal," Joe Del demanded.

The good father pushed his spectacles back onto the top of his nose and bellowed, "Why, that's preposterous." He quickly walked over to the fire and stirred a black pot being heated over the flame.

Joe calmly studied Father Delanda as he moved across the room. If any normal man had spoken to him in that tone, he'd probably be dead by now. Of course, this was no ordinary man. Even though the padre didn't have control over Joe's will like he

Document 512

did many of the other locals, Joe wasn't about to bite the hand that fed him. He needed to tread lightly. Joe respected the church even though it had cast him out years before, but he didn't let that influence him when it came to business.

He knew that this was going to be a difficult task no matter what. Joe Del's heart was deeply rooted in the ancient beliefs of his people. This took away the priest's most powerful negotiating tool: Joe wasn't going to be intimidated by any threats of spending an eternity in hell.

"Double your double."

"Ah, my son. You're much smarter than you look, but where is your devotion to the church?" Father Delanda opened a bag sitting next to the fire and pulled out one of the gold discs Huascar had delivered earlier. Then he nonchalantly tossed it into the kettle and continued stirring while whispering under his breath, "Do not turn to idols or make gods of cast metal for yourselves. I am the Lord your God."

Joe didn't get a very good look at the object from the bag. From his angle, all he could see was Father Delanda's black robe. He could smell something metallic in the air but didn't see anything unusual coming out of the fire. Besides, it was none of his business anyway.

"Your church is not my church," he said. "My church lies at Sacsayhuaman, it still shines at Tiahuanaco, and it will always exist at Machu Picchu, no matter how many of us are..." Joe hesitated before he finished his sentence. *Massacred* was a harsh word to swallow in any context. He gathered his thoughts for a moment and let the businessman in him take over. Offending the priest at this stage could only do more harm than good. "I will always follow my people."

The padre's eyes lit up. "Of course," he said under his breath, "Machu Picchu." With his back still turned to Joe, he gazed at the flame as the saucer slowly melted into a golden, glossy soup and said with a smile, "Have it your way, we'll double your double."

PART FOUR

THE CHASE

CHAPTER THIRTY-FOUR
DOCUMENT 512

The corner window at the *biblioteca* opened easily. The young boy returned his knife to its holder and slid through the small opening. A minute later, he opened a larger window off to the side and signaled for his two companions to climb through. Renee pulled her flashlight out and kept it low to the ground.

"This way," said Jason. "Keep an eye out for car lights. The local police patrol this area and they get pretty bored. If they suspect anything at all, they'll call in every cop within a ten-mile radius just for something to do."

"You sound like an expert on the subject," said the prince.

Jason nodded, "Yeah, I've spent many a night out on these streets. They don't hesitate to shake you down either."

"Shake you down?"

"It means that they'll take any money you have in your pockets," answered Renee. She and Tana exchanged smiles and then quickly turned away.

Jason began walking cautiously toward the rear of the building with his light pointing to the floor as the other two followed behind him. "Up those stairs."

He signaled with the light for the others to climb up as he stood guard. When they were halfway up the staircase, he followed behind them. Once at the top, he led them down the corridor until they arrived at the section where he'd been abducted earlier by the henchmen. Jason softened the glow of his flashlight with a bandana and began searching through the rows of books.

"It has a leather cover. It's worn away on the edges. There should be a piece of white paper wedged next to it."

They tried to keep the flashlights from reflecting off the walls and windows while they searched. Every time they heard a car nearby, they shut them off and stood still. It didn't take long before they found what they were looking for.

"Here it is!" exclaimed Renee.

She grabbed the book off the shelf and shined a light on the cover. *Document 512* was barely visible on the faded leather. The book appeared to be falling apart, yet the bindings were still intact. Even though the yellowed pages were fragile and eaten away in certain spots, they had a supple fabric-like texture to them that allowed them to turn with ease.

Jason extended his hand to Renee and said, "Good job. Can I see it?"

She handed it over and he thumbed through a few pages while holding the light. "Now I need to find where I left off, you know, before those thugs interrupted my reading session. The part about the cave and this shimmering light that covered a mountainside."

"Shimmering light?" questioned Renee.

"Yeah, why?"

Renee stared at the book. "I had this dream on the first night when we arrived in South America. It was, like, so vivid."

"Most of them are up here. Something about the altitude."

"Yeah, maybe so, but this one was special," she said. "There was that same number in my dream. I saw it immediately after we saw the shimmering rocks under the waterfall."

"Who's we?" asked Jason.

"I don't know. It was a man. Maybe you." She looked into Jason's eyes and added, "I think it *was* you."

Jason raised his eyebrows. He lifted up the book, pointed at the front cover, and said to Tana, "What does this number mean to you?"

The prince became uncomfortable as the other two closed in. He tried to look away, but it didn't help. "I don't know. It has no significance with my people."

"That can't be. Why would it show up in her dream and on this book?

"I don't know," said the prince. "Like I said, this number means nothing to me. There is a symbol, though, one of a union between…" He hesitated and just looked down to the ground in silence. They all stood there for a while until the prince finally spoke up. "*Señor* Jason, can you please read a little bit from this book?"

Jason could tell that something was eating Tana up inside and decided to not press the issue. He found the passage he was looking for and read aloud: *"Its entrance is through three arches of great height, and the middle one is the largest, whilst the two side arches are less. Upon the largest and principle we discerned letters, which from their great height could not be copied. There was one street the breadth of the three arches, with upper storeyed houses on either side; the fronts of carved stone already blackened; so…"*

"Why'd you stop?" asked Tana.

"The rest of the page is gone. Let me try another section."

He carefully turned to the next page and read: *"We went into this strange city on the valley floor, and we came upon a well set-out plaza, beside it, and in the middle of the plaza a column of black stone of extraordinary grandeur, on whose summit was a statue of a man with a hand on his left hip and right arm out-stretched, pointing with the index finger to the north pole. Opposite this plaza there runs very swiftly, a most deep and wide river, with spacious banks, that were very pleasing to the eye."*

"I know this place," said Tana. "I know it well. As a child, I used to play there."

"Akakor," said Jason.

"Please read on," said Renee.

"Of course," he replied. *"There was a strange man guarding this entrance, garnished with clothing, which were foreign to our eyes, including a medallion that draped down his chest. It was a peculiar piece of jewelry, which we all were amazed to see. One lined with several strings and circular in its shape. We exchanged greetings, as much as to be expected upon finding their bore no common language, and understood that he wished us to enter. Yet passage was only granted to one of my expedition, a fellow servant of the king whom which I knew little, except for surname and rank. After numerous objections, which we were unsuccessful at our attempts, thus remained outside, only to witness an event which bewildered and left one speechless in conveyance. Our host, with little break in time, disappeared before our eyes under a cloud of sparkling royal composition, leaving only those who waited beside me.*

"For days, we waited for his return, and admired also some lagoons full of rice, of which we profited, and likewise innumerable flacks of ducks which breed in these fertile plains. Upon consultation, and with great fear, not having found our comrade or his captor, which resolve of the matter otherwise must be left abandoned, it was decided to ignore the commands of this guardian and search the cave. When our party arrived, to where this original altercation resided, and with much surprise, discovered the entrance to be sealed off with rocks and boulders, having examined and determined to be impenetrable, at which we wondered about our own safety."

Renee looked up and said, "Did that book just say that the man disappeared before their eyes?"

Jason nodded. Down below they heard a noise. It sounded like a doorknob rattling. They extinguished their flashlights and remained silent. The boy scampered off like a dancer quietly gliding across a stage. He reached the top of the staircase and knelt down.

He saw a light shining outside of the building onto the walls. A silhouette of a man wearing an officer's hat passed by one of the windows. For a moment, the prince couldn't remember whether he'd shut the window downstairs or not. They heard the police officer walking away as Jason and Renee quietly shuffled over to where the prince was and knelt down beside him.

Jason ducked down for a better look and then turned to the others and said, "We need to get outta here."

CHAPTER THIRTY-FIVE
DIVIDE AND CONQUER

The three exited the library out the front door with the book secured in Jason's backpack and darted off to the first available tree. They kept their eyes peeled for any movement in the distance. When they reached a large oak tree, Renee leaned against it and said, "What now?"

Jason looked from side to side and answered, "We need to get to Machu Picchu."

"Why there?" asked Renee.

"That's where the entrance to Akakor is. I'm sure of it." Jason's eyes fixated on Prince Tana Nara and waited for a reply.

The prince looked down to the ground as different scenarios ran through his mind: Should he trust these two Americans? Was he exposing his people to grave danger by inviting them into his hidden world? Did he even have a choice? The world that he knew and grew up in was dying off fast.

The thick vegetation and rugged terrain of the Amazon jungle had protected his culture from the outside world for thousands of years. Many explorers and adventurers had tried to gain access by sending in expeditions, but none was ever successful. Corrupt government officials thwarted many of their efforts and local bands of thieves preyed on others. Those lucky enough—or unlucky, depending on whom you talk to—to make it deep into the rainforest were soon surprised to discover just how unforgiving the jungle really was. It was a little-known fact that ninety five percent of nutrients in the wild were used by the trees and vegetation, leaving very little to filter back into the soil. Stories of starving expeditions reduced to cannibalism from the lack of food were rampant from the 1500s up to modern times.

Eventually, some outsiders did manage to integrate with certain border tribes and establish contact. They lured the natives into the cities and exposed them to modern conveniences of all kinds. Over the centuries, that led to the extinction of countless tribes. Many others were pushed deeper into the forest by the encroachment of loggers and developers who were quickly stripping away their habitat. These outsiders built dams that altered the flows of their rivers, thus robbing them of a primary source of food. In the end, the few remaining factions united and moved to Akakor.

They were able to survive there by consolidating their knowledge and manpower into a hybrid society consisting of the best of each tribe. They knew how to live off the natural resources available to them. To the untrained eye, the forest appeared to be a lifeless counterfeit paradise void of wild game and edible vegetation. But to the natives, who knew how to lure monkeys out of hiding with a subtle whistle or stun dozens of piranha with a few drops of a milky juice extracted from a nearby plant, it was a way of life. They developed crops by building terraces on mountainsides and trained the rivers just enough to provide water and sanitation to their homes. Since the city was hidden deep in a valley surrounded by mountains, quicksand, and dangerous animals, they felt safe. It would have survived for many more centuries were it not for a new and unexpected phenomenon: global warming.

A slight temperature rise was all it took to change the breeding and migration patterns of many the birds and fish that had been staples of their diet for centuries. The constant flow of water from the Amazon tributaries was now shifting direction or drying up completely. Many of the precious plants that provided them with medicines and raw materials were disappearing too. What had started out as an off-the-cuff rumor among members of his tribe was now considered by many to be a fact: the Fifth Catastrophe, as predicted by their ancestors, had arrived.

The underground city of Akakor had existed since the beginning of written history. To them it was a gift from The Gods. Originally, it was created as a hideout for the first settlers who were evading capture from their enemies thousands of years ago. The tunnels system, ventilation, and lighting were all developed to sustain a civilization for a long period of time. Enough water from nearby rivers drained down to supply them with what they needed. Birds and fish were plentiful. They could even grow crops below the earth's surface.

The council of elders eventually decided that it was time to move all of the remaining tribesmen underground. Airplanes and helicopters were now constantly flying nearby and adventurers were getting much more sophisticated in their exploration methods. Before abandoning the city above ground, they destroyed many of its buildings and let the jungle take back the rest. Within a few years, most of what was left was buried under layers of vegetation.

Tana raised his head back up and said, "You are correct. We must be careful and observant, though. The signs are hard to see with the human eye."

Jason nodded and said, "Very well, then. We must go there tomorrow morning."

Suddenly, two blinding beams of light shined on their faces. They covered their eyes and followed them back to a couple of unmarked cars on the other side of the street.

A loudspeaker cracked and squealed, "*Todos quietos.*" Then a couple of *policia* approached with their guns drawn.

"What do we do?" asked Renee.

"We run," said Jason.

The prince quickly assessed their options and his instincts kicked in. "Follow me."

They ran back into the library and Tana led them straight to the rear exit. He shoved the door open and held it for the other two.

"Go, go!" he shouted. They sprinted down the alley.

"Which way?" Jason asked.

"That way," responded Tana. "I'll distract them."

"What?"

"You must. That's the way to the train station. Just walk slowly and blend in. I'll catch up with you later. Don't wait for me. We'll all meet up again."

"But why aren't you coming with us?" cried Renee.

"Don't worry. I have a plan."

He gently brushed away Renee's bangs and kissed her on the cheek. The gesture startled her. He started to walk away but Renee grabbed his arm. She wanted to pull him close and squeeze him as tight as she could, but instead she just said, "Please come back."

With that, the prince took off the other way down the alley and rounded the corner, heading straight toward the police cars. Jason and Renee heard shouting. He lightly grabbed Renee's elbow and said, "Let's go. There's nothing we can do at this point."

They casually walked the other way. At the end of the alley, they waited for a couple of tourists to stroll by and then fell in line behind them. Renee squeezed his hand as they disappeared into the night.

CHAPTER THIRTY-SIX
MACHU PICCHU

Lena wandered across the plaza to take in the view from the House of Three Windows. The misty cloud cover hovering over the mountaintops and drifting by the canyon walls was breathtaking. Each time she inhaled the pure mountain air, her body was invigorated. All of her troubles immediately subsided. The layers of plush green grass that carpeted the terraces and plazas were just as soothing to look at as they were to walk on.

She later peered down from Huaynu Picchu into the Urubamba Canyon. The impenetrable terrain of sheer vertical cliffs surrounding this ancient ruin was humbling. Deep green mountains shot up out of the ground and pointed toward the heavens as the fast-moving river cut a path through the valley floor below. It was easy to see how the Spanish never did manage to conquer this area.

As the day moved on, she returned to her favorite site, the Torreon, or the Temple of the Sun, for another climb. The snail-like structure perched atop an immense rock fascinated her. This ancient site reminded her of a modern observatory because of the way certain windows faced the sun and stars and how the stone pegs around these windows looked like they once held a rudimentary telescope. Then there was its mysterious alignment with the June solstice. But what really astounded her was the small cave housed underneath it. Local legend claimed that the cave was the birthplace for the whole Inca culture. That was code to Lena meaning that it was probably a secret entrance to the ancient tunnels.

She pulled out the yellowed map and stared at it again. Since arriving at Machu Picchu days before, she'd fully memorized every drawing and scribbled line on it. The excitement she once felt, though, about finally discovering its secrets had slowly fizzled away. It wasn't that she couldn't make out many of the locations. Her expertise in South American geography was substantial. The problem was with some of the symbols and lines. They just didn't make any sense at all.

The staircase symbol drawn above Cuzco repeatedly drew her attention. What did it mean? Was it a reference to the Torreon there at Machu Picchu or a hidden staircase buried somewhere in the nearby mountain range? What was the symbol next to it? To the laymen's eye, it appeared to be a maze, but that didn't make any sense. It must have had some other meaning. To the right of that marking was the outline of a mountain range with a straight line running along the bottom. There were also hieroglyphic letters scattered everywhere. Further to the east were two sets of dashes and dots leading away from the mountain ranges. She thought about the secret tunnel the Indians used to escape from Pizarro's men centuries before. The lines ended near a pyramid with columns that were surrounded by trees. None of these symbols had any resemblance to the markings on the pendant she now possessed. Even though she knew there was a connection, she hadn't even come close to figuring it out.

She pulled the necklace out of her bag and carefully laid it flat on the map. Ever since that first day at the ruins when she wore it around her neck, she'd been wary of even holding it. The pendant felt fine for a few hours, but as the day wore on, unusual things started happening to her. First, there was the avalanche of rocks that nearly crushed her into the side of the mountain on the

THE CHASE

trail from Machu to Huaynu Picchu. Then there was the feeling of vertigo that almost sent her teetering over the edge of a cliff as she walked on the upper pathway. She reached down and picked at the scab on her knee. That one came from a fall down the rock steps at the end of the second day; it was the clincher. She quit wearing the pendant altogether and hadn't had an incident since.

She slid the amulet from one side to the other, slowly moving it down the page. None of the intricate figures lined up with any of the markings. She flipped it over and repeated her movements. Still nothing. The frustration bottled up inside showed as she grabbed the trinket and squeezed it with both hands. With her head tucked under her arms and hands clasped together, she closed her eyes and wept quietly. The clues were right there in front of her, but she just couldn't put them all together. She needed to clear her mind and start over from the beginning.

With her eyes still closed, she imagined the sun on the horizon. It grew brighter and more intense. She almost felt the heat on her eyelids. This image usually calmed her down and helped her focus. Once she was in that zone, images of the past soon followed. Her thoughts meandered back to the place and time when her mind was clearer: the time during her childhood with her father.

She recalled the days when he would take her onto the army base. It was their alone time together. They would hang out at the officers' club, go down to the target range and shoot pistols, and then play around on the obstacle courses. He also taught her how to survive on her own and which items she needed to have and how to use them. All of the other officers treated her like she was one of their own. They brought her candy, showed her how to handle a weapon, and told her stories about the places they'd been around the world. It was there that her yearning for adventure was born.

The good memories were usually followed by the last memory she had of her father. It was the day he died. She was seventeen at the time and they were off with her younger brother on a road trip in the northwestern United States. Her mother stayed behind at the lodge that day because she wasn't feeling well. That happened quite often during family adventures that included Lena.

While driving back down a mountain, her father started having chest pains. Lena quickly realized that it was a heart attack and did her best to keep the car on the pavement. The winding road and steep incline were too much to handle, and the car ended up wedged into a line of trees overlooking a bluff. Her father died right there in front of them as they were pinned inside the vehicle. All he could do was put his hand on his chest and hold it because the pain was so severe. He looked to his two children and said, "Take care of each other. No matter what happens, take care of each other."

When the ambulance finally arrived, he'd been dead for a good hour and there was no way they were going to resuscitate him. The children were so traumatized that they didn't talk to anyone for weeks. The mother was also upset and withdrew in her own special way. It's easy to overlook the simple things a father does around the house: taking the garbage out, trimming the hedges, mowing the grass. None of this was being done after he died. If a toilet plugged up, they just didn't use it. If a lightbulb went out, they just read in the dark.

A few weeks after he was buried, an attorney presented the family his will, which her father had prepared years before. There were no long letters stating which person inherited this or that. It was very short and to the point. He left his wife a meager pension and his social security. She would, of course, keep the house and all of his possessions—with the exception of one major item: his life insurance policy. Surprisingly, he'd made his two children the sole beneficiaries of this money. Lena's mother was furious.

Over the next few weeks, she festered in her own resentment. Why didn't her husband leave the policy in her name? Of course, they both wanted their children to go to college, but didn't he trust her enough to make sure that happened? There must have been more to it than that. She slowly grinded up the facts in her own mental pestle and eventually came to a conclusion: Lena had planned the whole thing.

Lena must have known about the policy, she thought. A couple hundred thousand dollars could certainly go a long way for a girl her age. A little tug on the wheel at the right time and she'd be set for life. As these thoughts polluted her mother's mind, her next step became obvious.

The process started slowly, with a few drops of arsenic here and a tiny amount of castor beans there. Her mother knew Lena's favorite foods and which bedtime snacks she could bring up to her room. She made sure that transition was gradual enough to not alert any suspicions.

Yet as time passed by, Lena managed to hold on. She tried to stay active and hide her health problems as well as she could. It wasn't until she went on a weeklong trip with the school band that she began to figure things out. Within days of being away from home, her skin color returned and she wasn't throwing up any longer. After a week's time, she felt like a new person. Even her friends commented on how differently she looked. That's when she knew something fishy was going on at home.

From then on, she avoided anything her mother cooked. She tried eating before coming home from school, and when that wasn't possible, went for something either prepackaged or out of a can. She even thought about going to the police. They could run some tests and possibly link the chemicals to items in the house, but that still wouldn't be enough evidence for a conviction, she thought. No, the best way would be to catch her mother in the act.

The next night at dinner, she set her plan into motion. Her mother had made chili. After testing a few bites for that funny taste she knew all too well, she was ready to run out of the house and take the sample to the neighbor's house. At that instant, Lena had a "moment of clarity," as she would later write in her diary. Her younger brother was sitting at the table next to her mother laughing and smiling without a care in the world. The child reached over, kissed her on the cheek, and said, "I love you, Mommy."

As her mother reached over and squeezed her son tightly, Lena realized for the first time that being adopted wasn't the cause of all of her troubles. No, it must have been something else. After all, her brother had also been adopted ten years later than her. Yet, here she was witnessing a Kodak moment between the two while the only memories she had were of heartbreak and aggravation. That ultimately led her to only one conclusion: *she* was the problem.

The guilt and dismay overwhelmed and drained her emotionally. Everyone feels rejection at some point in their life, but this was different. This was the kind of emotion that sucked out your inner soul and lodged itself deep in your stomach, a gut-wrenching pain that never completely went away.

Her options now were very limited. If she went to the police, her little brother would grow up without any parents and probably in a foster home. If she did nothing, she'd eventually die. There was really no one to turn to for help with her problem. One of the cruel by-products of being an army brat was that she'd never really put down roots. As soon as she made a few friends and started building relationships, duty would call and she'd be off to the next army base far away.

She mulled things over and tormented herself for weeks. Ending it all kept coming up as the only answer. Then one night as she was watching an old TV cop show, an idea came to her. For her graduation present, she asked if she could go on a cruise to the Gulf of Mexico with her friends. Her mother was more than obliging to get her out of the house for a week.

On the fourth day of their trip, as they returned to the ship that was docked in Mexico, she made it a point of standing out when checking back in with the crew. First, she spilled a beer on a fellow passenger, then she threw up over the railing while boarding the boat, and finally, she pirouetted into a table, knocking over plates and dishes in front of the staff. After staggering off to her room, she snuck back off the boat just as it was about to set sail. The crewmembers didn't even notice another person dressed in a similar outfit walking toward the dock as they shoved off. She waved good-bye to a life of anguish and frustration with just the clothes on her back and a few dollars in her pocket.

Over the next few weeks, the money dwindled away quickly. Lena, being the trained survivalist, went into survival mode. She took odd jobs waiting tables or answering phones—just about anything that would put her in a warm bed at night. Finally, a con man came into her life and fell madly in love with her. He taught her the tricks of his trade as they traveled throughout the countryside pulling off scam after scam. In the end, his luck ran out in Cabo San Lucas when the *federales* picked him up during a routine traffic stop. Apparently, the bounty on his head was so big that it made any bribe pointless. When Lena heard the news, she skipped town and headed straight for South America.

She opened the palm of her hand and looked over the medallion once again. Then she lifted it up against the setting sun and angled it back and forth. Nothing. She pointed it in the direction of the mountains. "How did that girl get it to glow?" she mumbled under her breath. After a few minutes of swirling it from side to side, she gave up and put it back in her pocket.

The sunlight had already faded over a nearby peak and the last few tourists were leaving. She began the slow walk down the hill back to the lodge where she was staying. The chill from the night air was settling down onto the mountaintop. A nice, warm bath where she could soak her aching feet sounded awfully good.

She didn't notice the curtains being drawn in her room when she entered. Her mind was elsewhere. After locking the door behind her, she immediately went into the bathroom and drew a bath. She kicked off her tennis shoes and socks and then removed her shorts. At the sink, she unfastened her jewelry and stared into the mirror. The years had been kind to her even though she'd lived a pretty rugged life. There were no crow's-feet around her eyes and no real stretch marks on her hips.

It was usually at this part of her day when the loneliness set in. First, there was the reality check in the mirror. That was soon followed by the little voice in the back of her mind asking whether it was all worth it. Would it be better to just go back to the States and turn herself in? Her brother was an adult now and might understand why she did what she did. Still, nothing had changed back there except that she was a little older now. Even after all of these years, she wasn't ready to face her past.

She ran a comb through her hair and reached for a towel. When she pulled it off the rack, something was wrong. It was wet. How could that be? She'd been gone all day, and surely the maid had come in that morning. Without making a sound, she slowly walked over to her backpack and fumbled around for her knife.

"That won't be necessary," said a stern voice in the hallway.

CHAPTER THIRTY-SEVEN

ONCE BITTEN, TWICE...

Jason stepped into the bathroom with his knife in hand and pointed it toward Lena's backpack. "Just drop it to the ground."

Lena bent over and placed it down carefully. She felt his eyes undressing her body and staring at her legs. *Ah yes, every man has his weakness*, she thought. She tried to hide the smile and replied, "It's about time you got here. What took you so long?"

As she ran her finger up her leg and twirled it around her breast, Renee peered around his shoulder. She seemed bewildered by Lena's demeanor. "Oh, I didn't know you brought company."

"Your accent—it's different," said Renee. "You aren't German after all."

"I believe you two have met." Jason brought Renee to his side and put his arm around her. "Renee and I have a lot in common. Seems that we've both lost something very dear to us—to the same person."

He looked at Lena and stared into her eyes. While he was trying to read her reaction, a part of him was also looking for answers. There were so many questions that he wanted to ask her. *Why this?* and *Why that?*—but, in reality, it didn't matter anymore. Nothing she could say was going to change what had happened. That was all behind him now.

"How'd you find me?" asked Lena.

"The compass." Renee pulled it out from underneath her shirt. "It points right to the necklace."

Lena nodded and realized her mistake. The pitch of the bath water was rising, so she reached over and shut the faucet off before it ran over.

"Go ahead," said Jason. "It felt good taking a shower. I can imagine how beat you are after a long day of treasure hunting."

Lena looked over to Renee then back to Jason. "I think this might be just a little too uncomfortable."

"Oh, excuse me for being rude," he smirked. "Go right ahead, we won't mind. Let me get a couple of chairs from the other room."

He started to leave the bathroom when Renee grabbed him and said, "Let me get *a* chair."

She left the room and came back with one from the desk. "I'll watch some TV while you keep an eye on her."

"Deal," said Jason. He sat down and nodded to Lena, "Please proceed—and don't mind me."

Lena had him right where she wanted. This had worked every time before. She slowly unbuttoned her blouse while giving Jason a puppy-dog pout. After dropping the shirt to the floor, she reached around and undid her bra strap. Then she turned away and let it dropped down. Next, she bent over and slowly glided her panties down her legs and slid them off her ankles. Finally, she stepped into the tub one foot after the other, stretched sideways to slide the curtain behind her, and slowly sank into the water.

Jason wiped his eyes hard and brushed his hands through his hair. He found himself rubbing his palms over each other repeatedly. The temptation was overwhelming. Lena's silhouette moved across the shower curtain as she lifted up to reach for the shampoo. That was more than he could handle, so he grabbed the backpack and all of her clothes off the floor and then headed to the other room.

"I'll wait out here until you're done."

Lena just smiled and sunk her head down into the warm water.

CHAPTER THIRTY-EIGHT

THE DECOY

Prince Tana Nara paused at the end of the alley behind the *biblioteca* and began walking slowly toward the beam of light coming from the police car. It took a few seconds before the officers recognized who he was.

"*Pare, pare!*" they screamed.

The prince immediately stopped. As the *policia* approached, he backed up a few steps, keeping his eyes focused on them all.

THE CHASE

"Levante las manos"

When they sped into a full sprint, Tana twirled around and ran back to the alley. Jason and Renee were gone. That's all he needed to see. He raced off down the street away from the approaching posse. The officers were yelling and shuffling along behind him as the police car sped down the street with its sirens blaring.

Tana made it to the end of the street and turned the corner. Before his eyes could adjust to the dimly lit road, he knew he'd made a mistake. A tall, colossal figure standing before him reached out and grabbed his shoulder. Then he immediately spun the boy around and locked him against his chest before the prince realized what had happened.

Mean Joe Del lifted Tana's arm up into the air and examined the boy's hand. He counted the six digits stretching out while the boy struggled to escape. *So, the rumors are true*, he thought.

He raised the prince's other arm and turned to the man standing behind him, "Father, I have this boy."

"Well done, Joseph. Please place him in the car."

The first batch of police rounded the corner and immediately stopped in their tracks. The slower ones collided into them as they came up from the rear. The grumbling soon faded when they looked up and noticed Joe Del's new scar and haircut. None of them dared to move any closer.

After Joe placed the boy in the car and sat down next to him, one of the officers finally gathered up enough courage to speak. "To the station, Father?"

"No, that won't be necessary. I won't need your services any longer. We'll take him back to the cathedral." The priest jumped in on the other side and signaled his driver to move on.

Joe carried Tana into Father Delanda's study. He gently placed him in a chair next to the fireplace and secured both of his hands to the armrest with a rope. As instructed, he took special care not to injure the young man. After all, he did want to be paid.

The priest opened up the window shutters, allowing the first streams of sunlight from the dawn to highlight the walls behind him.

He nodded to Joe as he put the final touches on the bindings around the chair. Then he handed him a leather pouch and said, "Good work. We'll catch the morning train, so be back here in an hour."

"Where to?" asked Joe.

The good father glanced over to the boy and then back at Joe and said, "Machu Picchu."

Joe nodded and left. The priest locked the door behind him. He walked over to Tana and stood next to the chair.

"Are you hungry? A cup of tea?"

The boy remained silent and calm.

"Of course you are." The father walked around and sat directly in front of him. "I'll get you something shortly, but first we're going to have a long talk about your friends. You're going to tell me everything you know."

The boy looked up with a slight grin and said, "I'll gladly tell you whatever you want, but I doubt it will be anything you don't already know."

CHAPTER THIRTY-NINE
THE BRUSH-OFF

Don Carlos pulled up to the Cuzco police station and parked the jeep. Leslie got out and stretched her feet.

"That was the worst drive I've ever experienced in my life."

"Oh, there are plenty of drives like that here in my country, sister. You will get used to it."

"You say that as if I want to get used to it. Or that I will have to get used to it."

Don snagged his satchel from the backseat of the jeep and reached inside. There he found his automatic pistol and tucked it deep under the extra clothes. "You may have to if we are going to find your daughter."

They went inside the police headquarters and asked for the inspector. After a ten-minute wait, a man with dark bags under his eyes came out and said, "May I help you?"

Don Carlos began explaining that they'd called earlier about Renee. He introduced Leslie and told him about their long trip from La Paz. The inspector nodded and acted sincere. He shook his head and looked down when he explained what had happened to her husband. Then he offered her a tissue. When she asked where her daughter was, his mood changed.

"We are still searching for her."

"What do you mean?" said Leslie. "She was here at your police station earlier and somehow just disappeared?"

The inspector straightened up and gave her a stern look. "She didn't just disappear, Mrs. Gorman. She ran away with another man who was in jail at the time. It's believed that she actually helped him escape."

Leslie looked over to Don Carlos with disbelief. "Why would she do such a thing?"

Don cleared his throat and asked, "Do you have any idea where she went with this man? Maybe she was kidnapped or forced to go with him?"

"It is possible but very unlikely," said the inspector.

"May I see a copy of the report she filled out?"

The inspector looked at his watch. "It's not available at this time. Please leave your information at the desk and we'll notify you as soon as it's ready or if there's any other news." He then walked over to a coatrack and removed a brimmed hat. He placed it on his head and added, "I'm sorry, but I must be going."

After he left the room, Don whispered to Leslie, "This is going nowhere. Let's try something else."

CHAPTER FORTY
A CLUE

Jason rummaged through Lena's bag while she soaked in the bathtub. He smiled when he pulled out the map and tucked it safely into his pants pocket. Next, he removed the necklace and laid it on the table. Renee, who'd been mesmerized with a Spanish-speaking version of *SpongeBob SquarePants*, heard the sound of metal and knew exactly what it was. She crawled across the bed and sat next to him.

"That's it. I thought I'd never see it again." She lifted it up to the light. "It's so beautiful."

"May I?" asked Jason.

Renee admired it for a few more seconds before handing it over. Jason moved it closer to the small light sitting next to the table. He studied the markings for a long time. His fingers repeatedly traced the inside lines on both sides.

"You'd think there'd be more markings on the inside." He angled it in the light and added, "What are these strings supposed to be?"

"I don't know. My dad called them a *khipu*."

"*Khipu?* Never heard of it."

Jason pulled out his map and arranged it flat on the table. Renee drew in closer as they both sat and examined the clues from every angle. Jason's finger slid over to the square box near the lake and said, "You know, they recently discovered this strange formation in the Hayu Marca mountain region near Lake Titicaca. Cut into the side of a mountain is a square with a six-foot alcove in the middle of it. In this alcove, there's a small, circular impression about the size of this medallion. According to local legends, it's the place where great leaders pass through into a world of immortality. The natives call it The Gate of The Gods."

"*Puerta* means 'gate' in Spanish, right?" she asked.

"Correct, *Puerta de Hayu Marca*."

"Interesting." Now she understood why her father risked so much for this shiny piece of metal.

Jason glided his finger over to the staircase markings near the maze symbol, which butted up against a set of jagged and straight lines.

"That maze. I've seen it before," said Renee. "Back at Tiahuanaco."

"It's the symbol for *house* in some cultures. And that jagged line probably means a mountain—or possibly a lake since there's a line underneath it or through it. It's hard to tell."

"Really." Renee frowned and said, "I can't read them either. I wish I had a magnifying glass."

"I don't get it. There's nothing on here that even closely resembles the markings on that medallion."

"Maybe they're not supposed to. Where's your book?"

"You mean *Document 512*?" Jason pulled it out of his backpack and held it in his hand. "I glanced through it on the trip up here, and there's nothing else of interest in there except this one passage."

He opened it and read: *"Three days we journeyed down the river, and we stumbled on a cataract of such roaring noise and commotion of foaming water that we supposed the mouths of the most talked about Nile could not have made more trouble or booming or offered more resistance to our further progress. To the east of this waterfall we found several deep cuttings and frightful excavations, and tried its depth with many ropes, which, no matter how long they were, could not touch its bottom. We found some loose stones, and, on the surface of the land some silver nails, as if they were drawn from mines and left at the moment. Upon further observation, a vein of golden splendor appeared..."*

Jason looked up and said, "Then it ends."

"What do you mean, it ends?" asked Renee.

"I mean there's nothing after that. The rest of the page is gone. It's worthless." He tossed the book to Renee, but she wasn't quick enough to catch it. It smacked against the wall and a few half-eaten pages drifted onto the carpet.

"Jason, oh my God! This is an antique, you know. There're probably only a couple of copies of it in the whole world."

"Probably a good reason for that, you know."

She picked up the loose pages and started placing them back in the book as best as she could. When she lifted the last page, she noticed something different about it. It wasn't as discolored as the rest, and the edges weren't torn. The font style was also slightly different.

"Look at this. There's something strange about this page."

Jason quickly rose from his chair and grabbed it from Renee's hands. He perused it up and down and then flipped it over for another inspection. "You're right. This page doesn't belong. How come I didn't see that before?"

He examined the book again, flipping through it and then checking the front and back covers. "Look, it must've been hidden under the flap on the inside cover." He used his thumb to gently raise the leaf that was previously glued to the binding.

"What does it say?" asked Renee.

Jason sat back down at the table next to the light and began reading, "It's in Spanish. Dated 1659. 'I, Pedro Bohorques, of noble blood and ruler of ten thousand men, hereby decree that I have found the lost city of Paytite.'"

"What's Paytite?" asked Renee.

"It was thought to be a separate kingdom ruled by mysterious white men with beards who lived in the jungles. Legend has it that they were the protectors of all of the hidden treasures and cities. The Spaniards somehow linked it to the old myth of El Dorado and called it Gran Paytite, or the lost city of gold."

"Look at those symbols," said Renee. "There's a moon and a mountain drawn in there. I've seen them in my dreams." She stared at the writing underneath them and asked, "What's it say beneath that?"

Jason drew the page in closer and studied it for a minute before responding. "It says, *'You must stand in the shadow of your shadow when the eye of The Gods lifts and the earth is still darkened by night. Then the shadow of your shadow will point the way. It will show you the direction from the heart of heaven to the heart of the earth.'*" He looked up and said, "What the heck does that mean?"

"It's a clue, I guess—on how to read the signs."

"Well, what's it mean?"

"I don't know."

Jason squinted and drew the page closer to the light. "The rest is handwritten and hard to make out. It must be some kind of native language because they're not letters, they're hieroglyphics. Some of these symbols match the ones on my map. Here, take a look."

He showed Renee the page. "Yeah, I couldn't read them on your map, but these are easy," she said.

"You can read it?"

"Maybe," said Renee. She used the same method she'd discovered back at Sacsayhuaman of separating out each letter from the design of the symbol. Trying to decipher all the letters inside of each drawing was like playing an ancient three-dimensional version of Boggle. Some symbols made no sense at all, but others were obvious. "Here's that snail-like drawing again that you said meant *house* next to the jagged line. I think it says 'white house...'"

"By the lake," Jason interrupted. "Of course, now I remember. This whole story sounded familiar. This Bohorques character told everyone that he was some kind of aristocrat from Europe even though he was about as far from royalty as you could get. He convinced the natives that he was their king and set out looking for this lost city of gold. The Spanish government finally caught up with him and sent him to the gallows. Seemed he'd trained the Indians to hunt Spaniards for sport, which they didn't take too kindly to. In the book, he tried to buy his freedom by telling them that if they found this 'white house,' they'd find Gran Paytite. None of them believed him, of course, and they hanged him anyway." Jason looked Renee in the eyes and said, "Or maybe they didn't."

"Maybe he's the one who drew this map?" Renee added.

"Could be. It looks like it was drawn from memory since it's so out of proportion."

"Those symbols, though. They're not quite the same. A couple of things don't match up."

"What do you mean? Here, look at them side by side." Jason placed both the map and page next to each other. "They're almost identical."

"You have to remember, I, like, see things a little differently than most people. What you see as 'white house by the lake' looks like 'white house...'"

As she was about to finish her sentence, she saw a shadow rising on the curtain next to her. They weren't alone any longer. Over by the door was Lena, standing with a towel wrapped around her body and another on her head. Renee wasn't sure just how much Lena had heard, but she knew that anything was too much.

Lena sensed the uneasiness in the room and casually walked over to Jason while drying her hair. When she reached the table, she tossed the towel on the bed and said, "My clothes."

Jason handed her the backpack while studying her face. It was useless, as Lena possessed the best poker face he'd ever encountered. In fact, it was also the prettiest face he'd ever set eyes upon.

"I shall return shortly." With that, she went back into the bathroom.

"What do you think she heard?" he whispered. Renee shrugged her shoulders and shook her head. "I agree. There's no way of knowing, and unless we plan on killing her, we're going to have to come to some kind of arrangement."

"Arrangement?" exclaimed Renee. Her voice was lower than normal, but the frustration bursting out prompted Jason to reach over and place his hand over her mouth.

"I know, I know, but what other choice do we have?"

This time, Lena announced her entry into the room by humming an old Eric Clapton tune. That sealed the deal for everyone, as there was no longer any doubt.

CHAPTER FORTY-ONE

POKER FACE

The three of them went downstairs to eat dinner. The conversation was very light at first until Lena apologized. She didn't even try to explain her actions, as she knew that neither one of them would buy it.

This did allow Jason to get to the point, however. "OK, Lena, or Joanna, or whatever your name is."

"It's…"

"Uh, uh, uh, don't bother. Let's just leave it at Lena. There's no need to complicate matters even further."

Lena nodded, and Jason continued. "Obviously, we can't trust you, and I really don't want to have to kill you." Lena sat emotionless. Jason paused for a second to admire her fortitude. "The only other choice is to cut you in."

"Cut me in on what, exactly?"

"The treasure." Lena looked confused and waited for Jason to continue. "The lost city of gold that we were talking about back in the room. Don't act like you don't know."

Lena smiled and looked over at Renee. "OK, there's no reason to drag this on any longer. I'm in, but why are you still here?"

Renee blushed. Both sets of eyes were on her. Until then, she hadn't really even thought about it. The danger was over the minute she reached the police station back in Cuzco. Her mother would have showed up a day later, and tonight they'd probably both be sleeping in their own beds back in the States. Yet here she was eating dinner with two people she'd only known for a few days without a logical explanation as to why.

"I don't know," she said. "Maybe because I somehow feel obligated to find out what this necklace is all about." Her eyes watered as she continued, "Maybe I'm looking for a reason or some kind of justification for everything that's happened."

Jason put his arm around her and handed her a napkin so she could blow her nose. He looked over to Lena and thought, for a moment, that he'd seen a tear form in her eye. Lena looked down at the menu.

"There, there. We all want to find out why." He didn't know what else to say.

"I think I've found a clue," blurted Lena. "I've been all over these ruins, and there's one site that keeps sticking out like a sore thumb. I'd bet money that the hidden entrance is there."

"It's settled, then. We go there tomorrow." Jason extended his hand and said, "Partners?" Lena shook it and was ready to speak when Jason drew her in closer and whispered, "The next time you take off, I *will* kill you."

CHAPTER FORTY-TWO

THE STAIRCASE

The cool morning fog was still hovering over the mountaintops as they climbed to the entrance of Machu Picchu. At first glance, the site seemed no different than any other ruin in Peru, with its thatch-roofed huts and boulder-stair steps. The sparse crowd this early in the morning was made up mainly of nearby lodgers, as the train and buses had not yet arrived.

It wasn't until they turned the corner and witnessed their first full view of the ruins that they understood its majesty and why it was considered one of the seven new wonders of the world. The terraced platforms glistened in the sun as a thin layer of dew sparkled over the moss and grass. One could almost picture what it must have been like centuries ago walking into this sacred city and seeing a stack of temples and buildings bustling with activity. The fortress still looked impenetrable, though a good part of it had been reduced to rubble. Nonetheless, a warm vibe radiated from its carefully positioned trees and geometrically designed verandas.

They took in the views and visited the buildings for a few minutes. Then Lena guided them to her favorite spot. She stopped in front of it and said, "Here it is. The Torreon."

Jason looked up. "It's impressive—but what does that have to do with this map?"

"Look here," said Lena. "That staircase symbol. Couldn't that be Machu Picchu?"

"Yeah, but what about the other symbols around it? What do they mean?"

"I don't know, but I do know that there's a cave underneath this building."

Renee moved in a few steps closer and said, "Now we're getting somewhere. Caves usually mean tunnels." She walked around the Torreon slowly, sizing it up and looking for other clues. "Let's go on top."

They walked up the staircase and looked out over the ruins. There was a large building standing on a rock at the bottom of the hill. The cloud cover was still hovering over it. A *white house!* she thought. In one corner where several of the boulders were missing was a peculiarly shaped window. The morning sun was now peeking over the mountaintop behind her. She squinted and turned her head, trying to get a better angle on the figure. It was then that it dawned on her what she was looking at.

"The eyes of The Gods lift," she whispered. "Jason, those words from the manuscript. What were they again? You know, the part after 'the eyes of The Gods.'"

"I don't know. Something about 'your shadow will point the way…'" His eyes closed tightly as he tried to remember. "'The direction from the heart of heaven to the heart of the earth.'"

"You know what that sounds like to me?" said Renee. "It sounds like the directions to a secret tunnel."

The morning light was peeking over the mountaintops and blanketing the valley floor. On a hillside in the distance, a shape began to form. It was slight at first, but as the sun rose higher in the sky, it became larger. Then, it was there, in plain site. The same shape from Renee's dream and the same shape from the page that fell out of the book: a crescent moon.

"Look down there—at the building with the white cloud cover underneath. See how that figure on top is casting a shadow over on the mountain behind it? What's it look like to you?"

"Never mind the building down there," said Jason. "Look up on the top of the hill."

Above them, next to the remnants of a few buildings, were several men in uniforms. Next to them was a man dressed in a long robe while another man, twice his size, sported a Mohawk.

"Just like in my dream," gasped Renee. "Except there were three of them and only two of us."

"What dream?" asked Jason.

"The one that you were in that I told you about back at the library. We need to get over to the terraces and head down the steps."

"Why there?"

"Trust me."

Lena placed her hand on Renee's shoulder and said, "We need to do something, because they've spotted us."

CHAPTER FORTY-THREE
THE MULTIVERSE PRINCIPLE

They tried not to draw too much attention as they crossed through the village area and made their way to the terraces. The father and his police escort, meanwhile, were causing all kinds of commotion above them. Women screamed as Joe Del pushed them aside. The officers barked orders at tourists who were in their way. The men separated into two groups and headed down the mountain from both sides.

"Where to?" asked Lena.

Renee pointed and said, "To the bottom, past that white building."

They sprinted down along the terrace slopes as fast as they could, taking care not to twist their ankles on the rocks. The height between levels was much different from what Renee remembered in her dream. It would have been suicide to jump from one level to the next. Instead, they followed the path in the middle of the steep slope and tried their best not to slip in the grass. The men they'd seen at the top had regrouped and started their descent.

Within minutes, Renee's group was at the bottom of the terraces. Jason, who was out in front, hesitated and asked, "Where to now?"

"Keep going down into the woods."

Renee led them below the site and down a rugged path, which disappeared deeper and deeper into the brush. Behind them, Joe was gaining fast. He didn't stop to regroup in the middle like the others. Instead, he just pushed on forward. The thrill of the chase had overtaken his senses and was consuming him. His primal instincts were now in charge, and he hooped and hollered like an Indian warrior ready for battle. He knew the effect it would have on the party below. It was no longer about the money. This was a real contact sport and worth so much more than a few coins.

At the top of the mountain descending ever so gently was Father Delanda with Tana and a guard holding him on each arm. The priest was careful not to get too excited. After all, this boy was a little too eager to share all of the information he knew. He wasn't quite sure what his motives were, but he was willing to play along for now.

"Where are they heading, my son?"

The prince surveyed the scene and said, "I don't know."

The priest stopped and with a stern tone said, "This is not the time and place for games. I'd hate for something to happen to you out here—accidentally, of course."

"I don't know. This is not the way home."

Father Delanda studied Tana's face. There was enough sincerity in his delivery to be believable. He'd had years of practice reading the expressions and voices of those his congregation. This revelation made him a bit nervous about what lay ahead.

THE CHASE

Renee pulled on Jason's arm as she dragged him deeper and deeper into the foliage. She seemed to know exactly where she was heading. He would look back occasionally and try to gauge how far back the man with the Mohawk was. Just when he thought they'd lost him in the bushes, his shiny head would appear out of nowhere.

"How much further?" he asked.

"I'm not sure, but I know this is the right way," replied Renee, slightly out of breath.

"How can you be so sure?"

Renee kept talking but didn't stop moving. She slowed her pace just a little because the bushes and trees around her had thickened. "Back there. The map—and the page we found in the book." Her words were rushed. "I was trying to tell you about the inscription."

"You mean about the white house?"

"Yeah, but I didn't get to finish."

Jason caught a branch as it swung back and nearly smacked Lena in the neck. She smiled and said, "If I didn't know any better…"

"You don't," he interjected. "I just don't want you slowing us down." He resumed his focus on Renee. "Go on."

"The inscription on your map was too small to decipher. That's why people have been misreading it all of these years. That and the little secret weapon I have over most normal human beings."

"And what would that be?" asked Lena.

Renee looked to Jason, who understood that explaining it would be a bit embarrassing. "She's dyslexic. Apparently, the ancient Indian who wrote that inscription was dyslexic too. Maybe they all were, who knows."

Lena scratched her head and said, "You mean to tell me that the reason nobody's been able to find this place is because they were reading the words backwards?"

"Uh, maybe, but not exactly," said Renee. "Some letters and symbols are, like, backwards, but there's another trick to it that I'll explain later."

"How do you know which ones?"

"I just do."

As the words rolled off her tongue, she realized for the first time in her life that being dyslexic wasn't really a bad thing—or a weakness or a curse. Somehow, in this remote part of the world, seeing things backward was a gift. She tried to wrap her head around this concept but couldn't quite grasp it. It went against everything she'd ever known or experienced. Yet no matter how she looked at it, it was keeping her alive. That in itself was empowering.

As the forest thinned around them, they stumbled upon a cliff and peered over the edge. Hundreds of feet down into the gorge was the Urubamba River. They only heard the rush of the water when they were right on top of it. The brush and densely covered canyon walls had filtered out most of the noise on their approach.

Jason looked back for any sign of the crazy man chasing them. Heading back was not an option, and going forward appeared to be instant death. "We're trapped," he said.

"No, we aren't," said Renee. "That's what I've been trying to tell you. Back in the room, we were talking about the hieroglyphics on your map. The symbols didn't say 'white house by the lake.' They said 'white house *under* the river.'"

"*Under the river?* That doesn't make any sense. How'd you come up with that?"

"The jagged line you saw with the other line drawn below it. To most people it looked like a lake, but to me it looked like a river."

"You mean it was upside down or inverted?"

"Yeah, sort of. Anyway, I think it means that the white house is under a river and not by a lake."

Jason's eyes widened as he absorbed this new revelation, "Amazing. That one symbol changes everything. No wonder we weren't able to figure it out."

"Exactly. And then when I saw this crescent moon shining on the mountainside"—she lifted her arm—"pointing this way."

It all made sense, yet he still had his doubts. He turned to Lena for a second opinion. "What do you think?"

She leaned over the edge and peered down below. Then she looked back into the woods. "If that guy is half as dangerous as he looks, then I don't think we have a choice."

The yelping started up again. Joe was getting nearer. It was only a matter of minutes before he caught up to them.

"Let's do it."

They rotated their backpacks around and strapped them in tightly over their stomachs. "OK," said Renee. "We have to dive in and when you hit the water, keep swimming downward. Eventually, you'll go under a ledge and come out on the other side. I'm not sure what happens after that."

Lena and Jason nodded.

The bushes behind them opened wide. Standing there with a knife in his hand was the man with the Mohawk. A combination of blood and perspiration dripped off his new scar as he caught his breath. His smile revealed a set of crooked yellow teeth hungry for more action. He kicked away the last of the branches with a grunt and moved in.

Jason pushed the other two behind him. His knife was in his backpack, and he knew there was no way Joe would let him reach for it.

"What do we do?" whispered Lena.

"I don't know. Just wing it." Jason pushed the other two away from the cliff. Joe continued to close in, so Jason stepped to the side, trying to swing around him and reverse places.

Joe obliged and growled, "You can run, you no can hide,"

Jason removed his backpack and used it as a shield. He tried to pick up a branch off the ground but Joe was too quick. He lunged for him and managed to cut a small hole into the pack. Jason rolled onto the ground and barely missed Joe's second swipe. Renee reached down, grabbed a large branch, and tossed it over to him.

"Thanks."

Lena knelt down and picked up another branch. She lined up next to Jason, and they both slowly approached Joe.

Mean Joe Del just snarled, "Me like a good fight." His wolf-like eyes glowed with a yellow tint.

The two continued to move closer. Joe stepped back a few steps and grunted again. Renee finally understood what they were up to and found her own stick off the ground. Together, the three of them surrounded the crazy man and jabbed their spears in his face. Joe swung at them with his knife and kept taking small steps backward.

He caught Renee's spear in his hand and started to pull her in toward him. Jason screamed, "Now!"

They all lunged forward. Joe stepped back while still holding onto to Renee's branch. The ground behind him crumbled into the rapidly flowing water below. Joe finally realized where he was as he teetered on the edge of the cliff and held on to Renee's spear for dear life.

"Let go!" yelled Jason.

Renee let go of the branch and Joe's arms swayed uncontrollably as he tried to regain his balance. Lena plunged her stick into his chest. It didn't break the skin, but it was enough to send him down into the gorge below.

Then she grabbed Jason and hugged him tightly. Renee hugged them both.

After they caught their breath, Jason said, "It won't be long before the others come."

"You're right. We need to do this now."

On the count of three, they ran and dove straight down into the water below. As they traveled downward, Jason caught a glimpse of a figure hanging on a vine a few yards below the top of the ledge.

PART FIVE

MYSTERIES OF THE TUNNELS

CHAPTER FORTY-FOUR
DIVERS DO IT DEEPER

Renee was amazed at how long it took to actually hit the water. She hadn't gotten this far in her dream. There was time to reflect on the scuffle moments before and even contemplate what she thought she saw on her way down. When she did finally hit the water, she heard a loud splash and then silence. The impact came so swiftly that she didn't have time to inhale a last, deep breath. Panic set in as water seeped into her nostrils and her ears popped. She began swimming frantically, trying to go deeper and deeper, but her body was too buoyant. The ledge below was out of reach and she was out of air.

As her hopes exhaled with every rising bubble, something grabbed her shirt. It was Jason's hand. He held on with one arm and continued diving down with his legs kicking in unison. She saw a blurred image of Lena disappear underneath the ledge. Jason made it to the shelf and then swung Renee underneath it and followed behind.

When they reached the surface, Renee's lungs were full of water and her face had turned blue. Lena quickly dragged her on shore and pushed gently on her chest. Spurts of water shot into the air and Renee started coughing. Lena pushed her on her side.

"How is she?" Jason asked as he gasped for air.

"She'll be fine."

Lena was breathing normally. With a puzzled look, he asked, "How come you're not out of breath?"

"Swim team in high school."

As they decompressed, the sandy beach and gigantic white waterfall in front of them came into focus. It encompassed the whole area from left to right and top to bottom. Water gushed over a ledge above that was similar to the one they'd just swam underneath, creating the appearance of a waterfall. It was hard to determine where the sunlight was coming from, but it clearly illuminated everything around them. The dichotomy between knowing where they'd just been and seeing where they were now made no sense at all. It was as if they were in a world inside of a world, separated only by a layer of water.

"This must be the *white house*," said Renee.

Behind them was a deep, dark cave. A rush of cool air swept by them from the interior. Renee was now on one knee, lifting herself up with Lena's help.

"Was that who I thought it was hanging on the side of the cliff back there?"

Jason nodded and shined his flashlight into the black hole in front of them. "I doubt that we've seen the last of that guy."

CHAPTER FORTY-FIVE

THE BEST-KEPT SECRET

Jason carefully pulled the damp map out of his pocket. "Maybe we should let things dry out a few minutes before heading in. You never know, this map might come in handy again." He started removing items from his bag and laying them on the ground. "Does that compass still work?"

Renee lifted the chain out from underneath her blouse and tapped the glass cover. "Yep, still working." She removed her backpack, reached for the medallion, and held it next to the compass. "It's not pointing to the necklace any longer." The other two moved in for a closer look.

"Interesting," said Lena. "Why would it work above ground and not down here?"

"I don't know, but my feet are killing me. I think I've outgrown these shoes." Renee removed her tennis shoes and socks and then pulled a pair of flip-flops from her backpack.

"Your feet!" Lena exclaimed. "You have six toes!" She couldn't help but stare.

Jason knelt down for a closer look. "You never mentioned that little bit of information."

"Funny, huh? At least you didn't start laughing like most kids at school."

Lena realized that her staring was making Renee uncomfortable. "Sorry," she said. "It's just not something you see every day."

Jason rose up and said, "Must've been rough."

"Yeah, well, it was—or is. You never quite get over things like that." She took a moment and tried to clear her mind before adding, "Everything was going so wrong here with my father and all, so I didn't say anything. Plus, I didn't think it would be a good idea for Father Delanda to know either."

"Probably not," remarked Lena. "I wonder how the boy's doing?"

"He was trained well. He'll be fine."

"I hope you're right," said Renee. "When I saw his fingers, I knew there was a connection. My mother says that none of her relatives have six toes, so it must be a recessive gene."

"A recessive but powerful gene. Do you know what this means?" Jason waited for an answer but none came. "You're part of royalty, a descendent of kings and queens—at least, according to the legends around here. After meeting the prince, I'd say there must be some truth to it."

"That would explain the medallion," said Lena, "and why it only works with you and not others."

"What do you mean?" asked Jason.

"Try it. Hold it with both hands like you did back on the lake."

Renee clasped the necklace tightly. She held it there for at least a minute. "Nothing."

Lena moved in and sat next to her. "Try placing it around your neck." She picked up the pendant and drooped it over Renee's head. Again, there was nothing.

Lena ran her fingers over it. "I don't get it. It worked the last time."

"Maybe you were imagining things," said Jason. "The sun can play tricks on the eyes, you know."

"It also worked back at the cave in Tiahuanaco."

Jason and Lena both perked up and said in unison, "It what?"

"You never mentioned that either."

Renee looked a little uneasy. "It wasn't such a big deal. It just glowed a little bit when I first touched it on that creepy dead corpse."

Jason was now up and walking in circles, "An ancestor, maybe. But why did it glow at the lake?"

"Maybe there were ancestors at the bottom of that lake," said Lena.

"Maybe."

"We were passing an ancient burial site if I recall—the Island of the Sun?"

"How weird," said Jason. "Everything I've seen over the last couple of days contradicts the laws of physics. This necklace, and that compass—and that stupid number."

"What number?" asked Lena.

"'512.' It came up in Renee's dream and it's in the title of this book." He picked the book up off the ground—it had held up surprisingly well in the water—and looked at the cover. "It almost makes you go cross-eyed when you stare at it. See how the numbers kinda disappear and turn into a cross or *T* of some kind."

"Yeah, how weird. What's it mean?"

"I haven't a clue. Five-twelve is a common number in mathematics. You see it frequently with computer memory. They use it because its one of those convenient binary numbers that calculates out to two to the ninth power." He rubbed his chin. "You know, these tunnels seem to act like a computer or mainframe of some kind, when you think about it. But more like a computer that's lost its Internet connection—interesting."

He nodded as his mind processed everything he was saying aloud. This little trick was Jason's favorite way of resolving problems. He'd learned over years of being in the laboratory alone that when he talked to himself, both sides of his brain answered back. This usually meant that he came up with answers twice as fast.

"Although something tells me that it's not cyberspace it's trying to connect to," he continued.

"Oh, oh, here we go again," groaned Renee.

Jason smiled and replied, "I know, but these tunnels do sort of resemble *wormholes*, don't they?"

"I still don't see what that has to do with this number," Lena said.

"Yeah, you're right." He turned to Renee. "Anyway, Tana seemed to know more about this number than he was telling us back in the library."

"I think his silence said it all." Renee brushed off the dust from her toes and sighed. She could only hope that they'd meet again. There were so many questions that she wanted to ask him. Then a thought occurred to her: *Maybe no one knows.*

After they'd rested for an hour or so, Jason tossed the dried items back into his pack, folded up the map, and said, "I think it's time we start walking."

They set out into the cave, cautiously watching for booby traps or unusual-looking formations. The room remained at a constant temperature in the midsixties and had no natural light. Unlike the other manmade tunnels, its walls weren't cut into smooth ninety-degree angles but instead varied in height every few feet. The floors were rugged and rutted and had wet patches that made maneuvering slow and tiresome.

They traveled for a couple of hours, occasionally encountering pockets in which the ceiling stretched fifty feet into the air. Gold cups and plates littered the rocky floor from time to time as well. Jason didn't even bother picking them up. The last thing he needed was to be carrying extra weight. Since they hadn't planned on taking such a long trip, lunch consisted of a few candy bars and leftover jerky. Occasionally, a small animal scurried by and disappeared into a crevice.

Lena finally stopped and said, "If I didn't know any better, I'd say we're walking in circles."

Jason and Renee's eyes met. "I was getting that impression too. This same thing happened to us in Sacsayhuaman."

They walked for another minute or so when Renee whispered, "Do you hear that?"

They all stood still and listened. "Yeah, I can hear it—and see it," Lena said. "It's faint but I'm pretty sure I know what it is."

The two women took off running toward the light. Jason followed them. The noise grew louder when they rounded the next corner. There in front of them, shimmering and spraying a fine mist into their faces, was the same white waterfall they'd left on their way in.

"Great. Now what do we do?" asked Lena.

Jason looked over to Renee and extended his arm, "It's time to break out the compass."

CHAPTER FORTY-SIX

WITHIN THESE WALLS

They explained to Lena what they'd experienced in the tunnel back at Sacsayhuaman. "Just follow the compass. You'll see what happens."

Jason focused on the compass as the others followed behind. The compass pointed them in a southeastern path. Within a few minutes, the cave began to widen and dim. "Stay on course," he reminded them.

"It's getting darker, and I can't see the walls anymore," noted Lena. "But there they are again. Out of nowhere off to the sides—and now I can't breathe. Are you sure we should be doing this?" Her voice sounded deep and lethargic, almost hoarse.

"Yes, just keep going," Jason answered.

They continued to shuffle along cautiously while watching the compass. The tunnel's appearance slowly changed shape; its rough, uneven walls morphed into smoothly cut angles. Most of the stalagmite pillars and spiking stalactites disappeared along with the slippery cracks in the ground. A subtle glow reflecting off the walls soon grew to the point where they could now make out contours and lines without the help of the flashlights. Their pace picked up too as the floor descended deeper into the mountain.

Lena examined the shiny, flat walls that had transformed the room into something more resembling an office corridor than a cave. The pathway followed a jagged sawtooth pattern and had a series of golden discs spaced every few yards. "How do these things work?" she asked.

"Apparently, they reflect sunlight from above ground down to here," replied Jason. "Quite impressive."

"We must be getting close."

Suddenly, a group of Indians came running toward them from their left side. Their figures were slightly out of focus and distorted as they passed in and out of the serrated granite walls. It was as if they were running right through them or were somehow inside the walls but still visible. The friction created when they entered the rock blurred their images but didn't seem to slow them down much. They were a few feet higher off the ground and heading upward. As they sprinted by, the three ducked down for cover.

"What was that?" whispered Lena.

"Warriors," replied Jason.

"The same ones I saw with my father in Tiahuanaco. Did you see their eyes?"

"Not really," Lena responded. "I wonder why they didn't notice us. It was as if they were right next to us, but not really."

Jason ran his fingers over the rock and added, "Yeah, I didn't even hear them run by or feel the ground shake. I just saw them."

"That's true," said Lena. "I don't think they were in the same tunnel as us. They were on a different level or something—or maybe on the other side of the wall."

"That would explain a few things," replied Jason. "Maybe there are several paths you can take."

"Why didn't we see anyone in the first tunnel?" Renee asked.

"I don't know. Maybe it was abandoned."

"Did I tell you about the Indian drawings me and my dad saw on the walls?" asked Renee. "Their eyes seemed to change size and glow when we went by them. It was like they could see us and knew what we were doing."

"That's not comforting," uttered Lena.

They resumed walking and followed the compass as the room transformed before them. Occasionally, a rat would scamper by and disappear: it seemed to be running through the walls, heading up and down invisible ramps. Each time, the rats quickly vanished when spotted with a beam of light. The middle of the tunnel continued to slope down gradually while the group stayed fixated on the compass. As the minutes passed by, the light grew dimmer on the flashlight.

"We're running low on batteries," said Jason. "I don't think we need them anyway. There seems to be enough light down here now."

"Let's pick up the pace a little," Lena said. "It feels like we're descending deeper but the temperature hasn't gotten any colder. You'd think by now it'd be fifty degrees this far down into the ground."

Jason nodded, "That's true."

Lena hesitated and whispered, "Shhhh. Sounds like footsteps."

Behind them, they heard the patter of several feet coming their way. "The warriors," declared Jason. "Who else would it be?" They sped up, trying hard to follow the compass's direction and stay in the middle. The footsteps grew louder. "Faster."

Document 512

They were running at full speed now. The tunnel curved to the left and then jetted to the right. They hadn't noticed the dips and turns before, when they were just walking. Every once in a while, they heard a few voices grumbling and then the footsteps would start up again.

"There! I can see another path ahead," Jason shouted. "Keep running but stay in the middle." He looked down at his compass and said, "It's due east. Keep running east."

The middle of the tunnel widened as they raced through it. They felt the sides moving away and the walls vanishing in front of their eyes. The light was growing brighter and the temperature was rising.

Lena looked over and noticed that Renee was off to the side and half of her body was out of focus. She tapped Jason on the shoulder and slowed down. "Look, she's fading."

"Renee, get back on the path with us."

"I'm trying, but I can't." Renee moved in a few feet to the left but her fingers were still barely visible and her right shoulder was almost opaque. Lena reached out for her arm but couldn't hold onto it.

"Did you see that?" she asked. "Her arm felt like Silly Putty."

"Yes."

"I'm getting scared," cried Renee. "It felt weird to me too, and you guys are also out of focus."

The footsteps were much louder now. "Look," said Lena, pointing to tiny silhouettes off in the distance. "I can see them."

Jason peered down into the tunnel and said, "They're on one of our trails for sure. Which one I don't know. We're gonna have to try and outrun them. The first opening you see, take it and look for any kind of cover to hide under. It's our only chance."

They started sprinting back down the corridor. The Indians picked up the pace too and were yelling loudly. They were closing in. Jason couldn't run at full speed because Lena was holding on to his hand. Renee tried desperately to keep up but fell behind.

"I'm losing you two!" she shouted.

Jason looked back. The Indians were within a few yards. Their bodies were slightly out of focus and very similar to Renee's. He knew what that meant. Lena noticed it too.

"Renee, they're on your path and closing in. You need to make a run for it. We'll try to divert them somehow."

She nodded. "Promise that you'll find me."

"Of course we will," reassured Lena.

Then she dashed off down the corridor.

Lena grabbed Jason's hand and said, "What are we going to do? What if you're wrong and they're on *our* path?"

"Then at least one of us will get away." They ran around the next corner and stopped. He removed his backpack and pulled Lena down by her shoulders. "Stay low to the ground. When they get close enough, swing your bag in the air and try to knock them off their feet."

"Sounds good." She reached over and kissed him gently on the forehead.

Jason didn't know how to react. It was the last thing he needed to think about right now. He grabbed her hand and held it tightly. "Get ready."

The Indians came barreling around the corner and the two waited until they were right on top of them before acting.

"Now!"

They both jumped up and swung their packs at the same time. Instead of knocking them back, the bags sifted through the Indians' bodies with the ease of a comb clawing through a head of matted hair. The four warriors squirmed around and screamed in agony as the canvas backpacks riddled through their flesh.

The stunt immobilized the Indians only for a few seconds. When the pain subsided, one of them shouted at Jason and Lena and raised his spear.

Jason grabbed Lena's arm. "I think it's time we hit the road." He threw his backpack over his shoulder, looked down at the compass, and darted off like a sprinter leaving the starting blocks. She followed right behind him. The Indians gave chase, momentarily, but quickly realized that they were on another pathway as the two bodies grew less visible with every step. They spun around and shouted a few war cries before taking off in hot pursuit after Renee.

Jason and Lena raced on as the walls of the tunnel slowly transformed from solid back into a cloudy grayish-white. Soon the light grew brighter and the temperature started rising. They were getting closer to something, but weren't quite sure what it was. Just as they saw the end of the tunnel and a collage of green foliage appeared, they heard a scream.

CHAPTER FORTY-SEVEN
WHERE ARE WE?

When they exited the tunnel, they were greeted by a dirt trail lined with an arcade of exotic plants and wildlife. Trees shot up a hundred feet into the air and blocked their view of the sky. Birds chirped and fluttered above curtains of green and light brown. They caught glimpses of a few animal shapes and colors moving throughout the untamed arboretum. It was everything a tropical rainforest should be, minus the humidity and mosquitoes.

The light was evenly distributed—like at the cave at Tiahuanaco. There were no shadows. As they looked down into a valley, they could see a river meandering through the forest with colorful flowers and shrubbery hanging over it. Vibrant shades of yellow and red ran along its banks and easily marked its path.

"Look how windy it is," observed Jason. "It reminds me of the Purus River."

Lena took in the colorful palate around her and grinned. She thought these types of images only appeared on Hollywood movie screens. Losing Renee felt like a distant memory as her mind puzzled over what she was witnessing. "It's beautiful—but where are we?"

"I don't know, but look over there."

A large building resembling a palace was situated right in the middle of a plaza. Columns of huge black stones stood on each corner. Houses encircled it on all sides. Behind them was a wall decorated with gold and silver ornaments of all shapes and sizes.

"Does this place look or sound familiar?" Jason asked.

"Except for the missing statues, it sounds a lot like the place you described from your little library book."

"And a lot like the lost city of Akakor," he added.

"Are we still in Peru?"

"Probably not. One thing's for certain, though. We're deep in the middle of the Amazon Rainforest."

"But we didn't travel that far, did we?"

"That's hard to say. We walked a good five or six hours. It seemed like we were going in circles but maybe we weren't. Plus, the concept of time seems to have completely vanished down here in these tunnels. I'm hardly hungry even though we haven't eaten a full meal since yesterday—or what we remember as being yesterday."

As a waterfall rumbled off in the distance, they carefully moved through the brush, trying not to be spotted. There were a few children playing in a reservoir near an opening between two walls. A mist seeped out of a gap in the rock as water splashed into a pool below it.

"That's not the waterfall we first came through, is it?"

Jason squinted. "No, I don't think so. I'd bet this one is covering up that entrance. Lord knows how big it is on the other side."

While they were busy studying the opening, the ground began to vibrate under their feet. Off to the right, a group of Indians marched by rapidly. Renee was in the middle with her hands tied. Lena and Jason ducked down and peered through the bushes.

"Where'd they come from?" asked Lena.

"I don't know. I guess each path comes out of the tunnel at a different point here in this room."

"How weird. So when you go in, you don't know where you'll end up."

"Well, *we* don't know, but I bet the Indians have a pretty good idea. I remember seeing this drawing in a book that showed Akakor with twelve entrances. Every one of them headed toward the middle."

Lena pointed and said, "It looks like they're heading for the palace." She grabbed Jason's arm. "So, what do we do now?"

"Follow them."

CHAPTER FORTY-EIGHT
THE PALACE

Renee felt a hand from behind grab her shoulder. It wasn't spongy like Lena's but firm and strong. It stopped her in her tracks. The Indians quickly formed a circle around her and closed in. She couldn't help but notice how different they were from each other. Some had red skin and black hair and others were fair-skinned with blue eyes. A few even had red and blonde hair. They touched her clothes and exchanged a few comments. She couldn't understand what they were saying, but she did recognize a word or two that sounded like English.

One of them pulled out a rope and tied her hands together. As he was wrapping it around her wrist, he noticed her feet. He immediately pointed to the ground and started shouting to the others. They became ecstatic too. Renee became frightened.

The man then tugged on the rope and said, "*Mitgekommen.*" That definitely sounded German.

They marched across the compound, past the waterfall, and directly to the palace. The children playing in the water stood up and watched as the strange white girl walked by. It was unusual to see guards escorting anyone around their city.

The grounds were laid out in rectangles. Two main paths intersected the palace in the center and divided the city into four sections. The palace was in the shape of a pyramid stretching three stories high with a parapet wall and walkway on each level. The Indians guided Renee up a small staircase leading to the second story. From there, they climbed another flight of granite steps to an opening with no door and headed in.

The huge interior was well lit and ventilated with a series of large windows connected to a balcony running along the perimeter. There was a row of statues on each side of the room. At the front was a soldier wearing a helmet with wings and carrying a sword followed by an Indian warrior standing with a spear. After that was another Indian with a headdress sitting on a throne. Behind that Indian was a smaller man with a larger head and very wide eyes. Sitting all the way on the far end was an early caveman clothed in animal skin and holding a spear.

On the other side of the room was a set of animals beginning with a large elephant on one end and ending with a small snake on the other. The elephant seemed so out of place because its species wasn't found anywhere in South America. Next to it was a flying dinosaur similar to a pterodactyl followed by a camel-like creature with antlers. Behind that was a ferocious-looking jaguar whose eyes seemed to follow Renee as she crossed the room. That *Mona Lisa*-like quality made her nervous.

In the center of the room was a group of men and women sitting on beds of straw and wool. A mixture of white and red skin blended in with blonde, red, and black hair so randomly that no two people looked related, yet somehow they *all* looked related. A combination of animal skins, colorful necklaces, feathers, cotton shirts, skirts, and pants clothed their bodies. They looked more like a troupe of socialites ready to mingle at a costume ball rather than elders ready to conduct a meeting.

An older woman with white hair sat in the middle. Renee couldn't help notice that she was staring at her intensely. The other younger women around her seemed to be her servants or caretakers. A young man dressed in what looked like a brown uniform jacket with a pair of worn-out khaki pants walked over and whispered in the older woman's ear.

The lady turned to a red-skinned man wearing a thin laurel crown and relayed the message. Draped in a long, white linen robe, this tall Indian rose up and sauntered out of the crowd. He too looked out of place. Aside from the ruff of feathers tied around his waist, his garment more closely resembled that of a Roman senator than an Indian ruler. The band around his neck looked very similar to the *khipu* on Renee's amulet.

He bowed before Renee and said, "I am the high priest, Bartholomew." The dialect had hints of German in it, and he enunciated his words very strongly.

"You speak English?" she asked.

"Yes, among other languages. Our main tongue is a combination of Quechua and German."

"That explains a few things. But why German?"

He chuckled and looked to the other elders, then back at Renee. "Very well, I guess you deserve an explanation. Years ago, another tribe of men and women came to us from a distant land. They dressed very differently from any other tribe we'd ever known and carried powerful weapons. They spoke German. Over the years, they've integrated into our society and taught us many new things, just as we've taught them many things too. Naturally, their language became part of ours." He opened his arms and added, "I am a product of this union: half Incan and half German."

"Incan!" she exclaimed. "I thought they'd all been killed off."

Bartholomew nodded. "Yes, most of them were. Fortunately, there was one band of warriors that managed to escape and ended up here."

The man walked around Renee and studied her for a few moments before speaking. "It is very unusual for an outsider to make it this far into our community. In fact, it hasn't happened in fifty years or so. That's quite an accomplishment."

He then moved in closer for a look at her feet. The others gathered around and took notice too. They whispered to each other in a low but lively murmur. It was subtle yet jubilant.

Bartholomew continued to circle her as he spoke. "I understand that you're with two others. Where are they now?"

"I don't know. We got separated in the cave and…"

He gave her a long, inquisitive look. She guessed that he was somehow trying to read her mind or study her face to see if she was telling the truth. Either way, she didn't really care anymore. Her body was running on fumes at this point. His gaze moved to her backpack, and he ordered the guards to untie her.

"May I take a look inside?"

She removed it from her shoulders and handed it over. The high priest opened the flap and gently removed its contents. He tried the flashlight and nodded approvingly. Then he lifted her extra clothes above his head and exchanged a few words with the women in the congregation. When he came to the pendant, his eyes lit up. He held it up high for everyone to see and shouted a few words that she could not understand.

Bartholomew studied the strange markings inside the trinket. Then, for a long time, he stared at the *khipu* holding it in place. He nodded his head while deciphering its coded messages. Then his expression changed from delight to puzzlement. "How did you come by this necklace?"

"It's from a cave—in Tiahuanaco."

"*Tiwanacu?* You just found it in a cave?"

Renee wasn't sure how to answer this question. The wrong answer might get her into trouble. Yet she felt confident that their peculiar interest in her twelve toes was enough to keep her from any harm at this point. She lowered her head and replied, "No, my father kind of stole it. It was on the body of this dead king inside a tomb in this cave."

The others began murmuring again and seemed very animated. "This is wonderful news, my dear," said Bartholomew. "You do not know how happy we are to have this treasure finally returned to its rightful place. Please join us and tell us more."

Renee was placed in the middle of the group and passed around from one to the other. Each person hugged her and congratulated her for a job well done. She could make out the occasional English word and a few Latin roots, but it didn't matter. Their expressions said it all. After a lifetime of unanswered prayers and misunderstandings, she was beginning to feel good about herself.

CHAPTER FORTY-NINE

WHERE TO NOW?

Father Delanda yelled out for Joe once more. No answer. He was about to abandon the search when one of the officers shouted in the distance. The group hurriedly ran over to where the voice was coming from. By the time the priest arrived, the men were pulling Joe up by his arm and hoisting him onto the grass next to the cliff. The priest walked over and took a good, long look down into the canyon.

"Is that the way they went?"

Joe nodded. The padre knew that there was no way he could follow them. His body would never survive the jump. Joe caught his breath and recounted the events leading up to their escape. The priest listened intently while staring at the young prince.

When Joe was finished, the priest walked over to the boy and said, "It appears that your friends took some very daring steps in order to escape. What do you have to say about that?"

The prince rubbed his chin and replied, "A panther will eat his own foot off when caught in a trap."

"Do you know where this river goes?"

"I can only guess. I wasn't aware of such a path until today. There are other paths, though."

The priest smiled, "Then we shall try one of them."

He began to walk away, but Tana grabbed his shoulder. "Father, the path I know is very dangerous and physical. I don't know if you want to attempt it yourself. Many have died."

The good father narrowed his eyes and looked down at the young man inquisitively. The thought of more than one six-fingered boy existing in the Amazon was troubling. He knew what eventually needed to be done. He just wasn't sure when and where. The boy was still of great value and had to be handled with care. There were more urgent priorities needing his attention anyway, such as finding this lost city and finding out whether there were any others like this boy. Goose bumps formed on his arms at the realization that his final destination was almost within reach. He smiled and replied in a very stern voice, "A faithful man shall abound with blessings, my son."

"Well then, expect the unexpected."

The priest was studying the young man, trying to read between his words, when an officer trampling through the brush ran up to him and murmured something inaudible. Father Delanda looked to Joe and Prince Tana Nara and said, "We have company."

CHAPTER FIFTY
A CAN OF WHOOP ASS

When the group of officers exited Machu Picchu, there were two people waiting to meet them. Father Delanda was worn-out from the chase but managed to keep a wide smile while introducing himself.

"*Buenos días, mi nombre es Padre Delanda.*"

Don Carlos bowed and replied, "*Hola, Padre.*"

He explained who they were and how they'd gotten to Machu Picchu. It wasn't an easy task finding someone in Cuzco willing to talk to them. Finding anyone with actual knowledge of Leslie Gorman's daughter was impossible. In the end, they happened across an old woman villager who saw the priest get on the train to Machu Picchu. She said that she knew him personally through her son, Huascar.

Nina had been giddy to the point of hysteria as she patched together a story about the good father and why he left town. Even though it was so full of holes when it came to logic, that didn't matter. Don and Leslie were desperate for any kind of news at that point. Nina just waved as Don's jeep drove off and disappeared into the cobblestone street while repeating under her breath, "The Gods will have their revenge."

Father Delanda listened intently, and then placed a hand on Leslie's shoulder and said, "I'm sorry for your loss, my dear. I wish I could help you, but there's nothing that can be done on my end. I have no idea where your daughter is."

Leslie didn't take kindly to the priest's remarks. It was just enough to send her over the edge. She was tired and sore and pissed off to no end. Her whole family was missing and she'd had about as much indifferent South American hospitality as she could stomach. She wanted answers.

"Let me tell you something, Father. I am fed up to here with you and everyone else in this shit-for-brains country of yours. My husband's laying dead in a field somewhere and my daughter's being chased by every cop in Cuzco. Now I'm good friends with the head of American embassy in Lima and have already filled him in on a number of things. Either you come clean and tell me what the hell is going on or I'm going to bring down so much fire and brimstone upon your ass that you'd wish you'd never been born. What's it gonna be?"

The priest wasn't expecting such a spirited outburst. He removed his glasses and cleaned them while thinking of what to say. This tiny woman had more spunk and grit than any of the men in his posse, with the exception of Joe. He couldn't be sure if she was serious about bringing the ambassador into this. That would not be good. It would mean unwanted publicity and that might not set well with the church. He needed to nip this in the bud.

"Have it your way, Mrs. Gorman. I was just trying to protect you. We have a long and dangerous journey ahead of us. Some people will not be coming back alive. If you still wish to go then I will not stop you."

"I certainly do, thank you very much." She nodded and turned away.

By now, her heart was thumping so hard that it almost popped a button on her blouse. Something in her body had burst and was gushing adrenaline through her veins so fast that her words could barely keep up with her actions. Her verbal flogging of the padre had come out of nowhere. She had no idea who the ambassador of Peru was. It was the first thing that came to mind. Luckily, she'd always been good at thinking on her toes. It was a trait that had served her well over the years—and one she'd passed down to her daughter. In fact, she thought, it was probably the one thing keeping her daughter alive.

Don Carlos nodded approvingly and gave her an inconspicuous wink as she strutted by and exhaled. Out of the corner of her eye, she noticed the prince off to the side being guarded by two officers. When his hand went into the air, she did a double take. Then she zeroed in on his other hand. All of a sudden, her world became much more complicated. People with six fingers on each hand, a father she never knew, a husband and daughter mysteriously disappearing: What did it all mean? She had no clue right now, but deep down inside she had a feeling that this boy just might.

Meanwhile, Joe Del Diaz sat on a bench to the side and just watched and listened. He liked to see people's blood boil. It was good for the heart. This gringo impressed him. A worthy adversary for sure. This adventure had now taken on a new meaning. He wasn't quite sure what to think of it, but the first thing that came to mind was more money.

CHAPTER FIFTY-ONE
SIT AND WAIT

Jason and Lena watched Renee being escorted into the palace and decided to wait until after dark to make their next move. They needed to familiarize themselves with their new surroundings. The trees and birds all looked similar to those they'd seen in the Amazon Rainforest in the past. There was even an afternoon mist floating down that brought some relief from the heat. Yet the longer they studied everything, the more they realized that this place was nothing like anything they'd ever seen before.

There were no shadows stretching across the palace walls as the light grew dimmer. There were no crickets chirping after dusk or mosquitoes accompanying them. Unlike the jungle floor above ground, which usually greeted explorers with an unnerving array of taunting high-pitched screams or snarling growls, this night was silent. No moon rose over the horizon, and there were no stars lighting up the sky. The only light keeping the whole area from disappearing into obscurity came from a couple of torches by the palace.

"This place feels surreal," said Lena.

Jason looked over to Lena but could barely distinguish her silhouette from the bushes behind her. "Yeah, it's almost perfect—but a little too dark."

"I have a little pocket light," she said. "It's not much, but it's better than nothing." She went to turn it on, but Jason grabbed her arm.

"Not here. They're probably still looking for us."

He hesitated before releasing her hand. It felt nice and soft. *How easy it'd be to fall into this trap again,* he thought.

Lena sensed the uneasiness as he pulled away. His guard was still up, but she couldn't blame him. It's one thing to be swindled out of all of your worldly possessions, but it's another to be tricked into falling in love. It was the worst con in the business—but also the most effective. And, for that matter, the deadliest. Stealing someone's money can get you by in the short run; stealing someone's heart can get you killed.

"I'm sorry."

Jason remained quiet. He wasn't going to let her back in but she pressed on. "I'm really sorry. I mean it. I didn't want to hurt you. I, I just needed the money."

There was still silence.

Document 512

After a few minutes, she continued, "I could've left weeks earlier, you know. I knew where your stash was that first week we were together. It's just, I liked being with you and didn't want it to end."

"But it did."

"Yes, it did." Lena sighed and added, "I was getting scared. Scared that you'd find out who I really was and scared…" She hesitated but knew it was time to come clean. "Scared that I was…falling in love with you."

Jason repositioned himself in the grass and grunted. He knew better than to believe her. The only problem was he just couldn't figure out why she was saying all of this crap now. What kind of scam was she trying to pull off this time and why? He couldn't connect the dots.

"If you're trying to make me feel better, it's not working. Let's just leave it at that and move on. When this whole thing is over, you can go your way and I'll go mine."

A dozen guards wearing colorful outfits covered in feathers came marching out of the palace carrying torches and positioned themselves around the perimeter. The combination of bright lights and vibrant colors made it feel more like a Mardi Gras celebration than a changing of the guard. Lena moved closer to Jason and they both ducked down into the brush. The heat coming off the torches was so intense that they felt it from where they were sitting.

"Well, looks like we'll have to come up with another plan, because I don't see a way around them. Maybe we should try to get some sleep and wake up early."

Lena moved in closer and lay down beside him. "Sounds good."

CHAPTER FIFTY-TWO

REM

Renee found it hard to fall asleep. It was too quiet and too early. She yearned for the sounds of home. A car horn or plane flying low overhead would have made her feel more at ease. And how she missed those damn crickets. She knew that over time, she could grow use to the silence, but still, there was the palace itself. The cool stone walls did nothing to shield her from the night. Add to that the fact that there were two guards standing outside her door, and she had a recipe for a long and restless night.

She thought about her father. If only she could turn back the clock to that fateful day at Tiahuanaco. There were no mulligans in life, though, and she knew it. Then she wondered about her poor mother. She hadn't been able to talk to her in person since her father's death. Between the missed calls and garbled voice mails, she wasn't sure how much her mother knew. No telling what Don Carlos had told her, if anything? She must be going crazy right now not knowing what really happened. Hopefully, she had contacted the police in Cuzco, as that was their last destination on the trip. Then Renee wondered how much they would even tell her about her father's demise.

She did have confidence in her travel companions, though. They weren't going to abandon her after coming this far and getting so close. She knew that Lena was a bit unpredictable and hard to trust, but Jason, on the other hand, had been there for her. He'd risked his own life just to keep her out of harm's way.

One of the guards came in with a warm glass of a milky-looking substance and set it down on the side table next to her bed. She looked up at him and saw the same deep blue eyes high cheekbones she'd seen on Tana. Then she looked down at his fingers and counted; there were only five.

"Drink this," he said. "It helps with sleep."

"Thank you."

He stood silent for a moment and glanced over to the door. Then, when he felt comfortable that no one was listening, he whispered, "The prince—he will come back."

"How do you know?"

He tapped his finger on his forehead and replied, "Because I'm the one who trained him."

As he crossed the floor, the man looked back one last time and smiled. Then he closed the door and disappeared. The room was once again silent.

As she finally drifted off to sleep, the dreams came quickly and were more vivid than ever. At first, they were different versions of the past few days' events. There were tunnels that crisscrossed and paths through the jungle that never ended. The one thing that was missing from them all was that haunting nursery rhyme that had plagued her since childhood. It was gone—and so was the baggage that came with it.

Before long, everything was misty and light blue in color. She saw herself back on the beach lying next to the waterfall. The spray covered her body as clouds of steam rose into the air. A boy walked out and stood beside her. He reached down and lifted her up and then carried her into the cave. She couldn't make out his face, but she did see a pair of large blue eyes as they disappeared into the darkness.

The boy hesitated and asked, "Are you ready?"

She closed her eyes and replied, "No, but I'm willing."

The next thing she knew, they were flying through the air, physically passing beams of light and racing through the tunnels with ease. The tunnels soon turned into a series of circular tubes that vibrated like strings on a violin. The tubes crisscrossed each other up and down, left to right, and somehow back and forth as they shot up into the atmosphere and deep into the blackness of outer space. She held onto him tightly as he soared through the starlit abyss. Then she saw and heard the darkness tearing away and transforming from green to yellow to a familiar sky of blue with a layer of clouds cushioning their landing. Once again, she was lying next to a huge waterfall—alone.

At that moment, she awoke as a guard shook her and said in broken English, "Breakfast ready."

CHAPTER FIFTY-THREE
IN THE BEGINNING

The high priest was waiting in the center of the palace when the guards escorted Renee in. His entourage of elders from the day before was nowhere in sight. There was a spread of fruit and flatbreads on a table.

He motioned the guards away and said, "Please sit down and eat."

Renee nodded pleasingly and devoured everything in front of her. When she was done, Bartholomew cleared his throat and began speaking. "Our culture is an ancient one. It dates back over fifteen thousand years." Renee's eyes lit up. "It has gone through many changes and evolved so far over the centuries that I doubt our creators will even recognize us when they return"—he smiled and looked at Renee's toes—"except, that is, for one characteristic."

She looked down at her feet. "What do they mean—the toes, that is?"

"They mean everything to us. They are our connection to The Gods." He pointed to the row of statues of humans. "Our history tells us that in the beginning, man was more of an animal than a human.

Document 512

He walked on all fours and scavenged for food and shelter. Small groups lived together but didn't really communicate with each other except with a few simple gestures. Then a miracle occurred."

"Suddenly, golden beams filled the sky and the ground began to shake and The Gods appeared out from underneath the smoke. At first glance, they looked exactly like us from top to bottom, except for one detail: they had six fingers and six toes." He smiled at Renee's feet. "They came and freed us from the darkness we'd been living in and brought us light. They also brought knowledge that we'd never known before. Taught us the skills on how to gather food, hunt, herd animals, grow crops, erect stone buildings and weave clothes. Then they consecrated the new covenant between man and god forever by mating with us and creating a whole new race called Ugha Mongulala."

Renee's mind was spinning. She kept envisioning Tana and his six fingers, then the drawings in the cave at Tiahuanaco, then the book in her father's backpack about gods, and then the prince again. The stories her father had told her over the years all seemed so fantastic and unbelievable. Yet here was a man she'd just met claiming to have come from one of those imaginary places.

She rubbed her eyes and ran her fingers through her ratted hair. What she'd give for a nice, hot bath right now. She looked up to the high priest, pointed to the statues and said, "So what you're saying is, that I'm…one of you?"

"Not one of us, my dear." He looked to the ceiling and added, "You are one with The Gods. There have only been four generations of Ugha Mongulala throughout our history. Only four times have both a man and woman been born with six fingers or six toes within each other's lifetime. Each time these people have been joined together, great things have happened. We've been hoping for such a union for over sixteen years now."

An uncontrollable urge to smile came over her. After years of only seeing pity on the faces of her friends and teachers when they'd noticed her deformity, here was a man who saw hope. She could only imagine what her father would say if he'd heard these words. She knew that he'd be beaming with pride. Undoubtedly, he'd had a hunch that she was special in some way. Otherwise, he wouldn't have encouraged her so much with his whacky theories and carted her off to all of these ancient sites. And what about her uncle? He definitely knew something but apparently not enough, or else he would have handled matters differently back at the caves. She reached for the compass on her neck. It wasn't there.

"But what does the necklace mean?"

"Ah yes, the necklace. It is very powerful. It was stolen from our ancestors thousands of years ago by another tribe. This tribe separated from us during The Second Catastrophe. The one where mountains were swallowed by oceans and lakes moved like rivers. This tribe thought that it was a sign from The Gods and decided to part ways, never to return."

"But what's its significance?"

"Let me show you, my dear."

CHAPTER FIFTY-FOUR

THE LOST TRIBE

The expedition moved through the jungle in a single line. Joe had bought provisions, including a few alpacas to help transport supplies, and hired four extra Indian guides to help navigate through the thicket. It was always a precarious situation with hired hands, as you never knew whether you were getting experienced escorts or just lowlife swindlers waiting for the right opportunity to rob you blind. Joe eliminated many of the prospects with his own brand of judgment. One Indian, for instance, made the mistake of saying that he'd worked with a friend of Joe's years before. When Joe questioned the man a little further and caught him in a lie, he gutted him like a fish while the others watched. He was pretty confident that the crew who made the cut would be no problem.

The lead scout appeared out the of woods and raced over to him. They exchanged a few words about the path ahead as Father Delanda moved in closer. He'd held up pretty well on the journey considering his age. Although they couldn't convince him to relinquish the black robe, he did agree to wear boots instead of sandals.

"What does he say?"

Joe turned to the priest and replied, "He said there is a rock that's very big ahead."

The father looked over to Tana and signaled the two officers to bring him forward. The prince had showed no desire to flee his captors during the expedition. Instead, he'd seemed to completely relish every moment of the journey back into his homeland. Having donned a ponytail and painted red and yellow stripes on his face and chest, the young man gave off an appearance that not only frightened the officers but also terrified the guides. They knew that it was his way of communicating with the Indians hiding in the bushes and watching their every move.

"The scout says that there's a big rock up ahead. Are we on the right path?" asked the priest.

"We are," said Tana. "We should rest for a while and eat before moving forward. Once we're in the tunnels, there won't be any reason to eat."

Father Delanda hesitated to ask why. He didn't want to scare his men any more than they were already. They'd fought pesky insects, poisonous snakes, diarrhea, smothering humidity, and an occasional torrential rain over the past three days of traveling. This, along with the constant markers of skeletons hanging from trees on the trail, was enough to make them all a bit edgy.

"Very well, then, we'll rest for the night."

Joe dispatched one guide to gather wood to build a fire while the others erected lean-tos. He pulled the lever back on the chamber of his rifle and said, "I go find dinner."

Don Carlos and Leslie found a spot close by to sit. He'd managed to keep out of the limelight as much as possible on the trip. The Bolivian was used to long hikes, but tromping through the untamed rainforest was a little more than his plump body could handle. Between the small pimple-like lesions on his arms that itched to no end, compliments of a mob of almost invisible black pium flies, and the fungus fermenting in his shoes from the moist heat, he was noticeably miserable. Luckily, he'd brought his own stash of coca leaves to relieve the pain.

Leslie, on the other hand, showed no signs of exhaustion. She'd been so motivated by her ranting tirade to Father Delanda that it sparked something inside of her she never knew existed. Nothing this exciting had ever happened to her in her whole life. She recalled a few stories that her father had told about the war but they paled in comparison. She was also infatuated with Tana Nara. They'd spoken a few times on the journey, but it was mainly chitchat. The officers never strayed far enough away to allow her to ask the questions she really wanted answered.

She glanced over to the boy and said to Don Carlos, "I'm going over to visit with our new friend."

The boy was grinding a combination of plant leaves and the fruit from a nearby tree into a homemade pestle. He handed it to the officers and gestured for them to eat it. "Go ahead, it will get rid of your diarrhea." They sniffed the concoction and shrugged their shoulders. Anything would be better than the constant shivers, headaches, and bowel movements they'd been experiencing over the last few days. They both swallowed a couple of bites and looked at each other. At first, it tasted pretty good and went down easy. But soon, its healing powers kicked in. Within a few seconds, their faces turned blue and they took off into the forest to vomit.

Leslie sat down next to the prince and smiled. "You're quite the survivalist there. Did they teach you that back home?"

"They taught me the ways of many things."

She looked from side to side to see if anyone was watching. When she felt that the coast was clear, she whispered to Tana, "I've been waiting for those guards to leave so I could actually talk to you about my daughter."

"I know. That's why I gave them the medicine."

They both smiled. Leslie asked, "So what can you tell me about Renee?"

"She is kind and very strong. She will do well out here. Plus, she's with a man they call Jason. He's protecting her."

"Jason? Where'd they meet?"

"In jail, I believe, where Father Delanda put them. One was there by choice but the other was not."

Leslie looked worried. Her motherly instincts were telling her that she should be concerned. The thought of this strange older man running around the jungle with her daughter was more than enough to rattle her cage.

Tana laid his hand on her arm and said, "Don't worry, he's a good man. He will protect her."

Leslie nodded. "You're probably right." She was silent for a few seconds as this news sunk it. Then she lightly placed her hand on his and whispered, "I need to tell you something. I think we're related somehow."

Her statement slapped at him so unexpectedly that he leaned away. As the words sunk in, he wasn't quite sure what to think of this rambunctious American.

"What makes you think that?"

She leaned toward him and said, "Renee has the same number of toes that you do." Then she held up six fingers.

His eyes lit up. Leslie had no idea what this statement meant to him. As far as he knew, he didn't have any relatives. His elders had brought him up from childhood and told him that his family had died from yellow fever when he was very young. According to them, he was the only survivor and lucky to be alive. This had been a tough pill to swallow growing up. There were no memories, no stories, no brothers or sisters to fight with, and no family heirlooms to pass on. Even just having friends was a difficult task for an elite member of the Ugha Mongulala tribe. The few who had tried over the years never stayed around long for some reason.

No one could understand what it was like being constantly surrounded by priests and leaders prodding you and talking about you as if you weren't there. No one could fathom the pressure put upon a young ruler, who was "destined," at least in scripture, to lead his people and restore them to greatness.

He regained his composure and said, "How did she come about these six toes?"

"I don't know for sure, but it has something to do with my real father, who also happens to be Don Carlos's real father."

"I see. I wasn't quite sure what your relationship was with him. I mean brother and sister or cousin." Tana peered over to Don Carlos, who was cleaning out his boots and rubbing the lesions on his soles with salve. "Where does your family come from originally?"

"Don is from La Paz. He grew up somewhere over by Tiahuanaco."

The prince nodded. "That makes sense."

"Makes sense how?"

"There's a story about my people that has been handed down by word of mouth over the centuries. You won't find much reference to it in your books or libraries. Over ten thousand years ago, a catastrophic earthquake hit Peru. The ground shook so violently that the great Lake Titicaca actually moved thousands of feet away from Tiahuanaco. Not only did it move away, but it moved downward too. One of the Twelve Great Tribes was separated from the rest and left on its own there. When the leaders tried to convince them to come back, they refused. They believed that The Gods had sent them a sign to go it alone. Thus, this tribe—or might I say, *your* tribe—forever severed its ties with my people."

"Your story sounds a lot like the one we have in our culture about the city of Atlantis, which supposedly disappeared into the ocean."

"Indeed, they might have happened at the same time."

Leslie paused for a moment before asking, "What are they called—this tribe, that is?"

"They are called the Amautus tribe, or as you would say in English, 'The Tribe That Lives On The Water.'"

"And that explains the six toes?"

"Not completely. That's a story for another time."

CHAPTER FIFTY-FIVE
CONFIRMATION

The next morning, Joe Del Diaz awoke early. He'd been keeping a close eye on the prince during the whole trip. Now that they were near his homeland, the possibility that the boy would take off in the middle of the night was stronger than ever. Joe wasn't about to let that happen.

Tana had other ideas, though. He liked having home court advantage. In his own backyard, he was in complete control. All it would take is one signal of the hand and his warriors would be by his side in an instant. He'd heard their birdcalls and seen signs along the trail telling him that they were nearby. His plan would have worked perfectly had Leslie not shown up. That complicated matters. She could easily be caught in the crossfire of an attack or held as a hostage. That wasn't something he wanted on his conscience. He knew that Renee had already lost her father just days before. Losing her mother so soon afterward would most certainly send her over the edge.

They ate breakfast and gathered their belongings as a light mist began to fall. The two guards brought the prince over to Joe and the priest as instructed. Leslie and Don Carlos inconspicuously moved in closer to listen as the padre spoke.

"OK, my son, are you able to guide us from here?"

Tana nodded. Father Delanda was fully aware that he was taking a big gamble by trusting the boy. Everything was going too smoothly, and he knew how tricky the boy could be. He wasn't quite sure what Tana was up to yet, but he was willing to take it a little further. Besides, he didn't have much of a choice, as the prince was the only person who knew where they were going.

"This necklace that the German girl has taken. Should we be concerned about it?"

"I'm not sure," said the young Indian. "I haven't seen it. What do you know about it?"

"From what I was told, it was taken off an ancient Indian king from a cave in Tiahuanaco. I believe it has special powers." He turned toward Don Carlos and said, "Maybe our companion here can tell us more."

Don knew this moment would eventually come. He was surprised that it hadn't happened sooner. The fact that he'd managed to get this far into the jungle without being exposed made him feel confident enough that he'd be able to lie his way out of any situation. Still, the look on Leslie's face was hard to ignore. His cover was blown, and he knew there'd be plenty of questions later. He hadn't really thought of a good enough alibi to tell them, though. No matter what he came up with, it still didn't hide the fact that he was the one who took them to Tiahuanaco in the first place. So he decided to do what he did best: play dumb.

"Please, *señor*, you give me too much credit. I wish I knew more."

Father Delanda looked to Joe Del and nodded. His suspicions about the chubby Bolivian had been confirmed. Renee had told him enough about the ordeal in the cave for him to piece together the rest of the story. He'd concluded that Don Carlos knew plenty about this artifact and was probably behind her father's death. Something told him that this man was not to be trusted. Joe nonchalantly walked around the group, grabbed Don by his shirt, and lifted him into the air. Then he took out his knife and placed it against his left ear.

"*Un momento, un momento,*" Don cried as he cracked a halfhearted smile. "I remember now."

Joe lowered him to the ground but didn't let go of his shirt. Leslie moved away a few steps and was silent. The priest folded his hands together and said, "Please continue."

Don wiggled his shoulders and tried to get comfortable. "I remember seeing this necklace back in the caves. It was round and about so big with all of these strings hanging from it. It was rough on the edges but smooth inside. Looked like it was made of gold. It indeed has many powers—but I know not what they are."

Father Delanda reached down for his backpack, pulled out a picture, and said, "Did it look like this?"

He handed Don the worn-out photo from Sister Margarita. Don studied it for a few seconds and fought back the urge to show his emotions. It was almost exactly like the necklace from Tiahuanaco, except the markings appeared to be inverted. "It is very close, Father. This necklace looks larger, but the pattern looks the same."

He handed the photo back and the priest quickly returned it to his bag to keep it from getting wet. Leslie, who'd been very reserved up to this point, had seen enough and decided that she needed some answers.

"Hold on here a minute, Father. I think I deserve to know what's going on."

The priest looked to Joe, who'd released Don Carlos and was quietly approaching Renee's mother, and said, "You certainly do, Mrs. Gorman. It's quite simple, though. Your beloved brother here—or should I say, half brother—I believe is responsible for your husband's death."

Joe moved in and grabbed her by the arms before she could pounce on Don Carlos. Father Delanda continued, "Now, now, now, my dear, this is just speculation. The only person who really knows is your daughter, so until we talk to her we can't be sure."

He pulled the photo out of his pocket again and continued. "Whatever happened there in that cave had something to do with a necklace very similar to this one. A very powerful one." He lifted the picture up and placed it near her face. "Does this ring a bell?" Leslie gazed at the photo and shook her head. "I didn't think so."

He returned it to his bag. "I warned you not to come, Mrs. Gorman. The jungle is no place for a mother." At that moment, the slight drizzle that had been falling since daylight turned into a steady downpour. "You may still be of some value to us in finding your daughter, but I suggest that you mind your manners from now on." He motioned toward the prince and added, "Tie them both up—together."

Joe dragged Leslie over next to Tana and secured their arms together with a rope. The prince wasn't sure what to think of this. Was this the break he was looking for or the last nail in the coffin?

CHAPTER FIFTY-SIX

THE SIGN

The expedition marched off with Prince Tana and Leslie in front, followed closely by the two officers, Joe, the priest, and Don. The other guides made up the rear. Tana was loosely tied to Leslie around the waist. This prevented him from running away but also slowed the whole group down whenever they had to maneuver under a bush or tree. That, along with the newly formed mud puddles and never ending array of tree roots that slithered across the slippery pathway, made traveling that much more tricky. They heard a series of haunting birdcalls off in the distance followed by movement in the brush. When the prince raised his left arm into the air and grabbed his elbow with his right hand, the noises immediately ceased.

This spooked even Joe, as he knew exactly who was making the sounds. He'd seen the signs hanging from trees all along the trail and the remnants of old campfires. He'd also heard the stories over the years on how a tribe of wild cannibals protected the "chosen people" who lived underground. They were known to capture, torture, and eventually eat any trespassers who invaded their area. Why the boy was being so cooperative and complacent still mystified him. He kept a pistol pointed at Tana's back for insurance.

After a half hour of walking, the rain finally ceased, allowing streaks of sunlight to drip down onto the jungle floor. They came across a gigantic rock that stood thirty-five feet in height and was wedged firmly into the hillside, blocking the pathway. The prince stopped in front of it and addressed the group.

"Now comes the difficult part. We must climb."

"Climb. Isn't there a path we can take to the top?" asked the priest.

"No. It's not supposed to be easy, Father. If you wish, you can wait here."

Father Delanda shook his head, tightened his belt, and said, "I can handle it." He motioned for the two officers to untie Leslie and Tana. "Remember, we will be right behind you."

Tana grinned and returned his gaze to the rock. As he took his first step up, he shouted, "I must warn you, though. It's not the climb up that's treacherous. It's the climb down."

He started up slowly in a serpentine pattern, taking care to ensure that his footing for the next step was solid. Twice he almost slipped on loose rocks, sending them tumbling down on the others. The priest went next, followed closely by Joe, who helped him keep his balance and gave him an extra push when needed. The rest of the party tied off the alpacas and left behind what they couldn't carry. They climbed one by one to the peak, where they got their first glimpse of the valley off in the distance. It was hard to gauge just how large it was with the canopy of tall trees, overgrown vines, and thick brush blocking their view. Yet when they felt the wind blasting in their faces, they knew it was much bigger than it looked.

As they gazed down at the backside of the rock, they understood what the boy meant. The whole boulder was wet and covered with moss. A constantly running stream of water poured out onto the valley floor from a hundred different places inside the rock. Weaving underneath the miniature waterfalls was a series of canals and ridges meandering along and eventually draining into the pool of water below.

Leslie was the first to comment. "There's no way I'd make it down there without breaking my neck."

Tana chuckled and said, "Many men have—because they don't know the secret."

With that, he jumped with his arms out to his side and landed within a couple feet of a boulder on the bottom. Leslie gasped as he hit the ground, noticing just how close he came to cracking his skull on the edge of the rock. A short sucking sound reminiscent of a croaking frog followed as his body sunk up to his armpits into the mud. The only thing that kept him from submerging completely underground was the fact that he kept his arms out and steady when he landed.

He shuffled back and forth and found his way to the banks of the mud pool. Then he walked over to one of the small waterfalls and stood underneath it until all of the mud had rinsed off of his clothing. While shaking the water off his head, he looked up and shouted, "You try it. Just make sure you don't jump too far out—but make sure it's far enough away from the rock."

When Tana had jumped, Joe immediately fumbled around with his holster trying to retrieve his revolver. It almost fell to the ground as the sudden reaction also made him lose his footing for a brief moment. *This boy is very tricky*, he thought.

One by one, they plunged into the thick mud and then pushed themselves over to the shoreline. They tossed their backpacks and anything else that they wanted to keep dry to the others already on the ground. The shower felt good, as it had been days since they'd had a real opportunity to clean up properly. Everyone, including Leslie, stripped down to their underwear and rinsed out their clothing thoroughly. As they waited for their clothes to dry, the guides gathered snacks of fruits and nuts from nearby trees.

An hour later, the team packed up and moved on. A kaleidoscope of multicolored parrots and macaws shifted from branch to branch as they passed by. Off to the left was a large, booming waterfall that scattered a light mist into the air. Barely visible in the middle of that was a smaller waterfall that cascaded gently into the large pool below it. They descended into the clearing along a very narrow and dense path. A series of vines and roots on the embankment seemed to be holding hands with the vibrant river flowing alongside it.

"Stay behind each other," yelled the boy.

When they made it to the valley floor, an immense structure with three arches greeted them as the road leveled off. They began to notice peculiarly shaped rocks and formations under the layers of vegetation along the trail. Most had been completely swallowed up by the brush around them but a few exposed surfaces peeked out here and there. A column of black stone rising thirty feet into the air stood on each side of the path as they moved to the center. Under the straddling vines, they recognized the outline of a human body on a tall statue with obelisks positioned on each corner around it. What appeared to be an arm was stretched out and pointing north.

"What is this place?" said the priest.

Prince Tana Nara stopped and said, "This is the ancient city of Akakor. We are standing in the field where my people used to play games and gather. Up there is where the warriors would stand guard and look down over the valley. Over there is the palace."

"I don't see anything," said Leslie.

"Me do," said Joe. "Me see plenty."

The boy walked over to a mound of vines standing about fifteen feet tall. He ripped down the strands one after another until the gray surface of a structure appeared underneath. He kicked away a few more creepers and walked into a doorway.

"Oh my God," exclaimed Leslie.

She ran over to the building and entered behind him. A couple of bats flew out through the opening directly over her head, causing her to duck down quickly. Their ghastly sounding squeal echoed throughout the valley. Inside they found a few vines creeping along the cracks and window holes, but most of the room was still visible. There was a stove made of rock and mortar in the corner and a fireplace on the other side. A rock table sat in the middle. On the upper half of the walls was a thin plate of golden wallpaper stretching from one end to the other. The metal was pressed so closely to the rock that she could see the contours of the stone. The gold gave off a very warm yellowish glow that illuminated the whole room. There were a few drawings carved into the center. She brushed away the dust and tried to read the symbols but couldn't.

"Amazing. This room is lit better than my house." She rubbed the inscription and asked, "What's it say?"

Father Delanda, Don, and Joe were now standing by the doorway peering in. The prince looked at the wall and smiled. He knew very well how to read the ancient petroglyphs. In his mind, he traced the backward *E* and connected it to the *X*. Then he transposed the *P*, which crisscrossed the *S* and *E*. Finally, he disconnected the *T*'s and backward *A*'s.

The next symbol was different. It was made up completely of letters from another language that had been incorporated into his native tongue—just like the first word, but arranged differently. None of the letters overlapped each other but instead they connected side by side, creating one seamless line of scripture. Unless you knew where the letters began and ended, you'd be lost trying to translate them into words. The prince connected the Greek-looking letters, some of which were upside down, and completed the word.

"It says, 'Welcome home.'"

"Was this your home?" asked Leslie.

"I don't know. Maybe."

Tana wasn't expecting the question. He didn't know what else to say. As he felt the warmth of the light reflecting off the walls around him, he wondered if it really was his home—or, at least his parents' home at one time—and for good reason.

When he was twelve, a guard was given the task of teaching Tana the art of combat. For weeks, they met and worked above ground in Akakor for long hours until the prince was fully trained. One day as they were taking a break, the prince wandered into the stone hut. The guard came over and scolded the boy for leaving his side. He told Tana that he was forbidden from entering the house. When the prince pushed him for a reason why, the guard finally relented and said, "The ghosts that live here know you too well."

The guard wouldn't say anymore after that, but the boy knew what he meant. As the years went by, he managed to sneak back into the house whenever possible. Each time he did, a peculiar sensation came over him—a sense of calm and serenity, a feeling that someone was looking out for him.

"We should go," said the prince. "It's almost time."

Then he turned around and left the building. He continued leading them further down into the valley floor. The morning sunlight was beginning to filter in and trickle across the side of the mountain. He moved around in a circle and studied the light patterns as they slowly marched down to the hill. He sensed that the moment was near.

Located in the center of the valley was what appeared to be a square. In the middle was a column of stones covered with weeds and vines. Off to one side was a huge structure covered in dense foliage. Once they approached it, they realized that it was shaped like a pyramid. There were steps on each side leading up to the middle. It was four stories high.

On each side of the pyramid was a set of mounds about three feet in height. Most of them were covered with brightly colored purple flowers with long, yellow strands shooting out of the middle. Tana searched until he found the one mound with no flowers at all. Then he ripped off the greenery clinging to its sides and brushed off the top. It was a sundial of some sort.

The others moved in for a better look, but he waved them off. "Please do not block the sunlight." Tana looked up into the sky and positioned himself on the east side, away from the sun's reflection. "We must now wait. This will happen quickly so I'll need your help. I need everyone to stand in a circle around me but stand back about twenty feet."

The group followed his orders and spread out around the sundial. He directed a few of them to move even further away, over near a set of bush-like structures scattered throughout the area. Then he stared at the sundial and waited. After a few minutes, the sun's rays inched up onto the surface. He watched intently as they slowly blanketed the face of the rock.

When the sunlight reached the dial in the middle, he rushed up and studied it intently. Then he pointed to Leslie and said, "My friend, please clear off the boulder behind you to the left. The tall one."

Leslie hopped on top of a smaller rock next to it and started tearing off the vines. It revealed a dark black stone with several lines and drawings carved deep into its surface.

"OK," said Tana, "you can move away now. Thank you."

Leslie jumped down off the boulder and peered up at the tall black slab in front of her. The sunlight crept along the bottom of the rock ever so slightly. Tana quietly stepped toward it, and the others followed behind him. Within seconds, the light was reflecting off a few of the crevices, revealing lines and symbols. Most of the drawings remained dark, however.

The prince knelt down to the ground, grabbed a stick, and began drawing the symbols he was seeing. He drew frantically as the sunlight completely covered the black surface, turning it into a gigantic mirror. Leslie saw her reflection in the rock and noticed just how tattered her hair had become. She brushed it back with her hands but it did no good.

As the sunlight drifted away, the drawings faded with it. The prince stood and looked down at his sketches. Then he looked up at the mountain and studied it until he found what he was looking for. He smiled and said, "I know the way from here."

CHAPTER FIFTY-SEVEN

SHUFFLING THE DECK

Tana pointed up to the mountain off in the distance and said, "We must go up there."

They followed a path of loose gravel away from the valley floor and up the steep mountainside. It moved from side to side through the overgrown weeds and had even Joe panting before long.

When they reached the next landing, the boy surveyed the area until he spotted the rock he'd noticed from the ground. There were markings with lines and half-circles inscribed into it about a half-inch deep. No doubt they meant something to Tana, but to the rest of the group they might as well have been Chinese.

"Please stay in a single line," the prince said. "No one can enter any other way." He then walked over to a large boulder off to the side. While placing both hands on its surface, he slowly scanned the area with his fingers. Once he'd found the spot he was looking for, he repositioned his body so that it was perpendicular to the face of the rock. His shoulders sunk down as he dropped his head against it. With a gentle swooshing motion, his hands moved in a counterclockwise direction, almost like he was turning a dial. The boulder rumbled and began to move sideways. Behind it, a thin opening appeared. He continued to push until the tunnel was completely open.

No one moved. They were both apprehensive and in awe. Father Delanda's eyes lit up like a child's on Christmas morning. It was the moment he'd been waiting for. He looked back and nodded to one of the officers, who nonchalantly walked away from the group and ducked behind a boulder. Leslie was the only one who noticed the guard sneaking away, but she didn't say a word. The priest had made it perfectly clear that she was disposable. As the man vanished into the forest, she saw him pull something out of his backpack.

Don Carlos perked up too as soon as the opening appeared. He was perfectly capable of moving his own boulders; still, it was an amazing sight to see. He thought about how incredibly intelligent these ancient engineers must have been to come up with such a mechanism.

Tana walked over to the newly created entrance. He glanced at Joe just to see if the pistol was still pointed at his back. After sizing up the hole and determining that it was safe to enter, he said, "OK, it's only wide enough for one person at a time, so make a single-file line."

Joe moved up right behind the prince and entered with him into the tunnel. The priest followed behind. Intuitively, Leslie knew that she should be next. Call it female intuition or just a hunch, she quickly maneuvered herself in front of the other scouts and smiled. They politely let her pass, as would any gentleman. Don Carlos took that opportunity to squeeze in right behind her.

After entering, Tana stood off to the side of the doorway and watched the others come through. As soon as Don Carlos made it through the archway, he jumped to the middle and planted himself right in front of the scouts. The boulder shifted sideways with amazing speed closing the opening within seconds, and spinning the prince completely around the other way. The rest of the expedition was caught off guard. Their hopeless cries were heard for only a few seconds as the door slid shut in front of them. Then there was total silence.

Joe grabbed the boy's shoulders and said, "Why you do?"

Father Delanda stepped up and said, "Young man, you are trying my patience. Another stunt like that and I will let Joseph have his way with you. Do we understand?"

Tana looked up and said, "There are reasons for everything I do. Some of them are unexplainable, but they have to be done in order to navigate these tunnels. I don't expect you to understand and you can do what you want to me, but please realize that I am the only one who can safely guide you where we're going." He then glanced at each of them individually before adding, "Only so many people can enter the tunnels safely at one time. They would have not made it out alive had they all entered with us."

What he failed to mention was that the group of hostile Indians who'd been following them for the last few days would soon take care of the ones on the outside. They were not going anywhere.

PART SIX

THE LOST CITY

CHAPTER FIFTY-EIGHT
THE CHAMBER

The high priest led Renee down a flight of stairs to the lower level. He turned to the guards and said in his native tongue, "*Wächter punka.*" They acknowledged the order and marched back up the stairwell to stand guard and prevent anyone else from coming down.

She was given a golden garment to wear. Its design was something right off a fashion-show ramp, with wide and bulky shoulders and a midriff layered with different shades of yellow. She could tell by the fading on the elbows that it was old but the stitching appeared to be still fully intact. The fabric had a texture that was brawny yet soft—almost a cross between leather and felt.

"That belonged to Lhasa, the exalted son of The Gods. He ruled over our kingdom after the Third Great Catastrophe. The period where the waters rose and rivers ran backward."

"The Great Flood," whispered Renee.

"It was with his guidance that the kingdom was rebuilt and restored to greatness after the waters receded. Before the Third Catastrophe, our people experienced thousands of years of barbarism. These were called the Years of Blood: a very troubling time where many souls drifted and thousands of lives were lost. Lhasa brought us law and order and established the Twelve Great Tribes that ruled our kingdom. It is with this garment that you'll see your fate."

Renee was led into a chamber that seemed to defy the laws of physics. It was a fairly small area, but every time she looked in a different direction, she got the impression that the room was expanding. There were no real corners or edges to distinguish the walls from the ceilings, and everything had a dark blue tint to it. In the middle was a stone slab with a bowl of bread and a golden chalice sitting on top.

The high priest picked the food off the table and said, "These are the signs of life and death. Please, eat and drink."

He handed Renee a cup of juice and instructed her to drink it. She hesitated at first. "What is this?"

"San Pedro cactus, from the mountains. It will help you on your journey."

Soon, the hallucinogenic effects of the plant kicked in. She felt a little queasy, but Bartholomew gestured to her to eat and drink the rest of her food. That seemed to settle her stomach. He pulled the amulet out of his pocket and walked over to a nearby fire pit. Then he held the necklace over the flame until a black coal-like substance began to cover it.

As he dangled the medallion over the fire, he said, "When the great Inca emperor Atahualpa was being held for ransom by Pizarro's men, his wife used the Black Mirror to foresee his death. Not just anyone can summon its powers. It has to be created by the hands of a child—or a youthful virgin, which I assume you…"

Renee blushed as she lowered her head and nodded.

"Very good."

When the amulet was completely covered with black soot, he pulled it away from the flame. Then he returned to where Renee was sitting and said, "With this necklace you'll be able to see your place in our kingdom." He quickly touched the necklace to see if it had cooled enough and added, "I cannot accompany you on this part of the journey. You must do it alone. Please sit here until The Gods summon you. They will tell you what you need to do next." He placed the talisman around her neck and left the room without saying another word. Renee was now alone.

She sat in complete silence for a long time. The full effects of the cactus juice had infiltrated every part of her body. She found herself consciously forcing each breath in and out. When she forgot to breathe, her body shut down completely. Moments later, she would suddenly wake up and gasp for air. Eventually, she found her rhythm and relaxed enough to be able to breathe on her own again. Next, her vision went out of focus. She tried hard to keep her eyes open but to no avail. Several images of animals began drifting through her mind. There were gigantic birds flying through the air accompanied by a jaguar jumping from rock to rock. She saw all of the animals that were immortalized in stone statues from the main hall in the palace.

Right when she was beginning to feel comfortable with her surroundings, a voice in her head instructed her to rise and go to the next room. Instinctively, she stood up and knew which way to go. It was as if another person was leading her by an invisible leash.

This chamber was covered with many strange and colorful objects. The bright lights reflecting off the shimmering ornaments were dazzling. There were sheets of silver, gold and bronze on the walls cut into the shapes of rectangles, squares, triangles, and circles. Some were carved in the form of humans with heads that resembled the sun and stars. Images of serpents, birds, and pyramids were crudely engraved into other pieces. There was even a figure that looked eerily similar to a sperm cell floating in a petri dish.

At first, she wasn't sure where the lights were coming from. After her eyes adjusted, she noticed eight rectangular blocks made of a transparent material that looked to be about seven feet long and three feet high. There were beams of light radiating from underneath and dispersing throughout the chamber.

Inside of each block was a naked body lying down as if sleeping. She counted four men and four women. They were submersed in a yellowish liquid that rose up and covered their faces and chests. The bodies showed no signs of decomposition or aging. It was as if they were in a suspended state of consciousness between life and death. But what really caught her eye was the fact that each one of them had six fingers and six toes.

A voice inside her head instructed her to walk over to a table in the middle of the room and sit down. She then removed the necklace, held it in her hands, and began rubbing the black soot off onto her palms. Her hands worked tirelessly until every bit of dust was transferred to her skin and streaks of gold returned to the amulet. Then she placed it back around her neck and stared down at her cupped hands.

She gazed at them for a long time. After a few minutes, her pupils dilated to the point where her vision blurred. As she concentrated on her hands, they transformed the opaque, blackened contours of her skin into a glossy mirror. Her reflection was the first image that came into focus followed by several bright colors. Gradually other apparitions appeared that seemed to transcend beyond the boundaries of space and time. She simultaneously saw herself as a toddler holding onto her father's hand as they crossed a bridge and years later playing near a stream. As she stared into her palms and felt her body lift out of its skin, the walls around her began to speak.

CHAPTER FIFTY-NINE

REVELATIONS

The temple chamber glowed brightly. Renee felt the warmth on her face as white light shot out of her hands and the images grew more distinct. The coal-like reflective surface in front of her had softened its hue and now displayed these images like a miniature television monitor.

She heard a female voice say, "Welcome, my name is Oryana. I am from another world: a place free from feelings of happiness and sorrow, heat and cold; a place where no one can be destroyed by death; where no weapon can hurt, no fire can burn, no water can drown, and no heat can sear. By your presence here in this chamber, it is confirmed that you are one with us; you are Ugha Mongulala."

Renee moved her face in closer as sparkling lights soon appeared before her. Clouds of smoke descended onto the ground and people emerged from the smolder. The female voice began to narrate over the images. "We came to this world some fifteen thousand years ago to escape certain death. Our people had been defeated and overrun by foreign invaders. We managed to elude capture and break away right before they destroyed everything we'd known."

Her voice cracked as she continued. "Unfortunately, the invaders discovered our plan and followed us. Our only hope was to hide. We dug a series of tunnels deep under the earth's surface and hid there for many years. They could not penetrate the soil with their weapons and thus we were able to survive. But the attack caused catastrophic changes to your planet's landscape. The axis of the earth shifted dramatically, causing oceans to rise and temperatures to fluctuate."

The end of the Ice Age, thought Renee. She tried to absorb all of this new information while still keeping it in perspective. She wasn't sure if what she was seeing and hearing was actually happening or if it was just part of the effects of the cactus juice. She kept conjuring up memories of her father relating bits and pieces of stories he'd read in the Von Däniken books. At the time, she thought it was all gibberish but she still listened because she loved the way he told a story.

The voice continued as different images illuminated out of her palms. Holograms of men and women walked by her so close that she could feel their bodies' warmth and hear them breathe. Animals bounced from one finger to another and then leaped over her head. She could actually smell the ocean. It was as if she was physically in the center of each scene.

"Here we started a new life after the threat was gone. We taught your people many skills and lived amongst them. We fought alongside you in battles and survived several transitions. Eventually, we were able to reestablish contact with the survivors from our world using the resources available to us here. They told us that it was safe to return, so most of us left. But a few decided to stay. We knew that humans were destructive by nature and needed some guidance. Our brothers and sisters dispersed throughout the planet. Some settled in the Mediterranean, some in the Middle East, some as far as Asia.

"Around six thousand years ago, our people realized that their time here on earth was ending. After all, we weren't really immortal like your ancestors tried to portray us. It was decided that we must create a long-lasting bond with the natives in order to assure your success of surviving. Unfortunately, the consummation between humans and my people only bore a few offspring. Thus began the creation of Ugha Mongulala.

"As time went on and we slowly disappeared from the earth, chaos overtook the tribes. Thousands were killed and murdered as the tribesmen fought between each other and forgot the lessons they'd been taught by their ancestors. It was then that I knew what needed to be done. Your people were not ready to handle most of the knowledge we'd brought with us. Our tools were being used *against* each other instead of *for* each other. When my time had come, I left this world with that knowledge—and ensured that your ancestors would not find it again.

"Although there were few of Ugha Mongulala blood who survived the union, descendants did rise up from the dead and were born again. Every time a man and woman with the mark appeared together, greatness was restored to our culture."

Six fingers and six toes, thought Renee. It was now beginning to make sense.

"Only four times has a couple been born in the same generation with Ugha Mongulala blood. We now welcome you as part of the Fifth Union. Hold my hand and I'll take you through The Gateway into another world where you will learn about where it is we come from."

Images of a giant rock formation on a remote mountainside appeared before them. In the middle, a twenty-five-foot-wide square section was cut into the stone. Inside the square was an even smaller indentation almost a foot deep that closely resembled a *T*. Renee reached out for Oryana's hand but couldn't quite grasp it. It was mushy and rubbery—just like back in the tunnel when Lena tried to hold onto her. Oryana noticed that something was wrong too. It was then that she realized Renee only had five fingers. "Your hands. They're not complete."

"I know."

She looked at Renee's pendant. "There's something keeping our two worlds from becoming one. Maybe it's your hands, but maybe it's your necklace."

"What should I do?" asked Renee. She felt a coolness come over her, starting in her hands and soon spreading through her whole body. The room grew darker and everything again had a tint of blue to it.

"You must go to the land of seven chains covered with granite"—her image was now fuzzy and flickering sporadically; Renee felt herself coming out of the trance—"where a great lake lined with golden banks once lay, it...will...revealed..." There was more static. "Beware of the tunnels...The laws of our Gods...are not what they seem...remember...are not what they seem."

CHAPTER SIXTY
THE PATH WE TAKE

Joe Del Diaz pulled out his flashlight and clicked it on. After a few moments, he realized that he didn't need it because there was enough natural light coming in from somewhere. He knew better than to try and figure out why though. These were gifts from The Gods that couldn't be explained.

The group was still a little traumatized and absorbing what had just transpired. Father Delanda did a quick head count just to confirm what he already knew. None of the police and guides had made it into the tunnel. As their eyes adjusted to the lighting and the cavern's absolute silence calmed their fears, they started to move around normally.

Leslie rubbed her hand over the walls and exclaimed, "They're as hard as diamonds—and totally sealed." She walked a few steps further and added, "Look, air holes." Two cylinder ducts two feet wide and thirty feet tall jetted up into the ceiling in a spiral pattern. A swift breeze blew on her face as she inhaled a deep breath of fresh air.

The priest, meanwhile, studied the gold discs on the wall reflecting light. They were exact replicas of the two Huascar had given him back in Cuzco. Now he understood their purpose completely. A few feet over was a large bronze scaffold that housed a mirror six feet in height that was covered in dust. Father Delanda casually wiped away a spot and nearly lost his balance as a sensation of vertigo came over him. The startling images that he saw reflecting back appeared to be miles away. It was as if he was looking down a long, deep shaft.

"This is how we used to communicate with each other over long distances," said Tana. "Every month, a tribal chief would relay messages through the mirror using hand signals. It is said that if you look into the mirror long enough, you'll see your own soul."

"More pagan rubbish," the good father said as he peered into the mirror again. The thought of seeing into his own soul was intoxicating, but he knew his penance would be severe if he continued.

"This is amazing," said Leslie. "Where does it lead to?"

"It leads to the underground city of Akakor."

Father Delanda's eyes lit up as he tried to control his excitement. They were almost there. After a lifetime of dispelling rumors and harshly denouncing those who believed that this place existed, he was about to discover it for himself. The trap had been set and was almost ready to spring into action.

Father Delanda motioned the boy to lead them on, but before Tana did, he said, "Now that we're all inside, Padre, you must follow my instructions or else you'll never make it out of here alive. We need to move along side by side in a row instead of walking behind each other."

DOCUMENT 512

The priest knew something was up but couldn't quite figure it out. He stood right beside the prince as they began walking in step. The tunnel was just barely wide enough for all six of them.

The party traveled down into the tunnels for a good hour and a half. They passed by a few seats carved out of rock and a couple of small caverns strewn with eating utensils and blankets. Except for the sounds of their own breath and footsteps, it was absolutely silent. The prince managed to distance himself a few inches away from the priest and stayed very close to the wall. He knew this was his only chance at escape.

A few more minutes went by before Father Delanda noticed that something was wrong. At first, he thought it was just the lighting, but soon realized that the young man's body seemed to be disappearing.

Tana felt the priest's glare upon him and shouted, "Hurry, we're almost there." With that, he sped up. "Faster," he yelled to the others.

The tempo increased to a brisk jog. With every step he took, the boy faded away a little more. Some members of the group jogged faster than others, which allowed him to move even further ahead.

Finally, Father Delanda stopped and said, "Hold on, something's wrong here."

Everyone halted except Tana. He kept jogging along while saying, "Come on, quickly."

They'd all noticed the changes in him now. His body had an almost ghostly appearance to it where the fringes around his arms, legs, and head seemed to glow.

The priest shouted, "Stop!" He motioned to Joe, who reached down for his gold-handled knife and threw it with lightning speed. Leslie screamed as the knife hurled through the air and hit the prince squarely in the back of his rib cage.

Tana didn't immediately feel it. It wasn't a sharp pain like he'd expected. Instead, it felt more like an aching muscle. He reached back and felt a small patch of blood around the wound.

The others stared at the knife with bewilderment. The prince's body was barely visible but the knife was clear as day. When Tana turned and faced them, they could still see it in his back. The pain was discomforting, but not debilitating. He shuffled around a few steps then darted off into the tunnel.

"After him!" yelled the priest. Joe was already sprinting off before the good father could finish his sentence. As the boy ran deeper into the tunnel, his body increasingly vanished from sight. Within a few moments, he'd disappeared completely. Joe stumbled around in circles looking for any clue or sign but eventually gave up and pounded the walls in anger. The prince was nowhere to be found.

CHAPTER SIXTY-ONE
BOUNDARIES

The prince was out of breath. He stopped for a minute and rested. He no longer heard Joe's footsteps behind him. That meant that he'd successfully split away and made it down a completely different path. For a while, he was safe. It would only be a matter of time, though, before the others figured out the secret to breaking through the threshold.

He looked down at his arms and saw that they were there again, in full sight. The rest of his body had also come back into view. Although his breathing was still normal, he knew that the blade was dangerously close to his lungs. He tried to pull it out.

It wouldn't budge. He tried again. For some reason, the knife was stuck and not coming out. Finally, he gave up. It must have something to do with it being thrown from one path and landing in another, he surmised. It was as if the knife was suspended between two worlds and possessed certain qualities of each.

When he'd regained his strength, he set out down the path again. It was only a matter of minutes now before reaching the safety of his kingdom. The light was getting brighter in front of him. He was beginning to hear the familiar jungle noises again. A cloud of fog appeared and surrounded his body.

Then something unexpected happened. The warmth returned to the blood dripping down his back. He reached around and discovered that the wound was now bleeding profusely. The pain was more intense and his breathing became uneven. He staggered and lost his balance. The last thing he remembered before collapsing was the sound of a waterfall in the distance.

CHAPTER SIXTY-TWO

REUNION

"Shhhh...Did you hear that?"

Lena raised her head up and looked around. She'd unknowingly been lying on Jason's chest for most of the night trying to fight off the cold. Jason rubbed his eyes and opened them. His first reaction was to breathe in the sweet smell of her body as it draped over him. Then there was another noise.

He rose up onto his elbows and whispered, "I heard that."

They both got to their knees and peered through the bushes. Near the archway where they'd seen the waterfall was a young man on the ground lying on his stomach. They saw an opening behind him that appeared to be another tunnel exit. Jutting up from his back was a knife.

"It's Tana!" exclaimed Jason.

Lena stood up and brushed off her clothes. Jason and Renee had filled her in on their past encounters with him. By Renee's reaction every time they mentioned his name, Lena could tell there was a special connection. They ran over to the body where she placed her head by his mouth and announced, "He's not breathing."

Jason checked his pulse but there was nothing. "He's still warm." Then he gently touched the area around the knife wound. "He's lost a lot of blood."

Lena looked at Jason, "What do we do?"

"I'm not sure if there's anything we can do. We can try CPR, but that's not gonna replace a blood transfusion or stop any more blood from running out. I don't know if it's a good idea to pull this knife out either."

Jason noticed that the boy's hand was stretched out above his head. Drawn in the sand was the top half of a circle with a line running across the bottom. Next to that was an arrow pointing straight toward the circle. Tana's finger was lying next to the arrow, underneath which were a few marks that, at first glance, didn't resemble much of anything more than random scribbles.

"Look at this." He moved around the body for a closer view. "What do you think it means?"

Lena gazed over his shoulder and said, "I think that's a picture of the tunnel and there's an arrow pointing toward it."

"Yeah, but what's it mean?"

Lena looked back and forth from the boy to the opening and said, "I think it means that there's something in the tunnel we're supposed to see."

"Maybe." Jason stood up, gazed back at the tunnel, and said, "But I think it means there's something back there that *he's* supposed to see."

"Why do you think that?"

"Well, look at the lines underneath his finger. He was working on another drawing before, you know, he keeled over. If you look at what he has already"—Jason lifted up the prince's hand to get a better view—"then you can almost make out a stick person."

"You might be right. It does look like feet and a body."

"Let's move him, then."

They both grabbed an arm and dragged the boy back to the tunnel entrance. When they broke the plane of the opening, they heard a moan. Lena instinctively released his arm and jumped away. Jason wrestled with the added weight and nearly lost his balance.

"What are you doing?"

"I'm sorry. Did you hear that?"

"Yeah, I heard a moan. Let's get him in a little further."

Lena grabbed the boy's arm again. They dragged the prince in another twenty yards when they heard another moan. This time, she managed to hold on. The knife in his back had begun to changed form. It was lighter in color and a little out of focus.

"Look at that," said Lena.

"I see it."

"What's it mean?"

Jason lightly ran his fingers over the knife and said, "I'm not sure, but do you remember what Renee's arm felt like when we separated?"

"Yeah."

"Feel it. Is it the same feeling?"

THE LOST CITY

Lena tried to grab the handle but her fingers squeezed right through it. "Yeah, it feels like Silly Putty, like before."

There was movement. The prince opened his eyes for a few seconds and whispered, "Water."

Jason pulled out his canteen and placed it to the boy's lips. Tana gulped it down too fast and started coughing. He wiped his mouth clean and said, "Thank you."

Lena smiled and said, "Hello."

"You're the woman from Machu Picchu."

"Yes. I'm glad to finally meet you."

"Me too."

She wiped his forehead with a damp rag. "I feel like I've known you forever. I mean, from everything Jason and Renee have told me."

The prince glanced around and asked, "Where's Renee?"

Lena looked to Jason. He closed his canteen and said, "She's in the palace. We were separated in the tunnels and the warriors caught up with her."

The boy nodded. "She's safe, then."

Jason helped him sit up. "I thought we'd lost you back there."

"You did."

"That doesn't make sense. How?"

He struggled to sit up by himself while they both kept a firm grip on his arms. "Because it is the way of The Gods. Each tunnel has its own place in our world. The path you choose determines your fortune. Each one eventually ends up at the same place but a different set of events may follow you down that path. This knife was not from my path."

"I don't get it," said Jason.

"If the knife from the same path had been lodged in my back, then I'd have died in the tunnel. Because it came from another path, its powers were diminished—but only in the tunnel. When I left it, the knife became a regular knife again and, well, you saw what happened to me."

Lena nodded and said, "You said the knife came from another path. How did it end up in your back?"

"I'm not sure who threw it, but most likely it came from the same man who chased us in the church and chased you down the hill at Machu Picchu. I tried to run but couldn't outrun his knife."

"Oh dear," said Lena, "Who else is with him?"

"Just the priest, a man named Don, and Renee's mother."

"Renee's mother?"

The boy nodded.

"How did she get here?"

"I don't know," replied Tana.

"Who's this Don character?" Jason asked.

"I know," answered Lena. "He's Renee's uncle. The man who tried to kill her at Tiahuanaco."

"Well, that can't be good." His eyes met Lena's. They both knew that there was trouble ahead. He looked into the tunnel and added, "So how do we get you out of here?"

The prince was sitting up on his own now and feeling stronger. The pain was still there but not as sharp as before. He looked to his two friends and said, "You don't."

CHAPTER SIXTY-THREE

THE PRINCE'S PARADOX

"What do you mean?" cried Lena and Jason in unison. The prince did his best to smile. He didn't want to worry his friends but knew better than anyone what to expect. The ways of the caves were an intricate part of his people's daily lives.

They'd learned to accept the consequences of its idiosyncrasies just as they'd benefited from its powers.

"If I leave the tunnel, I will die."

"If you stay in the tunnel, you'll live?" asked Jason.

"Yes, at least for a while. I don't know how long," he said. "I'm still losing blood but not as fast as I was outside."

"Why can't we just pull the knife out and patch you up."

"I wish you could, but you can't."

Jason reached behind Tana and tried to grab the handle. The knife had little substance and slipped out of his hands every time he yanked on it. Lena could tell from the look on his face that it was hopeless.

"There's nothing you can do," said the prince. "The only way to remove it is to retrace my steps back to the point of entry. That's not as easy as it sounds. For one thing, the others are probably still looking for me. Plus, I have to follow the path back exactly the way I came. I don't remember much after the knife hit me."

Lena hugged Tana and said, "So what are we supposed to do? We can't just leave you here."

He looked up at her and said, "Can you find Renee and bring her to me?"

"Renee?" asked Jason. He seemed puzzled by this request but Lena understood completely.

"Yes, there's something very important that I must ask her before…well, you know."

"We'll find her," Lena promised.

The prince smiled. He then lay down on his side and relaxed. He needed to rest and save his strength. "I'll be here waiting."

In the distance, they heard footsteps. People were running toward them. They couldn't quite tell how many but it was definitely more than one.

Lena held her breath. She knew it was the search party looking for Tana. What she didn't know was who was on whose side. Renee's mother and maybe Don Carlos might be willing to help them out. The others were a different story. Her charm and good looks fooled the priest once but she was certain that it wouldn't happen again. That left her with only one other weapon: her wits.

"I think they've found the right path."

Jason nodded. The look in Mean Joe Del's eyes as he chased them through the church was still fresh in his mind. "We need to get the hell outta here."

The boy struggle to get up on his knees and said, "I need to disappear."

"How will you do that?" asked Jason.

He smiled and replied, "Just go, quickly."

The footsteps were now very close. They could almost make out the shape of a large man coming their way.

Lena brushed back the hair from Tana's eyes and said, "We'll find Renee. You just stay alive."

"I will," he said. "Please go now, before it's too late."

Jason shook his hand and pulled Lena away. They took off running down the tunnel. Joe's silhouette was slowly taking form. His Mohawk was the first thing Tana noticed. Then there was the revolver in his hand. Tana crawled over to the sidewall and slowly pushed himself up onto his feet. Then he pressed his body against the wall as close as he could while remaining still. His elders had taught him how to become invisible. He just hoped that they'd taught him well enough.

CHAPTER SIXTY-FOUR

THE WORD

The bright lights in the room dimmed. Once again, there was silence. The images Renee had been watching in her hands were now gone and the transparent blocks in front of her were no longer glowing. She reached for the necklace that was still around her neck. Now she knew why her uncle wanted it so badly.

There was commotion coming from the hallway. The high priest entered the room with a couple of guards. He rushed over to Renee and said, "Are you all right, my dear?"

She looked up and replied, "Yes, I'm fine."

They escorted her out of the room and up the staircase. Soon she was back in the main hall where the same crowd from the night before had gathered again. The high priest led her to them as a hush fell over the room. Some of them were on the edge of their seats.

"She has returned," said Bartholomew.

The old lady who'd been staring at her earlier spoke up. "*Iman geschah?*"

The high priest nodded. "They'd like to know what happened. Did you make contact?"

It now made more sense to her. None of them were able to do what she had just done. None of them were part of the bloodline of the original Ugha Mongulala tribe. From the looks on their faces, she saw fear.

"Yes, I did."

The group cheered. People hugged each other and danced around. There was loud laughter and smiles everywhere. Some of them were in tears.

The high priest asked, "Did they tell you what we should do?"

Renee was a bit puzzled with this question. She tried to recall the words from the woman in the chamber. She hesitated to respond. Her answer was not going to make them happy.

"Not really. They said something was missing and that I had to go somewhere…and that the laws of our Gods are not what they seem." She hesitated to say more. The details from the end of her vision, when Oryana's image started fading in and out, were sketchy.

Bartholomew rubbed his chin and said, "I thought that might happen. Something's missing. May I see the necklace again?"

Renee removed the amulet and handed it over. The high priest lifted it up to the light and said, "Yes, something's not right. What I'm not sure of is whether it's part of the necklace or one of the messengers." After studying it awhile longer, he repeated, "'The laws of our Gods are not what they seem.' What does that mean?" He handed it back to the girl and asked, "Can you please tell us if they said anything else?"

"They told me about who they were and where they'd come from—and who I was."

The old lady approached her and spoke again. "Excuse me for not introducing myself. My name is Elsa. It's a pleasure to officially meet you, my dear."

"Me too."

Elsa bowed and added, "Would you please tell us who you are, then?"

"They said that I was one of them."

The old lady smiled and said, "In good words and clear script, it is written. Therefore, it shall be."

"What do you mean?" asked Renee.

THE LOST CITY

The congregation gathered in a circle and conferred in a low murmur. There was heated discussion between a few of the members and obvious dissent, but after a few minutes they all seemed to settle down and agree on what they were going to do next.

The high priest approached Renee. "Years ago, the invaders came to our forest and started raping it of its beauty. Millions of acres were destroyed to make way for farmland and mining. Each time they moved in closer, we moved a little deeper into the jungle. Finally, we ended up at Akakor, the place where it all started. After living there became unsafe, it was decided by the high council to move back into the tunnels of our ancestors. We managed to survive here very well for many decades. Then the climate began to change. Soon, the animals and crops we'd survived on for so many centuries began to disappear."

A smile appeared as he resumed speaking, "Sixteen years ago, we were sent a miracle. Just when we thought our time was over on this planet, Prince Tana Nara came along and the legend of Ugha Mongulala was reborn. We waited and waited for a female to come along but it never happened. We thought that all was lost and eventually sent the prince into the city for help—and then you showed up."

Renee couldn't look Bartholomew in the eye and had to turn away from the whole congregation. She needed to think and digest everything he'd said. This was a lot to absorb in such a short time.

Bartholomew realized that these new revelations were overwhelming. Even so, someone needed to make sure that she knew what was expected of her. He looked to the old lady for guidance. She understood and walked up to Renee, held her hand, and said, "Throughout our history, the birth of both a male and female in the same generation with Ugha Mongulala blood has happened only four times. Each time, our culture has risen back from destruction and achieved greatness. We weren't sure if The Gods would accept you as one of them because you only have five fingers. But you confirmed what we were hoping. Your destiny is our destiny."

Renee could hardly breathe. This news was making her heart pound like a kick drum. She tried to take a few deep breaths and slow down the adrenaline rushing through her veins. She knew what this all meant: they had big plans for her with Prince Tana. Even though she had feelings for the boy, she hadn't known him that long and the scenario of being united together forever was too much to comprehend in such a short time. After all, she was only fifteen years old.

There were so many questions racing through her mind: What would her mother say? Would there be a wedding? Would she have to live underground forever? How could she get out of this situation without upsetting everybody? She didn't know how to respond, but she needed to ask one other question. "So what if I don't want to stay here with the prince?"

Elsa lifted Renee's hand to her chest and said, "Then my people will die."

A group of warriors burst into the room and rushed up to the high priest. They relayed a few words through the crowd that prompted Bartholomew to quickly shout back orders. Then he turned to Renee and said, "It seems that we have an emergency. Your friends are in trouble."

Renee grabbed his sleeve and said, "Then I'm going with you."

CHAPTER SIXTY-FIVE

CATCH OR BE CAUGHT

Lena gasped for air as they both exited the tunnel. There were no signs or sounds of anyone else following them. She bent over and placed her hands on her knees. "What now?"

"I don't know," replied Jason.

"If we get out of this alive, I want you to promise me one thing."

Jason looked away and said, "Let's concentrate on getting out alive first."

She pried her way into his arms and ran her hands through his hair. Then she wrapped a kiss around his lips with such intensity that he couldn't breathe. He could taste the salt dripping off her cheeks as the tears washed away his last line of resistance. There was no use in holding back. He'd never stopped loving her.

Lena laid her head against his chest and pleaded, "Promise me that someday you'll forgive me."

Jason held her close but couldn't speak. His mind was blinking red, yellow, and green all at the same time. He wanted to talk himself through the problem like he'd done so many other times before with his studies, but right now didn't seem like the time or place. Finally, he pulled away and said, "We need to get out of here and find Renee." From within the tunnel, they heard footsteps again. "They're almost here, let's go."

Before they could take off running, Mean Joe Del was upon them. He lunged for Lena and dragged her to the dirt with one arm. Jason stumbled a few steps forward and fell to his knee. He spun back around and dove on top of Joe. The blow knocked him back but the Indian managed to keep his balance. He twirled Jason around like pizza dough and tossed him to the ground. Jason tackled him and tried to knock him off his feet. It was futile. A few seconds later, Joe landed an elbow into Jason's jaw, sending his limp body to the ground.

During the struggle, Lena managed to backpedal a few feet while keeping an eye on the action. Joe looked up after delivering the knockout punch to Jason and liked what he saw. His eyes danced around the curves of her body while she tried her hardest to conceal the fear shivering up and down her spine.

Joe grunted and said, "You no can run." Then he pulled the revolver out from behind his back and pointed it at her chest. "You come here."

Lena kept backing up slowly. She knew that if he caught her it was all over. Dying wasn't going to be half as bad as the torture he'd put her through before killing her. She contemplated what to do when Father Delanda suddenly appeared from behind. He was out of breath and panting as he exited the tunnel. Joe spun around so fast that it startled him. With the revolver pointed at his heart, the priest yelled, "Joe, put that away."

After Joe realized who it was, he quickly refocused on Lena. She'd managed to get a few steps farther away and was about to make a break for it. It was now or never. Joe cocked the gun and shot a couple of rounds down at her feet. The blast made her jump.

"No move!" shouted Joe.

Lena froze.

The priest ambled up and greeted her with a panting smile. "It's very nice to see you again, my dear." He circled around and signaled Joe to lower his weapon. "I'm sorry that you missed your flight."

Lena relaxed her shoulders and let out a nervous chuckle. "Well, I had some unfinished business to take care of."

Joe stepped forward a few feet as Father Delanda said, "Be gentle, I think she'll be very cooperative." He looked into Lena's green eyes and said, "Won't you?"

CHAPTER SIXTY-SIX
PROCEED WITH CAUTION

Renee heard the gunshots and stopped in her tracks. An image of Prince Tana lying on the ground dead kept flashing through her mind. She remembered her dream from the night before and became nervous. Now she knew why her attraction to him was so strong. They weren't just sensual emotions like those she'd felt back in school when a boy asked her out. No, these were spiritual. Deep down, she recognized a connection in her soul that probably went back thousands of years.

The high priest stopped too and shouted orders to a few of his men. They dashed off into the jungle. He knew what gunshots meant and needed backup. It had taken his culture many generations and the slaughter of millions of innocent people to learn how to adapt to the influx of white men. Their weapons were superior and their hearts were soulless. Only in the last few years with the addition of the Germans was his tribe able to adapt. They taught them how to use a rifle and how to think like the white man. Yet, as with everything else in the jungle, the elements eventually rendered anything made of metal useless. Guns were nice to have when they worked but nothing could replace the dependability of a bow or spear. In the short run, though, it was better to fight fire with fire. He just hoped that his soldiers arrived sooner than later.

"That was gunshots," said Renee.

"Yes, and very close too." Bartholomew lifted his spear off the ground. "We must be careful."

He signaled a few warriors to split up and approach from different angles. The element of surprise was his only advantage. Back on the trail off in the distance, the old lady and a few others from the palace appeared.

The high priest raised his arm and said, "*Es gibt manchay wichay vorn.*"

The old lady, with the help of a cane, arrived next to Renee. She gently placed her hand on his shoulder and said, "I know, but I suspect that we're in more danger if we don't come."

"Please stay back, then."

Elsa nodded and the high priest barked out more orders. His men began to move out. He looked to Renee and said, "You should stay back too."

Renee immediately shook her head and replied, "Nope, I'm going with you."

The group moved out and headed toward the tunnel. They silently slid from one tree to another. After a few minutes, one of the scouts came back with an update.

Bartholomew leaned over to Renee and said softly, "We're close. We must be very quiet."

Beyond a group of low-lying bushes, she now saw the opening. A few feet farther and she heard the waterfall. There were two tunnels visible within feet of each other. In front of the first one she saw the priest, Lena, and man with the Mohawk. Joe was now holding onto Lena's arm while the priest walked around her.

The warriors crept in and stayed low to the ground while eyeing Joe Del. Renee and Bartholomew stayed back and watched. Joe had a devious grin on his face as his eyes studied Lena. Father Delanda seemed to be getting frustrated with her. Then a twig snapped in the brush near Joe's right. He shot a round from his revolver into a tree. A warrior fell fifteen feet to the ground and landed with a thud. Another warrior yelled and hurled his spear directly at Joe's chest. Joe moved to the side and caught it in midair. The high priest gasped.

Joe instinctively let go of Lena when he grabbed the spear. She tried to sneak away but wasn't quick enough. He seized her arm and swung her body around in front of him as his gun pointed to her head.

Bartholomew stepped into the clearing and waived for his men to come out. He looked at Joe and said, "You're surrounded. Put down your weapon."

CHAPTER SIXTY-SEVEN

THE WRATH OF JOE DEL

After a few minutes on the ground, Jason started to stir. It was hard to ascertain what all the commotion was going on around him, but he knew Joe Del was in the thick of it. His jaw hurt like hell but didn't feel broken. He saw Lena's feet shuffle around close by and then he recognized Joe's boots.

When the gunshot rang out, the pain vanished and the adrenaline kicked in. He rolled over on his elbows and slid in closer for a better look. Joe's gun was pressed against Lena's head. In the distance, he heard the high priest shout and tell Joe to put his weapon down. Jason slowly lifted up on one knee but stayed hidden in the bushes.

Joe shifted back and forth, making sure that all of the warriors were within sight and in front of him. He had no fear of dying and would just as soon take them all with him to his grave before surrendering. "You come more closer, I shoot the girl—and you."

Bartholomew signaled his men to stop. Joe was looking for a way out. While holding onto Lena, he quickly surveyed what was behind him. Jason ducked down as Joe noticed the other tunnel where the waterfall noises were coming from.

He'd just started backing up when someone shouted, "Halt!" Coming up from the left were four soldiers dressed in tattered gray uniforms straight out of World War II. Draped in long hair and necklaces with feathers, they looked more like a group of Ken Kesey followers than fighters. One was positioned behind a rock aiming a rifle while the others had pistols out ready to fire.

Jason heard Joe cock his trigger. It was one thing to fend off a group of warriors with spears but bullets were a little harder to catch. He was backed into a corner and Jason wasn't sure just how far he'd take this. There was no more time for thinking. He had to act now.

He knew that he only had seconds to make his move. Joe had the ears and nose of a fox. When Joe backed up a little more, Jason dove for the arm with the gun and pulled it away from Lena's head. At the same time, he dug his knee into the Indian's leg and tried to bring him down. Joe let out a groan and loosened his grip on Lena but managed to stay standing. She peeled away from his hands and ran toward the warriors. Jason wasn't about to wait around for another thrashing and sprinted off behind her.

Joe pointed his pistol at the back of Jason's head and took aim. This was going to be more fun than shooting fish in a barrel. Before he could get off a shot, two soldiers fired, hitting him in his right arm and grazing his belly. Joe looked at his shoulder and assessed the damage. It was minor. His waist, on the other hand, had been hit directly and the bullet had exited his back. The warriors raised their spears and approached cautiously. Joe kept them at bay with his gun and started walking backward toward the waterfall.

He glanced back one more time at the tunnel before firing on the Indians. They immediately ducked for cover. Then he unloaded the rest of his rounds toward the Germans. By the time the last shot rang out, he was off and running for the tunnel. The soldiers rose and started firing. A few warriors tossed their spears but were too far away.

Another bullet hit him in the leg but barely slowed him down. He limped into the tunnel and dove in under a barrage of gunfire. Still in one piece, he turned to run but was met head on with a wall of gushing water. This wasn't a tunnel at all. It was a trap.

He hobbled over, searching for a way out. The water was coming down hard and fast and everywhere. From the sound, it must have been falling at least a thousand feet or more. The mist drenched his clothes. He discharged the spent shells from the cylinder and pulled a few bullets out of his pocket. The spray was so intense that they kept slipping between his fingers. This wasn't working.

His only option was to go through the waterfall. Off to one side was an area with a little more sunlight coming through. He studied the plate of liquid glass rushing down but couldn't make out anything. He stuck his good arm out and tried to create a wide enough break to see through the water. The pounding force almost pulled him in so he recoiled quickly. Then he poked the barrel of his pistol in and caught a glimpse of a valley and mountain range off in the distance. *A way out*, he thought.

The soldiers had finally made it into the tunnel. They were yelling at him to stop but the cascading rumble echoing inside the cave drowned them out. He said a quick prayer to the ancient Gods—and to the Catholic God, just in case. As the men looked on, Joe tucked the gun into his pants and disappeared into the curtain of water.

The soldiers stood there in disbelief. They'd seen many men jump through the falls before. Unfortunately, none of them had ever lived to talk about it. They also knew exactly how tall it was and where it led. The odds were not good for this wild-eyed one-man wrecking crew. But then again, Joe Del Diaz was no ordinary man.

CHAPTER SIXTY-EIGHT
ALLE IN DER FAMILIE

Leslie Gorman stood at the exit of the tunnel and watched the drama unfold. She dared not make a move. Joe was acting crazy and was clearly capable of anything. She could easily become collateral damage with a man like that moving about.

DOCUMENT 512

When the soldiers returned from the cave, she came out with her hands up and said, "Don't shoot."

Renee heard her mother's voice and yelled, "Mom!"

She ran across the clearing and jumped into her arms. They hugged for the longest time before saying another word. Renee couldn't believe her eyes. They'd been four thousand miles apart from each other in the middle of an uncharted jungle with no means of communication, and yet here she was. There were so many things that she wanted to say but all that came out was, "I'm so glad to see you."

Her mother pulled back and took a good look at her prized possession. "Me too, honey. I thought I'd lost you for good."

Renee started crying. The words brought back the memories of her father. It was the first time she'd cried in days. The emotional dam had finally broken and for a few minutes, she was Mommy's little girl again.

"Dad. He's gone."

"I know."

Leslie had already dealt with her loss with a good, long cry back in La Paz. The events of the past few days had left little time for reflection as every waking hour was spent trying to find her daughter. She tried to control the inevitable, but the tears soon overtook her.

Lena walked over to Jason and held his hand. Then she placed a kiss on his cheek and said, "Thank you for saving me."

He groaned when she touched his jaw and replied, "Easy on the jaw. And you're welcome."

The high priest and the others made their way up to the visitors. Elsa stepped out and walked over to Lena and Jason. She couldn't help but stare at the young woman. Lena noticed and smiled back politely but was then immediately mesmerized by the old lady's eyes. They were deep green just like hers. Even though this woman was well into her eighties or maybe older, the similarities were frightening.

The old lady smiled and said, "You are German, no?"

"*Ja, bin ich.*"

Elsa responded with a slow nod and said, "I'm Elsa Brugger." She looked at Lena from left to right and added, "You definitely have the features."

Jason's ears perked up. This name sounded familiar. He recalled the caption on the back cover of *The Chronicle of Akakor* that he'd read over a hundred times before. Then he reached for his backpack but quickly realized that the book wasn't there. He looked around for Father Delanda but didn't see him anywhere.

"Did you say your last name was Brugger, as in Karl Brugger?"

Elsa grinned and replied, "Why, yes."

The woman studied his expression and understood. She knew of her son's book and the reasons behind his demise. She'd heard rumors over the years that he was looking for her through some of their contacts with the outside world. She was hesitant to tell these strangers the complete story of how her group of Germans had come to find themselves thousands of miles away hiding in the Amazon jungle. After all, did it really matter anymore?

They'd left society so long ago in order to escape the horrors of their war-torn homeland. To many, they were fugitives, but to the Indians, they were a sign from The Gods and were going to somehow save them from extinction. Over the years, both groups learned a great deal from each other, which, in turn, made them stronger.

Jason understood too and said nothing.

DOCUMENT 512

CHAPTER SIXTY-NINE

THE NECKLACE

A few warriors pulled Father Delanda out of the bushes and dragged him over to Bartholomew. The priest shrugged them off and straightened out his robe. Before he could say a word, Renee ran over and yelled, "Don't listen to him. He can't be trusted."

Bartholomew nodded and examined the defiant-looking cleric. He knew better than anyone what a man of the cloth was capable of. His history was filled with stories of Indians being burned at the stake or impaled alive all in the name of the Lord.

At that moment, a band of Chachapoya warriors came out of another tunnel dragging several prisoners by a rope. They were the guides hired by Joe and the officers.

Leslie and Renee backed away a few steps as the Indians marched up to the high priest and bowed before him. It wasn't the sticks jetting out of holes on both sides of their bushy beards that frightened them, nor was it the elongated tooth protruding from their leader's bottom lip. No, what made them take notice was the fact that every one of them, with their blue eyes and reddish-blonde hair, could have passed as one of their cousins. They were whiter than cotton.

"The Cloud People," Jason whispered under his breath.

The head warrior stepped forward and made a few signs to Bartholomew. The high priest bowed appreciatively and replied, "*Danka*."

"It seems that we've captured the rest of your party," he said, and then turned to Renee. "Is there any reason not to send them off to the mines along with your priest here?"

"What mines?" asked Renee.

"In due time, Your Highness." The high priest's words reverberated through the congregation: *Your Highness*. It wasn't until then had they fully understood the importance of this day. They were looking at their new leader and savior—and wondering what future lay ahead for them.

Never in a million years did Renee ever expect to be called "Your Highness." That title would have made almost any other girl beam with pride. It was something you only dreamed of as a child. But Renee knew better. She knew what responsibilities now went with that designation and it only made her uneasy. The longer she stayed in this kingdom, the harder it would be to eventually leave.

Lena and Jason looked at each other but were speechless. Leslie, on the other hand, wasn't shocked at all. She'd known for years that there was something special about her daughter and her unusual deformity. And though royalty wasn't the first thing that came to mind, it now made sense.

"Wait a minute," Leslie shouted. "This one here, I saw him pull something out of his pocket back on the mountainside before we entered the tunnel." She searched around in his pockets. "It's not here now." She looked at Father Delanda and noticed a slight grin on an otherwise stoic face. This was troubling.

Bartholomew removed the man's jacket and had him take off his shoes. "What is it that we're looking for?" he asked while staring into the officer's eyes. He could tell that the man was hiding something. "You know, my warrior friends here are awfully fond of Peruvian cuisine." He walked around the guard. "A man like you, so round and plump, would make a wonderful meal." The White Indians all grunted excitedly and stomped their spears into the dirt.

The officer looked over to Father Delanda, whose lack of expression said it all. He wasn't going to save him. The fear of being eaten alive was too much to handle so he blurted out, "It was a satellite phone. Father Delanda told me to turn it on once we got to the entrance of Akakor."

The high priest traded looks with Jason and Lena and asked, "What does this mean?"

"It means that someone else might know where we are."

Bartholomew understood very well what that meant. For the better part of fifteen thousand years, very few outsiders had ever penetrated their city or discovered its location. Yet over the last hundred years, protecting it had never been more difficult. When the Germans arrived, they brought with them strange-looking devices that buzzed and screeched. He knew that this satellite phone was very similar, and that scared him.

He looked off into the distance and asked the officer, "And did you turn this phone on?"

At that moment, Father Delanda broke free, pulled a knife out from underneath his robe, and thrust it into the officer's chest. "You served me well, my son," he whispered as the blade pierced the man's heart and left him speechless. The officer dropped to the ground gasping for air as the Indians quickly secured the priest again.

"What do we do now?" cried Renee.

Bartholomew gazed into her eyes and sighed. This girl was supposed to be their savior and here she was looking for answers. There was one hope though, one thing that might save them all. As it had been written with good words and in clear script, the Fifth Union of Ugha Mongulala was almost upon them. He peered off into the distance and said, "Where's Prince Tana Nara? Why's he not with you?"

Jason looked to Lena, then to Leslie, and said, "He was, but… he's still in the tunnel. He's been injured."

"Injured? How?"

Lena placed her hand on Renee's shoulder and spoke up, "There's a knife lodged into his back. I'm not sure how it got there, but there's definitely something unusual about it. I mean, it felt…

mushy…and was almost transparent. We tried to pull it out, but it wouldn't budge. He can't leave the tunnel either. If he does, then the bleeding gets worse and he…he dies."

Bartholomew turned to the elders as they gathered around in a circle to talk over this development. The look on their faces said volumes: any hope they'd had for salvation had been obliterated by this news. The old lady nodded to the high priest, and he addressed the visitors. "What you've witnessed is a phenomenon we call c*himpay*—when one's path crosses another. Unfortunately, uncrossing the path is very dangerous, if not deadly, at this stage."

"Deadly, how?" asked Renee.

Bartholomew held her hand. "Uncrossing the paths is nearly impossible, as you must reverse the order of every sequence of events that have occurred. That means everyone present in the tunnels at the time when the knife went into the prince's back would have to participate. Now that we've lost one person to the waterfall, that would make it impossible to do. Even so, people have been known to disappear or crumble like dust when trying to reverse a state of *chimpay*."

"So Prince Tana is lost forever?"

"I'm afraid so."

He tried to comfort her, but Renee just broke away and ran over to a clump of trees, crying. Leslie began to follow, but Lena grabbed her arm and said, "It might be best to let her be, at least for a while." Leslie nodded.

As Leslie watched Renee sulking in the distance and twirling the necklace in her hand, she remembered something from earlier that day. Something Father Delanda had shown her. She walked over to the warriors holding him and rummaged through his pockets. The photograph was still there. She carried it over to Bartholomew and asked, "Do you happen to know what this has to do with everything? The priest kept asking us about it and whether we'd seen it before. From the looks of it, he's been carrying it around for a long, long time."

Bartholomew stared at the picture, then flipped it over and read the inscription: "Sister Frida—Rio De Janeiro." With a solemn look he said, "I'm not sure, but it seems to be very similar to the necklace our young princess is wearing."

Jason peered over his shoulder and said, "So there are two necklaces?"

The priest looked up and replied, "Maybe, but I doubt it. Our scripture only talks of one necklace and its one purpose. It's more likely that there are *two parts* to *one* necklace."

CHAPTER SEVENTY
OPEN WOUNDS

Renee wiped her tears away and listened in on the conversation between Leslie, Jason, and the high priest. Then the stench of body odor wrapped itself around her so tightly that she had to gasp for air. She looked around from side to side but couldn't see him. Before she had the chance to say anything, Don Carlos grabbed her from behind. She screamed as he wrapped his arm around her and pulled out his pistol.

"Back up, everyone!" he yelled.

Don swiftly dragged Renee on her heels back toward the tunnel he'd just exited. When a few warriors started to stir, he pointed the gun to her head and said, *"No se muevan!"* The soldiers knew from his body language what it meant, whether they understood Spanish or not.

He reached around to feel Renee's neck. The chain was still there. Then he yanked it over her head and took a good look at the pendant. It was the same piece he'd been admiring and dreaming of holding for years. Finally, after so many failed attempts, it was his. He draped it over his head and let it fall on his chest.

The high priest gasped. This powerful heirloom, which had been theirs for only a few short hours, was now slipping away again—and with it, went the hopes of his people.

"Who is this man?" bellowed the high priest.

"I am Don Carlos of the Aymara Indians, and a member of the Amautus *tribe*."

"Amautus," whispered Bartholomew. He knew what that meant: the lost tribe that had separated from his kingdom thousands of years ago. He had no idea they still even existed. Rumor had it that they'd been wiped out when the Spanish annihilated everything in their path.

"What is it you want from us?"

"I have what I want, my friend. What I *need* is for you to stand down and let me leave peacefully. That way, the girl doesn't get hurt."

"We can't let you leave with the necklace."

"I don't think you have a choice here. Besides, it doesn't belong to you; it belongs to my people." Don scanned the area from side to side, making sure that none of the warriors were sneaking up on him. "This medallion has been with us for thousands of years. The young *chiquita* had no business bringing it here." What he failed to mention was the fact that he had no intention of returning it. He could almost taste the riches and powers it would bring him.

Father Delanda saw his way out. He wrestled with the warriors holding him and shouted toward Don, "Take me with you."

Don Carlos positioned the girl between him and the priest and said, "Why should I, Father? You haven't done me any favors."

"I can get us back to civilization safely—and I'm the only one who knows where the satellite phone has been hidden."

Don sized up his options. Getting back through the tunnel would be hard enough. Finding his way through the jungle would be even harder—and almost impossible without help. He couldn't see a problem with bringing the priest along. If he got in the way, then he'd just dispose of him along with the girl.

"OK, Padre. Just don't slow me down." Don motioned the warriors to release the priest.

As Father Delanda walked over to the tunnel entrance, he stopped in front of Bartholomew and said, "The photo, please." The high priest pulled it out and handed it over. Then he turned to Jason and said, "I'll take the map too, my son. It might still be of some value."

Jason hesitated to give it up again. He'd put so much time into studying it, guarding it with his life, and trying to understand its connection with Brugger's book. Yet it had served its purpose. It had led him to the lost city of Akakor, which, in turn, confirmed his belief that everything in *The Chronicle* was actually true.

"Don't make this any more difficult than it needs to be, young man," the priest grumbled.

Jason reached into his pocket and found nothing. Then he frantically dug into his other pockets and pulled out a lighter and a few coins, but no map. He fumbled through his shirt and exclaimed, "It's gone! I must have lost it on the way here." Then he glanced over to Lena, who winked and turned her head away.

Father Delanda ran his hands over Jason's body, patting him down and searching from top to bottom. He rummaged through his backpack then tossed it to the ground and growled, "Where is it?"

"I don't have the time to wait for you, Father. If you're coming with me, then you need to come now."

The priest took one last look around before shouting, "I'm coming." He glared at Jason and said, "This is not over. When I return with the rest of them, you'll be the first one I hunt down." Then he gestured toward the others. "Your days of pagan worship are numbered here on earth. Your fate has been sealed. The Lord has said, 'You shall not bow down to them or worship them; for I am a jealous God, punishing the children for the sin of the fathers to the third and fourth generation of those who hate me.'"

"Let's go now, Padre," shouted Don. "This is no time for a sermon."

As Father Delanda was confronting Jason, one of the soldiers with a rifle discreetly ducked behind a rock. He positioned the gun so that it was steady, lifted the sight up off the top, and zeroed in on Don's torso. When the fat Bolivian turned to face the approaching priest and exposed his left side, he fired.

The bullet hit Don square in the shoulder and knocked him forward a step. Don returned fire and positioned Renee in front of him. Then he looked back at the bullet wound. There was no blood and no pain. He felt around and put his finger through the hole in his shirt but still found no blood. The bullet entry hole was sealed completely and didn't seem to bother him one bit.

He lifted the pendant off his chest, looked to the priest, and laughed. "I think I've found the Fountain of Youth, Padre."

They both started walking backward toward the tunnel. The high priest and his men moved in closer. Some of them raised their spears. "Lower your weapons. Do not hit the girl," shouted Bartholomew.

Don Carlos kept the gun pointed at Renee's head while tugging her along. Father Delanda followed behind them both. When they reached the entrance, Don smiled and said, "*Adios, amigos.*"

As soon as his body broke the plane, blue and red sparks flew into the air. The crackling sound that followed startled Renee and made her instinctively duck down to the ground. The priest raised his robe over his head when he saw the shooting embers blast out of the tunnel.

It was as if someone had taken a bedsheet and ripped it into pieces. All they could do was watch as Don's body split in half. The back part of his carcass from head to toe tore off his frame and jetted into the depths of the cave, disappearing with lightning speed. The other half was a skeleton of tattered muscle and skin with a few remaining organs. They all stared in disbelief as it crumbled to the ground under its own weight.

CHAPTER SEVENTY-ONE
THE UNION

Bartholomew's men quickly ran up and secured Father Delanda. The high priest snatched the photo out of his pouch and shouted, "Take him away with the others to the mines, immediately." His warriors were careful not to get too close to the tunnel. They had no desire to end up like the Bolivian.

The others were silent. They watched the belligerent priest disappear into the distance, quoting scripture and threatening to return. They didn't quite know what to think of his actions. On top of that, any hope of reaching Tana before he died had now been erased after seeing what had happened to Don Carlos. It was too dangerous.

Leslie ran over to Renee, lifted her up, and squeezed her tightly. The young girl looked to the old lady and then to Bartholomew and asked, "Now what?"

"It's hard to say. When I hear this father's words, I'm concerned, but when I look into his eyes, I see a crazy man. Anyway, he won't bother us again once he makes it to the mines."

"Why's that?"

"No one has ever escaped from the mines."

"What if the others do come?"

"Just because they find this place doesn't mean that they will find us." The high priest looked to his warriors and added, "We should go back and assemble the high council. There's much to discuss. The Fifth Union may not be upon us after all."

When Bartholomew mentioned the Fifth Union, Jason remembered something that Tana had said back at the library—or at least started to say. He reached into his backpack and pulled out the tattered leather book. "What about this? Can it help?"

He handed it to the priest, who flipped through the pages. The symbol forming the "512" intrigued him. He thumbed through it, paying close attention to the inscription on the back about its origin. "I've heard that this book existed but wasn't certain until now. The stories about this group of explorers have been passed down from one generation to another within my people. They were the only other group of outsiders to ever make it this close to the city of Akakor—until you arrived."

Lena, Renee, Leslie, and Jason all looked at each other and beamed with pride. Who'd have ever guessed that a ragtag bunch like them would succeed where hundreds of other expeditions had failed?

Bartholomew continued, "This man's diary of his journey was never published. When this Francisco Raposo presented his findings to the governor of Peru, he was thrown in jail and his papers were seized. They ignored his stories of gold and silver and laughed when he said he'd found these tunnels and mines in a hidden valley. The government guarded his notes and kept them a secret from everyone. Eventually, they disappeared altogether. It was believed that the original Portuguese version was either shipped back across the ocean to your high priest or put under lock and key somewhere in Rio de Janeiro."

"The Vatican?" asked Jason.

"I believe so." Bartholomew ran his fingers over the cover and added, "Francisco spent a few years in jail until he repudiated all of the stories and swore never to talk about them again. He was forced to sign papers confessing his sins against the church and sent off into exile. Apparently, later on, as is obvious by the presence of this book, Raposo told his story to someone else and it was later transcribed into English and published by this Mrs. Burton. Whether or not he told them everything, we may never know."

"How do you know all of this?"

Bartholomew smiled and said, "Because we had a very special arrangement with the governor. He kept his men out of our rainforest and we presented him with many golden treasures. Unfortunately, that only worked for a few centuries. Now the governments have many other suitors to satisfy their thirst for greed."

"But what does that title have to do with me and Tana?" asked Renee.

"I'm not sure. Maybe this Franciscan saw the symbol in Akakor while he was there. After all, it appeared on many of the effigies in our city."

"What symbol?"

Bartholomew looked at Renee and said, "This symbol '512' as you call it on the book. It's intriguing how the design could be interpreted in so many different ways. This author was much smarter than I thought. One could just see the number and figure that it meant something special—or one could see the *T* in its center. Or maybe the kind of cross your people are fond of. In our culture, what we see is a symbol, the symbol of a union."

"What kind of union?" asked Jason. "I mean, is it chemical, physical, supernatural?"

"I guess it could be any kind—or many kinds. But here, I believe it means a Union between a Man and Woman, or as legend tells us, Ugha Mongulala."

"So what does this book have to do with Tana and Renee?"

"I don't know." The high priest looked at Renee and added, "Only The Gods know."

CHAPTER SEVENTY-TWO
CHOICES

Renee digested the high priest's words and tried to make sense of it all. After everything that had happened to her over the past few days, she knew this symbol definitely had something to do with her destiny. She also realized that a part of her soul was drifting away into the cloud of dust settling at the tunnel's entrance. Even though she'd only known the prince for a few days, her attraction to him was deeper than anything she'd ever experienced. She felt alive and, yes, maybe even *whole* when he was near. Now that he was dying, she couldn't help but feel that a part of her was dying too.

She knew now that she could never return to Illinois and live a normal life. This number, which had been haunting her from the moment she set foot in this country, was there for a reason. It had changed her life forever. It had also given her life new meaning. Even with the likelihood that she'd never see her soul mate again, she still wanted to stay. She needed answers.

She recalled a few passages from this cryptic manuscript. The part about the mysterious man wearing a necklace guarding the cave kept coming to mind. Was there a connection? She peered over at the medallion lying on top of Don's remains. All of the trouble this amulet had caused everyone. She'd seen its powers firsthand, but the only thing it had really gotten anyone up to this point was killed.

Then there were the tunnels. Were they linked to some past civilization that had left this planet thousands of years ago? She tried to piece together everything she'd learned from wandering through them over the past few days: how to interpret the symbols; how to move from one path to another; the unusual properties of gold inside their walls; and how they could not be trusted. She recalled the dream she had in the palace about flying through the air. Then she remembered what Jason said back in Sacsayhuaman. His theory about a lost Internet connection wasn't any more farfetched than the others.

Her thoughts soon wandered back to this leather-bound book. This number—or symbol—had to be the key. She remembered the author's description of the lost city and his never-ending search for gold. Who was the man that mysteriously disappeared in the cave? What was this "cloud of sparkling royal composition" the author mentioned? Then it hit her: maybe he was wearing a talisman—maybe the other half that seemed to be missing from the one atop Don Carlos's carcass. After all, her necklace had sent off sparks a few times—sparks of red and blue, in fact. The colors that make up purple, the color of royalty!

The pieces of the puzzle were all starting to come together.

When one of the warriors bent over to lift the medallion, purple sparks spewed out of the tunnel. Smoke poured over Don Carlos's body as they both ran for cover. Bartholomew looked to Elsa and said, "The spirits are restless. We must wait."

"Wait?" cried Renee. "How long?"

"Days, maybe weeks. It's hard to say with these conditions."

"What about Tana?"

Elsa hung her head down and replied, "I'm sorry, my dear, there's nothing we can do. You saw what happened to your uncle."

"He won't last weeks."

The high priest motioned his men to gather their belongings and replied, "If you enter the tunnel when one's spirit is moving on, many horrible things can happen."

"What do you mean?" asked Renee.

"Some spirits are good, some are bad. When they feel the presence of a human being dying, they get very excited and greedy. They'll try to steal anyone's spirit that's close by. This makes them stronger. Entering now is too dangerous."

"But…" She turned toward her mother and pleaded, "Mom…"

"Come on, kiddo," sighed Leslie. "You heard him. It's been a long day. Let's go home."

Renee didn't move. Instead, she looked to the ground. Protruding out of a hole in her shoe, like a four-leaf clover, was her extra toenail. In this strange lost world, this wretched curse, which had made her childhood unbearable, had somehow become a gift. She shook her head in disbelief. Yes, her uncle didn't get very far, but she wasn't anything like her uncle. She was *special*, at least to these natives, but in a good way.

As the group fell in line and began up the trail, she heard a sound coming from the tunnel—a familiar sound.

"Cinderella, dressed in yella…"

She turned back toward her friends and asked, "Do you hear that?"

"Hear what, honey?" asked her mother.

"Never mind."

Her senses were now being tugged and pulled and wrapped like taffy around so many different feelings that she wasn't sure what she was hearing. Just as before, the tunnels were playing tricks on her—taunting her, gloating, celebrating the loss of her soul mate and maybe even daring her to make the next move. Maybe it was over. Maybe everything Jason had said wasn't true. Yet, maybe, just maybe, these spirits were trying to keep her away from something—or somebody.

The twisted nursery rhyme lingered in the air: *"And tripped on her big feet falling in the wella."*

A cool breeze drifted by as the cave spit out a few more shards of blue and red light.

She recalled what Oryana had told her in the chamber: "The laws of our gods are not what they seem." What did that mean? If they weren't what they seemed, then were they really there at all?

DOCUMENT 512

"Renee!" called her mother.

The young princess looked to her one last time and said, "I'm sorry, Mom, but I have to do this. I'm the only one who can."

With that, she took off running for the tunnel entrance.

As soon as Leslie realized where her daughter was headed, her stomach tightened up. After everything that had happened over the last few days—losing the love of her life and almost losing her only child—here she was watching her world crumble around her again. Leslie's instincts kicked in and she sprinted off, yelling, "Wait!"

The chanting grew louder the closer Renee got to the opening. More sparks sputtered from the pile of her uncle's bones. She leaped over bushes and dashed under fallen trees without missing a beat until she was finally in front of the entrance. Then she glanced back, momentarily, to see that her mother was within ten yards of her. "I love you," she mouthed as she picked up the necklace and vanished into the darkness.

As Renee's body broke the plane, streams of blue and red lights shot out into the air. Within seconds, Leslie disappeared behind her, sending flashes of white light that trailed off in a cloud of smoke.

Bartholomew ran over but stopped well short of the archway. He gazed into the tunnel, looking for any signs of movement. Elsa walked up behind him and reached for his hand. With their prospects dimming and more danger on the horizon, they both stared into the endless black hole before them with only one question on their minds: *Whose side were The Gods really on?*

CHAPTER SEVENTY-THREE
CONSEQUENCES

Renee entered the tunnel and saw only darkness in front of her. She couldn't tell where she was going, but it didn't matter. It was a leap of faith at this point. She ran as fast as she could with her eyes closed. If this was going to be her destiny, then she wanted proof.

She ran until her feet hurt. The blisters on her toes were screaming to be untied from the cotton cages on her feet. *When am I ever going to stop growing?* she asked herself. She looked down at her feet and realized that they weren't the only part of her that was growing. She was definitely becoming a woman. Lying in the dirt next to her were several golden utensils scattered about. She walked up to one of them and kicked it away in frustration.

Whatever unknown force that was guiding her managed to keep her from running into the walls, but it did nothing to reduce the pain. It also did nothing to transport her to another place—a place where Tana would be waiting—like she was expecting. Instead, she found herself back in the same tunnel that she'd been traveling through all along.

As she caught her breath, she listened. There were no other footsteps. She thought she'd seen flashes of light and heard her mother call out to her on her way in, but there was no one behind her now. The silence was frightening. Even if she wanted to return, she didn't have a clue as to how to find her way back. Who knows what path she'd taken when she first came in?

Her heart was beating so loudly that it seemed to be echoing off the cold, glossy walls. A strange feeling came over her: complete isolation. Then a cool breeze brushed by and made her shiver. *A lost soul?* she wondered.

"Mom...Tana."

She waited, but there was no reply. It couldn't be that easy. As she rubbed her shoulders to fight off the chill, reality started creeping in. What had she done? She had little in the way of food or supplies and no idea on where to go. The consequences of her actions were obvious now. She was probably destined to walk these tunnels for the rest of her life.

She wanted to break down and cry but there were still no tears. Her body had been emotionally drained; every feeling had been dulled, every memory flushed clean. Even the pain in her feet seemed to want to cuddle up rather than ache. A part of her was ready to give up. She tried to revive a memory of what life was like before she and her father flew down to Bolivia but nothing came to mind. That life was over and no amount of tears was going to bring it back. There was only one life left for her now. One thought kept coming to mind as she stood there desolate, cold, and lost: Was this the end of her journey—or just the beginning?

CHAPTER SEVENTY-FOUR

NOW YOU SEE IT...

Leslie had almost caught up to her daughter when she saw the lights flash. Seconds later, Renee vanished along with everything else around her. Soon, Leslie became dizzy and felt like the air had been knocked out of her chest. When she tried to move, her body wouldn't respond. The walls blurred and began to ripple. She found herself floating in a dark pool of water that continually expanded as her body stretched out in every direction like a rubber band. Then there was a hole, a dark hole stretching as far as the eye could see, twisting and turning and burrowing its way through infinity. The whole time, her eyes were fixated on one spot, a tiny white dot surrounded by complete blackness.

She thought to herself, *This must be what death feels like.* The white light grew brighter. It brought back memories of movies she'd seen of people moving on into the afterlife. There was always a bright white light. The numbness, which rendered her immobile, seemed to confirm her fears. It was only a matter of time now before her soul left her body. Helpless and confused, all she could do was wait. Her vision blurred as streams of light swirled by and disappeared behind her. She could feel the centrifugal force against her skin keeping her in one place as she spun upside down, sideways, and even inside out.

The light continued to grow brighter, dispersing over her peripheral vision and bleaching out all other images. Her body swayed like a leaf riding a rapid-flowing stream as high-pitched sound waves floated around her, lifting and gliding in one clean motion. Then the light began to shred, with slits of red, blue, green, and yellow reappearing and dashing off onto the canvas and forming shapes before her eyes. The colors coagulated into figures and outlines that quickly turned into recognizable forms. Mountain peaks, clouds, trees, and bushes filled the space with more red and yellow blending into the sandy earth tones of the Andes landscape.

When it drifted by, she blinked a few times to make sure what she was seeing was real. This shape was vivid and saturated in exquisite detail. The image also made her heart skip a beat. It stifled her lungs temporarily, causing her breath to become irregular. She could feel her fingers and feet again and became more aware of her surroundings with every breath. There were voices in the background, people calling out to her, "Leslie, Leslie, are you all right?"

Her body shook as the voices continued. When the last glimpses of white light and noise disappeared, the darkness returned. She found herself lying on the ground with her eyes wide open. There were shapes and silhouettes above her while flashlight beams shined over her corneas. She squinted and covered her eyes.

"Leslie, can you hear us?"

"Are you OK?"

She recognized those voices. They were the two travelers who had accompanied her daughter. She rose to her elbows and said, "Renee. Is she here?"

Jason nervously glanced at Lena and answered, "No, she's gone."

"We need to get you out of here. These tunnels are not safe," said Lena as she lifted Leslie to her feet.

"Wait a minute. I saw something back there. I'm not sure where, but it was real."

"What do you mean?"

"There was a mountainside—not very tall—that kind of tapered off with boulders stacked on top of each other. On the front there was a large square cut into the stone that looked like a door. I don't know how, but then I found myself on the other side of the wall and there he was."

"Who?"

Leslie gazed into Lena's eyes as a tear rolled down her cheek and said, "My husband—alive!"

The silence that hovered over the room was absolute but far from voiceless. Leslie, worn-out and exhausted, tried desperately to recall every detail she'd seen of her husband and burn that image into her consciousness. Lena and Jason exchanged looks of doubt as they digested this information and wondered about the woman's mental condition.

Leslie could tell what they were thinking. "I don't know. Maybe it was all an illusion."

"Well, maybe so. These tunnels can play tricks on you. Let's get you out of here and back to Akakor."

Jason pointed to the light coming from the tunnel entrance and added, "Yeah, you need some rest, and we need to regroup and figure out how to find your daughter."

CHAPTER SEVENTY-FIVE

WITHIN THESE WALLS

A cool breeze of blue swept by Renee. *The spirits,* she thought. By now, she'd learn to respect the powers protecting these tunnels. The Gods had designed them not so much to harm people as to prey upon their innermost desires and fears. They knew that man was his own worst enemy.

Her necklace began to glow with a reddish aura around it. She looked down and lifted it up. It was warm. Then the blue smoke drifted down the tunnel. It spiraled from left to right like a serpent stalking its prey. As she watched it move, she caught a glimpse of a purple light off to the side about forty feet away. Each time the smoke spun around and came back to that spot, the light glowed.

Her necklace also seemed to become brighter when this happened. *What could it mean?* she wondered. When she took a few steps forward, the blue cloud stopped and hovered, completely stationary.

"Tana?"

She waited for a reply, but there was none. Then she took a few more steps forward and the blue smoke moved farther away.

Document 512

This time, the faint purple glow also moved a few feet away. It was as if these spirits were afraid to get any closer to her but had control over the light. Her necklace continued to radiate on her chest.

Renee wasn't sure what to do next. The aura emanating inside the wall was now even brighter and clearer. It pulsated like a beating heart. She was sure that Tana was inside there somewhere. The spirits knew it too. Time passed slowly as the game wore on—each side waiting for the other's next move. After a few minutes, the light began to fade. She had to do something quickly. She took a few steps closer and the brightness returned once more, but when the blue cloud backed away a few feet, the light moved with it.

This isn't working, she said to herself. Something was stopping her from reaching the light, yet it was also preventing the spirits from moving in—but why? She reached for the necklace and ran her fingers over the contours.

It made sense. The necklace was the key.

She knew what had to be done, but she also knew how dangerous it was. Without the amulet, she'd be completely vulnerable. The high priest's words rang out in her head as she felt the warmness radiate in her hand: "They'll try to steal anyone's spirit that's close by." As she watched the purple glow fade into the dark granite, it occurred to her that they'd soon steal Tana's soul one way or another.

Her options were few: wander through the tunnels until she withered away or take a chance with the spirits. The fact that there were so few options actually made it easier. Yes, the lesser of two evils was still an evil, but it was also still a choice. At this point, what'd she have to lose?

She slowly lifted the amulet off her head and placed it on the ground. The blue cloud swirled around and shot off a few sparks but didn't advance. "Good," she said under her breath.

Cautiously, she inched forward while concentrating on the cloud. It hovered in a circular pattern. The purple light was now diminishing a little bit with every beat. She picked up the pace. The smoke stood its ground and didn't move. It was almost as if the necklace had its own force field.

She whispered, "Tana, are you there?" The purple light flickered with fringes of red and blue that tapered off of it. Then she moved in closer. A faint silhouette of a body sitting on the ground inside the wall appeared.

Renee smiled and said, "Can you hear me?" The outline of an arm rose up and waved. She was now almost directly in front of the spot. She glanced over at the cloud to make sure that it was still stationary. Then she looked back at the necklace. It was glowing bright red as it lay on the ground. *So far, so good*, she thought. She took another step forward and then reached over and touched the wall. Her fingers penetrated the surface with ease. It was that same gooey feeling she'd experienced while holding Lena's arm when they separated in the tunnel.

"Can you reach my hand?" she asked. The silhouette on the other side rose to its feet. Tana's body was clearly identifiable now with his long hair and slender build. He lifted his arm and reached for Renee's hand. She felt nothing. Tana pulled back and maneuvered around, trying to pierce through the barrier at different angles. She moved her arm up and down, straining to connect with him. The light stayed bright around them as they struggled to make contact. Still nothing.

As time passed, the prince grew weary and lowered his shoulders. She could tell that he was fading away again. He took a step back and sat down when Renee shouted, "No! Come in closer!" She reached into the wall all the way past her shoulder. Her hand was ice-cold. "Don't give up!" she yelled.

Tana regained his composure and stood up again. Then he lunged with all his might toward her. The sound of crackling ice spread along the rocky barrier. Renee felt something. She frantically reached farther in even as a bitterly cold numbness crept up her arm. Finally, she felt his fingertips.

"Grab my hand!"

Tana clamped his fingers around her wrist. Renee grabbed his forearm and pulled. This time it was solid, and she felt something give. As his body slipped inside the dimensional divide between them, she felt a cool breeze come up behind her. *Oh no, a trap!* she thought. The blue cloud of spirits had swooped in and was sifting into the wall alongside her arm. A sensation of dry ice being injected into her veins flowed down her bicep into her forearm and made it almost impossible to continue holding on. He was losing his grip too and the noise was growing louder.

"Don't let go!" she screamed. She heard a faint groan but couldn't make out the words. The spirits had completely infiltrated the wall and were now circling around Tana's body. His fingers fell limp and slipped out of her hand as he took a step backward.

A loud thundering voice resonated inside the wall and roared, "Don't worry, my *chiquita*. I'll take good care of the boy." Don Carlos's face appeared in the blue smoke and circled around Tana's head. His spirit was now one with the others and leading them along.

"No!"

She pulled even harder but it did no good. She felt the whole weight of the prince's body as he slumped down and fell to his knees. Renee's heart was thumping hard as her body turned white and dropped in temperature. Her left arm was numb and her fingertips felt nothing. Don's image entered inside his body, causing the boy's eyes to roll back into his head. They were white and staring through her with a lifeless glare. She was losing him.

Out of the corner of her eye, she caught a glimpse of the amulet still glowing brightly on the ground. Was leaving it really her idea, or was she tricked by the spirits? After all, her uncle was one of them now. Bartholomew's words kept flashing like one cue card after another: *spirits, steal, makes, stronger.* She realized that she needed the necklace if she was going to have any chance of saving Tana. Without hesitating, she released his arm and fell back onto the tunnel floor. Tana was still visibly fighting off the cloud so that meant there was still a little time. She jumped to her feet and raced over to the amulet. Then she draped it around her neck and sprinted back to where she'd stood before. With all of her might, she plunged back into the wall and stretched out her arm as far as she could.

"Tana, reach for my hand!" she exclaimed as her arm searched for anything solid. He was halfheartedly swatting away the blue smoke floating around his nostrils.

The walls rumbled as Don's voice echoed around the chamber. "You cannot fight it, *señorita*, you are too weak. You do not know how to use the powers you've been given."

The prince's body was now taking on Don Carlos's shape. His stomach was twice its normal size and a dark moustache had sprouted on his upper lip. Renee kept searching for something solid to hold onto while slivers of flashing white light shot out of Tana's body. The cloud was pulling him away from the wall.

She plunged in even farther. This was exactly what Don was waiting for. When her fingers broke the plane on the other side, he quickly seized them with both of Tana's hands. Then he yanked her torso halfway through the wall. The crackling sound reverberating through her skull was unbearable; her body melded flesh into stone. She could smell hints of body odor sifting into her nostrils.

A calming numbness soon came over her. The blood flowing through her bloated veins tingled and continually expanded. She could feel Don Carlos's ghost seeping into her muscles and skin. As she tried to resist, his voice whispered in her ear, "Don't fight it, *chiquita*. It will only make it worse." At that moment, whatever willpower she'd been holding onto surrendered to the spirits. His voice was now her voice.

Document 512

Renee's head and shoulders hung lifelessly like a mounted deer on the other side of the wall. Her eyes were frozen and lost in some other place and time. The spirits clamped down with their hypnotic forceps, trying to suppress all conscious thoughts or feelings. Tana was still struggling and lingering between worlds. It was then that the prince's eyes connected with hers for one split second. That was all it took for him to realize what was going on.

With every last ounce of strength, he forced his head to twist in Renee's direction. He commanded his eyes to blink again and again while his mind urged them to succumb and close for good. Gradually, his colorless, dilated pupils began to show signs of life. He sensed that something was wrong even though his consciousness kept telling him otherwise. A voice in his head was repeating, "Bow down before your elders. Bow down before your elders." Yet the look on his companion's face was pleading for him to resist.

He watched as her limp body wrestled between both dimensions. Then he realized that it was his arms pulling her forward, his hands squeezing the life out of her hands—his body in someone else's mind. At that moment, something snapped and allowed him a brief moment of clarity. That was all it took. With all of his might, he grabbed Renee tightly and thrust himself back into the wall. A sharp, icy pain shot up into his brain but he kept on. The jolt nearly made him black out and caused a queasy feeling in his stomach, but he pushed on and managed to keep his balance.

Tana's sudden burst of energy also rattled the mental chains holding onto Renee and allowed her to break free from Don Carlos's grip. The prince reached out and squeezed her arm. When he did, visions from the palace chamber flashed before her in choppy, almost disconnected sound bites, freezing in some places and jetting forward in others, all with no sense of direction. A jaguar leaped off the mountainside that Oryana had guided her to, followed by flashes of white light funneling through the small alcove in the mountain's face. Lake Titicaca glided by like a fast-moving glacier spiraling downward into a riverbed of golden glitter.

Then Tana squeezed again and whispered, "It's me." It sounded like him, but how could she really be sure? After all, these tunnels had been nothing but trouble up to now. Then, as the voice tapered off and faded away, she heard it say, "Lead me where you want me." Now she was sure it was Tana.

She stretched out her fingertips and placed them around his hands. They were still mushy but much firmer than before. The necklace immediately glowed brighter and sent spurts of heat throughout her body. She could feel its warmth seeping into the walls. Renee heaved as hard as she could while Tana grunted and thrust headlong. As the cracking sound changed pitch and lowered in volume, his hand drove through the plane of the rock on the outside wall. They'd both broken through the barrier and were once again back in the tunnel.

Tana's body glided through the granite and tumbled onto the floor. The force also knocked Renee back and landed her on the ground next to him. An eerie silence came over the room as the blue smoke dissipated and vanished into thin air.

CHAPTER SEVENTY-SIX
REUNION

When Tana's body tumbled back and sent Renee crashing to the ground, her head hit the hard surface with an ominous thud. The prince immediately bolted up, placed his hands behind her head, and said, "Are you all right?"

Renee lay there without moving and stared into his eyes. Then she studied his face. Moments ago, he was barely able to find enough strength to fight off the spirits. Now he was vigilantly holding her in his hands like a lioness protecting her cub. It was more than she could handle. She just chuckled and squeezed him as tightly as she could.

Tana held on too until she repositioned her arms. "Ouch!" Her hand had bumped into the knife that was still lodged in his back.

"I'm sorry. I forgot." Then she put both her hands around his head and gently placed a kiss on his cheek.

He didn't blush this time, nor did he even try to turn away. He just laid his face against hers and held his breath for as long as he could. Then he slowly exhaled as the reality of the moment sunk in. He'd given up hours ago on ever seeing her or anyone else again. Yet here she was, holding him and lying with him as the prickling chill from the tunnel walls melted away.

They lay there for a few minutes and said nothing. Neither one of them were used to having another body snuggled up so closely. It felt good. Then Tana lifted up and said, "Your head. You hit the ground pretty hard."

Renee picked up the necklace off her chest and said, "I didn't feel a thing. I've got my lucky charm on."

He nodded and understood. This amulet's powers had been the subject of many fables and legends passed down from one generation to another in his kingdom. There were also the troubling tales surrounding it about the dangers that awaited anyone who possessed it. Although they were probably just as real, he thought it best not to mention them.

They sat up and filled each other in on the events that had transpired since their last meeting. He told her about how he felt the presence of someone in his body but didn't know it was Don Carlos. Tana's eyes widened when Renee told him of Father Delanda's bizarre behavior and the satellite phone. He knew what that meant, and it wasn't a good sign. There was trouble ahead for the kingdom of Akakor.

When she revealed the real meaning behind the number 512, he turned away. She slapped him on the shoulder and said, "You knew, didn't you?"

"I knew what it meant, but didn't know it meant, you know, I mean, that you…" He struggled to find the right words but couldn't. "Your mother, she told me."

"What?"

"On the trail. She came over one day and told me about your six toes. Then it all made sense."

Renee sat quietly and absorbed this new bit of information. She'd forgotten all about her mother up until then. Still, there were too many things to worry about and no time to fixate on just one. Although she now understood what her place was in the whole scheme of things related to this ancient phenomenon called Ugha Mongulala, she still had many unanswered questions. Her head ached as she tried to figure out what she and Tana were supposed to do in order to save his kingdom. What was this amulet's real purpose? As she pondered these thoughts, Tana sat quietly and studied her expressions.

Then, as she rubbed the necklace, another question came to mind: "Can we get out of here?"

Tana looked away and shook his head. "I don't know how. Unless we can get this knife out of my back, I can't go anywhere."

"How do we do that?"

He just looked down and shook his head. He knew many secrets about these caves but not this one. Even Bartholomew had gasped when he heard what had happened. He remembered what the high priest used to tell him as a child whenever they were about to enter a tunnel. His mentor would stop, look around, and say, "Expect the unexpected."

In this case, the unexpected had been Renee. Right before his eyes was the last hope of a dying nation—a savior, pure and true, just as it was written in good words and clear script. According to legend, the union was almost complete and a new beginning would reign over his kingdom. Yet at that moment, he felt powerless. Something was missing and he didn't know what it was.

Renee pulled the necklace over her head and placed it in the palms of her hands just as she had done back at the palace. She rubbed it and peered down intensely, hoping and praying that the Black Mirror would return and tell her what to do next.

Tana knew what she was thinking. Their minds seemed to be connected on a telepathic level now that they'd been reunited. Her thoughts were his thoughts and his were hers. Even though neither one quite realized what was happening, they were becoming *whole*.

She lifted her head to speak, but he responded before she could say anything. "It doesn't work that way."

She understood and nodded. "There's gotta be something that'll work. I mean, look at you. You look one hundred percent better just in the last few minutes." Then she lifted the amulet up and added, "It's got to be this necklace."

Tana reached out and said, "May I?"

Renee handed it to him and watched. He placed it around his neck and said, "Now, try to pull out the knife."

She jumped up and moved behind him. He quickly turned his head and said, "Be careful, though."

She patted him on the shoulder. "Of course." Then she maneuvered back and forth until she was firmly in place and said, "OK, get ready."

Tana took a deep breath and nodded, "Go ahead."

Renee firmly grabbed the handle, hesitating just long enough to say a few words under her breath, and pulled. The knife didn't budge. She tried again, wiggling it back and forth, but nothing.

"Go ahead!" shouted Tana.

"I already did. It's not working."

Tana rubbed his chin. "How unusual. I didn't feel a thing. Maybe it should be on you instead?"

"It's worth a try."

He removed the medallion and draped it onto her neck. Then he said, "Now try it."

Renee held the handle and squeezed. "It feels mushy." Then she yanked with all her might.

"Ahhhhh!" screamed Tana as his back arched upward.

CHAPTER SEVENTY-SEVEN
FATE OR SALVATION

"Oh my God! I am so sorry...I...I didn't know."

The prince stretched out his shoulders trying to relieve the pain and tenderness. The wound was bleeding again. Renee removed the necklace and handed it to him, "Here, put it back on."

When he did, the bleeding stopped as fast as it had come and the pain disappeared. He looked at her and said, "Amazing. It doesn't hurt anymore."

"At least we know it's still working. Unfortunately, it's not working in the way we need it to work."

"Something's missing," Tana said as he studied the amulet. "Something's just not right."

"That's what Bartholomew said."

"What?"

"Back at the palace, when I told him what The Gods said to me in the chamber. He said that something must be missing because they didn't tell me everything."

She recounted what the goddess had said about the missing part of the necklace and the seven chains of granite by a lake with golden banks.

Tana whispered, "Akahim."

"What's that?"

"It's a city, much like Akakor, that was destroyed hundreds of years ago. According to legend, all of the buildings were laid out in the shape of a constellation. If you find that constellation in the sky, then you've found The Gods."

"What about…"

"*Puerta de Hayu Marca*," Tana interrupted.

"How'd you know?"

"I saw it too. I mean, the image in the mountainside—when we connected inside the wall back there."

"So, if we find the other half of this amulet and this gate, we'll find The Gods?"

"Maybe."

"So what do we do?"

The boy mulled over everything in his mind. He didn't quite know what these connections all meant, but he was sure that it would be revealed in good time. Right now, there were more important things to worry about. There was something missing from the amulet that was making it work sporadically. The knife wanted to come out when Renee wore the necklace, but she couldn't get a grip on the handle. It did the opposite when around his neck. Somehow, they needed to combine these two parts together to get it to work.

"A Union between a Man and Woman," blurted Renee. This time, *she* knew what *he* was thinking. She shook her head and said, "That was strange. I don't even know where that came from."

"It came from me. From inside my mind, just like I read yours a minute ago."

The special union they'd heard so much about was actually taking form. They were becoming... *One.*

"I have an idea," he said. "I wanna try something. It's going to seem awkward, but just trust me on this."

His words catapulted her back in time to the night when she first arrived in La Paz. The night when her dream was so vivid and real that her body actually ached the next morning from mentally running down the hill. The night that number—that eerie-looking symbol, that spiritual beacon—came into her life. Those two same words, trust me, that showed up in her dream were now warming her soul. She was totally convinced that they were on the right path this time.

She tried to picture the man from her dream. Her memory had been shaken and stirred so much over the past week that it was hard to remember. His facial features were nothing more than a blur now. Maybe it wasn't Jason after all. It could have just as easily been Tana or maybe a combination of both. Nevertheless, it didn't matter anymore. What did matter was that she could trust him.

"I trust you. I always have."

Tana smiled and said, "Good, then I want you to lie down on your back and place the necklace in your hand."

Tana straddled over her and gently dropped down to where his chest was flat against hers. Immediately, their breathing patterns synchronized. He placed his hand on top of the amulet with hers and said, "OK, pull out the knife."

She reached behind him with her other arm and fumbled for the handle. It felt solid this time, so she gripped it firmly. Then she whispered in his ear, "Are you ready?"

Tana braced himself and whispered back, "No, but I'm willing."

The words echoed her sentiment too. They weren't only reading each other's minds now, but they were also experiencing each other's dreams and emotions. Even though there were so many things that could go wrong, she had a good feeling about it all the same. She closed her eyes and gently lifted the handle. The blade exited the wound in one smooth motion. As soon as it left his body, he exhaled loudly. Every ounce of fear and apprehension that he'd been holding onto over the last few days was now gone.

As his breathing began to return to normal, he uttered, "It worked. You did it."

Renee tossed the knife off to the side and said, "No, *we* did it."

Then she hugged him tightly. Her hand brushed by the hole where the knife had been. Heat rose up for a few seconds but then quickly dissipated. The blood dried up too. She felt around for the wound, but it was also gone.

"How funny. I don't feel the hole anymore." She continued caressing the area but couldn't even find a scab. "Amazing, there's nothing."

"Such are the ways of The Gods."

Renee moved her hand up to his head. She stroked his hair, and then pushed his bangs aside and just smiled. He smiled back. "What's next?"

"I have no idea, but we'll figure something out."

Even though she didn't have a clue as to what lay ahead for them, she was happy all the same. Her sense of emotional and physical existence had returned. All of her inhibitions about life and her past had vanished along with his wound. She didn't care about her learning disability, physical deformity, or about being the daughter of the crazy father who believed in aliens. Somehow, those things didn't matter anymore. It was all behind her now. She was finally at peace with herself and *one* with him.

Then there was the mysterious number that'd been with her from the beginning. An indelible birthmark with no true identity but multiple meanings. How could it be the title of this out-of-print manuscript and somehow connected to this legend of the

Fifth Union of the Ugha Mongulala? Something told her that she might never know for sure.

She was sure about one thing though: it wasn't the number leading her along this whole time. These last few moments with Tana confirmed that. No, it was the symbol hidden within—the cross, or the ancient sign of a Union between a Man and Woman—that was now guiding her. A union more powerful than any force of nature she'd ever known. Maybe it was, as Jason believed, a force that could possibly unite all of nature. She felt it moments ago with Tana—and felt it growing stronger by the minute. What that would lead to was anyone's guess. For now, she was content with just knowing.

As much as she worried about seeing her mother again or whether they'd ever find their way out of the tunnel, she wasn't afraid. Instead, she felt at ease. She stared into Tana's eyes and realized that everything would be all right as long as they were together. For the first time, her life had meaning.

"Shhhh, do you hear that?"

"Hear what?"

"Listen."

A faint but distinct sound could barely be heard off in the distance. At first, Tana didn't recognize it. He looked at her with bewilderment. But after seeing the intense look on her face, he held his breath and listened.

Slowly, the sound took shape. The random splattering of white noise began to follow a pattern that turned into a rhythm and eventually into a muted rumble. As their ears adjusted and finely tuned in the echoing vibrations, it became obvious what they were hearing. It also became obvious that her dreams were becoming reality. In a far-off corridor and almost out of earshot was the sound of a gushing waterfall plunging into a pool.

"I know that sound," whispered Tana. "There's only one waterfall around that sounds like that. You can hear the deep part easily, but if you listen carefully, you'll hear a very light metallic sound

Document 512

in the background. It's a double waterfall, and it's only found in Akakor."

Renee smiled and replied, "All I know is that it's the sound of freedom."

THE END

Made in the USA
San Bernardino, CA
07 June 2020

72935229R00202